MW01674040

Ranolf and Amohia

Anatiposi

Alfred Domett

Ranolf and Amohia

Reprint of the original, first published in 1872.

1st Edition 2023 | ISBN: 978-3-38213-336-8

Anatiposi Verlag is an imprint of Outlook Verlagsgesellschaft mbH.

Verlag (Publisher): Outlook Verlag GmbH, Zeilweg 44, 60439 Frankfurt, Deutschland
Vertretungsberechtigt (Authorized to represent): E. Roepke, Zeilweg 44, 60439 Frankfurt, Deutschland
Druck (Print): Books on Demand GmbH, In de Tarpen 42, 22848 Norderstedt, Deutschland

RANOLF AND AMOHIA.

RANOLF AND AMOHIA:

A SOUTH-SEA DAY-DREAM.

BY

ALFRED DOMETT.

LONDON:
SMITH, ELDER & CO., 15, WATERLOO PLACE.
1872.

—καὶ ἡ ἐλπὶς μεγάλη.

Plato : Phædo, 145.

RANOLF AND AMOHIA.

CANTO THE FIRST.

I.

"Glorious! this life of lake
And hill-top! toil and tug through tangled brake,
Dense fern, and smothering broom;
And then such rests as now I take,
In sunflecked soft cathedral-gloom
Of forests immemorial! Noble sport
Boar-hunting! yet that furious charge, the last
Of the dead monster there had cut it short
For me, and once for all, belike,
Had not his headlong force impaled
The savage on my tough wood-pike
That, propped with planted knee and foot,
Its butt against a rata-root,
From chest to chine right through him passed;
And nought his inch-thick hide availed,

Or ring-like tusks upthrusting through
The notches of his foaming lips,
By constant whetting planed away
To chisel-sharpness at their tips:
It weakened him—the knife-dig, too,
He caught when first commenced the fray;
When, as in haste I sprang astride
The narrowed gully—just a ditch
With flowering koromiko rich—
Between my feet the villain drove,
And fierce, with short indignant sniffs,
And grunts like muttering thunder, strove
To gain his haunts beyond the cliffs,
And foil the foes he fled from, yet defied.

" But Nim, my glorious bull-dog! Nim,
My mighty hunter of the boar,
Who never recked of life or limb
That old antagonist before!
That rip has finished his career—
His last boar-fight is fought; no more
He'll come to greet me as of yore,
Wriggling his lithe spine till his tail
Whipped his black muzzle in the excess
Of cringing canine happiness;
No more his genuine love express
With such dumb signs and tokens clear,
Mock bites and mouthings of the hand,
Easy as words to understand.
Strange, a mere dog should be so dear!
But he is dead, and—done with, must we say?
Poor victim of this universal demon-play
Of Life—*my* fate to-morrow, his to-day,

Which I, for sport, have sealed—as God (or *no* God, then
Say you ?) that of his myriad worlds and men ?
 And 'pluck' like his, that nought could quail ;
Good temper—honest, humble love and truth—
 These must not live again, forsooth !
 No future for the Dog—but why ?
Duty, our highest inborn feeling, who
Has stronger than this guardian true
To death ? or can we in our own rejoice,
As sprung from self-determined choice ?
 That Self with so much bias made—
 Our will by strongest motive swayed ?
 Scarce higher than his, *our* claims, I fear,
 To merit of our own appear.
 Then compound, too, not simple, he,
 A work complete no more than we,
 (If stuff for hope therein may be),
 Has not his nature, like our own,
Instincts at war, the lower with the high ?
With trusts to be fulfilled, obedience shown—
The longing for the ramble, game forbidden,
 Or bone, like miser's treasure, hidden ?
And if, instead of eyes that often so
 With solemn melancholy glow,
He had but tongue to speak with, who can show
 He might not tell of hopes, and dim
Perceptions, yearnings, that no longer dumb,
He, too, may rise to human, and become
Erect some day, a ruler and a lord,
 And, like his master, loved, adored,
 A visible God and Providence to him—
Though swayed, no doubt, full oft, by rage, caprice and whim.

* * * * * *

"Poor wretch! we read his failings at a glance;
All that in this life hinders his advance.
Ungifted to abstract, he can conceive
No clear ideal to aim at or achieve;
Ungifted to reflect—himself discern,
His depth beneath the ideal could never learn;
Had he both gifts, would want constructive brain,
To plan the way the high ideal to gain—
Want hands to work with, had he found the way,
So in his low estate perforce must stay.

"But are our organs that compare—combine—
Dispart and spin deductions fine,
Creations so exclusively divine,
They needs must be preserved compact,
By no harsh doom destroyed, dissolved?
When (though we match the Dog in eyes)
The precious, last, profoundest prize
They palm upon us for a fact,
In spite of all those starlit skies,
Is in our petty selves to see
And what from us (by what decree?)
Is still evolving and evolved,
The highest Being that can be?—
But truce to that preposterous claim—
I take it and stand by the same,
There is no God much worth the name,
Whate'er their scale, where'er their seat,
Would drop creations, incomplete;
Let any force his plans defeat;
The wants he caused, leave unsupplied,
Desires he gave unsatisfied!

Better believe all creatures—foul or fair,
One universal endless progress share;
In the procession headed by mankind,
  Only a march or two behind;
Each rank of God's grand army onward bent
To higher states and stages—who knows where?—
  Of free and fortunate development!"

II.

So mused a youngster as he lay at ease,
  Profaning (must we needs confess?)
With chestnut-glossed pet meerschaum the pure breeze:
Enjoying in delicious cool no less
The mighty shade of old majestic trees,
Whose tops the skies beneath our feet immerse,
  Down in a land, greenwaving, grand,
Upon our seeming world-medallion's rich reverse:
  The ruder Italy laid bare
  By that keen Searcher of the Seas
Whose tempest-battling, never-baffled keel,
Left half our planet little to reveal;
  But restless roaming everywhere
Zigzagged the vast Pacific as he prest
With godlike patience his benignant quest;
True hero-god, who realized the notion
Its races feign of mythic MAUI still,
And plucked up with a giant might of will
A hundred Islands from Oblivion's ocean!
Sea-king and sage—staunch huntsman of pure Fame,
Beating the waste of waters for his game,
Untrodden shores or tribes without a name;

That nothing in an island's shape,
Mist-muffled peak or faint cloud-cape
Might his determined thoughtful glance escape ;
No virgin-lands be left unknown,
Where future ENGLANDS might be sown,
And nations noble as his own.

III.

It was a wondrous realm beguiled
Our youth amid its charms to roam ;
O'er scenes more fair, serenely wild,
Not often summer's glory smiled ;
When flecks of cloud, transparent, bright,
No alabaster half so white—
Hung lightly in a luminous dome
Of sapphire—seemed to float and sleep
Far in the front of its blue steep ;
And almost awful, none the less
For its liquescent loveliness,
Behind them sunk—just o'er the hill
The deep abyss, profound and still—
The so immediate Infinite ;
That yet emerged, the same, it seemed
In hue divine and melting balm,
In many a lake whose crystal calm
Uncrisped, unwrinkled, scarcely gleamed ;
Where sky above and lake below
Would like one sphere of azure show,
Save for the circling belt alone,
The softly-painted purple zone
Of mountains—bathed where nearer seen
In sunny tints of sober green,

With velvet dark of woods between,
All glossy glooms and shifting sheen ;
While here and there, some peak of snow
Would o'er their tenderer violet lean.

And yet within this region, fair
With wealth of waving woods—these glades
And glens and lustre-smitten shades,
Where trees of tropic beauty rare
With graceful spread and ample swell
Uprose—and that strange asphodel
On tufts of stiff green bayonet-blades,
Great bunches of white bloom upbore,
Like blocks of seawashed madrepore,
That steeped the noon in fragrance wide,
Till by the exceeding sweet opprest
The stately tree-fern leaned aside
For languor, with its starry crown
Of radiating fretted fans,
And proudly-springing beauteous crest
Of shoots all brown with glistening down,
Curved like the lyre-bird's tail half-spread,
Or necks opposed of wrangling swans,
Red bill to bill—black breast to breast—
Aye ! in this realm of seeming rest,
What sights you met and sounds of dread !
Calcareous caldrons, deep and large
With geysers hissing to their marge ;
Sulphureous fumes that spout and blow ;
Columns and cones of boiling snow ;
And sable lazy-bubbling pools
Of sputtering mud that never cools ;

With jets of steam through narrow vents
Uproaring, maddening to the sky,
Like cannon-mouths that shoot on high
In unremitting loud discharge
Their inexhaustible contents;
While oft beneath the trembling ground
Rumbles a drear persistent sound
Like ponderous engines infinite, working
At some tremendous task below!—
Such are the signs and symptoms—lurking
Or launching forth in dread display—
Of hidden fires, internal strife,
Amid that leafy, lush array
Of rank luxuriant verdurous life:
Glad haunts above where blissful love
Might revel, rove, enraptured dwell;
But through them pierce such tokens fierce
Of rage beneath and frenzies fell;
As if, to quench and stifle it,
Green Paradise were flung o'er Hell—
Flung fresh with all her bowers close-knit,
Her dewy vales and dimpled streams;
Yet could not so its fury quell
But that the old red realm accurst
Would still recalcitrate, rebel,
Still struggle upward and outburst
In scalding fumes, sulphureous steams.
It struck you as you paused to trace
The sunny scenery's strange extremes,
As if in some divinest face,
All heavenly smiles, angelic grace,
Your eye at times discerned, despite
Sweet looks with innocence elate,

Some wan wild spasm of blank affright,
Or demon scowl of pent-up hate ;
Or some convulsive writhe confest,
For all that bloom of beauty bright,
An anguish not to be represt.
You look—a moment bask in, bless,
Its laughing light of happiness ;
But look again—what startling throes
And fiery pangs of fierce distress
The lovely lineaments disclose—
How o'er the fascinating features flit
The genuine passions of the nether pit !

IV.

Loose-clad in careless sailor-guise,
But richly robed in that imperial dress
Of symmetry and suppleness
And sinewy strength that Nature's love supplies,
When, at youth's prime, her work, superbly planned,
Takes the last touches from her Artist-hand,
Was he who rested in a forest near
Calm Rotorúa's ferny strand.
To him was not denied, 'twas clear,
That best of boons at her command—
A joyous spirit sparkling like the day,
Set in well-tempered, finely-fashioned clay.
His fair complexion, slightly tanned
By central suns' and oceans' glare ;
His eyes' gray gleams and amber hair,
Were such as brighten best where gloom and cold
And sombre clouds harsh northern skies enfold :
But curling locks and lip, and glance
Keen for all beauty everywhere ;

The straight harmonious features—though perchance
Squarer than pure proportion asked, in cheek
And brow, more thought and firmness to bespeak—
Of southern fervor and quick feeling told.
His love of the mysterious—vast—whate'er
Of solemn and sublime could bear
The soul aloft on wings of thrilling awe;
The restless daring that his reason led
To question all he heard and read;
The senses potent to divine the springs
Of pleasure in a thousand things,
Seemed from each clime some elements to draw—
Like Gothic metal run in Grecian mould.
In active body—vigorous mind,
Such seeming contrasts he combined;
Still, in his face whate'er expressions shone,
And to what moods soever he was prone,—
'Twas hardy gladness by strong will controlled—
A summer torrent bounding on incessant
Through rampart layers of glittering stone,
Seemed the habitual and abiding one.
Blithe Hope upon his forehead bold
Sate like a sunbeam on a gilt mosque-crescent;
And oft, in reverie, if he gazed apart,
His eye would kindle as in admiration
Of some past scene to fancy present,
Or glory glowing in the future distance;
As if one breaking morn of gold
Were round Life's whole horizon rolled;
As if his pulse beat music, and his heart
Clashed cymbal-bursts of exultation
In the mere rapture of existence.

V.

A shriek within the covert near,
A second, third, assailed his ear;
Straight for the sound at once he dashed;
Through tangled boughs and brushwood crashed,
And lopped and slashed the tangles black
Of looped and shining supplejack,
Till on a startling scene he came,
That filled his soul with rage and shame.

Her mantle flung upon the ground,
Her graceful arms behind her bound,
With shoulders bare, dishevelled hair,
There stood a Maiden of the land,
More stately fair than could elsewhere
Through all its ample range be found.
Two of his comrades, hired amid
The tribes whose chieftains held command
O'er all the vales those mountains hid—
Those western mountains forest-crowned—
Wild striplings, who, uncurbed from birth,
Deemed foulest wrong but food for mirth,
So that their listless life it stirred,
Were basely busy on each hand,
With flax-blades binding to a tree
The Maid who strove her limbs to free.
They knew her—for they oft had heard
Of that surpassing form and face;
They knew the hate, concealed or shown,
Between her people and their own;

The feuds, when open war would cease,
That smouldered in precarious peace ;
They knew the track by which the chase
Had lured them to that lonely place,
Was so unused, so tangled, rough,
They doubtless would have time enough,
And might without pursuit retrace
Their steps through mountain-woods, so dense,
No wrong would be suspected thence,
No outrage dreamt of ; so they thought—
If such a thoughtless impulse wild
Of mischief can a thought be styled—
They fancied, when the Maid they caught
At that secluded spot, alone,
With one slave-girl (who shrieking fled,
While after her a third accomplice sped,
Lest she the alarm too soon should spread)
It was a chance to win a name,
Through all the tribe some facile fame—
Let but their foreign friend agree,
If such a captive to their chief they led,
At his behest, dispose, to be.

VI.

Not more incensed—scarce lovelier in her wrath—
The silver-bow'd snow-Goddess seen
By rapt Actæon at her awful bath ;
Not prouder looked—scarce fiercer in her pride,
The yellow-haired Icenian Queen,
Stung by the tortures she defied—
Than did that flaxen-kilted Maid—

A warmer Dian—at her russet rise,
  Dun-shining through autumnal [illegible].
A young Boadicea sunnier skies
  Had into browner beauty kissed.
So flashed her eyes with scorn and ire,
They seemed, as deep in purple shade
The slanting sunbeams left the wood
And gloomy yew whereby she stood,
Two glowing gems of hazel fire :
And though a single sparkling tear—
Upon each lower eyelid checked,
Whose thick silk fringe, a coalblack streak,
So darkly decked her flushing cheek
In mellow contrast to its clear
Rich almond brown—alone confest
Some softer feelings lurked among
The passions that her bosom wrung ;
Yet indignation's withering flame
So towered and triumphed o'er the rest,
Did so enkindle and inform
Her heaving breast, her writhing frame,
Just then, you would almost have deemed,
Her very tresses as they streamed,
With lightnings from that inner storm,
And not with flecks of sunset, gleamed.

" *Slaves!*" she was saying : "*this to me!*
Me, Amohia! Know you not
The daughter of the 'Wailing Sea?'
Is TANGI-MOANA *forgot?*
When he shall this vile outrage know,
Your homes shall blaze, your hearts'-blood flow;
A life for every hair shall pay
Of her you've dared insult this day!"

Swift to her aid our Wanderer sprung,
Aside those ruffians roughly flung;
Cut, tore away, the bonds that laced
Those tender arms, that slender waist;
Reproached, rebuked with sarcasm strong
The culprits for their coward wrong;
The Maid with soothing words addrest—
Regret and deep disgust expressed
At what disturbed her—so distrest;
By every gesture, look, declared
How much her grief and pain he shared;
Urged all that might with most effect
Her anger stay, her grief allay,
And smooth her ruffled self-respect.

And if, while thus the Maid he freed
With eager haste, and soon replaced
Her mantle, tagged with sable cords
Of silky flax in simple taste,
He could not choose but interfuse
Some looks amid his cheering words,
Keen admiration's natural meed
To one with so much beauty graced;
Think you, this stranger's form and mien
Could fail to make their influence felt;
Unconscious though she might have been
Of their magnetic power to melt,
Pierce, permeate her spirit's gloom,
And all her brightening breast illume,
Till docile, ductile, it became
To his persuasive voice's sway—
Mild breathings of discretion, reason's claim;

As on a summer day
The silent sunbeams sink into and fill
A snowy cloud, and make it lighter still
For gentlest breeze to bear away?
And pleased was he, surprised to mark
How swiftly vanished every trace
Of passion so tempestuous, dark;
Its shadow floating off a face
Where, sooth to say, at any time
It seemed as alien, out of place,
As some great prey-bird's, haply seen,
Not mid the awful regions where he breeds,
Sky-sweeping mountains, towering peaks sublime,
But in a land with daisied lawns and meads
And rippling seas of poppied corn serene.

VII.

And all her story soon was told;
How she had left Mokoia's isle
That central in the lake alone
Rose high—a bristling mountain-hold,
With fort and fosse—a dark green boss
On that bright shield of azure-stone—
Had left the isle, the time to while
With one companion in her light canoe;
While in a larger came a fisher-crew
She wiselier should have kept in view;
But they two of the sport had soon
Grown weary in the glaring noon;
So landed, from the sun's attacks
Their splendour-puckered eyebrows to relax

In the refreshing grateful shade
A clump of trees not distant made;
Thence to a spot amid the level hills
Of Rangikáhu, where a hotspring fills,
Near a deserted settlement,
A square stone-tank ('twas Miroa's whim), they went
To boil some sweet roots which they found
As they expected in a patch
Of old abandoned garden-ground:
That done, they strolled the forest through,
And strolled to little purpose too;
Had tried a parrot for a pet to catch
In vain; had seen, by marshy glade
Or woodside brake, look where they might,
No tangle of convolvulus to twine
Into rich coronals of cups aglow
With deep rose-purple or delicate white
Pink-flushed as sunset-tinted snow;
No clematis, so lovely in decline,
Whose star-flowers when they cease to shine
Fade into feathery wreaths silk-bright
And silvery-curled, as beauteous. And they knew
The early season could not yet
Have ripened the alectryon's beads of jet,
Each on its scarlet strawberry set,
Whence sweet cosmetic oils they press
Their glittering blue-black hair to dress
Or give the skin its velvet suppleness:
So they had loitered objectless,
And chaunting songs or chatting strayed
Till by his rude associates met.
Her simple story told, the Maid
Asked in her turn the Wanderer's name;

Tried to pronounce it too—but still,
With pretty looks of mock distress
And scorn at her own want of skill,
And tempting twisting lips, no stain
Of tattoo had turned azure—found
"Ranolf" too strange and harsh a sound
For her harmonious speech to frame;
So after various efforts vain
"Ranóro" it at last became,
The nearest imitation plain
Her liquid accents could attain.
Thus, when at length they reached the shore,
Had found and freed and comforted
The damsel who at first had fled
(Poor little Miroa, weeping sore),
And launched the small canoe once more,
'Twas with a farewell kind and gay
She bade the stranger "Go his way;"
'Twas with her radiant ready smile
She started for the mountain-isle,
Which then, one mass of greenish gold,
Shone out in sharp relief and bold
Against the further hills that lay
In solemn violet-gloom—grim, dark and cold.

VIII.

So towards his tent his steps he bent;
Nor marvel if as home he went
His thoughts to her would still recur:—
"—But Amohia! what a glorious creature
In every gesture, every feature!
Such melting brilliant eyes! I swear

They cast a shadow from whate'er
They rest upon! I do believe they throw
Such shifting circlets of soft light
On what she looks at, as a sunbeam weaves
On the green darkness of the noonday woods,
Through chinks in the transparent leaves!
And then her hair! to see it but unbound!
Such black abundant floods
Of tresses making midnight all around
For those twin stars to shine through! while between
In glimpses the fair neck was seen
Just as at night upon those white
And windheaped hummocks of glimmering sand—
Thickflowing sand—so finely sifted
By the gales whereby 'twas drifted—
Soft patches of pale moonlight stand
Beside their sable shadows. Then her teeth!
All things that most of whiteness boast
How dull and dim beside them! The far wreath
Of snow upon those peaks eternal;
The sea-foam creaming round the coast—
The wave-bleached shell upon it tost—
No, none of these—perhaps the kernel
Of a young cocoanut when newly broken
Would best their blue-white purity betoken.
But what were graces so inviting
Without the soul—the spirit's charm
That from some well of witchery internal
Comes dancing up, delighted and delighting,
Comes sparkling through them—bright and warm!
How frank and noble is her face!
And what a sunny pride and sweetness lies
In those open brilliant eyes!

Her voice chimes like a merry bird's—
How winning are her cheerful words!
With what a blithe and stately grace
She drew her glistening flaxen mat,
  With chequered border decked,
Into the hollows of her wavy form
  And stepped away erect!
  A maiden of a million that!"

Strange power of Beauty! in a moment's space
It photographs itself upon the brain,
And though with limnings soft as light, imprints,
Burns in, such deep encaustic tints,
  The finest line, the tenderest stain,
  No future impress can displace,
  No wear and tear of Time efface.

CANTO THE SECOND.

I.

But this "Ranoro"—Ranolf—who was he?—
Let us a brief while turn aside and see.

Sprung from a race of hardy mountaineers—
At the remote extreme of Britain's isle,
Where rugged capes confront the Arctic sky,
Now faint beneath the pale and tender smile
Of Summer's lingering light that sadly cheers;
Now through rent chasms of the storm-cloud's pile
Seen lurking lone in grim obscurity;
Where whirlpools boil, and eddying currents scar
The tides that sweeping from the Atlantic far
In finest season at their gentlest flow
Swarm up a thousand rocks, shoot high in air—
Columns of cloud a moment towering clear—
Then sink at once plumb-down and disappear,
While all the shining rocksides, black and bare,
Are streaked with skeiny streams of hurrying snow
Like stormers beaten back that headlong go;—
There was he born; did there his childhood pass
Mid wastes of purple moor and green morass.

His father, last of a long race decayed
Of pastoral chiefs, when all their land was gone
Had manlike set himself to humbler trade;
And something more than competence had made
From calcined kelp, and that free-splitting stone
Which in sea depths or silent cliffs, unknown
A thousand centuries, unquarried lay
Stored up and fashioning for the future beat
And ceaseless tramp of busy millions' feet
In that enormous World-Mart far away;
But most from fisheries, filling all the bays
With ruddy shifting sails in sun or haze,
When rippling loud, with myriad gleam and glance
And rustling shiver o'er its wide expanse,
The liquid mass of seething Ocean seemed
Quickened to silvery life that one way streamed.
  Such sights and sounds inspired the growing Boy
With wondering exultation; and the joy
Of deeper thought and loftier feeling lent
To the mere gladness of temperament.
But books and fancy and old fishers' tales
Of glorious climes beyond these mists and gales
Soon made the youngster restless—stirred his blood
With impulses resistless, such as drive
That insect-dragon scaly-winged to strive
And struggle through his chasmed channel's mud,
And reckless dash into the splendour-flood,
The new wide pool of light he feels and sees;
Such longings, as, when Summer's searching heats
Find out the butterflies in their retreats,
They yearn with, till, unvexed by any breeze
The velvet-winged ones at her sweet command,
Sole, or in slow-revolving twos and threes

Float in a crimson flutter through the land.
Thus the Boy fevered till his sire's consent
He gained to gratify his natural bent
Towards sailor life, and follow o'er the main,
Although the favourite son, his brethren twain.
So from his schools, and tasks, and tutors free,
Away he went at twelve years old to Sea.

II.

But what preceptor like the mighty Ocean
To kindle thought and manifold emotion?
Majestic in its every form,
Stupendous calm or terror of the storm;
For ever to the dullest sense
A symbol of Omnipotence;
Yet like that Oriental notion,
That Deity of old devotion,
Omnipotence so lightly roused to ire,
And fickle as a flame of fire.

And with this fierce Sublimity, despite
The terrors of its treacherous might,
Its ruthless rage or sleek perfidious play,
As 'twere with some tremendous beast of prey
Half-tamed, the Sailor lives from day to day,
Lives cautiously familiar, hour by watchful hour
For ever in its presence—in its power.

But what a hardy pride his bosom warms
The while he runs the gauntlet through the storms,
Playing with such a foe in wary strife
A match whereof the forfeit is his life,

The gain, more than his own, another's pelf;
With such apparent odds against himself,
The seeming desperation of the game
Hardens the coarser soul it cannot tame
Into a blind oblivion of the morrow,
A stoic mirth that laughs at vice and sorrow;
While he of nobler mind and loftier aim
Is nursed by consciousness of danger, still
Escaped by foresight or subdued by skill,
Into a calm unboastful strength of will,
A sober self-reliance, firm and grave;
And feels as o'er vast Ocean's baffled wave
Triumphantly he steers from clime to clime
Elate with something of its own sublime.

And many a vacant hour, on many a theme,
Our thoughtful Sea-boy found to muse or dream;
Those vigils which the sailor needs must keep
In the sky-girt seclusion of the Deep;
Oft when the playful billows, lightly curled,
Run past the ship, and quiet seems, as sleep,
The lone retreat that roams about the world—
That white-winged monastery moving still
Of rugged celibates against their will;
Or when in darkness, towards her goal unseen,
On moonless midnights mournfully serene,
She seems, as by some instinct, self-inspired,
Still pressing on her eager quest untired;
While, the obscurely-branching clouds between,
Crossed stays and braces—silent rocking spars
Seem mingling dimly with the dancing stars;
Or when, if steady-breathing trade-winds blow,
No shift of sails for days required, the crew

About the deck their quiet tasks pursue ;
The dragging sail with rudely-skilful hands
They patch, or splice the rope's stiff-plaited strands,
Or twirl with balanced backward steps and slow
The whizzing yarn, still pondering as they go
The long-drawn tale it types of blended joy and woe ;
Or when, her topsails squared, with plunging ease,
The ship goes reeling right before the breeze ;
And he who has the watch, relaxing now,
May lean and mark, with thoughts far elsewhere, how
The bowsprit weaves great circles on the sky—
Down sinks the deck with all its life—up fly
The wide horizon and dark Ocean's plain ;
And then the buoyant deck ascends again :
While speeding after, ever and anon,
A huge blue watery hill comes roaring on,
Tiger-like, open-mouthed, in furious chase ;
But near the flying stern with slackened pace,
And lowered crest, seems first disposed to see
What the strange winged Leviathan may be
That dares amid these boisterous brawlers stray ;
And, fearful the encounter to essay,
Falls back in a broad burst of foam, and hissing slinks away.

No lack of change each feeling to employ !
How his eyes widened with a solemn joy
When on some witching night
The jutting corner of the gibbous Moon—
A golden buoy
That weltered in a sable sea of cloud
(One level mass extending wide,
The firmament all bare beside)—
Shed an obscure and ominous light,

And fitful gusts scarce dared to moan aloud :
    How was the heart-leap of his exultation
    Sustained—sublimed by thrilled imagination
When, if a storm came veiling all the noon,
    Old Ocean, rising in gigantic play,
    Marshalled his multitudinous array
    Of waves tumultuous into ridges gray,
And sent them whirling on their headlong way,
    Host after host of crested cavalry
Charging in lines illimitable, urged
By trumpet winds whose deafening bray
Drowned the sharp hiss of myriad-lancing spray,
Into the horrible white gloom profound
That gathered, thickened all around !
And when the dimness of the squall was gone,
    Haply, to some far region bound,
The great whale went majestically by—
Plunging along his mighty course alone,
    Into the watery waste unknown ;
Cleaving with calm, deliberate speed,
The battling waves he would not heed ;
    While at long intervals upthrown
Successive jets of spouted brine,
Decreasing with the distance, in a line,
    Told how he ne'er diverged
An instant from his haughty path
Into the black heart of the tempest's wrath,
That like dense smoke before him scowled,
For all the clamorous coil of winds that howled
And waves that leapt around him as he past
And flung his foamy banner to the blast.

III.

But with these Ocean-scenes the Sea-boy fed
On others fruitful both for heart and head;
Had glimpses of strange lands and men as strange;
Saw with each clime their minds and manners change:
Learnt how on God by various names they call,
While God's great smile shines equally on all;—
Allah, unimaged, One; Brahma, Vishnu,
And Siiva—monster-imaged One in Three;
Ormusd—'Ahuramasda'—name profound—
'Living I Am'—that splendour! One of Two
At war—dark Ahriman his throne invading,
Piercing with evil first the shell so sound,
His cosmic Egg-of-Order's perfect round;—
Manitou, mistlike with his pipewhiff fading;—
Buddha—prince, mystic, moralist—at last
Made God for teaching that no God can be:—
Arab—Hindu—Red Indian—Jew—Parsee;
Chinese Joss-beater, little reverent, too—
That cracker-loving creature of the past—
Blithe spirit—soul a lifeless leaden cast;
Who with high-sublimated Gods, a store,
His Buddha, Fo—Confutzee's Tien—Taou
That pure God-Intellect of Lao-tse,
Breathes blinding fog—Convention-fixed of yore—
Of grossest superstition. With the rest,
The necromancing negro of the West,
The terrorist of Obeah. These he scanned;
And many a charm on each delightful land
Lavished by Art's or liberal Nature's hand:
Inhaled the breath that through dense mist distils
From green spruce woods and all the sea-air fills

With sweet sour odours from Canadian hills :
Dwelt with enraptured gaze on Hindostan's
Umbrageous bowers of spice and spreading fans,
And glistening ribbon-leaves and arching plumes ;
Her starry palms and sacred peepuls set
On many-fingered roots, a snaky net ;
Or propping their highroofed magnificence
On pendent pillars ; clustering gorgeous glooms
Whence pointed domes of marble mosques and tombs
Emerge—from that deepbosoming defence
Blackgreen—into the burning atmosphere ;
Or gilt pagodas rise above the shade
Like spires of thick cardoon-leaves closely laid,
All in blue tanks reflected, still and clear.
Or else that tropic Isle of Springs entranced
The lad—who revelled in its noonday glare
And silence deep, so tremulously hot—
So gently interrupted when it chanced
A sudden and soft fluttering in the air,
Like silverpaper rumpled, startlingly
Whispered some flying rainbow-fragment nigh,
Darting in downy purple golden-shot ;
Or, as suspended by his long bill's tip
On viewless wings a-quiver poised, to sip
A crimson cactus-bloom—the honied dew
Which from that silky breast, so fit in hue
And texture fine, the airy suckling drew.
Safely that land of merry slaves he saw
Late ruined by a half-completed law ;
When thoughtless theorists had flung aside
The evil bonds by ancient Custom tied,
Nor better bonds they wore themselves, supplied ;
Had left to tyrannies of grovelling sense

The victims of their vain benevolence;
Left them still basely free from forethought, care,
And loftier loads the self-dependent bear;
Left them untaught to welcome Labour's pains,
More nobly slaves to all a freeman's chains;
To feel, the highest freedom all can reach
Is but the highest self-restraint of each;
True freedom is a grave and sober thing,
With loyalty to Right crowned inward king;
While laws of Duty made despotic, make
The *only* freedom mobs nor kings can break.

IV.

So four years passed: to him a happy time.
Meanwhile his brothers both in youthful prime
Had perished; one, the pest of that fair clime,
The demon lurking in its loveliness,
The yellow fever's swiftly-withering flame
Had caught up and consumed: and that distress
Scarce over, from the Storm-Cape tidings came
Doubtful, which soon for doubt left little room,
The other must have met as sharp a doom—
Himself, his ship and shipmates whirled away
In Ocean's wild tempestuous embrace
To some unknown unfathomable Tomb.
Then did the anguish-smitten Father pray
The youngest, last remaining of his race
To leave a calling where such risks were rife,
And live at home, his age's staff and stay.
So, with what grace he might, though grieving sore,
The stripling gave his dutiful consent

Henceforth to follow some pursuit ashore,
Where Death, the Shade that dogs the steps of Life,
Upon his prey though equally intent,
Because less startling, seems less imminent.

V.

To tutors now and long-left tasks restored,
The sea-emboldened, self-reliant Boy
Soon grew enamoured of his new employ.
And many things those tutors never meant
Into a mind of such inquiring bent
His classics and his metaphysics poured.
But most he loved, could ne'er enough adore
The Godlike spirit of that grand Greek lore
That first taught Man his glorious being's height;
Taught him to stand, the Universe before,
Erect in moral, intellectual might,
And brave, in strength of Soul, the adverse infinite.
How would their strains his kindling bosom warm,
Those daring darling Poets, who enshrined
The freest Spirit in the purest Form—
In matchless Beauty such consummate Mind.
How would he triumph with the Theban Maid
Who, in no armour but instinctive sense,
The panoply of conscious right, arrayed,
Her lofty sentiment her sole defence,
Risked all the murderous rage of tyrant force
To snatch a burial for a brother's corse;
Though all the gods—all worldly wisdom's saws,
All cherished loves and all Convention's laws,
Denounced herself and spurned her holy cause.
Antigone could teach him that the test
Of right and wrong lay in his own free breast;

That right was right, despite high-seated wrong
And throned Authority by Custom strong!
That Man of all external aid bereft,
Had still himself and staunch endurance left;
Could stand above all Circumstance elate
And trust high Nature in the fight with Fate.
And when he read the agonizing cries
That vulture-tortured Giant in the skies
Utters in deathless and sublime despair,
Doomed for his love to Man that woe to bear;
And all the sad majestic converse, round
The pinnacles of Caucasus snow-crowned,
Swelling like solemn Music, and again
Dying along the illimitable air,
As, one by one, supernal visitants
Come floating up to watch the ghastly pants
And writhings of the Titan, and with vain
Compassion, taunts—temptations vainer still—
Assail his grand unconquerable Will,
And bid him break his voluntary chain,
Abandon Man, scorn that vicarious pain,
And hail the gloomy Tyrant's selfish reign;
When all the student's sense of justice rose,
Stirred by the dauntless Poet's great appeal,
In wrath against the author of such woes,
And his young heart would passionately feel
For the doomed donor of the god-wrung fire;
Think you he ne'er was tempted to inquire,
Was that outworn Olympian rule of Zeus
The only tyranny men called divine?
Was there no other nature-startling use
Of absolute power—no other punishment
Of love, inflicted on the innocent

At which instinctive Justice would repine?
But most his soul was wonderstruck to see
To what a height humanity could reach
In that divinest hemlock-drinker—he
Who welcomed Death less evil than the breach
Of fealty to his country's laws, or scant
Reliance on the faith he came to teach;
The truths his nature *forced* him to proclaim—
The necessary outcome of his frame,
Mental and moral—by the innate law
Of evolution for its excellence
Provided—as inevitable thence,
As from the sap of each peculiar plant
The special blossom earth and air must draw—
Trust absolute in the perfect Power above,
His perfect goodness; and what these must prove
(For with the ill around, what other just
Conclusion could he reach, with such a trust?)
That sole relief of every human want,
Soother and solace of the general sigh—
The soul's unbodied immortality.
And where was ever a sublimer page
Than that which paints the Godsent Prophet-Sage
Cheerily urging with his latest breath
His lofty creed upon his weeping band
Of friends—his very gaoler too, unmanned;
Then standing forth, and with dilating eyes,
That look straightforward—bold and calm—'bullwise'
Into the dread Eternity so nigh,
With one libation to the gods on high,
Drinking the Elixir both of life and death!
And as the deadly influence upward stole
And sobs broke forth he could no more console,

Lifting the mantle from his failing sight,
Just ere his soaring spirit winged its flight,
To make with accents faint his last bequest—
While haply in those eyes supreme o'er pain
A moment's humorous glimmer shone again—
That votive cock to the medicinal God
Of herbs—his soul's last evidence to be
Of joy at shaking off this mortal clod,
And his triumphant gratitude attest
To one whose potent drug had set him free.

VI.

Next with uprooting Metaphysics toyed
The youth—their tangled subtleties enjoyed;
Nor, as his tutors counselled would confine
His tasks to careworn, truth-adoring Locke;
Eager to learn what "paying out more line"
Where Locke had cast it, led to—solid rock,
Mud, quicksand, or the fathomless profound.
The more line ran, more depth there seemed to sound.
It took him, as you know, to that rare creed,
Etherial, beautiful—the fertile seed,
First dropped by Locke, our goodly Bishop caught
And sowed and reared into rich food for thought,
Heavy with ears of amaranthine gold
That yet may yield their glorious hundred-fold.
"All possible ideas are mere sensations,
Or our reflections on them," LOCKE insists;
"But half the first are Sense's own creations,
No faithful types of what in truth exists;
Not in the rose the red, nor in light-rays
Its texture splits, but in the eyes that gaze;
Not in the fire, but in our frames, the heat;

Not in the honey, but our tongues the sweet;
Not in the thunder, but our ears, the roar;
These are impressions on the brain—no more:
But form, solidity, extension, power
To move or rest, are Matter's genuine dower,
Her real outside existence." "Nay—pursue
Your doubt," cries BERKELEY; "probe them through and through,
And you will find these qualities you flatter
Yourself you prove essential in this Matter,
No more substantial than its red and blue."
And then the mighty mitred Analyst,
Silk-aproned but sincere Psychologist
And Sage—by few believed, by all beloved,
With subtlest power "unanswerably proved,
What no man in his senses can admit,"
(The phrase of little truth and not much wit,
Is Reid's—though Hume had first acknowledged it)
Proved that all things we hear, see, feel around,
Have no such base as Matter—only hold
Existence in pure Spirit—their sole ground:
Forces are they, from Infinite Mind proceeding,
Spiritually active, wheresoe'er it be,
On finite mind to print, in order due,
Sensations, not deceptive nor misleading—
But spiritual coin as spiritual Coiner, true,
And real with Spirit's sole reality.
So Berkeley said and proved his flawless case.
But HUME came sliding in with smiling face,
Veiling the grimmest strength in easy grace;
The pleasant playful Giant—gentle Chief
Of sceptics, dealing blows without a sign
Of effort—slashing with a sword so fine—

Killing with lightning-touches bright and brief;
So wise, so good; whose adversaries found
His silken glove a Cestus iron-bound,
When staggering all the gladiator press
He proved—or seemed to prove—to their distress
And ours, that Thought itself and Consciousness
Had no such base as Mind—which only meant
Trains of impressions and ideas that went
And came *in nothing*—neither more nor less;
For no recipient spirit could be perceived,
And Matter was already gone and shent;
And he had settled to his own content
(To such a dogma, ye who *can*, consent!)
No Cause did ever yet *produce* Effect
However Custom may the two connect.
Therefore for pictures we within us find,
No Power without—above—of any kind
Need be, or could be, as their cause assigned.
So must we Matter, Mind, God, Soul, alike
Out of the ranks of real existence strike:
And yet as Mind and Matter both, without
Or spite of Reason, *must* be still believed—
Nature took care of that—that much achieved—
The only clear conclusion was dim Doubt.

Thus Locke by Berkeley—Berkeley thus by Hume,
Was pounced on in retributive swift doom,
Hand over hand, as children play, so pat,
Each crushing his great predecessor flat:
So swiftly hurried down the eddying tide
Of speculation which began to flow
In the far East three thousand years ago
When doubting dusky Sages threw aside

Their faith in those symbolic wheelspoke arms
And double heads of deities of Ind ;
And some mild paddy-fed pale-blooded crew
Of subtle theorists argued nought was true,
Nought real but Brahma—him in whom inhere
All magic-lantern shadows that appear
As living shapes in this illusive sphere.
Then Brahma's essence, subtilised and thinned,
In Kapila's self-styled " Perfect Wisdom " grew
To Absolute Spirit—Thinking Substance pure
And abstract as that pure unworldly Jew,
The spiritual Spinoza, ever drew.
But earlier still, in wild recoil more sure
From Brahmin tyranny of creed and caste,
The o'er-refining Orient fancy passed
To dreams the maddest ever Reasoning spun,
In that high-moralled faith that still has charms
(Because its founder's self, made God, replaced
And vivified so soon for vulgar taste
The No-God he had taught) to sway such swarms,
Dusk Aryan and Turanian tawny-skinned ;
That fullest-millioned Faith beneath the Sun,
Which Sakya Muni—princely eremite—
First saddened into—sickened with the sight
Of sorrow and pain inseparable seeming
From life—his own a pleasure-sated blight
With high desire forlornly through it gleaming ;
So with a proud deliberate despair
Conceived his monstrous method of redeeming,
By guiding, souls back to their primal night
Of non-existence ; which his pupil and friend
Kásyapa teaches they already share,
Therein are based—begin—and ought to end ;

Nor rests, like Hume, content in doubt to pause,
But from his metaphysic "Basket" draws
Negation of all spirit—God—first cause—
Brahma or Absolute Being—all and each
Creator and created—matter—mind—
Alike chimeras ; wisdom's highest reach
To know this nothingness ; the soul's true aim
To lose existence and partake the same ;
Extinguished then, with consciousness consigned
To darkness—blown out like a taper's flame,
To enter so "Nirvana"—there to be
Absurdly blest with blank Nonentity.

VII.

Well—posed with that result of logic-fence,
Our student tried the school of Common Sense.
But soon the irreverent youth came bouncing thence :
"What," cried he, "is it not a false pretence
That makes of Metaphysics but a name,
And theirs to Science a preposterous claim
Who dare their doughty reasoning begin
By begging—nay, with beggars' impudence
Demanding the one point at issue here ;
The only one that Logic seemed to hurt—
Dare for superior density assert
The victory their acuteness could not win ?
O REID and BROWN, my crafty friends ! 'tis clear
You found when sorely gravelled by this Hume
'Twas harder far to prove than to assume ;
An easier feat for souls of sluggish pace
To seize the palm-wreath than to run the race ;
Boldly to claim the stakes—while beaten they
Throw up the game their business 'tis to play !"

VIII.

How gladly then he roved from such chopped hay
To fields that seemed all clover, green and gay
Though hedged with worse than Indian orange-thorns—
Sharp subtleties for Doubt's intrusive horns.
Did not those free-souled Germans point the way
To regions bathed in Truth's unclouded day?
Where Knowledge hampered by no faintest trace
Of Doubt might soar secure in pride of place,
And Faith fold Science in a fond embrace?
Did not great KANT in pedant's jargon show,
As mathematic truths from Reason—so
Do moral from the inborn Conscience flow
By mere necessity?—those mightier facts
And fixed conditions in which Reason acts—
The Soul—the Universe—but pre-suppose
And force you to the grand Idea behind
Whence both must spring, wherein are both combined—
To God—the source of all that thinks or knows,
All Being's boundless origin and close?
Was not that cold, cloud-cleaving Aeronaut,
Potent, with swoln balloon of subtlest thought,
With Logic's self, triumphantly to lift
Man's deathless Hope into an atmosphere
Serene above the wayward dust and drift
Of Logic—from Sensation's vapours clear?
Did not poor Faith, doubt-prest from shift to shift,
Find a safe refuge in that "Reason pure?"
Trusting ensconced in Science so obscure—
A pachydermatous Philosophy
Of scarce pronounceable hard names, to be
Both scoff and sceptic proof: and might not she,

That lofty Hope, in such environment
Of prickly briars of Thought—a tangle rude—
Sit like the Beauty in the long-charmed wood,
Secure—supreme—inviolable? pent
In hard, repellent reasonings that defy
Assault—and there kept living safe and sound,
Like bright-eyed toad with rock encompassed round;
Buried in chaff of dialectics dry,
A chrysalis (like that with reeled-off floss,
Bared of its dress, all amber gleam and gloss,
The careful schoolboy hides in homely bran)
Whence a new Psyche should emerge for Man?
Like Psyche's self, say—from blue Italy
Prepared to cross the rude rough-handling sea,
Laid up in wood and iron, sound and safe
In naked beauty from all chance of chafe—
So closely presses round her spiritual face
And limbs of tender marble and white grace,
The hard-caked sawdust of her packing-case.

But, O conclusion lame and impotent!
O rage of vigorous reasoning vainly spent!
Those great ideas—Time, Space and Cause—'tis plain,
Though notions connate with the nascent brain,
Have in essential fact no solid ground—
Only within the human soul are found;
Though necessary bases of our thought
Are from no prototypes beyond us brought!
That God is but a sort of ghost confined
To haunt the shadowy chambers of the mind!
As if within a glass-roofed palace grew
Some strange grand Tree of mystic shape and hue,
With various virtues wondrously arrayed—

With mighty fronds and majesty of shade,
And towering crest sufficiently sublime;
Within those vitreous walls compelled, no doubt,
By nature's laws luxuriantly to sprout,
But with no fellow—no resemblance known,
Or able to exist in any clime
Mid the green glories of the world without;
A most magnificent, yet monstrous cheat,
Proud overgrowth of artificial heat,
And that peculiar edifice alone.
"Why, if this God's a product of our own,
Which ends in us, though there perforce it breeds,
A doubtful light which but to darkness leads,"
Our student thought—"what waste of toil and time,
These more than acrobatic feats to climb
Such crags precipitous, such slippery heights,
Where no rewarding view our toil requites;
No vision of the City long-desired,
Though brief as that in Moslem myths—perchance
Seen standing—sudden—silent—sunrise-fired,
Before the desert-wanderer's awestruck glance,
Far stretching multitudinous array
Of gilded domes and snowy minarets,
And tiers of long arcades, rich-roofed with frets
More delicate than frostwork! then, again,
Gone—vanished! and a hundred years in vain
Resought, but gladdening nevermore the day;
Not e'en such glimpse, O mighty Kant!—at most
When we have reached your height at so much cost,
In densest fog we see a finger-post,
You say directs us to that City fair;
But is no proof of any City there!

Some letters on its arms obscurely seen
Your spectacles discover; what they mean,
In worse than three-tongued wedge-rows sealed up fast,
We have to take from you on trust at last.

"And, then, that 'Reason practical'—that creed
Of Action that its own high laws must breed;
'Will must be free, whatever you may prove;
Run where it lists, yet always in a groove—'
Why, we are drifting back to Brown and Reid!"

IX.

So to that Spirit erect and pure, he next
Resorted (with these fancied failures vexed)
The march majestic and the genuine ring
Of whose high eloquence on one high theme,
How best aloft the expanded soul may wing
Her way, and best sustain her flight supreme—
Had all the warranty a life could bring,
The faithful mirror of his faith—sublime
In self-dependent stateliness severe,
And steadfast single eminence of aim;—
Fichte—whose name recalls a dearer Fame—
A trenchant towering Spirit as grand and true!
Of those who think, profoundest and the prime;
He whose capacious soul's ascending Sphere
Oft looms obscure while flashing brightness through
Dull mists it kindles till they disappear;
Who, rolling back the ponderous stone of Time,
Makes the dead Past, upstarting from the gloom,
In Truth's rough Poesy lightning-bathed, outbloom
The living Present, whose loud shams—with might

And hammer like his own white-knuckled Thor's,
And love that for the culprit's sake abhors
The crime,—his prophet-hand was sent to smite !—
Fichte—great voice to rouse, great heart to cheer !
This greater could not hear it and not leap
In unison, "Deep calling unto Deep"—
Could not from such a credence and career
Withhold the dower of his undying praise ;
Which saw therein the far-reflected gleam
Of high-endeavouring old illustrious days—
Heard solemn echoes or the etherial flow
Of Attic pacings of the Portico
And whispers from the groves of Academe,
Where Truth alone by sages world-renowned
Was sought, and made Life's rule at once when found ;—
FICHTE struck out once more for truths that shine
Instinctive and immediately divine.
In consciousness is all of God we know ;
But consciousness proclaims him ; neither dim
Nor doubtful He ; all Being's source and stream ;
Nature exists in us, and we in Him.
For "Me" and "Not-Me"—Universe and Soul
Are one—not two—and Consciousness the whole :
Nature its passive, Soul its active side ;
In Consciousness are both contained—allied ;
And from the Soul though Nature takes its rise,
It limits none the less and modifies
That worker, whose material it supplies ;
Spirit is all—and Matter there is none
But part and product of the Soul alone.
And what ideal does Consciousness proclaim
As all we know of Him whom "God" we name ?—
That active principle, which clearly seen

Is working out, whatever intervene,
The triumph in the Universe and Man,
Of all that's useful, beautiful, and good ;
That Force which forwards its consummate plan
Of progress endless towards the perfect Day
Of moral Order's universal sway ;
And to the Soul above all tumult cries
Of one high Duty still to be pursued,
With that "Divine Idea" to harmonise
The Will, and all its faculties subdued
Into devout co-operative mood,
Press forward freely to the ennobling prize.

High thoughts ! yet haply Hindu still ; so like
The course—nor much unlike the goal—to those
The later Buddhists for the soul propose,
Dropping the dreary nihilistic phases
Of Sakya's faith too purely insane to strike
The fancy of the myriads, else its foes ;
Backsliding into healthier dreams and brighter,
In Burmah or Nepaul ; or such as lie
Obscurely hidden in the mystic cry,
The shaveling in red robes and yellow mitre,
In snowy Thibetan devoutly raises
At Lama-ridden Lhassa, when he phrases
In one short shibboleth his prayers and praises :
"Gem in the Lotus-flower, Amen !" whereby
He breathes his aspiration to proceed—
His soul's intense desire to wing its flight
Through Æons of blest Being—height o'er height,
Till evermore suffused with purer light
It merge—from death, disease, old age and need,
And all the griefs of gross existence freed,—

Perfect, in Buddha's Soul—its boundless meed—
Absorbed in that All-perfect Infinite !—
A heterodox "Nirvana," worthier far
By ages of vast virtue to be won ;
No 'taper-flame blown out'—a blissful star
Lost in the splendour of the noonday sun.

"True," thought the lad, "this Man was true, indeed :
A noble Teacher of a noble Creed !
But should a sage so lofty lapse again
Towards pure assumption's unassured domain ?
Revert to doubtful regions long resigned,
Basing our Berkeley's Universe of Mind
On Common Sense—though of a nobler kind
Than puzzled Reid could for poor Matter find ?
'What must be, must'—'It is because it is'—
Is proud Philosophy reduced to this ?
Yet, to persuade us how the Soul may climb
Triumphant o'er material Space and Time,
Stronger than all that dialectic strife,
His most convincing logic was his life ;
Of truths the stern philosopher had taught
Proof most profound, perhaps, the patriot brought,
When, finishing his last great fight for God,
And many a rapt impassioned period,
Down from his desk the mighty Master came,
Unmoved by murmur low, or plaudit loud,
Or fervent blessing from the student-crowd ;
And left the loved arena of his fame
With shouldered musket in the ranks to stand,
And fall or conquer for his Father-land."

X.

Then SCHELLING plies the metaphysic ball,
Which Reason's racket still will strike aloft
To overfly Sensation's bounding wall,
Though to the ground a thousand times it fall.
Those two Ideas we prate about so oft,
The Soul—the Universe—are really two,
And are identified—O, not in you,
Nor any finite Consciousness so small,
But only in the Absolute—the All.
Spirit is Matter that itself surveys;
And Matter, Spirit's undiscerning phase;
They are the magnet's two opposing poles,
And each the other balances—controls:
Both in a centre of indifference rest,
Which their essential being is confest:
As in the magnet's every point—we see
In all the works of Nature just these three;
But that which bounds them all and each degree,
The Absolute—the Magnet's self—must be,
Except at Being's most exalted height—
Impersonal—unconscious—infinite;
For God—that Absolute—still strives in vain,
In Nature's blind inferior works; nor can
In any form Self-Consciousness attain,
Save in the highest reasoning power of Man,
That central point, which Soul and Nature gain;—
Unconscious else the Universal PAN.

Behold, then, three-and-twenty centuries passed,
The stately Ship of Western Thought at last,

Striking and stranded on the barren shore
Where struck that Buddhist bark so long before,
Left high and dry with all its phantom freight;
Thither impelled by that satiric fate
That dogs our intellectual pride, and brings
Shipwreck with its conviction shallow and vain,
That 'tis a storm-charmed cruiser, this poor brain,
Built, rigged, and manned to circumnavigate
The mighty round of all existing things.
So Schelling digs where Kásyapa had dug;
Magniloquent, yet microscopic elf,
So makes all Nature but the high-plumed hearse
Of God gone dead; so, whipping out his cord,
O metaphysical and monstrous Thug!
Strangles Creation's life out; in a word,
Finding the Universe within himself,
Leaves nought but Self within the Universe.

"Alas!" thought Ranolf, "were it wrong to call
This the most drear of metaphysic dreams—
The most revolting, mean result of all?
The Being, then, of highest worth it seems,
Which that World-ghost, that blind and senseless force
Evolves in its uncaused unconscious course,
Is but this inefficient soul of ours—
The one God, Man—for all his boasted powers
A clay-clad, wingless, weak ephemeral,
A worm upon this earth-speck doomed to crawl.
Is *he* the sole Intelligence? can he
The crown and climax of all Being be
Throughout that million-starred immensity?
Prove it by demonstration flawless, strong;
The wild conclusion proves some premiss wrong;

Absurd, as if those dwellers by old Nile
Had, in mere Scarabeus-worship vile,
Crowned with a beetle their great Pyramid—
The Monarch Builder out of sight and hid."

XI.

To mystic depths and mistier. HEGEL shrouds
Himself and Faith in denselier-rolling clouds,
Like Arab genie sore opprest in fight;
His splendour flashes through redoubled night.
Thoughts are the same as Things; and what is true
Of one must be so of the other too;
So Non-existence, as a thought, must be
Like pure Existence, a reality.
Of Being absolute, and uncombined
With qualities of any form or kind,
What can we know or predicate aright?
Is not Non-being in the self-same plight?
The positive and negative descried
In all things, must be these and nought beside;
For each Idea or Object (which you please—
Both are the same) developes into these;
But these destroy and shut each other out,
A negative is all they bring about:
But as the idea is there, and must remain,
That negative must be denied again.
As Abstract Space, for instance, cannot be
Conceived as boundless, or as bounded either;
Yet must be one, to be at all, you see,
Then cannot be at all, because 'tis neither;
A negative that meets denial clear,
For space *is* something after all, and *here*.

That last negation, then, the Idea revives,
And real essential Being to it gives
In the "Conditioned" where alone it lives.
Those magnet-poles, the two extremes, are gone,
And in the central point survive alone;
Object and Subject, Universe and Soul,
Are in that centre, one and real, and whole;
Each in itself a nothing we may call,
But their relation to each other—all.
Like alkali and acid, they attract
Each other, meet, and perish in the act—
The effervescence rests the only fact.
So the "Becoming"—the immediate spring
From Nought to Somewhat, is the vital thing;—
"Well, well!" broke out our student here, "at least
It cannot be denied this great High Priest
Of metaphysic Mysteries, has the wit,
The ant-lion boasts who scoops his coneshaped pit
In subtlest sand, and there securely hides;
And when into the trap the victim slides,
And strives in vain to climb the slipping sides,
Down, deeper down, the crafty digger goes,
And o'er his prey such blinding dust showers throws,
He triumphs quickly, and the intruder draws
Bewildered into those remorseless jaws."
But when unflinching Hegel flatly laid
The axiom down he would not have gainsaid,
Disdaining compromise—dispute—or flout
(Settling so coolly Hamlet's staggering doubt)
"To Be is Not-to-be"—and "Not-to-be
"To Be"—agree to that, or disagree,
"'Tis Logic's first great axiom, and most true!"
What *could* a youth with risible organs do,

At this, Philosophy's last grand exploit?
But "ding the book the distance of a quoit"
Away, and with a shout of laughter loud,
Take to his pipe and blow—as clear a cloud.

CANTO THE THIRD.

I.

For, as he whiffed and watched above his head
The dainty spirals float and curl and spread,
"Well then," he thought, "if we perforce must dub
These German Giants with their Logic-club,
Unwieldy champions much too prone to beat
The air with ponderous weapons, to defeat
Those agile Jacks of Science, or to screen
From errant Knights of Scepticism keen
The beauteous Truths they clumsily immure
In cavern dim or castle-cage secure;
If, like the bristled monstrous minims seen
To jerk and writhe and wriggle goggle-eyed
Within the lighted circle on the wall
Thrown by the microscopic lantern's sheen—
These crabbed and cribbed Philosophers go near
To craze, because the Apparent's magic sphere
So hems them in; and Hegel above all
Seems, like the fabled Scorpion girt with fire,
With his own logic-nippers to inflict
A bite that kills himself, in mad desire
And effort to escape from bonds so strict,
That radiant round of the Phenomenal—

What then?—the grand mysterious *outside*
Is *there*—there still, and cannot be denied:
Howe'er the thing we may define or name
The 'Unapparent' still exists the same.

"For grant it may be made by reasoning plain
That all the fair impressions on the brain
Are not the pictures of such things around,
Where no realities are like them found,
But from those decorating Senses gain,
In passing through them, all the dædal dress
Of qualities we fancy they possess,—
'Not in the rose the red—nor in light-rays
Its texture splits, but in the eyes that gaze;
Not in the thunder—honey—fire, the roar,
The heat or sweetness we perceive; all these
Lie in the Sense that hears, tastes, feels or sees;
Well, it remains as certain as before
The *causes* of these feelings lie without,
Beyond us still; for who pretends to doubt
We do not, cannot of ourselves excite
These manifold sensations?—by what right
Is it asserted, then, *that* outside sphere
Of causes is not varied, powerful, bright
And beautiful as aught we see or hear
Or any way perceive *within* the Mind?
You say, 'Light—colour—sound—taste—smell,
Are states of consciousness, but none can tell
What in themselves they are!' So far 'tis well.
'Nature in her insentient solitude
But as eternal Darkness must be viewed,
Eternal Silence.' Wherefore thus decide?
What if your bold conclusion be denied?

'The Light is in ourselves' say you—
Well, so must be the Darkness too.—
'All Nature dark without the eye,
Silent without the ear!' But why?
The Silence and the Darkness you must own
Are *our* alternatives alone,
Not Nature's!—when the Light and Sound are gone
From us, the causes of the Sound and Light,
Are these effaced because they cease to smite
Our organs? or must these become the same
Ceasing to act upon our consciousness,
As what within that consciousness is left
When ceasing to be acted on?—the things *we* name
Silence and Darkness? states we feel, bereft
Of those mysterious agents that no less
Are active—glorious—infinite—divine—
Ever impulsive—eager to impress
On other Souls whom other organs bless,
Say (for their nature none of course can guess)
Lights gorgeous, jewel-tinted, more than shine
For us—for our beholding all too fine;
And melodies of such entrancing tone
As would outravish all to mortal music known!
What! make the wondrous Universe depend
On *our* perceptions—there begin and end?
Must Senses like our own exhaust its powers?
May there not be more Senses too than ours?
Does the Sun cease to be a Sun, and die,
Hurled from his throne in yon majestic Sky,
Whene'er the Worm that grooves the flowery fret
Of pulpit-work—or Spider at his net
On some rose-knotted oak-carved canopy
Within a great Cathedral's gloom and grace—

May lose the few faint rays it feels through panes
That serve to bound, e'en while they brighten, all
Its tiny being's scant-accorded space—
Dim rays half quenched in that transparent pall,
Yet rainbow-rich with saintly blazonry
And dusky with a wealth of Angel-stains?

II.

"Well! if this non-apparent Something still
Exists, nay seems the Universe to fill,
Producing all we are and all we know;
And if its Sphere be such, the human brain
Must never hope an entrance to obtain
For Science to its wonders—overthrow
Or undermine its jealous walls—or gain
At least some glimpses of the fair domain—
By observation or deduction slow,
By force of *Intellect*—perhaps too poor
A tool to burst the Imperial Palace-door—
(Though I for one will never cease to think
The endlessly-expanding sphere allowed
To Man's Experience *must* one day supply
Some solid basis, starting-point or link—
Though many a thousand years it take, whereby
Science Demonstrative shall pierce the cloud
And back with glittering spoil come laden gloriously!)
But if *this* may not be, what then is clear?
What is the worst we then should have to fear?
Why, to confess, that Supernatural sphere,
That Unapparent region, must be such,
For Intellect thereon to logicise,
Would be to try rich colours with the touch
Or test melodious sounds with keen bright eyes—

As Dante's *heard* the sculptured Widow's speech—
On that white frieze-like Purgatorial bank
Whose end each way his eyesight could not reach—
Ask death for her son's murderer as she sank
At Trajan's feet, and ceased not to beseech
Till his roused virtue had vouchsafed her prayer;
Then *saw* the sound of visible replies
The marble Emperor made her voiceless cries.
That feat we would not ape, but rather dare
Confess that in an atmosphere so rare
The leaden wing of Logic cannot rise;
That by Emotion, not Reflection, best
The Soul is borne aloft in that fine air—
Feeling, not Thought, her fiery chariot there!
The highest Sentiment were then confest
The base whereon the highest Truth must rest
True till a higher Truth were felt or found
And by the beating hearts of men around
As such accepted—welcomed—honoured—crowned;
Still raised, refined, as Science purged away
What films of Error might obscure its ray;
Aught from that lower realm that might alloy
Its gold, would Logic fasten on—destroy;
And everything she honestly disproved,
Must be relinquished—howsoe'er beloved.

III.

"One truth we feel is safe at least—that Mind
Was ne'er by Matter compassed—caused—designed;
Or any chance or law, unconscious—thoughtless—blind.
No Logic e'er can prove—no healthy brain
The monstrous opposite can entertain:
Intelligence must have a Cause—'tis plain;

And so the Mind is framed, it *must* consent,
That Cause must be itself intelligent.

"Nor much avails the talk against 'Design.'
True, to use means, consider and contrive
And step by step slow towards an end to strive,
Has more in it of human than divine:
Yet at one flash to will and have it done,
To make conception and completion one;
Is not this justly to be deemed a sign
Of more—not less—of that peculiar might
Of forethought—adaptation—infinite
Resources in one faculty combined,
Glimpses of which we call, whene'er they shine
In finite creatures, consciousness and mind?

"But if that primal Cause, as means, employ
Growth—progress—evolution, does indeed
This fact, that other of 'design' destroy?
If Clime or outward Circumstance succeed
In forcing life into its myriad Shapes
Of beauty, fitness, symmetry so rare—
Scarce for an instant candid thought escapes
Of that designing mind its former need.
For who gave Circumstance this genius vast,
So wisely to select, extinguish, spare—
Turn out such wond'rous mechanism at last?
Whence the mould's power to shape each cunning cast?
Chance is no Chance that leads to ends as fine
As boundless Skill or Science could design.
'Law,' 'Method'! these still need the Something higher—
Designing Mind and purpose, still require.

And should you prove the human race began,
Forsooth! in manlike ape, or apelike man,
(Though why the Ape is not advancing now,
Through ages can no hair-breadth's progress show
To higher aims—let those explain who can!)
Are not Man's soaring spirit and its claim,
Its maker, mystery, miracle, the same
As if in that more vulgar conjuring way
He sprang at one great leap from ruddy clay?—
Truly, the rudimentary display
In lowlier forms, of organs—powers—we meet
In loftier—of design gives proof complete:
And were, to show design, the thing designed,
How for our finite could that infinite Mind
A more conclusive, clearer method find,
Than thus to let the self-same pathway lead
To his great ends, whereby he had decreed
Our minds designing, should themselves proceed?
And as a Painter somewhere in the dark
Leaves on his pictures his distinctive mark,
Or, haply, best the authorship to tell
Of earlier works that fond in memory dwell,
Might give to quiring Seraphs as they gaze
Enraptured on the beatific blaze
Of present Deity's immediate rays—
Haloed with every heavenly attribute—
Some favourite form of viol, harp, or lute
His less ambitious art had oft bestowed
On blind old Minstrel begging by the road;
Or peasants revelling, rid of creaking drays
And milk-white ox-teams and their latest load,
Last shaking purple hill of vintage-fruit;

The grand Designer thus, to prove when done
His works harmonious and the Worker one,
Might thus his works initial—thus impress
Ignobler traces of the lower and less
On loftier works of one Almightiness;
And show how such excess of plastic skill
Can with one method—one material still
Stop at the low or reach the high at will.

IV.

"But of that conscious Cause—what next declare?
Must we attribute, by deduction fair,
But just so much of power for good or ill
To this mysterious Being's deed or will
As in the Universe *we see* displayed?
That were indeed to limit and degrade
All possible Existence to a range
Lower and narrower (a conclusion strange!)
Than what poor finite Mortals can conceive.
In spite of Hume—'tis harder to believe
He who has done so much can not do more,
And all the evil that exists retrieve
With compensating good somewhere in store—
Than that the fault lies with the human Mind,
Too weak and narrow the true cause to find
Why from the first throughout the universe
The best has not excluded all the worse.
And more preposterous it is to dream
The Universe is an abortive scheme,
Worked by a Power unequal to its task,
Or to complete a plan it cannot mask,

Than to believe that Power—so great confest,
Spite of apparent flaws we seem to trace
In all its works—is far beyond the best
And mightiest our conceptions can embrace—
And therefore (though so much we take on trust)
Perfectly wise, good, powerful, loving, just."

V.

Well—this fresh faith in God and Good, no more,
For such a soul—so healthy, bold, and bright,
Shrivelled or shrunk in metaphysic blight—
Wherein it flourished greenly as before,
As if from deeper source unreached it came—
Than dewy grass through window-panes descried
Waving unscorched in vivid flickering flame
Reflected from the fire that burns inside.
No! strong and joyous—so he ran,
Bright and joyous like the Sun,
His free course from Boy to Man.
Evil in its thousand forms,
Fester as it might, without,
Failed to drive that heart so stout
To the fiends—Despondence—Doubt;
Deadly Serpents he could shun
Or their writhing coils repress
With that hardy hopefulness
Almost infantine, which strangles
In its cradle crawling worms
So lethal, loathly. So he found,
Though as yet 'twas theory, crowned
Only by experience slight,
Evil—sickness, pain and peril,
All that sinks cold hearts and duller,

Into icy creeds and sterile,
Like the sardonyx or beryl,
Like the prism's crystal angles—
Could but make the pure white light
Of the Good that lurks around
Everywhere and infinite,
Flash in rays of richer colour,
Streaks and stains more exquisite—
Pity—Patience—Self-denial—
Love—Endurance through all trial,
And a thousand virtues—feelings—
Gaining thence their sole revealings.

Sanguine, say you, his temper !—If his blood
Coloured his reasoning, 'twas at least as good
As props the atrabiliar doctrines dyed
So darkly on the melancholic side.
We *ground* on those mudbanks of Doubt alone
In the ebb of the world's heart or our own ;
Tangled in shallows of Despondence dark
Only when life is at low-water mark.
Not in our healthiest, our completest state
Do such misgivings our wise joys abate :
And youth's glad trust is worth most mental wealth ;
For Confidence is Life—and Hope is health :
At least his seemed so—who with pipe renewed
This way his dry soliloquy pursued :
"What ! fear we hopeful Confidence is blind ;
That the Heart's sunshine needs the clouded Mind !
Must Reason then be spurned from her high seat,
Or that most natural passion held a cheat ?
That thirst for deathless life, that high desire
With which all wakened Intellects aspire,

As the dread Serpent of Eternity
Had bitten them with fangs like those accurst
Once fabled of the dipsas—causing thirst
That quenchless burnt for ever! must this be
Held a mere lure to lead the human race
Through the long ages to some loftier place,
And from the myriad generations spent
And wasted in the wearisome ascent,
Evolve some sample of consummate skill
Whom powers with instincts harmonized should fill—
The clearest Reason and the purest Will?
That perfect race—must *it*, too, have its day,
Rise, growth, and culmination, and decay,
Then, like its predecessors, pass away?
What! could your great Contriver, then, contrive
No better shift his vast machine to drive,
Only at such a failure to arrive?
Either prevent illusive Hope's uprise,
Or make the illusion's fathomless disguise
At least impervious to human eyes?
What kind of God would show for one short hour
Such want, yet waste, of Goodness and of Power?
If such the Universe, at once declare
Some Demon-Bungler has been busy there;
Willing and yet too clumsy to deceive,
Creating spirits to aspire and grieve
And die without redemption or reprieve;
Myriads on myriads fleeting like a breath,
Endless vicissitude of Life and Death;
The swarming star-shoals coming—going—whence
Or whither? without object in the dense
Infinitude of futile impotence!

Nor boots it that the central, primal Cause
Itself might boast of permanence or pause,
Be an eternal Now—a boundless Here—
Nor like his vain creations disappear.
No! any God I would believe or teach
Should be at lowest competent to reach
The good of All through happiness of Each;
Each life progressive, and the last result
In bliss unqualified should all exult;
Perfect as well as permanent should be,
Creation's glorious Crown, and every glad degree.
Nor call God's goodness other than our own,
Different in kind, not in degree alone;
If so, let nothing be denied, averred;
Vote all assertions on the theme absurd,
Give it no thought, nor waste on it a word."

VI.

So, as we said, still high and clear forthstood,
For this inquirer's cheery thought and mood,
God and the great predominance of Good;
So could his heart retain its joyous tone;
Run over in a worship of its own;
Nor, as the taper's wax in wintry room
Melts, but congeals in winding-sheets of gloom,
Would for a moment feel its fervid flow
Chilled by keen Scepticism's cheerless page,
Or the cold spirit of a critical age
Into ill-omened dreams of hopeless woe.
If, in an argument it e'er befell
His reason baffled, made a feebler stand,
His haughty senses settled it off-hand,

Perhaps with greater reason—who can tell?
Once when, with pro's and con's eternal tired,
Some good materialist had talked him dead—
"Here try this lovely disputant—I SMELL
God's goodness in this damask rose," he said;
"O listen to the luscious miracle!
With such convincing fragrance 'tis inspired,
With such an eloquent glow—with hues so rare
And useless—arguments beyond compare,
Its crimson beauty burns upon the air!"

VII.

Yet not for this could he the more incline
To cramping creeds, or any partial shrine;
His heart was but one endless protestation
Against the slightest shackles on free Thought;
Rather than not attain the end he sought,
His strong intolerant love of toleration,
His towering spirit of tyrannous liberty,
Had *forced* all mental bond-slaves to be free.
Then all for Nature! "She alone for me!"
"*What!*" he would cry in his impetuous style,
Climbing, perhaps, some mountain-peak the while,

"*What need of Temples!* All around,
Through Earth's expanse, through Heaven's profound,
A conscious Spirit, beauty-crowned,
A visible glory breathes and breaks,
And of these mountains, moors and lakes
A Holiest of the Holies makes!
Above—around—where'er you be,
The true Shekinah shining see!
With ever-fuming Incense there

An Altar burns for praise and prayer!
Whence better to the Lord of Love
Can sorrow waft its wail above
Than from some desert-waste forlorn,
Where sadly, of all splendour shorn,
Creeps-in the stilly-dripping Morn?
Why not in deep prostration groan
On God for help when all alone
Where forests make their mighty moan?
Why not the exulting burst of praise
Pour forth where hills their great tops raise
Majestic in the silent blaze
Of Sunset over Ocean's haze?
What! shall the Spirit only draw
Near that unknown and nameless Awe
Where, beauteous though it be, there stands
Some puny work of human hands?
But I, O mystic Might! no less
As thy all-hallowed home will bless
Sublimest Nature's loveliness!
But I will dare, O Power Divine!
Revere One true transcendent Shrine
This flashing Universe of Thine!"

VIII.

Enough of this.—'Twas time for him to turn
To some profession now, and haply learn
How in the hungry press of strugglers best
The means of life his own right hand may wrest.
But better is the narrow, humble sphere
Which sets from childhood's days before the eyes
Some calling which to climb to were a prize—

Which, difficult to win, is therefore dear—
Than wider means which leave the cultured lad
Himself to choose what path of life to run—
Let Fancy tell what Duty should be done,
Make worthless what can be for wishing had,
And prove how too much choice is worse than none.
And this felt Ranolf—puzzled sore to name
Church—Physic—Law—which most attractive seemed,
Or rather least repulsive should be deemed.

What marvellous study like the human frame!
What webs and tissues by that living loom
Woven to rarest texture, richest bloom;
What wefts and warps of flexile ducts that wind
In never-tangled courses intertwined;
What mechanisms intricate, exact,
In orderly profusion ranged and packed;
What cunning cordage curiously inlaced;
What delicate engines of supply and waste;
What fine concoctions and witch-juices strange
For metamorphosis and magic change;
What subtlest forces balanced and combined;
Leaving poor human skill so far behind,
All Art seems artless, all Invention blind!
But then how saddening, that superb array
No more in healthy and harmonious play,
But festering in disorder and decay!
What grander triumph can Experience show
Than the cool surgeon's, who, in conquering strife
With fell disease, with science-guided knife
Dares open wide the dreadful door of Life
Some perilous moments, and his dexterous feat
Of desperate rescue rapidly complete

With sure decisive stroke, lest the grim Foe
Should entrance gain and all his work o'erthrow!
"Aye!" thought our student, with a transient glow,
"For object so exalted who denies
The labour of a life were well bestowed?
But then, alas! to that proud power the road
Through fetid chambers of Dissection lies
Whereat a very Ghoul's foul gorge would rise."

Well, cannot Law awake some genuine spark
Of true ambition—pay for patient toil?
What spectacle more pleasing than to mark
Some Master of inimitable fence
Strike Falsehood to the heart through every foil
And feint of scoundrel skill? mark learning, sense,
And trained acumen flash their sunlike rays
Through all the vile, perversely winding ways
Of vice; illuminate the burrowed maze
And crannies Craft and Cunning know to shape,
And stop their every earthhole of escape!
Is not the Law a mighty mesh to snare
The many-shifted meanness of mankind?
Of cheated Innocence the Champion fair
Against all wrongs by tyrant Wealth designed?
Its task, what nobler since the world began,
To sort and settle by right Reason's plan
All deeds Man does or duties owes to Man?
To stamp the drill and discipline of schools
On the rude progeny of fertile Chance;
Through Time's still widening wilderness to chase
With the slow hounds of principles and rules
(Though mostly distanced in the dubious race)

The ever-doubling hares of Circumstance?
Nay! may not even youth's impatience glance
With pitying interest or perhaps with praise—
At that mole-eyed devotion of old days
Which with such mousing perseverance strove—
Such creeping subtlety and crabbed love,
To fit dead forms to living ages, lacking
Responsive facts that made their sole defence;
In search of reasons, dull inventions racking
For aims that had to reason no pretence;
And stretching Ingenuity to cracking,
To reconcile absurdity to sense?—
"Fine theories all!" thought Ranolf—"but that bowl
Of Law—what golden bias guides its roll
We know; how riches crush the right—how long
Perverted learning bolsters up the wrong:
And doubtless as distasteful it must be
To dabble in diseased morality
As physical corruption. Is it true
Besides, that Wrong, like Right, to get its due,
Let Justice fairly judge between the two,
Must have its Advocate—whate'er he feel
To brawl and burst with simulated zeal?—
'Twere odious as, for those sly silent fees,
To cant condolement with high-fed Disease,
Paddle with Luxury's pampered pulse—and steal
Through sham sick rooms with cat-like pace and purr
Sleeking palled Fashion's pleasure-ruffled fur."

Try then the Church. "What Church?" our youngster sighed:
"Is there within the world's circumference wide
A Church or *any* Temple—in this dearth
Of Faith, with half her heavenly cables snapt,

Hope's anchor scarcely left—has life or worth
To make its intellectual votaries feel
What in old days they felt ; that martyr zeal,
Forgetfulness of present self and rapt
Possession of the Infinite on Earth
That gave a grandeur to the Life it scorned ?
But who would brook a church if unadorned
With absolute love of Truth ? unless it gave
To Thought the utmost freedom it could crave ;
Followed where'er it led, true Reason's light ;
Avowed itself to Truth an utter slave,
Truth ever and Truth only—come what might ?
And who that loved his own free soul could bear
To work, a digger in the dark gold mine
Of spiritual Truth, or bold researches try
Where scientific Doubts with deadly shine
Like Icebergs freeze, or Faith's bleached fragments lie
Whitening the hot Saharas of Despair—
Handcuffed and fettered with the leaden links
Of dogmas stereotyped—creeds cut-and-dry
And double-dry ? heart-paralysed by dread
Of all but what smooth smug 'Society'
That feels by fashion and by custom thinks,
Gives pass and permit to ? Whose Soul so dead
As dare assume the glorious character
Of Soul-Deliverer, trembling lest he stir
Some wash-tub of Formality about—
Dumb till it rage its tiny tempest out ?
Or who with strangely grovelling Quixotry
Would think to quell the Evil all about
With candlesticks and censers ?—satisfy
The crave for Infinite Good that cannot die,
With trim and tinselled haberdashery ?

Who, in a fight so fierce in such an age,
With lackered shields and silvered wooden swords
Of ceremonious mummeries would engage?
With pagan posture-tricks such warfare wage
And pantomime, in place on Thespian boards—
Stage-twirlings in the death-tug! Who could dote
In imbecile expectance to assuage
Sharp pangs of soul with prayers run up by rote
In self-complacent trills with pompous throat?
Would any heart remorse had desperate driven.
Or milder sense of 'Sin' abased, on heaven
In accents guided by the gamut call,
And *do-re-mi-sol-fa* the God of All?"

His youthful scorn would graver minds endorse?—
A priesthood's duty is as great, of course,
Old Truth admitted to apply—enforce,
As to explore the Universe for new.
But how much priestly truth is granted true?
Will Science check Truth's still increasing flow,
Whether it drown a drowsing Church or no?
Should not the eye be open?—hand be free
To seize at once whate'er the eye may see
Of nascent truth, and let the dying go?
What, if like Shepherds more than half asleep,
Over the gold-brown gloss a Priesthood keep
Vain watch, while half their sheep a-hungered stray
To succulent green pastures far away?
For Forms of Faith, though beautiful they be,
If e'er the Truth, their living spirit, flee,
What are they like but cold and stony flowers,
These geysers boiling up through emerald bowers
In far-off islands he was soon to see,

Clothe with a sparry spume, that hardens white
Around the perished plant concealed from sight,
But still retains in delicate array
Each form of tiny leaf and tender spray,
Cold, crumbling, colourless—in lifeless pride—
No growing green, no circling sap inside !

IX.

Well, ere his choice was fixed—his father died,
And left the youth with more of gold supplied
Than would for his immediate wants provide.
So to the Sea, his passion all the time,
He took. To rove from clime to clime,
At least would gratify his ruling taste :
At least, he knew upon the watery waste
His buoyant spirits kept in play would be—
His soul unfettered still, his fancy free.

CANTO THE FOURTH.

I.

And now, behold, this Ranolf once again
Tossing, a Student-Sailor, on the main.

Here are some fragments written home from sea,
Two in his earlier Sailor life, and three
His later. Of his character they show
Some traits, perchance. Then pardon us, although
Beguiled, dear Reader, at this stage too long,
(Alas, for sins of inartistic Song!)
O prithee pardon, if with little skill
We fling these scraps together—skip who will!

I.

* * * * * *

"A noble sport—and my delight
That reefing topsails! just to make all right,
Ere the wind freshens to a gale at night.
See! clambering nimbly up the shrouds,
Go, thick as bees, the sailor-crowds;
The smartest for the post of honour vie
That weather yardarm pointing to the sky:

They gather at the topmast-head
And dark against the darkling cloud
Sidling along the foot-ropes spread :
Dim figures o'er the yardarm bowed,
How with the furious Sail, a glorious sight,
Up in the darkness of the Sky they fight !
While by the fierce encounter troubled
The heavy pitching of the Ship is doubled ;
The big Sail's swelling, surging volumes, full
Of wind, the strong reef-tackle half restrains ;
And like some lasso-tangled bull
Checked in its mid career of savage might
O'er far La Plata's plains,
It raves and tugs and plunges to get free
And flaps and bellows in its agony !
But slowly yielding to its scarce-seen foes
Faint and more faint its frenzied struggling grows ;
Till, by its frantic rage at length
Exhausted, like that desert-ranger's strength,
Silent and still, it seems to shrink and close ;
Then, tight comprest, the reef-points firmly tied,
Down to the deck again the sailors glide ;
And easier now, with calm concentred force,
The Ship bounds forward on her lightened course."

2.

* * * * * *

"Once, 'twas my watch below, (worse luck !)
A sudden squall the vessel struck :
With half my clothes about me thrown
I rushed on deck—what havoc there !
The topsails from the bolt-ropes blown,

Topgallant masts and royals gone,
And huddled sails and shattered spars
And tangled tackle everywhere ;
While all amazed, our gallant tars
Stood at the sudden wreck aghast,
Nor seemed to heed the swift commands
The Captain shouted through the blast.
The heaving staysail swagged and swung
As from the strained jibboom it hung :
Of course with some sharp words addrest
To two or three, our smartest hands,
Forward I jumped to do my best.
They followed quick ;—the lightest, I
The bowsprit's end could safest try ;
We grasped the frail spar like grim death,
And shut our eyes and held our breath,
Clinging with tightened arms and knees
When o'er us dashed successive seas
And blinded, ducked, and drenched us, till
Seizing the chance of every lull
To look and lash and tug and pull,
We furled the sail and got it still ;
Though no one knew as there we clung
How badly was the bowsprit sprung.
But when I 'lighted on the deck
Shaking the water off, the good
White-headed Master, who had stood,
He told me since, in breathless mood
(His heart was in his mouth, he said
While looking on, for very dread)
Threw his old arms about my neck,
'God bless you !' cried he, 'my brave Son !
Twas nobly, beautifully done !

The safety of my Ship and Crew
This blessed day—I swear 'tis true,
Is owing, under God, to you!'—

Mother! ten times the risk I'd run
To have such praise declared my due,
By such a gallant Seaman too!"

3.

* * * * *

* * * * * * *

"How grandly—when throughout the silent day,
Some ample Day, serene, divine,
Beneath the glowing Line
Our helpless Ship had hung as in a trance
In light-blue glassiness of calm that lay
A wide expanse
Encircled by soft depths of ether clear,
Whose melting azure seemed to swim
Surcharged and saturate with balmiest brilliancy—
How grandly solemn was the Day's decline!
Down as if wholly dropped from out the Sky
The fallen Sun's great disc would lolling lie
Upon the narrowed Ocean's very rim,
Awfully near!
A hush of expectation almost grim
Wrapt all the pure, blank, empty hemisphere;
While straight across the gleaming crimson floor,
From the unmoving Ship's black burnished side,
There ran a golden pathway right into the core
Of all that throbbing splendour violet-dyed;
Whither it seemed an easy task to follow
The liquid ripples tremblingly o'erflowing

Into the intense and blinding hollow
Of palpitating purple, showing
The way as through an open door
Into some world of burning bliss, undreamt of heretofore.—
Whose heart would not have swelled, the while
Deep adoration and delight came o'er him
At that stupendous mystery, close before him!
Not less, but more stupendous that he knew
Perchance, whate'er the subtle surface-play
Of Science had to teach of level ray
Reflected or refracted; and could say,
Nay, almost count the millions to a mile,
How far away
That pure quintessence of dark fire, deep-lying
In fathomless Flame-Oceans round him flying,
His inconceivable circumference withdrew:
Knew all about the fringe of flames that frisk
In ruddy dance about his moon-masked face,
Set on like petals round a sunflower's disc—
Each glorious petal shooting into space
Ten times as far as Earth's vast globe is thick:
Aye! or could prate about full many a world
Worn out, and, crushed to cinders, flying fleet,
Or in cold black rotundity complete,
Into his burning bosom headlong hurled,
Just by collision to strike out fresh heat,
And feed with flame, renew and trim,
And keep for aye from falling dim
That monstrous and immeasurable wick—
Say rather—everlastingly keep bright
That awful, mystic, God-created Light!"

4.

*   *   *   *   *   *   *

"Naraka—Niflheim—Tartarus—or Tophet!
From what dead heart and poor unpicturing brain,—
Too dull to see or realize
Its own demoniac phantasies—
Of Bonze, Skald, Brahman, talapoin, or prophet—
Goth, Syrian, Greek, or old Hindu,
Of Aryan or Semitic strain—
Came singly or from all upgrew
That rank arch-blasphemy and dream insane
Of torture-gulfs where Infinite Love
All human guess or gauge above
Preserves in fiery suffocation
The myriads of its own creation?
I care not—I; but when I came
On deck in darkness yesternight,
That very place appeared to be
Laid bare before my startled sight:
For far and wide in pale effulgence dire,
One boundless ghastly welter of white fire,
The Ocean rolled; a hoary Sea
Of awful incandescence rolled and broke away
In bursts of firespray—tongues of lambent flame
That writhed and tossed in burning play,
And with a baleful glare
Put out the stars—quenched what mild radiance fell
From the clear skies, as that unhallowed spell
Of blighting Superstition can outblaze
With its fierce coruscations of despair
The genuine rays

Of light from Heaven that fall like dew,
Divine illuminings serene and true.
And yet such thoughts did ill beseem
This vision—so would any deem,
And other lore and wiser learn,
Who o'er the taffrail marked the excess
And marvel of the loveliness
Of those swift-whirling volumes of soft light
Fast-flashing with gold star-drops sparkling bright
In myriads through the alabaster glow—
Those spangled gyres and wreaths of dazzling snow
That still in wide expanding trail
Went roaring off her stern
So grandly as our Vessel through
The surging phosphorescence flew,
Streaming behind her, as the snowy plumes
Of those rich birds the Aztecs old
Reared at their royal Town of Gold,
Stream when at dusk they slowly sail
Streaking the depth of Amazonian glooms.
Ah ! surely no sound heart these glories seeing
Would thence derive the notion of a Being
Creating only to destroy ;
Or framing Phlegethons and fire-washed caves
Swarming with frenzied Spirits thicker than these waves
With millions of medusæ all alight with joy !"

5.

* * * * *

"St. Lawrence ! yes, I well remember
Thy Gulf—that morning in September.—
Fast flew our Ship careering lightly
Over the waters breaking brightly ;

Alongside close as if their aim
Were but her vaunted speed to shame,
Sleek porpoises like lightening went
Cleaving the sunny element;
Now where the black bows smote their way
How would they revel in the roaring spray!
Like victors in the contest now
Dash swift athwart the flying prow;
Or springing forward three abreast
Shoot slippery o'er each foamy crest—
Shoot upwards in an airy arc
As three abreast they passed the bark:—
Pied petrels coursed about the sea
And skimmed the billows dexterously;
Sank with each hollow, rose with every hill,
So close, yet never touched them till
They seized their prey with rapid bill:—
Afar, the cloudy spurts of spray
Told that the grampus sported there
With his ferocious mates at play.
Meanwhile the breeze that freshly blew
From every breaking wavetop drew
A plume of smoke that straightway from the sun
The colours of the rainbow won,
So that you saw wherever turning
A thousand small volcanoes burning,
Emitting vapours of each hue
Of orange, purple, red and blue.
The Sky meanwhile was all alive
With snow-bright clouds that seemed to drive
Swiftly, as though the Heavens in glee
Were racing with the racing Sea:
Each flitting sight and rushing sound
Spread life and hope and joy around;

Ship, birds and fishes, Sky and ocean
All restless with one glad emotion !—
But what a change ! when suddenly we spy
Apart from all that headlong revelry—
Pencilled above the sky-line, like a Spectre drear,
A silent Iceberg solemnly appear,—
Pausing ghost-like our greeting to await.—
The crystal Mountain, as we come anear
And feel the airs that from it creep
So chilling o'er the sunny Deep,
Discloses—while it slowly shifts
Now blue, faint-glistening semilucent clifts,
Now melancholy peaks, dead-white and desolate.
But comes it not, this guest unbidden
This wanderer from a home far-hidden,
Dim herald of the mysteries of the Pole
With tidings from that cheerless region fraught—
Comes it not o'er us like the sudden Thought,
The haunting phantom of a World apart,
The blank and silent Apparition
That, ever prompt to gain serene admission,
Lurks on the crowded confines of the heart,
The many-pictured purlieus of the Soul ;
Nay, sometimes thrusts its unexpected presence
Upon our brightest-tinted hours of pleasaunce ?—
That Polar realm is ransacked—known—
And all the World of Matter, still
Lies pervious to determined will :
And shall the World of Spirit never
Its secrets yield to true endeavour ?—
Five thousand years have doubtless shown
But little of that Spirit-zone :
For Science is a Child as yet
At hornbook rude and primer set :

And Man is just emerging from the past
Eternity of Darkness ; from the vast
Æons and ages of a measureless Night,
Rubbing his eyes at the unwonted light :
  How should *he* read all things aright
And say what can or cannot be—or utter
Out of *his* heart the Universe, whose growth
And whole existence yet is but the flutter
    Of an ephemeral water-moth ?
  Take fifty thousand years—a span
  In the conceivable career of Man ;
Think you, with riper knowledge—skill profounder—
  No grand explorers, bolder, sounder,
    Will break into that Spirit-zone—reveal
  Not iron-bound realms of ruthless ice and snow
  Or narrow straits where freezing waters flow,
    No shooting lights, or shifting gleams—
  But prospects trustier than the dance and play
  Protean of those dumb magnetic storms—
  Auroras lovelier than our sanguine dreams
  Of fondest Inspiration—Forms
  Of Being more essentially divine
Than all that in Thought's topmost triumphs shine ?
  And prove how *real* the region whence our stray
  And shadowy intimations find their way ;
  With what *true* signs and tokens rife
Those glimmering dreams and fine forebodings steal
  Into the circle of our little day,
Into the glad familiar Sea of Life ?"

* * * * * * *

II.

'Twas some few months before our tale began.
Bowling before the fresh fair breezes ran
Our Ranolf's stately Ship ; and now was nearing
A range of rugged hills whose olive-green,
Sleeked over faintly with a sunny sheen,
  Upon the starboard bow was seen.
Obliquely towards one shadow she was steering
That, darklier-painted, showed a harbour's mouth,
  Because between her and that goal
  There stretched a hidden dangerous shoal.
For towering topmasts of the Kauri pine
The Ship had voyaged to the verdant Isles,
  The Sea-girt El Dorado of the South
Whose mountains famous since for many a mine
Of marvellous wealth, and reefs of riches, stand
The golden baits from bygone ages planned
To draw the swarms that, sweltering in distress
Cannot be won by nature's simpler wiles,
From climes where Life in very overstrife
To live chokes out redundant rival Life,
  To this remote sweet wilderness,
This Life-deserted, Life-desiring land.

    In deep blue sky the sun is bright ;
    The Port some few miles off in sight ;
    The pleasant Sea's subsiding swell
Of gales for days gone by may tell,
But on the bar no breaker white,
Only as yet a heavier roll
Denotes where lurks that dangerous shoal.

Alert with lead, and chart, and glass,
The Pilot seeks the well-known pass;
All his familiar marks in view
Together brought, distinct and true.
Erelong the tide's decreasing stream
Chafes at the nearer bank beneath;
The Sea's dark face begins to gleam
(Like tiger roused that shows his teeth)
With many a white foam-streak and seam:
Still should the passage, though more rough,
Have depth of water, width, enough.—
But why, though fair the wind and filled
The sails, though masts and cordage strain,
Why hangs, as by enchantment stilled,
The Ship unmoving?—All in vain
The helm is forced hard down; 'tis plain
The shoal has shifted, and the Ship
Has touched, but o'er its tail, may slip:
She strains—she moves—a moment's bound
She makes ahead—then strikes again
With greater force the harder ground.
She broaches to; her broadside black
Full in the breakers' headlong track;
They leap like tigers on their prey;
She rolls as on they come amain,
Rolls heavily as in writhing pain.
The precious time flies fast away—
The launch is swiftly manned and sent
Over the lee, with wild intent
To anchor grapplings where the tide
Runs smoother, and the Ship might ride
Secure beyond the raging bar,
Could they but haul her off so far.

The boat against her bows is smashed ;
Beneath the savage surges dashed,
Sucked under by the refluent wave,
They vanish—all those seamen brave.
On—on—the breakers press—no check—
No pause—fly hissing o'er the wreck,
And scour along the dangerous deck.
The bulwarks on the seaward side,
Boats—rudder—sternpost irontied
With deep-driven bolts—how vain a stay !
The weight of waters tears away.
Alas ! and nothing can be done—
No downward-hoisted flag—no gun
Be got at to give greater stress
To that unheard demand for aid
By the lost Ship's whole aspect made—
Herself, in piteous helplessness,
One huge sad signal of distress.
Still on—and on—the tide's return
Redoubling now their rage and bulk,
In one fierce sweep from stem to stern
The thundering sheets of breakers roar,
High as the tops in spray-clouds soar,
And down in crashing cataracts pour
Over the rolling, tortured hulk.
Death glares in every horrid shape—
No help—no mercy—no escape !
For falling spars dash out the brains
Of some—and flying guns adrift,
Or splinters crush them—slaughter swift
Whereof no slightest trace remains,
The furious foam no bloodshed stains :

Up to the yards and tops they go—
No hope—no chance of life below!
Then as each ponderous groaning mast
Rocks loosened from its hold at last,
The shrouds and stays, now hanging slack,
Now jerking, bounding, tensely back,
Fling off the helpless victims fast,
Like refuse on the yeast of death
That bellows, raves and boils beneath.
One hapless wretch around his waist
A knotted rope has loosely braced;
When from the stay to which he clings,
The jerking mast the doomed one flings,
It slips—and by the neck he swings:
Death grins and glares in hideous shape—
No hope—no pity—no escape!—
Still on and on—all day the same,
Through all that brilliant summer day
Beneath a sky so blithe and blue
The wild white whirl of waters flew,
In stunning vollies overswept
And beat the black Ship's yielding frame,
And all around roared, tossed, and leapt
Mad-wreathing swathes of snow! affray
More dire than most disastrous rout
Of some conceivable array
Of thronged white elephants—as they
Their phalanx broke in warfare waged
In Siam or the Punjaub—raged
And writhed their great white trunks about,
With screams that shrill as trumpets rung,
And drove destruction everywhere
In maddened terror at the shout

Of turbaned hosts and torches' flare
Full in their monstrous faces flung ;—
Wide horror ! but to *this*, no less,
This furious lashing wilderness,
Innocuous-seeming—transient—tame !
Still on—still on—like fiends of Hell
Whiter than Angels—frantic—fell,
Through all that summer day the same
The merciless murderous breakers came !
And to the mizen-top that swayed
With every breach those breakers made,
Unaided, impotent to aid—
The mates and Master clung all day.
There—while the Sun onlooking gay
Triumphant trod his bright highway ;
There, till his cloudless rich decline—
Faint in the blinding deafening drench
Of salt waves roaring down the whine
And creaking groans each grinding wrench
Took from the tortured timbers—there
All day—all day—in their despair,
The gently brave, the roughly good,
Collected, calm and silent stood.
That hideous doom they firmly face ;
To no unmanly means give way,
No frantic gestures ; none disgrace
With wild bravado, vain display,
Their end, but like true men await
The dread extremity of Fate.
Alas ! and yet no tongue can tell
What thoughts of life and loved ones swell
With anguish irrepressible,
The hearts these horrors fail to quell.

The Master urges them to prayer,
'No hope on Earth—be Heaven your care!'
And is it mockery—O but mark
Those masts and crowding figures, dark
Against the flush of love and rest
Suffusing all the gorgeous West
In tearful golden glory drest—
Such soft majestic tenderness,
As of a Power that longs to bless
With ardours of divinest breath
All but one raging spot of Death:—
For all the wide expanse beside
Is blushing, beauteous as a Bride;
And a fierce wedding-day indeed
It seems, of Life and Death—with none to heed.

And now the foam spurts up between
The starting deck-planks; downward bowed
The mighty masts terrific lean;
Then each with its despairing crowd
Of life, with one tremendous roar
Falls like a tower—and all is o'er.

III.

One of the worn despairing ring who round
Their chief upon the mizen-top had found
A dizzy shelter in the pelting spray,
Had Ranolf borne that dreadful day;
Down with the headlong mast was thrown;
And as his consciousness flashed back again
(A moment in the act of falling gone)
He found himself almost alone
With desperate clutch still clinging to the top

Beneath its lee that fenced the lashing rain
Of breakers off—else all had been in vain.
'Mid tangled rigging, to the vessel's side
With violent efforts he contrived to glide;
Then, by the chains protected, in the shade
Of the green flying roof the wild waves made,
In that dark hollow's gloom a hideous space,
Steadying his thoughts and strength he clung,
While in his ears the roaring ceaseless race,
The driving avalanche that knew no stop,
With stunning dread reverberation rung.
Beneath him frequent timbers swung
In fragments to and fro; so, quick as thought,
He seized a lucky chance to drop
Into the weltering foam, and caught
A floating piece of plank, and kept
Half hopeless his determined hold,
While it and he like lightning swept
To where the waves less wildly rolled:
A larger fragment next he gained;
Then, with what failing strength remained,
Straight towards that dear-bought harbour strained.

Scarce half a mile the favouring tide
Had forged his drifting plank ahead,
When in the gathering gloom he spied
A big canoe with bulwarks red;
And heard the beat of paddles plied
With strong recurrence—right good will.
Half dead with cramp, fatigue, and chill,
He called; the paddles all were still.
He called again; a cheery strain
Gave answer as the rowers sung;
And forth the bounding vessel sprung

And shot his wayward plank beside
With swirling swiftness as a coot
Or wild duck will alighting shoot—
Ere it can stay its headlong way—
Along the ruffled water. Then
An eager crowd of deep-voiced men,
Dark-visaged, wild—in unknown tongue,
Their hoarse congratulations cried,
As safe on board the backed canoe
With rapid talk and much ado,
That kindly crew the Stranger drew.
With fiercer chaunt they pulled ashore ;
There from his clothes the water wrung,
Lit fires, brought food, and on the floor
His bed of fresh-pulled ferns, o'erlaid
With clean elastic mattings, made ;
Tried all that care or kindness can
Of genial Earth or generous Man—
Though one half desert, one half savage—
To smoothe and smile away the pangs
Of grief and bodily pain and dread
Of horrible Ocean's wreck and ravage,
Whose shadow like a nightmare hangs
O'er one who lives, of many dead,
Just rescued from her ruthless fangs.

IV.

So ended that death-stricken day.—
But how felt Ranolf as he lay
Rescued and weary—and could scarcely deem
'Twas real, what seemed a wild tremendous dream,
That all his comrades bold had passed away ?
Bursting with thanks, O doubt not, to the Power
Whose laws had let him live through such an hour ;

And yet—to think of all that life so marred
And mangled, swept away like worthless chaff
While merciless mocking Nature did but laugh !—
" This pure Benevolence hits somewhat hard
It must be owned," thought he, " or rather say
Inexorable laws must have their way.
Were any breach of law allowed, who knows
What infinite disasters would ensue !
Such certainty is safest, we suppose,
For creatures such as Men are. Trite and true !
Yet such a hell of havoc as we saw
To-day makes one half-dubious of such law ;
Results so dire, alas ! who would not call
Demoniac still—if what we *see* were all ! "

V.

When from the beach with swollen corpses strewn
Like seaweed, 'mid the waste of wreck upthrown
His sea-chest had been brought, and honestly
Returned him—as he much desired
More of this people and their land to see—
To the far neighbouring continent he sent,
(To pay for food and service as required)
For woven stuffs and many an implement
And trinket these barbarians most admired.
Their language then he set himself to learn
With zeal, until the vessel's slow return ;
And when in that, and their strange customs versed,
With followers often changed and cheaply paid
From place to place and tribe to tribe he strayed
Amused and loitering, till his way he made
To Rotorua, where we found him first.

CANTO THE FIFTH.

I.

A FINE old sturdy stalwart stubborn Chief
Was Tangi-Moana, the "Wailing Sea":
  Both brave and wise in his degree.
In Council calm, no wordy waterspout,
  He loved with some bold figure brief
In words—or blunt symbolic act without,
To clench and quench discussion quietly.
But there so careless of distinction, he
Was a conspicuous, restless, fiery guiding-star
  And rock-like rallying-point in war.

His many merits how shall we repeat?
In all that most adorns a Chief, complete.
Highborn—of ancient perfect pedigree,
The carved and saw-notched stick, his family-tree
And roll heraldic, where each tooth expressed
A male progenitor, concisely showed
How still through these his lineage proud had flowed;
  For not a single gap confessed
The rank did ever in a female vest,
Since, from that blissful Isle divine
Far o'er the azure hyaline—

That sunlit vision seen sublime
Faint glimmering through thick mists of Time,
The cradle of his race, in legends yet
Embalmed, a fond ideal for regret—
Since from Hawaiki, tempest-driven,
Or roaming restless for a wider home,
  Five hundred years ago had come
  The mighty Founder of his line,
Commanding (one of those primeval Seven)
His old hereditary grand canoe.
To all the unkempt Aristocrats around
  Who could a better model be
  Of all befitting their degree?
For costlier mantles, richer in design,
No chief more carelessly possessed:
  None with a choicer feather-crest
Would, when occasion needed it, be crowned;
Had those rare plumes in heir-loom chest preserved
More richly carved, more elegantly curved;
There, with green nephrite pendants safely hid,
Though loose its oval-shaped, oil-darkened lid—
His sole "tapu" a far securer guard
Than lock and key of craftiest notch and ward.
  And none gave ampler feasts—displayed
  War-clubs of more transparent jade:
And finer closer spirals of dark blue
Were never seen than in his cheek's tattoo;
Fine as if engine-turned those curves declared
No cost to fee the Artist had been spared;
That many a basket of good maize had made
That craftsman careful how he tapped his blade,
And many a greenstone trinket had been given
To get his chisel-flint so deftly driven.

II.

Now at the time whereof we tell,
The white man's creed—the potent spell
Of civilised communion had begun
Their work about the borders of the land:
Before that higher light, and influence bland
(As night recedes long ere you see the sun)
The most revolting vices of the race,
Among ev'n those who never would embrace
The new belief—child-murder and the feast
That sinks the cannibal below the beast,
His better there—the ghoullike foul disgrace,
Had slunk away abashed and wholly ceased.
As, when you turn upon a sea-creek's shore,
  Some limpet-crusted boulder o'er,
The reptile life that swarmed and skulked beneath
So close that nothing there had seemed to breathe—
Sea-centipedes and purple crabs and worms
Threadlike, blood-red—and limbless fleshy forms,
Swiftly or slowly—all before the light,
Shrink—wriggle—scuttle sidelong out of sight—
So had those viler vices taken flight.

And Tangi and his tribe thus much had gained,
Those vices lost, but all their gods retained.
A love of change was never fault of his,
And least he fancied such a change as this.
Once when a zealous teacher from the North
The terrors of his creed had thundered forth—
Unfolded with keen zest and kind desire
To save his hearers from so sad a fate,

His pleasant faith in everlasting fire,
And painted all the pangs the damned await—
While horror blanched the cheeks of half the crowd,
Old Tangi roared with laughter long and loud :
That Hell of theirs, he said, might be a place
Wholesome and fitting for the white man's race,
No Maori was half bad enough to be
Doomed to so horrible a destiny :
Had a good Spirit destined for such woe
His children after death, he long ago
Had sent some trusty friend to let them know ;
But he for his part would have nought to do
With any *Atua*,* whether false or true,
Who could delight his direst foe to see
The victim of such monstrous cruelty.
And when he learnt what adverse sects prevailed
And how each other's doctrines they assailed,
He held his hand out, with the fingers spread—
"So many ways to heaven you teach," he said ;
"When you have fixed the right one and none doubt it,
"'Twill then be time for *me* to think about it."

Sometimes indeed when young hardheaded minions
From seaside tribes would urge these new opinions,
Our Chief, for argument was not his forte,
With calm remonstrance tried to cut them short :
What all their ancestors and his believed
Why could not they? that which was good enough
For *them*, might well content, as he conceived,
Such youngsters ;—husky grew his voice and gruff :
"What ! give up all our good old ways—the charms
And ceremonies practised all our lives

* *Atua*—God or Spirit.

To make our Men all warriors, brave in arms,
Our Women skilful, chaste, industrious wives—
Give up our wars—war-dances—*tauas* *—taboo,
Whence all our wealth, and power, and fame accrue,
For these new notions! were they all to cease
For this effeminate creed of love and peace!"—
But when the good old Chief found all he felt
So strongly had no power to move or melt
His tough opponents, he the point pursued
No further—but with self-complaisance stout
Closed with that comfort—wherein oft no doubt
Much abler controversialists conclude—
"'Twas self-sufficiency—'twas downright mere
Conceit that would not see a case so clear—
'Twas rage for talk, or love of contradiction,
That would not be convinced"—by *his* conviction!

And so a hearty heathen he remained,
And those new whimsies quietly disdained;
He fed his Gods and fee'd his priests so well,
What was to him the white Man's heaven or hell?
A Priest himself and half a God or quite,
Did not the elements confess his might?
At least all said so—and if failure wrought
Misgiving, still desire constrained his thought;
The failure proved the counteracting spite
Of rival Gods into collision brought,—
Against his own pretensions argued nought.
Nor wonder this should be; when low and base
Man's notions of a God, and vain and high
Those of himself, as with a barbarous race
And minds uncultured ever is the case,

* *Taua*—a war expedition.

Men may believe their own divinity :
Manhood and Godhood come so near together
They may be made to mingle and agree
Without much stretch of Faith's or Fancy's tether.
And thus our Chieftain felt ; if he excelled
In attributes for which his Gods were held
Divine—might he not be their equal too ?
Could he not at his pleasure save or slay,
A Lord of life and death as well as they ?
And for those elements—'twas but mistaking
The still unknown and so obscure relations
Between the Spirit mystical outbreaking
Through all the manifold manifestations
Of Nature, and the surer Spirit illuming
His own as mystic Being, and mastery thence,
In pride of his superior excellence,
Over that other phase of Spirit assuming.

III.

Such was this Tangi—such "The Wailing Sea ;"
Of form almost gigantic he—
Bull-necked, square-jawed, firm-lipped, bold-eyed, broad-browed,
His looks proclaimed his character aloud :
And when he stood forth in full height and pride
In flowing vest of silky flax, undyed,
But crimson-spotted with round knobs of wool,
Black points of cord, alternate, hanging free ;
And o'er it, down to the brown ancles bare
A mantle of white wild-dog fur well-dressed,
Its skirt's broad rim tan-hued ; his snowy hair
Crowned with a jet-black arching crest

  Of hoopöe-feathers stuck upright,
  Their tips a crescent of pure white;
And in his hand, to order with or smite,
The greenstone baton broad of war or rule,
Green, smooth and oval as a cactus leaf—
Did he not look, aye, every inch a Chief?
Did not each glance and gesture stamp him then,
Self-heralded a God-made King of Men?

IV.

A thunderstorm was sweeping o'er the Lake,
The hills had whitened off in sudden mist
That soon grew leaden-livid; flake on flake
The fine spray smoked along the watery floor—
Till plumb-down rushed the rain's impetuous pour;
A thousand claps of thunder seemed to break
Confusedly all at once—with clattering roar
Tumbled about the air or groaning rolled,
As if some race Titanic, storming Heaven
From ponderous unimaginable wains
On rocky grating causeways headlong driven,
Shot crashing mountains on the skiey plains;
Or if the tumult for a moment stopped
You heard the torrent rain how loud it hissed,
As if a hecatomb of bulls at least
Were broiling for some sacrificial feast;
And all about the liquid lightnings dropped
In points like grapestones shaped, of molten gold.
But Tangi, while the tempest raged, was told
That where his daughter might be no one knew—
They feared, upon the Lake in her canoe.
Straightway the stoutest of his clansmen staunch
He sent in search of her their boats to launch;

Then set himself to charm away the Storm ;
And it was rare to see the grand old Chief
Now in the haughtiness of fancied power
To cope with Nature in her fiercest hour,
Quick pouring forth wild-ringing chaunt on chaunt
To bid Tawhiri—God of Storms—Avaunt !
Now in a rival storm of rage and grief
Threatening—reproaching—all his stalwart form
Dilating with defiance : outstretched arms
And head thrown back and milk-white fleece of hair,
And blooodshot eyes and dark-blue visage bare
Lit up by fits in the blue lightning's glare.
So plies he his monotonous rude charms—
So on the Storm his vehement passion vents,
Hoarsely upbraiding the hoarse elements.

V.

But soon the light Canoe they saw
  Come bounding o'er the breaking wave ;
There sate, while mixed delight and awe
  Beamed from her face, the Maiden brave !
With rapid change from side to side
A native youth the paddle plied—
A stranger, and his hearty will
Seemed matched with equal strength and skill.
Attentive to his least command
The Maiden grasped with one firm hand
The sheet that held the shortened sail
That strained and tugged beneath the gale,
And with the other strove to bale
Fast as she could the water, still
Threatening the little bark to fill.

Begemmed with spray her dark hair streamed ;
Her beauteous cheek no paler seemed
Though rain and spray-drops o'er it teemed
And all around the lightnings gleamed :
For neither lightning, rain nor spray
Could turn her from her task away.
Still stood the sail and bending mast,
And they the beach were nearing fast.
Then through the waters' boiling strife
The clansmen rushed at risk of life ;
A struggling, swimming, diving crowd,
They seized with acclamations loud
The gunwale of the light canoe ;
On either side, a dancing row
Of rough black heads now rising through
Now sunk beneath the foamy snow,
With great triumphant shouts they bore
Canoe and Maiden to the shore.

VI.

And now the youth announced how he
To Rotorua's Chief of high degree
From Tapuae by Taupo's Lake, his home,
A messenger of great sad news was come :
How he by chance upon the other side
Had Amohia's bark espied
And she had offered him a cast across.
And then he told the lamentable loss
Of great Te Rehu, Taupo's Chief—to whom
That Maiden as they knew so well,
From the first promise of her matchless bloom
Had been betrothed and "*tapu.*" It befel

In this wise. Sometime since, continuous rain
Softening a mountain, it had slipped amain
Down and across a deep ravine and dammed
A running stream, and all its waters jammed
Between the hills, till thus repressed and choked
Into the porous mound they slowly soaked;
And one fine night when all was still and dim,
The saturate mighty mass had burst away,
And rushing down the vale, while fast asleep
Te Rehu and his nearest kindred lay,
Least dreaming such a doom, had swallowed him
And them and their whole village in a deep
And stifling yellow mass of fluent clay,
So overwhelming, sudden, viscous, they
Could neither float, nor rise in it nor swim.

VII.

Astonished, shocked at such a tale,
At such a death for so renowned a man,
Low murmurs through the crowding hearers ran:
And when the storm had to the hills retreated,
Though still it rumbled, lumbering heavily
In the back chambers of the sky,
With downcast looks in treble circle seated,
And grief, if false yet truly counterfeited,
The summoned clansmen sung their song of wail:
One, standing in the midst the slow sad chaunt began:—

"Death, degrading, mournful, gloomy!
Death unfit for song or story,
Death for a dog—a cur—a slave—
Not for the brave!—"

And all took up the chorus harsh and strong,
  In perfect time discharging groan on groan,
While rolled a distant thunderpeal along
  In kindred and scarce deeper tone:

  "Death, O Death, how hateful, gloomy!
  Death for a dog—a slave—a slave!"

Then rose the single voice in prouder strain,
Just as the lightning flashed again:

"Had you died the death of glory
On the field of battle gory,
  Died the death a chief would choose,
  Not this death so sad and gloomy—
Then with tuft and tassel plumy,
Down of gannet—sea-king's feather,
Gaily-waving, snowy-flecking,
Every deep-red gunwale decking—
Then a hundred brave canoes—
    With elated
    Warriors freighted,
Like one man their war-chaunt chiming,
Fierce deep cries the paddles timing,
While the paddles' serried rows
Like broad bird's wings spread and close—
    Through the whitening
    Waves like lightning
Had been darting all together,
Forward through the foam together,
All in quest of vengeful slaughter
Tearing through the tortured water!"

And from the dusky figures seated round,
With savage satisfaction in the sound—
A stern deep pride with sadness shadowed o'er,
Like volleys fired above a soldier's grave,
Rang out the chorussed thundering groans once more:

"*Ha! a hundred brave canoes—*
Crowding, crashing,
Darting, plashing,
Darting, dashing through the wave!
Forward—forward all together,
All in quest of foemen's slaughter,
They had cleft the foamy water
Seeking vengeance for the brave
For the brave—the brave—the brave!"

VIII.

But while with stern staccato notes this song
Of simulated sorrow rolled along,
A genuine gladness cheered one secret breast,
One with a grief as genuine was deprest.
To Amohia 'twas pure joy to be
At length from that detested contract free,
Released from nuptials the reluctant maid
On various pretexts had so long delayed.
For the good Chief could ne'er be reconciled
To use coercion with his darling child,
Who by the dreadful "tapu" firmly bound
Moved—a bright creature, consecrate and crowned,
Inviolate and charmed, to ali around

IX.

The "tapu" was a fearful spell,
Potent as creeds or guards or gold
The power of Priest and Chieftain to uphold.
The terrors of that ever-present Hell
Outdid the threats of distant ones
That faintly flame in far futurity—
As might the roar of pointed guns
A word would on your body bring to bear,
The noise of thunder in the sky.
And never did despotic cunning plan
A fouler system for enslaving man,
Than this mysterious scheme of fear and hate,
The basis of their savage Church and State.
True, the strange custom had its brighter side
When for good ends resistless 'twas applied :
What could compel the masses to combine
Like it, their labor for each grand design—
The great canoe—the long sea-sweeping seine
Or hall for council where the chiefs convene ?
Where could true rights a trustier guard procure,
Corruptless and invincible and sure ?
Yet most 'twas used as stronghold and as stay
For the Aristocrats' and Hierarchs' sway ;
For though swift-gathering relative and friend
Would prompt upon a culprit's tribe descend
And, plundering by strict rule with much ado,
Avenge each *minor* breach of this 'taboo,'
Yet, let but rank or priesthood be profaned,
A direr doom the wretch who sinned, sustained,
More terrible than dungeons, gibbets, chains,
Material penance, penalties or pains.

No high divinity that hedges kings
Could with this sheltering deviltry compare,
Or forge for tyranny a subtler yoke.
For Chief and Priest at will or whim could dower
Sticks—stones—most treasured or most trivial things
With deadliest excommunicative power:
And whoso touched them and the "tapu" broke
Became anathema—accursed and banned—
Infected and infectious; with a pang
Of livelier terror shrunk from—shunned—than e'er
Plague-spotted patient—canine madness—fang
Of rattle-snake or cobra: Fiends were there
To torture them; obedient, at the Chief's command,
The "Wairua," Spirits of the myriad dead—
And all the other invisible Spirits dread,
All mystic powers that fill the Earth and Air,
The "Atua"—waited but a hint from him
To dart into their victim—waste and tear
His stricken vitals, cankering life and limb.
Had not the boldest who from want of heed
Some solemn "tapu" had infringed, been known
When conscious of the sacrilegious deed,
To die outright from horrible fear alone?—
  So well these savage Lords had learned
How nature's mystic terrors might be turned
To means their own dominion to increase;
Unseen executors of their caprice,
Agents impalpable upheld their cause;
The world of Spirits was their dumb Police,
  And Ghosts enforced their lightest Laws.

X.

But he whose grief was most sincere
The news of that unwonted death to hear,
Was Kangapo the "Tóhunga"—a Priest
And fell Magician famous far and near;
A Thaumaturge regarded with more fear
Than any living or than most deceased.
Men whispered that his very body swarmed
(Crammed as a war-canoe with warriors armed)
With evil spirits rustling thick
As blue-flies buzzing in a wayside corse:
And some more credulous would trembling tell
How when demoniac inspiration quick
And strong, in frenzy and full force
Rushed on him (it was vouched for well)
The grass would wither where his shadow fell;
Or, were the sliding shutter of his door
Just then left open, by the river side,
Such deadly emanations would outpour,
Mere strangers chancing in canoes to glide
Beneath the house, had stiffened there and died.

These tales were Kangapo's delight and pride.
And yet his mien that dread renown belied;
So calm and mild; his eyes deepset and dark
Abstracted still and unobservant seemed;
But those who dared to watch him long would mark
How those dim eyes would on a sudden shift
And glitter like a lizard's; then again
Fall still and calm; and yet that glance so swift
Seemed quite enough, as rapidly it gleamed,
To single out and give his scheming brain

All they would wish to hide or he to see.
His voice was gentle too, and low, and sweet ;
So men compared him to the tutu-tree,
Whose luscious purple clusters hang so free
And tempting, though with hidden seeds replete
That numb with deadly poison all who eat.
And then his pace was stealthy, noiseless, soft,
So that a group of talking people oft
Turned round and found him, none knew how or whence,
Close by them, with his chilling influence :
As that great wingless loathsome locust bare,
That scoops from rotting trees his pithy fare,
With elephantine head and horny jaws
And prickly high-propped legs—is sometimes found
Upon your limbs or clothes, in sluggish pause,
Inside the house ; though none upon the ground
Have marked him crawling slow from his retreat,
The fire-logs, when dislodged by growing heat.

But Kangapo had reason to bewail ;
For had he not a hundred times foretold
That should those Western Tribes *his* tribe assail,
Those famed Waikáto, foemen from of old,
Stout Tangi in the contest should prevail ?
And whence derived he confidence to make
That prophecy so clear, beyond mistake ?
'Twas from the doubled strength his tribe he knew
Would gain from an alliance close and true
With the brave borderers of the central Lake.
And what inducement could be found so strong
To that alliance as the union, long
Desired and schemed for, and as long delayed,
Of Taupo's Chief with this surpassing maid ?

But now his plans were cut up, branch and root :
And he must task his plotting wits again
To find some other project to maintain
The safety of his tribe—his own repute.
For if he failed so notably, a stain
Would on his fame indelibly remain.
One thing was clear ; he must not lose this lure,
This bait, some splendid Kingfish to secure
Among the Chiefs—this matchless girl, on whom
Himself, o'ermastered by her beauty's bloom
Had sometimes cast a longing eye, in vain ;
For not his utmost art could passage gain
Even to the threshold of her fair regard ;
His calm, insidious, slow addresses barred
Their own access : her very flesh would creep
Antipathetic, shrinking to its ward
Instinctive, from his flatteries sly and deep.

XI.

So anxious now his auguries he plied
For some forecast of fate his course to guide.
First, by the solitary shore, he drove
His gods into the ground ; each god a stick
Knobbed with a carved and tattoo'd wooden head,
With fillet round the neck of feathers red ;
Then to each idol he attached a string ;
And in monotonous accents high and quick
His incantations wild began to sing :
But still the impatient patient Sorcerer strove
With frequent jerks to make it yield a sign
Whence might be drawn an omen of success :
Nor this so difficult as you divine,
Nor need the gift his Atua much distress.

The slightest hint a Priest for answer took;
Let but a grass-green parrakeet alight
To pluck from some wild coffee-bush in sight,
And nibble with his little moving hook,
The scarlet berries; let some kingfisher
Slip darting from the post whose summit grey
He crowned—a piece of it—the live-long day—
Long bill protruding from his shoulders high,
Watching the lake with sleepy-vigilant eye—
Looking so torpid and so loath to stir,
Till that faint silver twinkle he descry;
Let, gold-cuirassed, some hard ichneumon-fly
Drag with fierce efforts to its crevice nigh
A velvet-striped big spider, sore distrest,
Struggling in vain and doomed to be the nest
And food of that wasp-tyrant's worm new-hatched;
Nay, less significant the sign might be
For which the keen-eyed Sorcerer sung and watched;
A passing cloud—a falling leaf—the key
Might offer to unlock the mystery,
Which with his wishes surely would be matched.

Nor could our Augur set his mind at ease
With simple divinations such as these:
And he was almost tempted to invoke
The Spirits of the Dead who sometimes spoke
Through him, the Arch-Magician and Adept;
Half tempted in his own case to accept
Answers his own ventriloquism feigned;
Ready to square his faith to his desire,
And half believe supernal spirits deigned
To prompt his organs and his speech inspire:—

Could nothing, think you, less than mind unsound
Sensation with volition thus confound?—
But this he chose another Priest to try.
So in their midnight haunted chamber they
Summoned the dead, and drank in mournfully
What the faint hollow voices seemed to say;
Now like the nightwind through the crannied roof
In longdrawn whistling whisper sighing bye,
Swelling and sinking, near and then aloof;
Now melancholy murmuring underground,
Then dying off, up in the starry sky.

Such the success impostors still achieve;
Such Nature's final Nemesis for all
Who teach to others what they half believe,
To keep them fast in Superstition's thrall,
From such a doom dreaming their own reprieve:
Into the pits themselves have dug they fall,
Their own deceptions do themselves deceive.

CANTO THE SIXTH.

I.

WITH merry laughter rang the air
And feminine soft voices sweet ;
And acclamations here and there
Of loud delight at skill more rare,
Some happy hit or dexterous feat ;
And little shrieks at failing luck,
The baffled aim, the striker struck ;
As Amohia on the ground
Amid her damsels, scarlet-crowned
With kowhai-flowers, a lively ring
Playing at '*poi*,' sent flying round
The ornamented ball o'erwound
And worked with vary-coloured threads,
And loosely hung with dangling string
Made fast above their rich-tressed heads—
Fast to a single lightsome yew,
One lone totára-tree that grew
Beneath the hillside rising high
Mid rocks and flowering shrubs. Hard by
A little summer-dwelling peeped
Deep-red, from foliage o'er it heaped

Deep-green and lustrous—trees that bore
In tiny flowers their promised store,
Large berries of autumnal gold.
Verandah-pillars, barge-boards broad,
And balcony and balustrade,
All rough and crusted with a load
Of carved adornment quaint and bold—
Concentric fret or face grotesque
In rich red-ochred arabesque
Relieved with snow-white touches—shewed
Gaily against that glittering shade,
The thick karákas' varnished green.
This cheerful cot, when days were hot,
With its interior cool and clean,
Its floor, for fragrant orange-scent
With faint tawhiri-leaves besprent;
Its roof, and walls, so neatly lined,
Between pilasters white and red,
With tall pale yellow reeds close-laid
And delicately intertwined
And diamond-laced with sable braid
Of leaves supplied, when split and dyed,
By that thick-tufted parasite
Which with its fleshy blossom-bracts
The native as a fruit attracts—
This cot was Amo's chief delight:
And now while yet the day was new,
And scarce the sun had dried the dew,
She and her handmaids sported there.
Quick hand and eye they each and all
Displayed, as, arms and shoulders bare
From side to side they whisked the ball:
Nor is much need our lay declare

How she, the Mistress-Maid, in face
And form superb, and waving grace
Of lithe elastic limb, whene'er
The more erratic ball she tossed
Or caught—or proud with easy air
Regained her balance seeming lost,
Outshone them all beyond compare.

But see! at once the game is stopped,
Each mantle, in its ardor dropped,
Snatched quickly up, at once replaced:
In coy confusion, giggling haste,
Up start the girls of lower grade,
As in his sailor-garb arrayed,
Emerging from a neighbouring patch
Of pinky-tasselled milky maize,
A glimpse of Ranolf's form they catch,
And, pausing, he the game surveys.
But Amohia calmly rose
With courteous mien and gentle pride;
A moment's blush she could not hide,
Within her eyes a moment's light,
Upon their lids a tremor slight,
Alone lent import to the greeting
She gave to him whose image bright
Had left, since that first forest-meeting
Her busy fancy no repose.

The youth had come prepared to stay
With presents and persuasive speech
Results he feared that luckless day
Might lead to; for the violence shown
By his companions to atone:

The "Wailing Sea's" just ire appease,
And heal if such there were, the breach
Between his former friends and these.
But as they scaled the steep ascent
Up to the village rampart-pent,
With high embankments, ditches wide
And fighting-stages fortified;
And passed the crooked entrance made
Through double post and palisade
With crossing withies braced and tied,
The prudent Amo gave her guest
A hint to let the matter rest;
And then he learnt how she had laid
Injunction on her babbling maid
To hold her peace; and strange to tell
The girl had kept the secret well.

With blunt good-humoured haughtiness,
A sturdy, proud and easy air
Of sway unquestioned, frank no less,
Did Tangi-Moana declare
In briefest phrase how glad was he
The stranger at his place to see.
And then, the proffered food declined,
To pipes and parley he resigned
Himself, in sunshine while they basked;
And many things it sorely tasked
The hoary chief, the youthful friend,
To illustrate, or comprehend,
Attentive heard, acutely asked;
About the white man's home and land,
Why Ranolf left it, yet so young;—
The tribes he knew—had dwelt among;

The seaward chiefs and what they planned ;
Who were their friends and foes—and most
The guns and powder they could boast,
And all the wealth at their command
From ships that trafficked on the coast.

II.

Their meeting over, Ranolf strolled
About the flat where gardens gay
Bright in the morning sunbeams lay,
With large-leaved roots and basking fruits
That lolled on beds weedfree and clean
As fairies had the gardeners been.
Then with the younger folk, a few
By Amo led, and one or two
Most brisk or curious of the old,
Crossed, paddling slow a large canoe,
The gleaming Lake's unrippled floor
To woody Nongotáha's shore,
To wing the hours of sultrier heat
With converse in a cool retreat—
A hillside hollow, whose sun-parched
And slippery grass of golden hue,
Green, like the half-ripe orange, grew
Where feathery locust-trees o'erarched
A little plot, an airy spot
Their yellow-blossomed branches laid
In luxury of emerald shade.
There Ranolf flung him down, at rest,
With that expansion of the breast
Exultant—all that unrepressed
Abandonment to glad emotion—
So fair a clime, a life so free,

With health and strength and buoyancy
Of spirit in supreme degree—
And more than all, and all enhancing,
That blooming Child of wood and wild
With shadowy hair and radiant face,
That glossy glancing thing of grace
With eyes in liquid splendour dancing,
Or calm, as if from some high place
Of bliss above this earthly scene
Her soul looked forth with light serene
No time could quench, no sorrow dim—
Might well excite, excuse in him,
A careless castaway of Ocean.
Before him lay no water, say
A hollow Sky inverted—blue,
With flecks of sun-illumined flue,
And mountains hung in crystal air
With peaks above and peaks below
Responsive—every feature fair
Reversed, in that transparent glow
Deep mirrored ; every ferny spur
Each puckered slope, and wrinkle sleek
That creased their glossy forest-fur,
Sure at the water's edge to meet
Its upward-running counterfeit,
Exact as roseate streak for streak
Some opened Venus-shell displays,
Bivalve with answering spots and rays.
Far round were seen, o'er thicket green,
By sandy shore, in darksome glen,
Cloud-jets of steam whose snowy gleam,
But that they moved not, you would deem
The smoke of ambushed riflemen ;

But peaceful these, nor passed away
For wind or hot refulgent day:
White, bright, and still, o'er wild and wood,
Like new-alighted Sprites they stood,
Pure in the brilliant breathlessness;
For breathless seemed the earth and sky,
Real and reflected; none the less
Because at times there wandered by
Over the sun-bathed greenery
A soft air, lifting like a sigh
Some tree-fern's fan, as if in sleep
It stirred in the noon-stillness deep,
Then sank in drowsy trance profound—
That faint distress the only sign
Of life o'er all the glorious sweep
Of verdure streaming down the steep.
So hushed the deep noon-glow around,
So splendour-bathed that vault divine,
The atmosphere so subtle-clear
'Twas rapture but to breathe it!—well
Might these have made more sober, staid,
Or pensive souls a moment fear
To break the soft luxurious spell,
The dreamy charm that wrapt the scene—
With utterance, even the most serene.

III.

But Life with too much force and heat
In these young hearts impetuous beat
For Silence; so the livelong day
The stream of converse grave or gay
From springs redundant flowed alway.

Their superstitions, legends, lays,
Could endless disquisitions raise;
And our Adventurer, still inclining,
Though neither sad nor very serious,
To all that bore on Man's mysterious
Links with the Life there's no divining—
Learnt how for them, invisible throngs
Of Spirits roamed all visible Space:
All Nature was a human Face—
A Sybil with a thousand tongues
And teachings for their priests to trace,
Excite, evoke with charms and songs:
All Matter was all symbol—fraught
With Love and Hate—with Will and Thought:
Within a Man's own frame—without,
Above, below, and all about,
Nothing beyond his will that stirred,
His limbs in dreaming, beast or bird,
Insect or thing inanimate,
But 'twas oracular of Fate:
The wild bird's song, the wild dog's bark,
Were mystic omens, bright or dark;
A leaf could wave, a breeze could blow
Intelligence of weal or woe;
Let but the wind creep through your lifted hair,
Some God was present there;
And if a rainbow overspanned
A hostile band,
Already 'twas as good as crushed.—
And then their legends—once again
Recastings from the ancient mould;
Gods, demigods and heroes old
Of giant bulk and dwarfish brain.

Greek, Gothic, Polynesian—all
Primeval races on a train
Of like ideas, conceptions, fall;
Their supernatural Beings still
Are but themselves in ways and will;
And still the Superhuman race
Keeps with the human steady pace;
What Man would be—what Man has been,
Through magnifying medium seen
Still makes his God or Gods that grow
With his Soul's growth—its reflex show
By grand Imagination's glass
Dilated; its best thoughts—the mass
Of noblest feelings that exist—
Projected with expanding rays
Upon Eternity's dim haze,
Like Brocken Shadows on the mist.
And was it not so planned to give
Mankind a fit provocative,
At every stage from birth to age,
The best devised to speed the Soul
Towards Adoration's utmost goal?
To guide his infancy and youth,
Too weak to see the summits fair,
Up an ascending mountain-stair
To highest hidden peaks of Truth?
And so Religion's self endow
With that continuous life and glow
Discovery lends, though painful, slow;
That interest ever fresh and warm
Which Science boasts her greatest charm?
Though slow indeed Religion's rise
Even to a glimpse of purer skies;

Though foul and stagnant if you will
The fens and swamps that clog her still.

But here the legendary lore
The stamp of earliest ages bore ;
The stories told were wild and rude,
Insipid mostly, pointless, crude :
The simple guile, the childish wile,
With savage deeds of blood and ire,
And treacheries dull for vengeance dire ;
Gods, giants, men, all blood-imbrued.
Uncouth the wondrous feats rehearsed,
With lighter fancies interspersed :
Recounted frankly, best and worst,
Since none were met with sneer or scoff :
—How Maui fished these Isles up first,
And Kupé chipped the islets off ;
—How Tinirau—vain Chief ! the same
Who broad transparent pools outlaid
Of water, which the mirrors made
Where he his beauteous shape surveyed,
Was yet of giant power to tame
The great Leviathan he kept,
A plaything and a pet, who came,
Obedient from his boundless home—
Through sinking hill and swirling trough
Of Ocean, black through snowy foam,
With ponderous swiftness crashing swept—
Whene'er he summoned him by name ;
Or rolling over, at a sign
From him, would smash the level brine
Into great clouds of powdery spray,
With thunder-slaps heard miles away.

—How Pitaka would noose and draw
Out of Earth's bowels by main strength,
Out of his mountain-dungeon fell,
Like periwinkle from its shell,
The bulkiest time-worn Taniwha;
Undaunted by his tortuous length
Of notched and scaly back—his jaw
Wide-yawning, and obscenest maw
With bones and greenstone trinkets filled,
And weapons of his swallowed prey—
Men, women, children, countless killed
By this, of ancient tale and lay
The wingless dragon—rather say
Iguanodon or Lizard vast,
Some caverned monster left the last
Memento of a world bygone
Earth's grinding changes had o'erthrown,
Downliving with still lessening powers
Into this foreign world of ours:
—Then, too, how Márutúa drew
His dragnets round a hostile crew,
The thousand men he snared and slew—
Beguiled to feast upon the strand
And lend their seeming friend a hand
In some great fishing-bout he planned:
—How Hátu-pátu, as he lay
Couched in a rimu-tree one day,
Still as a tufted parasite,
A mere excrescence, not to fright
The birds that would close by alight,
Nor mark his lithe and bending spear
Along the branch more near and near
Creep slowly as a thing that grew,

Until with sudden thrust and true
The noiseless weapon pierced them through—
Himself was quite unconscious too,
As thus he lay like one spell-bound,
What long-curved claws were slowly stealing round
The stem—or cautiously withdrew—
Slowly retracted—then again protruded
Amid the leafy shadows playing
Upon the sunny-chequered trunk,
Noiseless as they and unbetraying
The lank and gaunt Witch-giantess
That wholly hid, behind it slunk;
Until he found himself, the watcher,
Grim-clutched, and not the poor fly-catcher;
Then in her cavern-home secluded
Was kept in cruel-kind duresse
To be as best he might, moreover,
That Patu-paere's pet and lover!

IV.

And next, fair Amo's handmaid—she
Whose gaze of wondering curious glee
Would Ranolf's gestures, looks—pursue,
So pleasant seemed they, strange and new;
Who, if his lively, joyous glance
Alit upon the little maid,
Would start half-back, as if afraid
And half-disposed to run away,
With look averted though so gay,
And face half-hidden, and a play
Of giggling blushes, bright and shy;
Then with brown eyes—that all the day
Would else with mirth and mischief dance,

Keeping a sheltering friend close by,
Would snatch a serious look askance,
As quickly turned aside again
Lest she be caught in that assay;—
All with an artless sympathy,
An interest undisguised and plain—
Such fresh unconscious coquetry!
Though little noticed by the rest
Because with fancies of their own,
Thoughts, feelings hitherto unknown,
Too much amused and prepossest;—
This shy and saucy Miroa told,
With fluttering breath, slight-heaving breast,
Looking at any but the guest
To whom her story was addrest—
How merry Rona, reckless, bold,
Wetting one evening in a stream
The leaves to make her oven steam,
Cursed the fair innocent Moon aloud,
Because she hid behind a cloud,
And Rona when the light was gone,
Struck her foot against a stone;
And how the solemn Moon in anger came
Broadening and reddening down, and wound
Her bright entangling beams around
The affrighted Maid in vain resisting,
Like a vast Cuttlefish around her twisting
A hundred writhing trunks of chilly flame;
Then rose with basket, Maid and all,
And fixed them in her amber ball—
"And this is fact for certain—doubt who will,
Wait only till the Moon shall fill
Her horns—there's Rona with her basket still!"

"A pretty fancy, pretty one!"
Said Ranolf when the tale was done;
"Come here, my child—let me repay
Your story—it will suit your hair
This ribbon, though not half so gay,
So beauteous as the wreath you wear."
And as the laughing girls beside,
Caught, pushed her forward, held her there,
The ribbon round her head he tied,
For some such purpose brought; while she
A-tremble with delighted pride,
With pettish mock reproaches, aimed
At them, not him, seemed, half-ashamed,
Half-angry, struggling to get free.

V.

Then Amohia, tapping Ranolf's arm,
Said, "Listen, Pákeha!"*—and with lifted hand,
Rounding—Enchantress-wise,
When double soul she throws into a charm—
The solemn archness of her great black eyes,
Deep lighted like a well,
An ancient legend she began to tell
Of one God-hero of the land,
Of which our faithful lay presents
Precisely the main incidents,
Diluting only here and there
The better its intent to reach,
The language, so condensed and bare,
Those clotted rudiments of speech:

* Foreigner.

"Once a race, the Pona-turi—in the oozy depths of Ocean,
Fierce, uncouth, in gloomy glory, lived where light is none, nor motion.
More than anything created, Light, their bane, their death, they hated;
So for Night they ever waited ere ashore they seal-like clambered
To their house Manáwa-tanë—their great mansion lofty chambered;
Whence, if e'er a windy Moon had caught them, you would see them hieing
Homeward—sable shapes beneath the crisping silver floating, flying,
Swift as scattered clouds on high their snowy courses gaily plying.

"Young TAWHAKI, well he knew them—did they not his Father mangle?
Hang his fleshless bones, a scarecrow, ghastly from their roof to dangle?
Keep his Mother too, a slave, each day to give them timely warning
Ere dark Sky from Earth uplifting left the first gold gap of morning?

"Vengeance with his Mother then he plotted. So by daylight hiding
In their houseroof-thatch he couched, his slimy foes' arrival biding.
Darkness comes; they land in swarms; their spacious House they crowd and cumber;

Revel through the midnight reckless; drop at last in weary slumber.
Like the distant Ocean's roaring sinks and swells the mighty snoring.—
Out then steals Tawháki chuckling; long ere day begins to brighten,
Stops up every chink in doorway, window, that could let the light in:
And the snoring goes on roaring; or if any Sleeper yawning
Turned him restless, thinking, 'Surely it must now be near the dawning,'
Growling, 'Slave, is daylight breaking? are you watching, are you waking?'
Still the Mother answered blandly, 'Fear not, I will give you warning—
Sleep, O sleep, my Pona-turi—there are yet no streaks of morning!'

"So the snoring goes on roaring. Now above the mountains dewy,
High the splendour-God careers it—great TE RA, the TAMA NUI.*
Sudden cries Tawháki's Mother, '*Open doors and windows quickly!*
Every stop-gap tear out, clear out! On them pour the sunbeams thickly!'
Through the darksome Mansion—through and through those Sons of Darkness streaming
Flash the spear-flights of the Day-God—deadly-silent—golden-gleaming!

* Te Ra—the Sun. Tama Nui—the "great Son" of the Heavens and Earth.

Down they go, the Pona-turi! vain their struggles, yells and fury!
Like dead heaps of fishes stranded by the Storm-spray, gaping—staring—
Stiffened—so astonished, helpless, lay they in the sunbeams glaring:
Fast as shrink upon the shelly beach, those tide-left discs of jelly;
Fast as leathery fungus-balls in yellow dust-clouds fuming fly off,
So they shrink, they fade, they wither, so those Imps of Darkness die off!—"

"Manáwa-tanë! '*breath or life*
Of Man'—no doubt; a *race at strife*
With Light!—were this a German tale,
Not artless Maori, who could fail
To hit its sense, extract its pith,
So pregnant, palpable a Myth!"
Thought Ranolf listening. "Darkness breeds
A swarm of superstitious creeds
That crush Man's Spirit till it bleeds;
His Father—God! yes, him they clearly
A terror make, a scarecrow merely—
High up—unmoved—dry bones or worse
To his abandoned Universe:
His Mother, Earth—her wealth—her worth—
Her schools—thrones—churches—mind and might—
Enslaved so long, set day and night
To warn and war against the Light,—
Free Thought, the beautiful, the bright!
Whose Sons not seldom from their eyes
Shut out, dissemble and disguise

Its full results—half-veil its rays
(Till they shall gather to a blaze?)
And fondly feign they nurse no seeds
Of death to all those narrow creeds:
Howe'er that be, the Sun *will* soar!
His foes may slumber, rave, or roar—
Yet Dayspring spreads o'er sea and shore—
And now, even now, for all their din,
The killing LIGHT is streaming in!—
But I attend. Bright-Eyes, proceed;
Your Myth seems one who runs may read!"

"Now, of heavenly birth to cheer him—beauteous from those blue dominions,
HAPAE came—divine—a damsel—floating down on steady pinions;
Came, a moving moonbeam, nightly lit with Love his chamber brightly:
Till that Spring-time of her bosom flushed out in a baby-blossom.
Infant, it had infant's failings. These as once he eyed the bantling,
Scornfully Tawháki jeered at. Straightway all the mother mantling
In her heart, her treasure Hapae caught up; to her plumy vesture
Pressed it nestling; then upspringing with reproachful look and gesture,
Sailed off to her skiey mansion, vanished in the blue expansion,
Like an Albatross that slides into the sunset,—whitely fading
With its fixed rare-winking vans, away into the crimson shading.

Only ere she parted, while the lagging Westwind she invited
Flapping her broad wings, a-tiptoe on the mannikin alighted
(Red, with arms akimbo on its knees, the gable-apex crowning)
One advice she waved Tawháki, more with grief than anger frowning:
'If you ever feel the Child and Mother to your heart grow dearer,
Ever wish to follow and to find us, O unkindly sneerer,
And would climb by tree-dropt trailers to the Sky a little nearer,
O remember, leave the loose ones; only take and trust to surely
Such as hung from loftiest treetops, root themselves in earth securely!'

"Many a moon he mourned—Tawháki. Then he started to discover
Where they grew, those happy creepers, that could help a hapless lover.
Many a moon he roamed—Tawháki. And his heart was sore and weary
When he found himself despondent in a forest grand and dreary;
(Ah! that wildering wild wood—who can tell how dense it was and tangled!)
Where in wanton woody ringlets many a rope of trailers dangled.
Rapt, absorbed in her pursuit, a blind old Crone those creepers tended;
Caught at, groped and felt for any that within her reach descended.

He, an ancestress discerning, ere for counsel he implored her,
Touched her eyes, a charm repeating, and to sight at once
restored her.
Then they found a creeper rooted, finely for his purpose
suited.
Up he went exultingly, bold-hearted, joyous-eyed, firm-footed.
At the treetop, see ! a tiny spiderthread upshooting shiny,
Wavering, viewless half, yet ever held aloft by mere endeavour !
With a beating heart, Tawháki, muttering many an incanta-
tion—
Wild with hope so high it takes the very hue of desperation,
Clasps the clue so evanescent ; then with yearnings deep,
incessant,
Seeing in the vault above him only Hapae's eyes that love
him,
Up and up, for ever upward mounts he dauntless—nothing
scares him,
Up through azure bright Abysses still that thread in triumph
bears him !
Suddenly a sunny grove is round him—cheery people working
At a great Canoe, appear. All day he keeps the thicket,
lurking,
Till when balmy Shadow veils them and serenest Sleep
assails them
Stripping off his youthful glory, out he steals, an old Man
hoary ;
Strikes a few swift strokes, and magic-like the work is ended—
Graceful with its lofty stern, with open-circled fretwork
splendid,
Lo ! the great Canoe completed ! To his copse he then
retreated ;
On another hollowed trunk next night the wonderwork
repeated.

—Those Celestials marvelled greatly; yet reflecting in their pleasure
Such a worker were a treasure as a Slave beyond all measure,
Watched and clutched that Old Man wilful—so decrepit yet so skilful,
And to their great Ruler bore him.—O delight! who sits before him?
'Tis his beautiful benign One, 'tis his downy-plumed divine one,
Hapae! will he now deride her or the subtle Elf beside her!—
Kindly greeted, with caresses he the Child allures and presses
To his heart no more to sever. Then, as he flings off for ever
That disguise's dim defilement, Hapae smiles sweet reconcilement;
Swift, the Child they bathe, baptize it, lustral waters o'er it dashing;
And Tawháki—breast and brow sublime insufferably flashing,
Hid in lightnings, as he looks out from the thunder-cloven portals
Of the sky—stands forth confest—a God and one of the Immortals!"

"More myth and deeper"—murmured he
As Amo rose and bid them wait
Her quick return: "But how translate
In German style the mystery?—
Shall Hapae our URANIA be?
The 'meaning not the name' were she?—
And if Philosophy Divine
Whose radiant features wont to shine
With heavenly splendour, hopes so rare,
To Man's enfranchised Soul resign

Her charms celestial ;—if their Child
Hight Science seem at first defiled
With taint its infancy may wear—
Materialism—foul Despair—
Shall he the wondrous birth despise ?
Perhaps of those imperial ties
With Reason, free Enlightenment,
That marriage made in heaven, repent—
Until his fair Urania flies
Despondent to her native skies ?
No, but from her he cannot sever—
Can ne'er resist the lofty lure
Of those aspiring eyes so pure !
His must she be, to forfeit never,
His hopeful, heavenly One for ever !
But where to seek the Angel flown ?—
Can that dark forest overgrown
Be Metaphysics ? And the crone
So watchworn, Kant or Hegel is't ?
Some mighty Transcendentalist ?
Or some serene Sensationist
With both his blinkers on ? content,
Nay proud, with his old-fashioned bent
(Anile, perhaps ?) to take and teach
Just what his eyes and hands can reach ?—
Well ! *let* the climber cling through all
To truths they call 'phenomenal,'
Well-rooted in the circle small
Of our perceptions ; and ne'er doubt,
That, sown and springing from *without*,
These parasites upon the Tree
Of shadowy-leaved Humanity,
(Like those depending trailers, sprung
From floating seeds sky-dropt and flung

Upon the bark wherefrom they shoot
And reaching Earth take firmer root)—
These, even these, shall point the way,
The outlet find, some happy day,
By triple-plied deductions, say,
Or if by subtler clue it be,
Some thread of fine analogy,
To regions fair and fertile, where
Undimmed by dense refracting Sense,
Far in the Unapparent shine
Truths and assurances divine
Of God and deathless life confest,
Where the sad Wanderer sore distrest
May glad once more upon the breast
Of his regained Urania rest !—

"With yet more truth the legend teems.
Man's heaven's a heaven of *Work* it seems ;
Yet though his matchless Art reduce
The World of Matter to his use ;
Carve out that grand design, until
Its primal Force start forth compliant,
His Science-Lamp's good Genie-Giant,
Ardent to help him at his will,
Achieve whate'er that will may dare,
To walk the sea or ride the air—
Nay, though his potent patient skill
Work subtler witcheries, stranger still—
Take weeds and turn their downy fluff
To magic mirrors that retain
Whate'er impress of loveliness
May, flitting by, their surface stain ;
Take light, and its fine rays unravel

Till they betray the inmost stuff
The stars are made of whence they travel;
Through continents and Ocean-caves
Whisper a lightning-language; yet
Not this alone his nature craves—
All these a loftier race may set
As tasks and triumphs fit for slaves
Who cannot reach a nobler goal
Nor conquer truths that touch the Soul!

* * * * * * *

"All fancy this! invention pure;
That credulous complaisant whim
With its foregone conclusions trim
To which no Oracles are dim,
No doting prophecies obscure.
Myths may be construed many ways;
Things take a hundred shapes in haze;
In this world, like as Child and Mother,
Matter and Spirit ape each other,
Into each other shift and run—
(Both, better known, may turn out one)
And type and antitype around
In all things may be feigned or found.
Yet for all this, most true it is,
That savage story strangely rings
With echoes of profoundest things;
Glows with the old celestial yearning;
Nay glimmers with a faint discerning
How nought can stifle or repress
Man's upward tendency—the stress
Towards ampler Being, nothing less
Than high immortal Happiness."

CANTO THE SEVENTH.

I.

THEN Amohia, who, her story ended,
Had left the group, returned, not unattended.
A sturdy stripling by her side,
Te Manu, to herself by blood allied,
Coal-curled, brown-cheeked, with beardless chin—
Good-humour broadly shining in his wide
Black eyes and teeth white-glistening through a grin—
Came from the beach where the canoe was tied,
And on the ground before the Stranger placed,
That he the first might touch and taste,
In flax-wov'n basket for a dish,
A dainty pile of delicate fish
In native style deliciously steam-drest,
Like whitebait some; some boiled bright red,
The small cray-fish in myriads bred,
With sunk fern-bundles lifted from the Lake:
Next, roasted fern-root pounded to a cake,
Milkwhite and floury; and the choicer roots,
The new potato and its substitutes,
The *kúmara* and *táro*. Then a store
Of jellies, ruddy-clear as claret, pressed
And well preserved from fruits last season bore,

Rich clusters of *tupáki*, luscious sweet;
With water mixed their noontide thirst to slake,
An innocent beverage truly! Rude the light
Repast, and simply wholesome at the best;
Yet scrupulously clean withal, it might
Have satisfied a more fastidious guest.

II.

And when the talk began again,
Said Ranolf, "How do you explain,
You Maori, how the heavens were hung
Up there? who spread the azure main?
Whence Man and all things living sprung?"

Prompt was an ancient Dame's reply,
Of wrinkled cheek yet lively eye,
Who took the pipe from her blue lips
And sate in grizzled dignity,
Proud of her crest that towered so high
Of heopoe-feathers, black with snowy tips;—
Prompt was that ancient Dame's reply—
Compact her scheme of rude Cosmogony:

"There was NIGHT at the first—the great Darkness. Then
PAHPA, the Earth, ever genial, general Mother,
And our Father, fair RANGI—the Sky—in commixture unbounded confusedly clave to each other;
And between them close cramped lay their children gigantic—all Gods. He the mightiest, eldest, the Moulder
And Maker of Man—whose delight is in heroes—TUMATAU—the Courage-inspirer, the Battle-upholder;

TANGAROA, far-foaming, the Sire of the myriads that silvery
cleave the cerulean waters;
And the solemn and beauteous TANE, who gathers his
stateliest, ever-green, tress-waving daughters
Into forests, the sunny, the songster-bethridden; then RONGO
—the peaceful, the kindly provider
Of the roots that with culture are milkiest, pithiest; he too,
who flings them in wilder and wider
Profusion uncultured, nor needing it—HAUMIA; lastly, the
fiercest of any, the Rider
Of Tempests—TAWHIRI, joy-wild when his sons—when the
Winds multitudinous rush with the rattle
Of hail and the sting of sharp showers and the hurry of
turbulent clouds to aerial battle.
All these did the weight of vast Rangi o'erwhelm; there
restlessly, rampantly, brother on brother
Lay writhing and wrestling in vain to get free from the
infinite coil and confusion and smother;
Till the forest-God, Tanë, with one mighty wrench irresistible
prized his great parents asunder—
With his knotty and numberless talons held down—held the
Earth and its mountain magnificence under,
Heaved the Heavens aloft with a million broad limbs shot
on high, all together rebounding, resilient:
Then at once came the LIGHT interfused, interflowing—
serenely soft-eddying—crystalline—brilliant !—
Now the Sons all remained with the Earth but Tawhiri; he,
sole, in tempestuous resentment receding
Swept away at the skirts of his Father—the Sky; but swiftly
to vengeance and victory leading
His livid battalions, returned in his terrors, his kindred with
torment and torture to harry:
Tangaroa rolled howling before him—even Tanë bowed
down; could his blast-besplit progeny parry

His blows, or withstand the full pelt of his torrents that flung
them o'er wastes of white Ocean to welter?
Could Rongo do more ere he fled than conceal in the warmth
of Earth's bosom his children for shelter?—
No! they shrank from the Storm-God amazed and affrighted.
One brother—Tumatau—alone durst abide him,
Tumatau and MAN stood before him unswerving, deserted by
all, disregarded, defied him!
But Man that defection still punishes daily; with snare, net
and spear still their offspring he chases,
Tangaroa's and Tanë's—the feathered—the finny; still turns
up and tears from her tender embraces
All that Rongo has laid in the lap of his Mother; while
fiercely Tawhiri still plagues *all* their races—
Ever wreaks his wild anger on blue Tangaroa, and whirls
into spray-wreaths the billows he lashes—
On the Earth whose rich berries and blossoms he scatters
and scathes; on the forests he splinters and crashes;
And on Man who stands firm when his thunder is loudest
and laughs when his lightning incessantly flashes!"

III.

Said Amohia, "In your heart you laugh;
You think all this is nonsense, *to-e*, 'chaff;'
Nay then, O Stranger, answer in your turn,
For still the Sun is riding high,
Of *his* beginning—of the birth
Of all things, Sea and Sky and Earth,
What from their Sages do the white men learn?"

Silent he scanned an instant's space
The open eyes, the candid face
Of the enquiring earnest Maid;

Then as a half-satiric smile
Twitched at the corners of his mouth, the while
Lurked in his eyes a sly malicious twinkle,
Rushed off into a wild tirade—
Not caring if his words were clear or dim,
Only obedient to the moment's whim,
Somewhat like this ;—for we must sprinkle
With phrases freer, fuller and more flowery,
Than match the rudeness of his simple Maori—
Omitting interruptions too
And explanations not a few—
The terms the careless youth employed
To give to her whose wonder he enjoyed,
Some notion of the Deity—the greatest
By Science hit on—or at least, the latest:

"*There's a God they call* MOTION ; *a wonderful Being,*
Omnipresent, omnipotent! thinking and seeing,
All life, birth, existences, creatures, conditions,
Of his versatile skill ever-new exhibitions,
Are but phases his phantasy, subtle or simple,
Condescends to assume ; from the faintest first dimple
He indents in the vapour that veils him—beginning
As he slides to a pirouette graceful and winning,
Such a whirl of Creation, such Universe-spinning—
To his last of developments dense or ethereal,
When as Consciousness crowned with a halo imperial,
Though but grovelling in granules and cells ganglionic
In the brain of Mankind sits the grand Histrionic!
'Tis the strangest and stoutest of creeds and convictions—
'Tis a God that defies and disdains contradictions:
His adorers, though puzzled perhaps to say whether
He is *they*, or they *he*, they are mixed so together ;—

Though himself best proclaims his own glory Protean
When as lightning he dances with worship Judæan,
Or intones as deep thunder his own Io-Pæan ;—
Though reluctant and shy to acknowledge, avow him—
Yet with all that is precious and priceless endow him.
At the shrine of this Pagod they immolate gaily
Aspirations Humanity feeds upon daily ;
There consume, with serene suicidal devotion
Whole heart-loads of lofty and tender emotion,
All the foredawn of gold over Life's darksome ocean :
And they vary his victims with Logic—no little ;
Never spare Common Sense—not a fraction—nor tittle ;
Show no mercy for Sciences, moral or mental ;
And for Metaphysicians—the tribe transcendental,
Would burn them to cinders—a holocaust ; striving
On the ashes to keep their Divinity thriving.
For strange though it seem, this Almighty Mechanic,
Undesigning Designer of all things organic,
Comes from nowhere himself : his own Father and Mother—
Never caused though all-causing—derived from no other ;
And arranges, combines for such orderly courses
His myriad myriads of multiform forces,
By accident only—repulsion—attraction—
Into beautiful symmetry, uniform action ;
By merest unconscious haphazard produces
Profound adaptations to infinite uses ;
And as helplessly, stolidly stumbles on wonders,
With as little intention, as others on blunders ;
Deaf and dumb, and stone blind, can make eyes, ears and
voices,
Till with Beauty—Light—Music—all Nature rejoices ;
Nay, unconscious beforehand arrives in due season
By dint of mere going, at Thought, Sense and Reason ;

With *no* Mind, makes *all* Mind—that fine consummation,
That can trace the back steps of the blind operation;
Aye can soar on the wings of sublime calculation
O'er the flaming far ramparts of star-filled Creation.
So this Fetish—this Stock-God, this Impulse unguided,
With no aim and no sense, yet success so decided,
Still is fashioning Matter by no one provided
Into Minds like vast Mountains a World overviewing:—
With no better notion of what he is doing,
Hits off Shakspeares and Newtons and Cæsars and Platos—
Than the logs on the ashes which roast your potatoes:
And the men who consider this creed satisfactory
And would smile with mild pity on Sceptics refractory,
Poor crawlers who crowd to a house with a steeple,—
Are—*some of the wisest and best of our people*."

To this effusion nought replied
The listeners; only said aside,
"The Stranger mocks us;" quietly—
Too courteous for expressed dissent,
Too proud to show astonishment
Or ignorance of their Guest's intent.
That laughing lunch-purveyor, he
Only to Miroa muttered low:
"A *tito* this—a fib, I know;
'Tis nothing like what Mapou says
Of their white Átua and his ways;
And *he* can tell, who visits most
And learns all news that reach the coast.
This Stranger too,"—and here the grin
Grew broader,—"by his dress at least
Is not a *Tohunga*, a Priest;

For Mapou says, *they* always go
In shining black from top to toe,
With two white plumes beneath their chin,
Just like that *Tu-i*, Mapou thought."
And Ranolf smiled, whose quick ear caught
The fancy, as he saw just then
The bird they spoke of, down the glen
Come dashing, with its glossy coat
Like jet-black satin shot with green
And blue reflexions—at its throat
Two dainty-pencilled plumes of snow;
And once again admired, as oft
Before, its lively ways and note;
As flitting, shifting to and fro
It ransacked every kowhai-tree
In yellow bloom, and loudly coughed
And loudly whistled in its glee,
And turned quite over, bending low
Its busy head to reach and dip
Into the pendent flowers and sip
Their juice, in fluttering glad unrest,
Unceasing in its honey-quest.

"That may be true," said Miroa, "too;
For 'tis averred they are like a bird
In this (although it seems a joke)
They cannot *speak* like other folk,
But always *sing* what they would say,
E'en when they to their Átua pray."
—But here that feather-crested Dame
Who this light chatter overheard
Rebuked them—feeling it became
Her sage experience to repress

Such sallies of mere sauciness:
"Oh foolish you! *we* always do
Ourselves in all our prayers the same!
Do we not *sing* for all we want?
May *they* not know some potent chaunt
To charm their Átua from his haunt,
As we coax eels to leave the mud?"—
  Such reasoning they could not gainsay,
It nipped their satire in the bud.

IV.

Meanwhile, another Guest had been
Among them, though unnoticed and unseen;
Joining their converse with no audible tongue,
And speaking mystic Music without sound;
On whose mute melodies the listener hung;
Whose viewless Presence brightened all around.
Who should it be but that Consoler dear,
Heartwhispering Paraclete of priceless cheer—
Who but the Enchanter—Love? whose witchery flings
Fresh life round Daybreak's life-enlivening springs;
Heaps Noon on Noon for fervour; double-dyes
For deeper pathos Eve's empurpled skies.
Did he not use his artless Art that day
With slightest means most meaning to convey?
Some idle question asked as if in sport,
Some falter in the tone or breath drawn short—
Some touch of tapering fingers—touch so fleet,
They seem, just *seem*, as they a moment meet,
To linger ere they leave the contact sweet?
Or scorning all less subtle ministries
Did He not speak through Amohia's eyes,
Whose lids and raven lashes though they fell

Dark as a closing bird's wing o'er their light
Upon her rich warm cheek, could never quite
Shut in their lustrous tenderness, nor quell
Their rebel glances eloquent of Him,
More than the mother-bird can fold with hers
Her crowd of small quick-running loiterers
So closely, safely, that no single one
Of all the nestling, jostling train
May slip a moment out into the sun,
Although next moment gathered in again ;
Whene'er that brooding mother sees
The stiff-stretched hawk across the blue vault swim ;
  As once or twice amid the trees
Had Amohia marked the Priest appear,
(Though vanishing almost as soon as seen)
With eyes inscrutable and dim
Watching herself and Ranolph ; though with mien
Not threatening now, malignant nor severe,
  Whatever cause she had to fear.
—But who could tell what hatred fell,
What dark designs might not be found
Within his heart whose face no less
Was such a smooth and placid screen ?—
  How many a man amid the press,
Is but a walking Wilderness,—
Like some fierce Ameer's hunting-ground
By lofty walls concealed, confined :
Caverns interminable wind,
Abysses yawn, those walls behind ;
There wild beasts prowl and moan and howl
Of lust and greed and all excess ;
They peer and pry who wander by—
The smooth fair walls are all they spy.

But little of his looks recked they,
Which though they keenly glanced their way
Did yet no ill intent betray.
So from redundant springs all day
Flowed streams of converse, grave and gay.

CANTO THE EIGHTH.

I.

O'ER all the East the sunset's flush
From plain to peak began to rise;
That slowly-fading fever flush
Of beauteous Day before she dies.
The friends again had reached the Isle
And for a little space had parted;
Those elder women kindly-hearted
About the evening meal employed:
Their guest had strolled away awhile,
And by the Lake the painted eve enjoyed;
There, tempted after all the sweltering heat
By the cool water glistening black
In shade behind a green spur's shelving back,
Which seemed a place for bathing meet,
Had passed some wooded rocks upon his right
Into a thicket where karakas veiled
The path in gloom almost as dark as night—
When from behind he felt himself assailed
By ambushed men unseen, unknown;
Before he could resist was overpowered;
A mantle o'er his head was thrown,
His arms and feet fast pinioned; nor availed

His stifled shouts, the threats and taunts he showered
Upon his dastard foes, who answered nought
But with determined silence and one will
Their struggling captive rapidly conveyed
O'er rocks and rooty paths (he thought)
Where branches oft their way opposed
Into some place from outer air enclosed ;
For cooler seemed and yet more still
The atmosphere ; and on his sense the smell
Of the dried rushes used in buildings fell.
There on the ground the luckless youth they laid ;
And when a sliding panel was made fast
With cautious footsteps out of hearing passed.

II.

Now left alone, the youth contrived to free
His head, and strove his prison-place to see.
All round was sombre darkness ; but it teemed
With great white ghastly eyes that strangely gleamed
With pink and silvery flashings here and there,
And seemed to float and throb in the dun air ;
Then by degrees grew motionless, and fixed
On *him* one savage and concentred gaze ;
And slowly he discerns, those eyes betwixt,
Features gigantic—furious—in amaze ;
Wild brows upbranching broad, yet corrugate
With close-knit frowns ferocious ; blubber lips
Stretched wide as rage and mockery can strain
Mouths—monstrous as the Shark's, when 'mid the ship's
Exultant crew he gnashes in dumb pain—
That grin grotesque, intense and horrible hate,
And thrust out sidelong tongues that from their root
The very frenzy of defiance shoot

So, with malignant and astonished stare
They gaze, as if the intruder's blood to freeze.

At length, accustomed to the gloom, he sees
What dwarfish forms those ponderous heads upbear;
Their crooked tortoise-legs, club-curved and short;
Their hands, like toasting-forks or tridents prest
Against each broad and circle-fretted breast;
And all the fact discerned at last, he knows
These pigmy-giants form red-ochred rows
Of rafters and pilasters to support
A spacious hall;—some carved in high relief;
While others standing from the walls aloof
Piled up in pillars of squat monsters rise
Perched on each others shoulders to the roof.
The tribe's great Council-Chamber this should be,
Their Whàre-kúra, Hall of sacred Red,
For worship—justice; where the most adept,
The glorious deeds of their ancestral dead,
And pedigrees that back for centuries crept,
Safe in their memories by rehearsal kept;
Those forms were effigies (he might surmise)
Each of some famous ancestress or chief;
But to his fancy now the crowd appeared
A Gorgon-eyed and grinning demonry
Whose fiendish rancour his misfortune jeered.

And bitter were his feelings as he lay
To dark forebodings, anxious fears a prey:
What could have caused this outrage? whose the deed?
Or what its object? in his utmost need
Where could he look for succour? how escape
The doom that threatened him in some dread shape

He scarce could doubt, although the thought might strike
His cooler mind, so unprovoked a wrong
Done by these islanders, was little like
(As all his past experience would attest)
Their usual treatment of a peaceful guest.
And though the tide of his regrets ran strong
With self-reproaches that a careless hour
Had placed his life within their savage power,
Mokoia's Chief he felt could never be
Privy to such a wrong!—The 'Wailing Sea'
Had spurned such crafty craven treachery.
His natural spirits at the thought revived;
And he resolved forthwith to be prepared
The moment that his unknown foes arrived
And loosed his bonds, to spring upon them—dash
Between them—struggle—lose no slightest chance,
But do and dare whatever might be dared
Or done, however desperate, wild and rash,
That might accomplish his deliverance.
Or if no opening should occur for swift
Decisive force or dexterous agile shift,
He still would try what gentle means might do—
Never despair! in worst extremes he knew
So many chances to the brave accrue,
Hopes to the true heart come so often true!
  But should all fail, and he be doomed to die,
Ah, could he help but feel,—no soul so dull
As *not* to feel—how deep the misery,
The bitterness to leave a world, so full
Of vivid beauty, varied life and joy,
'Twould scarce the wisest even in ages cloy!
Yet even then he had the heart to rest
In trust the great All-giver would invest—

Out of the infinite exhaustless store
Of Life he loves with lavish hand to pour
Thick as a mist of dew-drops over all
The inconceivable array of star-worlds, more
In number than the sands on oceans' shore—
His soul with new existence; though to dust
This apparition of mere clay should fall,
Its present phantasm. What, 'Is man more just
Than God?' that immemorial chime
Asked out of Arab wastes in earliest time;
And why not ask, Is he more generous, too?
Should not God's great beneficence outdo
What Man could in conception and in will
Be equal to? should He not spare
Another life—a hundred if need were,
To beings into whom his loving care
Did such deep longing for the boon instil?
Yes, he would trust in this his extreme need
The INFINITE; who if infinite indeed
In aught, is infinite in Love as well
That must our own heart's highest love excel.
So with firm patience he resolves to wait,
Whatever be its form, his coming fate.

III.

Two hours or more had dragged their weary way
While cramped with chafing bonds in pain he lay;
Those stony eyes had faded from his sight
When deeper fell the shades of growing night.
Far, far away his mournful thoughts had flown
To friends and scenes in happy boyhood known—
When—hist! a rustling sound that softly falls
Upon his ear, his wandering mind recalls;

He listens—all is silent—then again
The rustle and slight creak are heard—'tis plain
Some cautious hand has thrust aside the door—
Some noiseless foot steals light along the floor;
The form that owned them had a moment hid
The patch of moonlight where the panel slid
Away—too briefly for his eye to trace
Its outline—guess its purpose; to his side,
So stealthy, swift and noiseless was its pace,
The shadowy Shape seemed less to walk than glide.
Could this some midnight murderer be? his heart
Beat quick as over him that Shadow bent—
Quick as the sweet breath felt upon his face,
That Phantom's breath, that quickly came and went
As if in his emotion it took part.
A soft voice whispered: "Stranger—hist! no word—
'Tis I—'tis Amohia!"—Then she fell
To her kind work, and every cutting cord
Sought out and severed with a sharpened shell.
Upsprung the youth, to life and joy restored;
And rapturous thanks had to the Maid outpoured,
But that her hand upon his lips was laid,
But that her lips in briefest whisper prayed
What her unseen more eloquent looks implored:
"O for your life no sound! but follow me—
Who knows how near your deadliest foe may be!"

So through the doorway stealing in the dark,
She makes the panel fast, and he may mark
Less-pleased, that silvery blue solemnity
That mingles with the bowery trees hard by.
Then in the open, silently they creep,
They, and their shadows thrown so sharp and deep.

Upon a terrace half way up a cleft
Or hollow on the mountain's northern steep,
'Mid tufts of flax, tall-bladed, bright as glass,
And ferny tree-clumps, stood the house they left.
See! by a hut which they perforce must pass,
Across their very path, three youths, asleep
In the warm moon upon the sun-dried grass
Are lying!—'twould be ruin to retreat:—
The Maiden's heart, he almost hears it beat!
Each foot placed firm before the last is raised,
They step between the knees so nearly grazed:
And soon are safe beneath the blessed shade
By trees—themselves as still as shadows, made.
Then round the island's end, that fear allayed,
Beneath its woody western slopes they steal,
Where they may speak secure, and she reveal,
The cause and author of the base assault
Her friend had suffered. Kangapo's the fault—
That priests', and not her father's, she averred:
For Kangapo's sole aim, he might have heard,
The one great passion that his bosom stirred,
The main pursuit in which his life was spent,
Was, next his own, their tribe's aggrandizement.
For this, by his advice, almost from birth,
Herself had been made '*tapu*' to her grief,
To Taupo's Lord—an old whiteheaded chief,
Of mighty power, no doubt, high rank and worth:
And though this marriage of her dread and hate
That landslip had relieved her from of late,
Yet much she feared—the Priest already planned
Some other proud disposal of her hand;
So jealously he watched, so little brooked
The slightest glance of any youth who looked

With any (here she checked herself)—at least
Of any one who talked with her awhile:
And so that day when she observed the Priest
Eye them so keenly with his crafty smile,
Although deceived a moment by his guile,
It roused suspicions, strengthened when she saw
Again, on their returning to the Isle,
He noticed Ranolf from the group withdraw
At sunset; and himself stole off so soon
By the same pathway towards the western wood;
She followed; for the thing could bode no good;
But by another track; had seen him meet
Four men to whom his slightest wish was law,
Then to a copse of mánuka retreat
Where they could safely, secretly commune;
Had crept close-up on tiptoe—overheard
Their vile atrocious project every word;
To seize, bind, bear the Stranger to their great
Runanga-house; there leave him bound and wait
The setting of the Moon, till they could take
Their captive to the middle of the Lake,
Where they would throw him overboard, still bound;
And tell her Father next day how they found
The Stranger at his evening meal—with food—
Aye, *food!* beside the monument that stood
High carved in their most sacred burial-ground
O'er his most famous ancestor's dead bones:
And though a bird sung on it all the while—
Doubtless the spirit of that Chief renowned,
It still could not prevent the outrage vile:—
Would not such impious sacrilege astound
The boldest?—how aloof the crime they viewed
With hair on end, tongues to their palates glued

In speechless horror, motionless as stones :
But how his Ancestor's insulted Shade
With vengeance dire the deed profane repaid ;
For when the Stranger launched his boat again
There was no ripple on the watery plain ;
Yet scarce a spear-flight had he left the bank
Before his boat without a breeze capsized,
And with it—he with scarce a struggle—sank ;
For all his powers that Spirit had paralyzed.
This was the plot concerted then and there ;
And next she noted where his boat they hid
To make all points of their narration square ;
And Miroa was to bring it, as she bid,
Round to a spot they presently would reach—
Yes ! there she saw them waiting on the beach !
The rest he knew. "But now, O Stranger, haste !
Fly to your skiff—O not a moment waste
In words—already, see ! the Moon is low—
Away, before your flight those traitors know !"

He turned to thank her—would not take her nay ;
Despite her struggles clasped her to his breast,
And ere from his embrace she broke away
Upon her lips a shower of fervent kisses prest.

IV.

O in all climes and every age a token
Of one bright link for suffering mortals left
With the Eternal and Divine unbroken—
By all Earth's strain and tears untarnished and unreft !—
O tempting—time-worn—ever-during theme—
That first fond kiss of Love ! first dazzling gleam
When two surcharged electric Love-clouds meet—

Flash Paradise into the mutual dream
Of rapt twin-spirits in a lightning stream,
And blend in blissful rest their soul-entrancing heat!—
Most surely is the Heav'n-glimpse visible there,
When some young creature, innocent as fair,
Supreme Civilization's tender heir,
Such first faint utterance of true love may dare.
The wondrous, pure, envelopment divine
Of fearful awe and maiden scruples fine—
That trembling kiss has broken through it now,
Like the first crocus peeping through the snow;
Oh timid touching of a terrible joy
Whose sweet excess would almost ask alloy!
First hesitating step within the range
Of unimagined worlds—enchanted—strange!—
Ah! break off there, young throbbing hearts! Ah stay,
Let that ecstatic dawn ne'er darken into day!
The quivering brilliance of that hour so tender,
Love's disc emerging o'er the horizon's rim,
Does not its molten palpitating splendor
Leave vulgar Noon and its refulgence dim?
Oh might that Morn its freshness ne'er surrender,
But still in blinding innocency swim!—
Vain thought!—save one such bud of bliss, unblown—
And laws that rule the Universe were gone!

But now, the kisses prest with youthful passion
On Amohia's lips were not alone
The first those lips from one she loved had known.
They were the first she ever felt at all!
A novel mode—a strange too fervent fashion,
Of salutation or caressing this!
What aid, what safeguard to her side to call,

This subtle soft assailant to repel,
This cunning and insidious foe—a kiss!
Was it not thrice too thrilling? might not well
This meeting of the lips and breath appear,
Spirit to spirit—soul to soul to bring
Too dangerously close—too fondly near?
Through joining lips heart seemed to heart to cling;
And had not breath and spirit but one name—
In hers, as many a rougher tongue, the same?—

But she has torn herself away—"Oh go,
Ranoro, only go! haste—haste, or they
Will track us here!" She could,—she would not say
For fear more than those choking words, although
Such briefest farewell seemed a knell of woe.
"Farewell, then, dearest! till we meet once more!"
He said, and pushed off quickly from the shore.

V.

She gazed unmoving—watched his boat depart,
With desolation dragging at her heart.
Just then the ill-omened Moon withdrew behind
A sable cloud-stripe, sudden, as if dropped—
Dead Nun! into a coffin snowy-lined.
Then swelled her heart with tears her pride had stopped;
Weeping she stole the silent trees among,
Weeping reproved her weeping with a song;
For the spontaneous song her sadness moaned,
Provoked the very weakness it disowned;
Racking her bosom with its feigned relief,
And bitter comfort that redoubled grief.

I.

"Leave me! yes, too dear one, leave me!
Better now, when least 'twill grieve me!
While unrisen, unconsuming,
Love's red dawn is but illuming
With faint rays our spirits glooming—
Oh while we can bear to sever,
Let us part and part for ever!
Part with wishes—vows unspoken,
Tears unshed and hearts unbroken!

2.

"O this feeling! who shall cure it—
Teach the Maiden to endure it?—
Where is he, whitebearded, holy,
Who shall lead his daughter slowly
To the waters melancholy?
Lead his love-afflicted daughter
To the still, estranging water?—
Where the pool so gloomy-shining,
Can relieve this love-repining?

3.

"She has let it charm too dearly,
Lull too fondly, touch too nearly,
That sweet sorrow; now unwilling,
In the wave so soothing, chilling,
Pure, translucent, passion-killing,
He must lave her—chaunting faintly
Hymns so piteous, hymns so saintly!
Then shall cease this yearning—sighing,
With the mystic measure dying."

VI.

So parted they—and so they strove apart
Each to repress the risings of the heart ;
Each to rake out, ungerminant, ungrown,
The seed in fertile soil too richly sown.
Yet in her own despite, it seemed, the Maid,
Was still recalled to something done, or said,
By or about the Stranger ; to her breast
Tidings of him, like wild birds to their nest
Would fly, it seemed as to their natural rest ;
The slightest news that floated in the air
By some attraction seemed to settle there ;
Nor ever seemed there lack of such, or dearth
Of Fancy's food ; for desert wastes of Earth
Blush nectared fruits, and the blue void above
Rains mystic manna but to nourish Love !

Nor yet could Amohia, in that pain
Of stifled passion, though she strove, refrain
From stealing sometimes to a lonely spot
Where all before her lay the Lake serene ;
And she could see the glimmer of the cot
Her heart divined was his ; and there with mien
Expectant on the mountain-side unseen
In thick red-dusted fern would couch, until
From the dim base-line of the opposite hill
A white speck disengaged itself and grew
Into a sail ; or sometimes—for to while
The time when sport was slack or weather bad,
With help from native hands, our sailor-lad
Had fitted up a light canoe,

With keel, mast, sails, and rudder, too,
And sculls in European style—
Sometimes a dark spot she descried
With flashing twinkle on each side
That neared and neared till clear in view
The light skiff, in a mode so new,
Its single occupant, though backward going
At once with two long paddles rowing,
Came skimming the blue calm, and still
With sharp keel seemed to slit the thin
Glazed surface of the shining Lake
That shrank apart in widening wake
As shrinks beneath the sacrificial knife
Some forest victim's opening skin
Discoated of its fur and warm
From the last pants of its wild woodland life:
There as she sat alone and long,
Like one who murmurs low some potent charm,
In fervid words her love would simmer into song:

I.

Now should He come, whose coming for a while
Will make all Nature smile.
O bless my longing sight,
Dear one! whose presence bright
I hail with more delight,
Than birds the sunrise thrilling through each rapture-ringing cover,
Than trees the spring-time when they glow with gladder green all over.
The Sun is dim without thee, dearest,
Joy's self looks sad till thou appearest!—

See, he comes!—O dull, dull Lake!
How canst thou sleep so blue—nor wake—
Nor rise and wreathe with loving spray my own, my darling lover!

2.

O slim white Sail, whose every curve of grace
So fondly now I trace,
Each silver shape you try
Only to charm his eye
Ah, happy Sail! and fly,
Because you know, howe'er you strain, he still is with you steering—
Nay! but you only feel, slight Sail, the faint wind's fickle veering:—
That envied Wind! that hampered never
Might fondly fold my Love for ever
Wholly in one airy kiss;
Yet coldly can renounce such bliss,
And on your disenchanted way go heartlessly careering!

3.

You vapory columns that from hotsprings rise
(As from my heart such sighs)
So white against the green,
And through the day serene,
Now this, now that way lean,
And easier postures seem to take for silent contemplation,
O why not always turn towards him in speechless admiration!
But you, dark Clouds! that grate with thunder
While on the leaden gloss thereunder,

Silvery rings the fishes make,
Are glistening, fading on the Lake—
Turn, murky Clouds, O turn from him, your muttered indignation!

4.

O Sail, O Bark, O happy Wind, O Lake,—
All happy for his sake,
Why cannot I too rest
Indifferent, unopprest,
No aching at the breast—
Why not behold a beauteous thing with heedless airy pleasure,
Sleep, sport or speed away like you, untortured by the treasure!—
But I must moan and writhe and languish,
And almost envy in this anguish
The poor fishes, for they die,
But close to him—beneath his eye:—
And death with him to life without, O who its bliss could measure!

CANTO THE NINTH.

I.

1.

"*Tears, tears!—Oh do not trickle down,*
Oh sleep within your fount unknown!
Oh rack my heart but rise not, lest
Cold eyes discern you, and divine the rest.

2.

"*Oh for some cavern unespied*
Whereto I may escape and hide!
Lest my deep love, in my despite
Leap up, and break away into the light!—"

Such was the burden of the ancient lay
Sad Amohia murmured as she sat
Apart from her companions one bright day
Making a broidered border for a mat.
From sloping roof to earthen floor
Two staffs were fixed the Maid before;
Upon a line between them strung
Fringe-like the flax-warp loosely hung;
She worked the woof in thread by thread;
Inserting deftly, plaiting, tying

Into the web as on it sped
More coloured threads beside her lying :
Her task without a model plying,
She wove with interchange ornate
Of spaces crimson black and yellow—
Triangular or tesselate,
Responding each one to its fellow—
The silky fibres intricate :
Like some Pompeian pavement's old
Mosaic, rich with contrast bold
Of vivid colours, tasteful, true,
The fair design her fancy drew
Beneath her nimble fingers grew.
But ever and anon she stopped,
A thread was tangled, missed, or dropped ;-
What but some ill-concealed distress
Could mar such manifest address
With quite unwonted awkwardness ?
How could she speed her at her task so trim,
With thoughts so wandering and with eyes so dim ?

II.

Then in this fever of despondence, finding
Her restlessness she could no more restrain,
Struggling her mien and movements to compose,
Though scarcely able to refrain
From rushing—out into the air she goes.
She steps into the noon-glare hot and blinding—
But what a gush of gladsome sound
At once assails her !—like the winding
Of tiny watches numberless, all round
Unceasing streams the loud-vibrating hiss
Of gay cicadas in their summer bliss.

O it tormented her—it pained
Her soul, that emulous shrill monotony
Of exultation so persistent and sustained.—
She turns to where the Lake, a mimic sea,
The pebbled beach with pleasant murmur laves ;
Hastily she hurries onward now,
Now rests as wearily—wearily watching how
Distorted by the heaving crystal, the bright stones
And tremulous streaks between them clear,
Still float up, vanish, reappear
With endless iteration as the little waves
Keep rolling—rolling in. O then she moans
In very impotence to bear
The placid, playful happiness,
The obstinate calm contentment they express
As if in mockery of her despair.
She flings herself upon the grass
With passionate floods of tears :—Alas,
But who can weep away a woe?
Tears for each flood are readier to reflow ;
Or if with the worn frame at length
Exhausted, still revive with its reviving strength.

III.

Now the long splendours of the day were past ;
The gorgeous tints of Eve subsiding fast :
The Western hill-tops touched with solemn rays ;
Their slopes in chestnut-hued and chocolate haze
Thin-veiled, that melted downwards into gloom
Blue as the ripened plum's white-misted bloom :
While the reflected roseate richness steeping
The East, slunk fading up from lake and shore,
From mountains next, and last the sky, before

The purple gray of shadow upward creeping;
All the flushed sunset sobered into boding awe;—
When Miroa, coursing quick from side to side,
Tossing to any one she saw
A merry word her aim to hide—
With careful shew of carelessness—
Her anxious flutter anxious to repress—
Her object to seem objectless—
Came like a quivering flittermouse,
Came darting through the gathering dusk to Amohia's house.
Bursting with news she longs yet fears to tell,
The darkling room she first examines well,
Lest any listener be lurking near;
Then whispers in that Maiden's ear,
How all day 'twixt her father and the priest
The close and covert converse ne'er had ceased:
Till they determined there should be despatched
An embassy to Nápuhi's famous Chief
With offer to bestow her—Amo's hand
Upon his son Pomáre: how, in brief,
She for young Kárepa had watched,
Who to the mission was attached,
Waylaid him on the road and wormed
His secret from him—as she well knew how;—
He teased her with his love so often now!
But had not Kangapo with truth affirmed,
No match more advantageous could be planned
For her—none give her Sire such right to stand,
With unconstrained and equal brow
Proudly amid the proudest of the land?—
This was a marriage,—must she not confess
The priests would all conspire to bless;

Aye, raise to frenzy-pitch their rival tune
Of incantations to the Sun, the Moon,
The winds, and all the powers of Earth and Air,
To be propitious to the bridal pair?

Shocked—terrified—the Maiden heard
The tale with obvious truth averred;
She flushed and paled; her blood suspended,
All life seemed fading from her brain;
Then the hot current spirit-stirred,
Back from her strong heart rushed again,
And high she rose above her pain.
Her doubts, her hesitation ended,
This—this—she felt had sealed her doom:
O dread! to-morrow well she knew
Once more she might be made taboo:
And what could break that hideous chain!
The threatened fate she could evade
Only by flight—swift—secret—undelayed!
All the sheet-lightning that had played
In pointless passion round her soul so long,
Condensed by this compulsion strong,
Shot into arrowy purpose, clear against its gloom.

As through the land when some dread Earthquake thrills,
Shaking the hidden bases of the hills;
Their grating adamantine depths, beneath
The ponderous, unimaginable strain and stress,
Groan shuddering as in pangs of worldwide death;
While their long summits stretched against the sky
Rough-edged with trackless forests, to the eye
A double outline take (as when you press
The eyeball); and the beaten roads below
In yellow undulations roll and flow;

And in broad swamps the serried flax-blades lithe,
Convulsed and tortured, rattling, toss and writhe,
As through them sweeps the swift tremendous throe:
Beasts howling run, or trembling, stand and stare,
And birds, as the huge tree-tops swing and rock,
Plunge scared into the more reliable air:—
All Nature wrung with spasm, affrighted reels
Aghast, as if the heavy chariot-wheels
Of God in very truth were thundering by
In too intolerable majesty:—
Then he who for the first time feels the shock,
Unconscious of its source, unguessing whence
Comes flying o'er him, with oppressive sense
Of irresistible Omnipotence,
That boundless, strange, o'erwhelming influence,
At once remote and in his inmost heart—
Is troubled most, that, with his staggering start
All the convictions from his birth upgrown,
And customary confidence, o'erthrown,
In Earth's eternal steadfastness, are gone:
Even such a trouble smote in that wild hour
Our Maiden—such revulsion shook her soul,
As o'er her swept that sense of doom
And dire compulsion spurning her control!
All feelings that had been her life-long stay
Seemed from their deep foundations wrenched away;
No more could her convulsed, afflicted breast,
On childhood's loves or home-affections rest;
Her Being all upheaving seemed to be
Cast loose and drifting towards an unknown Sea;
Her heart's young world, uptorn—receding fast—
Far rolled the echoes of the fading Past;
She stood alone—herself her sole support at last.

IV.

'Tis Night;—the Maiden steals along the shore;
How lone the aspect at that hour it wore!
How shelterless from all dread things—so deemed
Her superstition—wherewith Darkness teemed!
All the familiar friendliness of Day,
And all its life and stir, subsided—sunk—
Within that circling fence shut up and shrunk,
Where, snake-like coiled, the sleeping Village lay!
Miles distant now its very precincts seemed.
She speeds to where her people use
To leave afloat their red canoes;
A new misfortune! all and each
Are high and dry upon the beach;
The lightest well she knew would prove
Too heavy for her strength to move.
Was she distrusted? her design
Betrayed? she cares not to divine:
Her spirit not a moment falters;
Not once her cheek its colour alters:
As he who desperate only tries
To strike one stroke before he dies,
And hardly wincing, never heeds
Some fresh deep wound as fast he bleeds—
So this last stroke the Maid receives;
So with impatient patience shuts,
Though to her heart it keenly cuts,
Her heart against it; if she grieves,
That grief can silently repress
With one sad smile of bitterness,
(The choking at her throat no less)

While to her aim she calmly cleaves.
Shall this defeat her fixed intent?
The Lake her purposed flight prevent?
Her favourite haunt, almost from birth
In many an hour of fearless mirth,
Her life beside it had been spent,
'Twas like her natural element!
With throbbing breast, with lips comprest,
She flings her quick and lighted glance
Determined o'er its dark expanse:
That further shore was distant—dim—
  But better death than turning back!
No way but one! yes, she will *swim*—
Her daring path unaided track
Across that plain so still and black!—
Did not her own great Ancestress
Once swim that Lake in like distress?
Might she not dare and do the same?
Did she not feel as true a flame?—
She keeps before her mind, despite
The spirit-haunted gloom of night,
That hid its waters shadowy-bright—
Its daylight image, tempting, dear,
Light blue and beautiful and clear!—
She tries in vain to recognize
The rolling mountain-slope, where lies
The hut that holds her love—her life;
But as with daylight details rife
She bids the cherished picture rise,
She feels the spell of kindly eyes;
One kindly voice inviting cries;
One living presence sweeps from view
The distance and the darkness too;

Before its thrilling influence driven,
All scruples to the winds are given!
What to her is far or near?
What has SHE to do with fear!—
Her light dress lightly flung aside—
See! she has dashed into the waters wide!

Delicious to her throbbing heart—
Delicious to her fevered brain
Was that cool loving water! Eagerly
She dipped her head, again—again—
As if it could appease the inward smart,
Could charm away the choking pain.
Then fully conscious first she seemed to be
How she had launched upon her lonely way;
As from a dream first perfectly awoke
To all the dangers of her bold essay.
So singling out and noting well
A star, that near the mountain's verge
Obscure and vague, hung just above
The spot, as even in darkness she could tell
Whence she had seen his boat emerge
So oft, as on her hill-top she would bask
On that forlorn look-out of Love,—
She fixed upon its twinkling spark
Her course to guide, her goal to mark;
Then with a calmer pulse and steadier stroke,
Gave herself up to her adventurous task.

CANTO THE TENTH.

I.

Swim, Amohia, swim!—with strong swift grace she swims;
Lightly in silence cleaves the pathway smooth.
The water's gurgle from her waving limbs,
Only its ripple from her flexile limbs—
  Seems less to break than gently soothe
The hush of solemn Silence as she swiftly swims.

And now the cooling lymph more calmly breasting,
    She comes upon some wild-fowl resting:
  And as soft plashing she intrudes
  Into their glassy open home so wide,
    And feels the solemn still impress
    Of sweetly-sheltering loneliness—
      "Safe in their gleaming solitudes"
  She sighs, "each bird with what it loves allied!
      How well doth for his trusting broods
      The Spirit of the Lake provide!"
      With startled glance their heads they raise,
      One movement quick from side to side,
      Then far into the dimness sail
      With shrill wild cry and dripping trail.

As each into the still air dashes,
Its level-flapping wing-tips make
Upon the else unruffled Lake
A double row of silver splashes
Spurting a moment in its wake.
She smiles: "Ah, had I wings like you,
Could be so soon love-nestled too!
Dread Spirit! help me too as well,
Whom no irreverent thoughts compel
Unwillingly to break the spell
Of Silence lone wherein you dwell!"

II.

Lightly along her liquid path she presses;
Nor yet the toil her buoyant frame distresses.
Anon, as patiently she sped,
There came as of itself into her head
An old and simple lay,
She oft had sung in many a happier day,
About a maid her home for love forsaking;
And the recurring rhythm making
The effort of volition less,
And so preventing weariness,—
Though scarce a meaning to its phrases linking—
She kept into her spirit drinking
The metre's chime—a kind of rest from thinking;
And steadily aside the crystal waters flinging,
Kept murmuring the old rhyme in time—she had no breath for singing:—

I.

"The freshet is flowing,
But growing quite clear;

The full river flashes
And gurgles and dashes
With tinklings and plashes
How pleasant to hear!
The tiny bright billows
That lately were whirling
So turbid and dun,
Are playfully curling,
And merrily glance as they dance in the Sun!—
To the current confiding
My little canoe,
See! joyously gliding
My course I pursue.
Look! carelessly twirling
The paddle I sit,
The river deciding
Which way we shall flit:
I sit all alone,
No fear have I, none!
For I know to what quarter its waters will run!

2.

And see how, while speeding,
A Maiden unheeding,
Wherever those curling
Crisp billows are leading—
Never raising a mast or
The light sail unfurling,
But leaving my boat free to float as it will;
The rich breeze comes after
To drive her the faster—
The faster to waft her

To where out of sight
Stands a cottage so bright;
(Ah well do I know it,
Rush-wall and red rafter
And carvings so gay!)
Which oft far away
I have watched half the day,
When the sunbeam would show it
One spot of red light
Beneath the deep-glooming, far-looming blue hill.

3.

No obstacles stay me,
No dangers delay me!
The streams,—where the river
In summer dividing
In silvery threads,
Slips hurriedly gliding
O'er glittering beds
Of shingle,—all mingled, you nowhere can see!
All the rapids wherever
The water ran creaming,
And—flashing and gleaming
From humps and from shoulders
Of obstinate boulders,—
Snow-tassels offstreaming
Would flutter and quiver—
They have vanished—replenished to let me go free!
And the broad yellow spaces
Where lost were all traces
Of the creaming, the flashing,
The streaming, the dashing,
The stir and the strife;

Where you heard not a murmur,
No chatter or churme or
Low musical plaint ;
Where the gravel-beds wholly
Concealing it, slowly
The river went oozing
Beneath, and gave life
To a few dainty bosses
Of pallid gray mosses,
Such fragrance diffusing
Delicious and faint—
They are gone—they have vanished—all banished for me !

4.

The ranks of green rushes
With their brown knobs of down,
Where the stream's overflow
Creeps dimpling and slow—
How gentle their stirring
As softly conferring
They murmur so low !
In a moment 'tis done ;
They are still every one !
As they stand in a row
And watch me, I know
Why it is they are so—
I know each green lisper
Fears even a whisper
May show where I go, who the rover must be !
And the louder flax-bushes
With their crowding and crossing
Black stems, darkly studded
With blossoms red-blooded—

Their long blades are tossing
As the breeze comes up quicker
(So wantonly spilling
The honeysweet liquor
Their ruddy-cups filling) :
Hark ! pattering, playing,
They rustle in glee ;
And I fancy them saying :
 'O fondly, O fleetly
She flies—never heed her,
For Love is her leader ;
And fairly and featly
He steers, who but he !
Then mind her not—hinder not—let her go free !'—
And brighter and higher,
Like flames of pale fire,
The great plumes far and wide
Of the sword-grass aspire ;
In their grace and their pride
They are all on my side !
See ! feather to feather
How bending together
They seem to try whether
My flight they may hide ;
'We know where she hies to—
We know what she flies to—
Droop thickly—wave quickly—that no one may see !'

5.

Then, Father, why chide her,
Your darling, your pride, or
Lament at her going
Whatever betide her !

For though your eyes glisten,
O how can she listen—
To such a fond lover the rover has flown!
Unavailing the wailing,
And idle to chide her,
When breezes freshblowing,
When waters quickflowing,
All fair things upgrowing
And waving beside her,
Will but guide and confide her to *one* heart alone!"

Thus, not without a sense forlorn and dreary
How doubtful her own flight and fate
Beside that maiden's, speeding to her mate
With answered love and confidence elate,
Poor Amohia swims till she is weary.

III.

A welcome rest! Above the surface, see,
Projects the stump of a long-sunken tree:
Last remnant of a forest-giant
That once with outflung arms defiant,
With all his green fraternity
Stood shouldering out the dappled sky
On this same spot, and shed around
Noon-twilights, where in leafy shade
The golden tremors sparely played;
Or in the echoing hush profound
At intervals the soft quick beats
Of the wild-pigeon's winnowing wing,
Subsiding whisper-like, betrayed
Where high up in his green retreats,

He flitted leisurely at feed.—
The mighty forest like a weed
Has withered—vanished like a dream!
The sky is bare, and everywhere
Above you spreads the empty air,
Around the lonely waters gleam:
Where insects burrowed, hummed and swarmed
The wildfowl dips; and, unalarmed,
In silvery shoals the minnows stream,
Their thousands moving with one will;
Or, lying motionless and still
On tiny fins self-balancing,
Like spreading arrows shoot away
If any swimming Maiden may
Perchance their crystal-folded slumbers fray.
Such wondrous change can compassed be
By Ru, the Earthquake-God's decree,
Who lifts and lowers the groaning land
As in the hollow of his hand.

To this old timeworn stump unsought
Her slightly devious course had brought
The unconscious Maid, direct and true,
So that perforce it was descried.
She found a footing on its side,
And as a long deep breath she drew,
And firm her panting bosom prest
The filmy weeds that o'er it grew
Light green, and dangling rose and fell,
Listless in the lapping swell
Her swimming left—her arms she threw
Around it, grateful for the timely rest.
Spontaneous gratefulness—to whom and why?

Wondrous, with no one to be grateful to,
That thus the natural heart should ever fly,
Thus gravitate, as 'twere, if left alone,
To something all unseen, unknown :
That its perennial lights, intense or dwindling,
To bold clear Love and Adoration kindling,
Or dimly down to Fetish fear declining,
Keep pointing to a polestar—nowhere shining !
You pity her—untaught and rude
To know how blind such gratitude ;
Who threw away vain thanks because
Her own proceedings and intent
Just then fell out coincident
With the fixed working of cast-iron laws ;
And so o'erlooked in ignorance
That principle, to minds profound
So much more rational and sound,
Her real benefactor—Chance !

IV.

But right the sentiment or wrong,
It was not one to hold her long.
To her deserted Father flew
Her thoughts—his anguish when her clothes they found :
What if his Child, his grey hair's pride were drowned !
Her loss how would he brood upon and rue ;
With dim eyes, in the sleepy old canoe,
With pole and hoopnet as he used to do,
Fishing perhaps the long day through—
Unconscious half, in his distress
And heedless of his ill-success.
To think of his despair her bosom bled—
Yet how could they upbraid her that she fled ?

Could they, if all were known, bid her contend
Against a fate she could not help nor mend?
Was *Love* to be resisted? Could they blame her
If that insidious Power o'ercame her?
Because they could not see nor feel
The spell whose tyrannous control
Absorbed, entranced her mind—her soul,
Should they expect she could reject
Its might, her heart against it steel?
As well—(for as her feelings rose,
The oriental fancy, bred
And born with her, and through all joys and woes
With metaphor and song for ever fed,
At once in some remembered chaunt
Springing so ready to her want,
Again to Natures' ways and shows
For vindication and example sped)
As well upbraid the feathery clouds of Morning,
Because the unrisen Sun is out of sight,
For not in cold impassive pallor scorning
The first faint touches of his cheering light;
As well expect their snowy fleeces,
As upward from his seahid cave he rushes,
Not to be heart-struck into burning blushes;
Or as he nigher comes and nigher
And the soft-flowing splendour still increases,
Though all his disc be hidden yet,
As well expect the basking brood
No further to drink-in the blissful flood,
But fling it eddying back, nor let
The rosy blushes rapture-kindle into golden fire.
"Ah no!" she thought, while her full bosom heaves
A sigh—"with me no more than these—Ah no,

It cannot be—it never can be so!
Him I was born, compelled to love—I know;
Him I *shall* love—him ever—till the day
When with thick coronals of freshest leaves
The maids and matrons to my funeral go!"—
In fresh resolve the passing pang she smothers,
And dashes, as it starts, the tear away:
Then with a half impatience and mute pain
She turns into the yielding Lake again—
Again the Lake's mild breast receives her like a Mother's.

CANTO THE ELEVENTH.

I.

Swim, Amohia, swim!—with patient toil she swims,
In solemn silence, night, and loneliness.
Steady the star-reflexions, every flake
Like dropping arrows, golden, motionless,
Hang on the shadowy polish of the Lake;
Only the waving of her lithe young limbs
Sets them a little trembling, or bedims
And quenches them, as through their glittering trails she swims.

Once more the Maiden's vigour flags;
Wearily now her languid frame she drags;
So on her back to rest her arms she turns,
And with her feet alone the water slowly spurns.

But when at once right o'er her swung
The whole enormous lighted dome of Heaven,
What feelings in her bosom sprung?—

II.

Not fraught indeed for her the glorious vision
With all the myriad miracles 'tis given
Our tutored sight to marvel at therein—
Thickstarred Immensities—to which all fields Elysian,
Softswarded glooms of Paradise
Fire-streaked with glancing lovelit eyes—
Or that pure Empyrean where the bards divine—
Of Albion or the Florentine,
In world-entrancing everliving dreams,
Saw jacinth-downs and topaz-spurting streams
And uplands opaline ;
Champaigns of sheeted pearl with rosy-green
Reflections shot, and mildest rainbow-sheen,
Where snowdrifts of blest Angels spread and swarm
And scatter, on the rolling grand Hosanna-storm
Uplifted—floated—borne away !
Or rounded to a snowy world-wide rose
With golden heart where God's own brilliance glows ;—
All seem but tinselled stagework—transient—mean—
Poor craft of some mere mortal mechanician !
—Nor could her fancy science-guided stray—
From those bold fires that here and there
Like vanward sentinels low hovering hung,
Rejoicing in some kingly trust,—
Through an immeasurable array
Of evervarying mingling lights
Pausing in multitudinous troops
On still retiring higher heights
As on some vast celestial palace-stair ;
Or poured forth infinite in scattering groups
And endlessly-recurring shoal on shoal ;

With luminous depths on all sides leading
To deeper depths that evermore receding
And evermore reopening lose
Themselves in labyrinthine avenues
Of glory unspeakable! a maze
Of vistas intricate that everywhere
Away and upward roll
Into a dimness splendid with a dust
Of Suns—a gleaming haze,
A visible shining cloud,
Of specks invisible—all worlds—and all avowed
Only a handbreadth of the outstanding Whole!
O not for her the eternal flood
Of worlds in bloom and worlds in bud;
The lightning-speeded cataract of Creation
Boundless and bounding on for ever;
Chaotic mass or cosmic—brood on brood
Evolving, intermitting never,
To dash and daze the strongest-winged imagination:—
Full many a sun-thronged Universe that dwindles
To a tiny film of light,
So far off in the Infinite!
Full many a flying Ocean of bright Mist that kindles
At its deep core eddy-curled
And whirls and thickens to a world,
Or at its vasty margin thinning
Drops lagging vapour-belts and luminous rings
That shrink apart, like breaking strings
Of jewels, into moons and satellites,
Fresh-starting on their separate flights,
And on new centres spinning;
—The trailing spawn of Systems vapour-tangled;
And seeded masses of stargrain like roes

Of fishes, so the congregated clusters close—
Aye, golden ovaries of great globes in myriads—all
By distance inconceivable comprest
Into the semblance of a swarming ball
Of pin's-head spiders in their whitewebbed nest :—
—The swallow-swoop of Comets as they flee
In the wild race of revelry ;
Each like some mad enamoured Bayadere
That darts from out the throng to where
Sits in full-diamonded pride
Her mighty Rajah awful eyed,
As if, athirst for his caresses,
To fling herself upon his blazing breast ;
But catching as she comes anear
The kingly-chilling glitter of his glance,
Swerves off abashed in full career
Again into the reeling dance !
So, down upon their Sun-God dashing
With sudden shift these couriers swift
Still scour away into Infinitude—off-flashing
With all their hundred million leagues of luminous tresses
Into the fathomless abysses
To make amid the astonished spheres
Their sportive circuit of a thousand years !
Or say, 'twere but the wake they trace
Lashing to foam-light as they race,
Quiescent force asleep in space—
Still—still they spurn all resting-place !—
—Then all the sensitive Planets as they float,
In their enormous solitudes
Troubled mysteriously—the changeful moods
Reflecting of their kindred most remote ;
So delicately alive to and returning

Each faint and far off sister's finest yearning;
In their elastic orbits wheeling
Eternal rounds of sympathetic feeling.—

Not these—not all the vast sublimities that lurk
Within the visible sphere—the o'erpowering whole
Disclosed by the optic tube that dares to thrust
The flaming portals wide asunder
And shew the great Creator at his secret work
So silent—boundless—beautiful, it strikes the Soul
Into hushed tears of awe and ecstasy and wonder!
Yet fires it with impatient thirst to be
Knit somehow nearer,
In vision clearer,
Communion dearer
With the impenetrable mute Mystery
That flings such glories freely all around us
Not for the sake of such a mite as Man;
Yet as he made them ours,—
Gave us such powers
So wide a portion of his works to scan
And apprehend—not comprehend—a plan—
Ah! not at least to baffle and confound us!—
For shut out from the eyes of wiser Sense
That palpable Omnipotence,
And in the flashing face of it descend
To doughtiness of reasoning—where will end
Your task—to what conviction tend?
Will not the oneness of the Law all through
And fitness of our intellect thereto
Pronounce in spite of metaphysic brawl
One Will—one conscious Mind—the cause of all?
Or call it Force, self-causing—if you will—

'Tis Force that infinitely varying, still
Through myriad myriad evolutions ranges;
Into a million simultaneous streams divides;
At once through all without confusion glides;
And keeps their mystic momentary changes
Springing in mutual fitness forth—agreeing
As each the fresh results of all foreseeing:—
What powers has Mind such Force does not possess—
What knowledge proper to self-consciousness?—
But not for slow deductions—wrong or right—
Those marvels gleam transcendant—but to flood
The Soul with inspiration—but to smite
Into the heart a rapture bright
Of reverence and devotion and delight,
And leave for its ecstatic mood
No outlet, no expression, no relief,
But in *one* grand conviction in whose blaze
Poor Logic withers with her creeping ways,
And stands confest an attribute
Lower and fitter for the brute,
For things that creep and things that plod--
But in one blinding Truth and chief
Of truths—unprovable—above all proof—the *feeling*, GOD!

III.

Well—though there rose not to the Maiden's mind,
Such visions with such thoughts entwined,
She could not fail
Awestruck to mark how vast a bed
Of brilliants was above her spread,
As 'twere the sediment and golden grail
By some great Sea of upper Light deposited:

Nor all the finer showers of gems that far away
Fused into fainter light-wreaths lay
Marbling the mournful depths of solemn blue :
Nor how across it all meandering wide
Went a pale, luminous smoke that swarmed
With sparks, as from the unseen fires it rose
Of some vast spectral beings that performed
Their unimaginable rites outside :
She wondered too
At those mysterious stains of darkest hue,
Unfathomable shafts of blindest vacancy
Like scathing tracks of Demon dread
Before whose flight the myriad brilliances
Shrank blighted—marred—as shrink and close
Rock-purpling tribes of sea-anemones
Beneath the careless tread
Of one who by the side of Ocean goes.

But shunning all that glorious Company
There, furtively and swift, a Meteorite, see!
Slides into light a moment, and is gone!
Of all unnoted, noting none ;
In stealthy chase (she thought) or bent
On secret mission—but apart, alone—
And utterly absorbed in his unknown intent.

All was so solemn, vast, etherial, strange—
Complete within its wondrous self—removed
So far from our dark world of chance and change,
From all she hoped, or feared, or loved,
The longer on the scene she dwelt,
More helpless still the maiden felt,
More feeble, specklike, in the gleaming dumb Immensity.

What, though she had been taught to trace
Amid the million throbbing hearts of fire,
Ancestral spirits of her race
Whose fame had won them that high place,—
Those steady stars, unwinking, bold,
That well might souls of heroes be,
From *them*, so proud, and calm, and cold
How could she look for sympathy?
But where were they, so gentle, clear,
Sweet innocent spirits in timid lustres shrined,
Whom oft at twilight she would mark
Come trembling through the melting dark,
As then, then only confident enough
(Like fawns upon the point to turn and fly)
With fluttering heart to hesitate so nigh?—
They must be, sure, of tenderer stuff,—
Have souls that pity could inspire!
Ah, idle seemed the fond desire
Amid the thronging hosts to find
One kindred heart from whom a Maid
Might look for love or hope for any aid!
For if her glance for many moments rested
On any single group of all that sprinkled
The skies, the fancy then her brain infested,
They were tall radiant Figures downward peering
From shining strongholds, high and free
And safe above her, while behind them leering
Still more and more kept crowding in to see,
With eyes that with malicious pleasure twinkled
At her poor puny efforts. And her guide,
Her pilot star could be no more descried;
So by the glorious vision more deprest

Than strengthened by the partial rest,
She turns again,
And plies her weary shoulders with increasing pain.

Poor outworn Amohia!—world-abandoned Maid,
Thy brave strong heart is now thine only aid!

"Ah! if at last I sink—"
It blanched her cheek to think
The thought—her heart a moment ceased to beat—
"Oh might I then on that dear shore be thrown
And by Ranoro found alone!
And if he loved me with a love like mine
Ah, would not even then my bosom own
Some feeble flutter of a joy divine
When frantic he would clasp, the cold, cold form
With vain caresses warm—
No love returned, no answering heat;
Then curse the intolerable light—nor stay—
But dashing out his life in some quick way
While the loathed Universe whirled off his brain,
With fainting fervour strain
Our dead and dying hearts together—never to part again!

* * * * *

But if, as once I think you said,—
Laughing at what I told you of the gloom
And sordid horror of our Reinga dread—
The white man hopes a better doom
For spirits of the dead,
Oh would not mine low hovering for a while,
Linger for yours, Ranoro! Then, O bliss! to speed
Together to that happier land—

For they would rush together freed,
And wondering with a pensive happy smile
At all the maddening care and heed
That vexed the senseless forms entwined upon the strand.

* * * * *

Nay, live, Ranoro! live—and sometimes give
A thought to your poor—lost—" The bitter tear
Was checked before it reached her eyes;
And that throat-agony forbid to rise:
With resolute will
She bids the unnerving visions disappear;
And the brave Maiden tries
To rally her spent force with thoughts of meeting,
With the deep rapture of Ranoro's greeting.
Alas, though feebly struggling still
With patient anguish on her brow,
Poor gallant Amohia is exhausted now.

IV.

But see! upon the hillside glows,
Unmoving, bright, a sudden light!
Oh joyous sight, 'tis *his*, she knows!
New hope, new life, new strength she gains;
It feeds her brain with will—with warmth her veins:
And now she is aware how on the right
A mountain spur, as if in friendly guise
Has stolen forward to surprise
And catch—say rather, to embrace her!
How high the hills that darkly face her
Have grown! the darkly-branching trees
Are mingling with the stars, she sees:

A kind of gentle stir is in the air—
Faint sounds of life, though life at rest, are there.
Two loud harsh notes assail her ear—
The night-hawk's! harsh but yet so *near!*
She blest them! to her present plight
Seemed never song-bird's notes so dear,
So sweet, as that melodious screech
Startling the darkness with delight.
With desperate strokes she presses forward fast—
She feels that they must be her last.
With downthrust foot she strives to reach—
O joy! O bliss—she feels for and has found,
Can touch that deep salvation—the firm ground!
One stroke—one other yet—a moment more
She staggers, falls—upon the pumice-whitened shore.

V.

Cold, shivering, stiff in every limb:
With pulse scarce beating, eyes that droop and swim;
With deep-drawn pants and gasping sighs
Long prostrate on the ground she lies;
But gleaming in the Moon's new-risen beam
She sees not far a little puff of steam;
She struggles towards it slowly—half-alive—
That lucky spring will soon her languid frame revive!

It was a sparry basin, smoothly tipped and fringed
With snowy stalactite, just tinged
With a faint delicate flush
Like that white rose, the maiden-blush.
The water seemed a liquid piece of heaven—so blue—
Of midmost heaven a lonely piece
Laid bare by a slight breach in the summer-fleece;

And look what sparkling crowds of bubbles through
Diaphonous azure, fast and ever
Escaping in the fountain's fever
Are trembling up with timorous haste to greet
And deck with diamond grail the beauteous guest,
As down she sinks into her lucid seat
And in transparent sapphire makes her warm and liquid nest.

CANTO THE TWELFTH.

I.

THAT evening, with a feeling half forlorn,
With him unusual, Ranolf musing sate,
And listened listless to his followers' chat.
It was the hour for sleep ; but though outworn
With hunting, now with reckless zest pursued
In his unsatisfied and restless mood,
Little for slumber felt the youth disposed.
Outside their hut beneath the stars reclined,
Or pacing to and fro, he let the Night—
Its soft black-brooding Spirit-wings outspread,
Its myriad-winking eyes of mystic light
Exulting in their secret undisclosed—
Sink down into and soothe his working mind :
" It was so still and breathless," as he said,
" You almost heard the stars throb." One by one
His comrades to their mats retired to rest ;
Till Tareha was with Ranolf left alone,
Who at a legend all his tribe outshone :—
Of many, this was one he told his guest :

I.

MUTARA'S fame filled all the land ; what foeman but would fear
The crashing of his battle-brand—the whirlwind of his spear !

One dread opprest his haughty breast, lest he should die at last,
And leave a name some Warrior's fame among the dead surpassed.

2.

Far as the Reinga's* self erelong—down to those very dead,
Like flames in fern when winds are strong, his widening glory spread;
His sire Patito's heart grew dark; beneath his gloomy frown
His eyes' grim ire flashed lurid fire, to hear of such renown.

3.

One eve Mutara chafing strode along the Ocean shore,
While flew the Tempest all abroad—for Peace his heart-strings tore:
Blood-tinged with Sunset struggling through black Storm-clouds branching free,
Came roaring in with splashing din, the boiling hissing Sea!

4.

Wind-swept, a waft of sea-birds white went scattering up the sky,
As storm-opprest to rocky rest they staggering strove to fly;
For scouring wide, the hollow winds rushed frantic in despair,
And spray-wreaths grand and wreaths of sand tossed their wild arms in air.

5.

With firmer foot and dinted heel Mutara onward went,
And clenched his teeth with rage to feel so baffled and besprent.

* Reinga—place of departed Spirits.

"Oh, could you take," he muttered deep, "*here*, *now*, a human form,
Soon would we see who'd Master be, O blustering, bullying Storm!"

6.

Scarce was the reckless challenge given, before with tenfold wrath
The furious frenzied gusts were driven across his difficult path:
As round him thick fly sands and spray, a Figure looming large
Seems in the drift approaching swift the Challenger to charge.

7.

Two lightning gleams shoot through the gloom—O horror! he descries
Fierce-flashing through the whirling clouds, his Father's spectral eyes!
The frantic winds with hollow scream seem sounding in his ear,
"There, boaster, there! see if you dare abide your Father's spear!"

8.

Aghast, amazed—yet still he raised his lance and forward leapt;
But o'er him black the maddening rack of the whole Tempest swept;
And down the eddying wind hoarse shrieks of laughter rolled in scorn,
As he was left of sense bereft, stretched on the sands forlorn.

9.

They found--revived him—sung his praise—the One who with the Dead
Alone had dared to fight unscared ; and all our Elders said
That had Mutara won the day on that tempestuous shore,
The Reinga's power and Death's dark hour had conquer'd Man no more.—

"Death conquer Man no more !—but how succeed
In conquering *him !*" said Ranolf ; "Strike *him* low
But once, that were the feat of feats indeed !
But had you never hero could o'erthrow
That bugbear—beat that universal Foe ?"

"Well, *Maui** tried it, long enough ago :—

11.

"You have heard, have you not ? of great MAUI ? how he
Lay at first on the flat rocky reefs of the sea,
In that land of our fathers, Hawaiki the blest—
'Mid the vast ropes of weed that in endless unrest
Crawl, welter and toss on that surf-snowy plain
Serpentining in long undulations of pain,
And glistening black, as they writhe in the tide ;
Or if haply their monstrous contortions subside,
Still uneasily stir in their comfortless bed ;—
They are tresses, they say, that Taranga outspread
Round the Infant she left on the sea-shore and fled :—
But those tangles, they dandled in sunshine and storm,
And nurtured and kneaded the Babe into form.
Then scathless to keep him from sea-bird and worm,

* Pronounced "*Mowee.*"

The jelly-fish wrapt him all fresh from the brine
In their discs of soft crystal, that streaked with such fine
Radiations of scarlet transparently shine.
So he grew up a Giant; and gave his great days
To glorious deeds and the winning of praise.
The red seeds of Fire he was first to discover;
And dared in his longing for light to lean over
The mountainous walls of the uttermost West,
The Sun in his headlong career to arrest:
There in spite of his fast-flashing struggles, he noosed
The far-darting limbs of that Lustre; reduced
The perilous speed of his ruinous race
To a steady, majestic and orderly pace;
And compelled him in warmth and mild splendor to steep
The Isles Maui's hook had first fished from the Deep.
But how small was the worth of his glory and power,
While the monster, black Death, could all Being devour;
And Man who elsewhere could such victories gain,
Of his villanous maw must the victim remain!—
No, if *He* were unconquered, all conquests were vain.

Now Maui had seen how the Sun every night
Sunk wearied and worn from his sky-cresting height;
While a legion of Clouds oft exultingly stood,
Like a crowd of base foemen all stained with his blood,
O'er the dying great Chief as he sunk in the flood:
Yet the Hero next morning, revived and renewed,
Rose in glory again and his journey pursued.
It was down, then, beneath the deep Sea and this Earth
He was steeped in fresh vigor, endowed with new birth.—
Might not Maui descend to this Life-spring and bathe
In its waters, and shake off the scorn and the scathe
Of this tyrant, this Death, and delighted reswathe

His limbs in the glory and gladness of youth
In those mystical depths?—He would try it, in sooth!—
But, to find where those springs of vitality flow
In what ultimate gulfs and abysses below!
Could it be where the Mountains' foundations are laid
In the realm of red Ru, or the Reinga's deep shade?——"

"The realm of Ru—the Earthquake God!
More awful realm, i'faith, than e'er was trod
By jinn or gnome must Ru's have been!"
Cried Ranolf—"fancy what a scene!—
What bellowing Caverns measureless and dread—
With rents in thunder running overhead;
Far seen through low-browed arches glimmering red.
A Sea perpetual agitation frets and churns
To foam, that luridly illumined burns!
Then wide and wider yawn the branching rents
That through the black impending granite spread;
And lo! the vast Abyss hurled upward vents
A maddening Chaos of all elements—
An infinite ruin of red fire
And flying rocks fire-molten—tumult dire
Of roaring steam and sulphurous blasts and lava seas
And forests of upshooting flame and tower-trunked trees
Of pitchy cloud and sky-hung cinderous canopies—
All the fire-entrails of that cavernous pit
Whirled upwards through one vast volcano-rift!—
'Tis Ru! 'tis Ru! with red wild eyes,
And blazing far-coruscant hair,
And frowns that blacken half their glare,
Outrushing from his burning lair
Into a realm for his disporting fit!—

For see! whene'er the hurricane drift
Of heaven-outblotting ashes swift
Breaks off, the ensanguined dome of cloud
Seems shattered, frittered to a crowd
Of fragments small of uniform shape and size,
As by some shock that ran at once through all
The shivering Earth and shuddering skies!
See! far and near—see! great and small
His band awakening at his call!
How their volcano-fires appal!
Here, white, intense and awful and half-hid
By upheaved strata, lifted like the lid
Of some enormous, black half-opened tomb
Within whose jaws condensed it glows self-fanned:—
There, shot up silent—sudden—athwart the gloom,
Pillars of ruddy light unmoving stand!
And many a sheaf of vivid flame up-showers,
Crested with scarlet flowers
Of red-hot scoria:—level stripes of gold
Afar in lakes the Lava sleeps,
Or like a swarm of deadly serpents creeps,
Or down the shaking mountain-steeps
Dashes in crimson cataracts uncontrolled:
And peaks and pinnacles and ridges bold
In fluctuation terrible are rolled,
And rise and sink like sea-waves; underground
A deadened roar goes on for ever with a sound
As if a hundred Giants waking would have risen,
But bumped and thumped their heads against the roof
Of their too-cramping subterranean prison!
A world's artillery crashes near—aloof
Reverberating thunders rumble round
The mountain-filled horizon—But I stay

Your story—let us hear how Maui found
Down to those life-springs his adventurous way!"

"Well, Maui resolved to descend to the womb
Of original Night—to the kingdom of gloom;
For 'twas there that this water, these life-springs must flow
And its mouth is beneath the dark tide, as you know,
In the uttermost North, at the end of the land,
Where a rocky long causeway of pinnacles grand
Breaks off mid the waves' ever-restless commotion
Far away in the lonely and limitless Ocean.
So direct to the mouth of that darksome abode
O'er the mountains from summit to summit he strode;
And his legs as he stalked on his wonderful way,
Caught sight of beneath the broad cloud-skirts of gray,
Might have seemed the dim rays, wide aslant, which the Sun
Flings beneath him sometimes ere his bright course be run;
And his Form when full seen, swept toweringly by,
Reared aloft like the waterspout whirling on high
In a dark-waving column from Ocean to Sky.
So he strode through the clouds to the terrible pass.
Then, although his vast might had availed, in a mass
To uplift from the Sea the whole rocky-backed Cape—
As blue in bright distance, long headlands will gape
On a sleek summer morning, warped up from the main,
Like the snout of some monster, just raised from the plain
As he listlessly crawls in slow length from his lair,
And pauses a moment to sniff the cool air—
Yet determined its natural terrors to dare,
Or fearing the road so subverted to miss,
Head foremost he plunged down the pitchblack abyss.
But when great Mother NIGHT, *Hinë-Nui-te-Po*,
Perceived her inviolate regions below

So profaned, a deep shudder of horror and dread,
Through the cavernous realms of the shadowy Dead,
Round their sombre and silent circumference ran;
That was just as bold Maui his passage began:—
But when still he persists in his daring endeavour
The shudders, the horrors grow wilder than ever!
A more terrible spasm, a desperate shock
Contracts and convulses those portals of rock;
And ere his great head and vast shoulders get through
They cut the gigantic Intruder in two!—
So ended great Maui—so vanished his dream,
And in spite of him Death was left tyrant supreme!"

"Well, these are genuine Myths at last,"
Thought Ranolf, "samples from the Past
Of modes men caught at to record
Notions for which they had no word;
So clothed, unable to *abstract*,
Emotions deep in fancied fact;
To else unutterable thought
Imaginative utterance brought:
So these expressed, to souls untaught
Thought from some Mind that thought, to part,
And feeling from some feeling Heart—
How futile every effort still
To fathom Death's mysterious ill;
How of all phantoms of Despair
Frowns one, no noble heart can bear,
A ghastly horror, nothing less,
Beyond relief, without redress,
The Nightmare of pure Nothingness:
How hateful, spite of all endeavour,
How utterly repugnant ever,

No tongue can tell to what degree,
It is to Being not to Be.
Aye! none the less for that mad scheme,
The Buddhists' nihilistic dream,
Spurned by the masses wholly—since
Ev'n he—its half-crazed Founder-Prince,
(If e'er the tenet was his own,
Not Kásyapa, his friend's alone)
Was forced in self-despite to teach,
A million ages' high persistence
In virtue must elapse, ere each
Or any could attain, evince
Capacity for non-existence—
Mere power of soul-extinction reach.
These wiser Savages at least were true
To one grand Instinct—somehow felt and knew
Nothing but conscious individual life—
No 'mingling with the visible Universe'
Or 'painless sleep for ever'—worse than pain—
Will satisfy the everlasting strife
That must be waged without it; what a curse,
A mockery this Existence (if no worse)
Did future Nothingness for Man remain;
The highest feelings, then, he can attain,
The best delights, but traps and lures would be
To cheat him into madder misery."

III.

The night wore on—his friends were gone;
Still Ranolf paced and mused alone.
It chanced, a little lad who slept
In his men's hut that evening—come
For change' sake from his neighbouring home—

Felt thirsty; from his mattings crept,
The yellow calabash to find,
Which, hollowed out, a hardened rind,
Was mostly full of water kept.
'Twas empty: looking out, "'Tis light
(He thought) almost as day:"—so quite
Forgot his native fear of Night,
And to the spring beneath the hill
Set off his calabash to fill.

The spring was close beside the path
To that quick-bubbling crystal bath
Where Amohia rested; she
Could in the moonlit distance see
The cot and its karaka-tree,
And Ranolf now emerge, so clear,
Now in its shadow disappear.
And she had marked the little lad
Set off *her* way with heart how glad;
And when he neared her bright retreat,
That heart with high expectance beat.
Hard-by there grew in snowy bloom
Thickets of aromatic broom;
Within whose green impervious screen,
Stand but a yard, she ne'er were seen.
Into the copse she quickly slipped,
Three steps from where the fountain dripped.
There, breathless, stirless, on the watch,
She formed her little scheme—until
The thirsty lad had drunk his fill,
And held his calabash to catch
The water of the trickling spring.
Then in a warbling voice, low sweet and wild,

That intertwined with its harmonious plash,
The hidden Girl began to sing
A ditty to the startled Child
About "a fountain" and "a calabash:"

1.

"Golden water! golden water!
Flowing freely, flowing ever,
Flowing since the World began;
What shall we pour it in—
Heedfully store it in?—
If your calabash be not quite clean—if any foulness begrime or besmutch it,
O you never will catch the clear rillet—it will shrink away as you touch it!

2.

"Golden water! golden water!
Flowing coyly, dried up never
Since Tumátau moulded Man;
Flowing so tamelessly,
Seeming so aimlessly!—
Would you catch it with hands unsteady, or a heart with passion fretted?
Would you guide it in spouts of flax-leaf as you please?—Oh, you'll only get wetted!"—

The Child, at first too terrified
Even to run away, stood there
Holding the calabash in air,
With cheeks all blanched—mouth gaping wide,
And eyes outstarting; reassured

A little now, he seemed to gain
Some heart to list the simple strain;
But 'twas the voice that most allured,
And most his confidence secured.
Had not the Maid been ever known
And loved for that melodious tone?
And was it not at birth instilled,
That voice like Music? when they killed
In numbers at her name-day feast
The *Korimáko*, sweetest bird
Of all that are in forest heard?
That so, with prayers of chanting priest,
The spirit of their sweetness might
Upon the happy Child alight,
And her maturing accents be
Unmatched for kindred melody?—
So doubtful if to run or stay,
He stood—while she resumed her lay:

3.

"Crystal water! crystal water!
Glistening out, then disappearing;
Blinding those who wink and blink:
How to get near it, then?—
Forward, ne'er fear it, then!
Sharp eye and free step—no crawling or creeping sideways like a shellfish—
All else like an innocent Child—confiding—straightforward—unselfish!

4.

"Crystal water! crystal water!
Chilling often, often cheering,

Numbing those who cease to drink:
How can we use it well?—
Drink and diffuse it well!
If in finely-carved cisterns you try to enclose it securely—
Tiny monsters will breed there and wriggle—it will stagnate impurely.

5.

"Diamond water! diamond water!
Warbling to all tribes and ages,
Welling near us yet apart:
Who is it guards it so?
Watches and wards it so?—
If you fear any Spirit too much, you'll ne'er see it though flowing close by you—
But revere you no Spirit at all?—what you drink will but petrify you.

6.

"Diamond water! diamond water!
With still, lucent eye of Sages,
But with Childhood's open heart;
So may you light on it,
Thrive and grow bright on it!"—
Here Amohia from the thicket springing
Whisked from his hand the flask it clung to, singing:
"Though your calabash be battered, bruised—yet fear not you to fill it—
For the better 'twill hold, the fresher keep, this flitting, magical, rillet."

—This was a song, in fact, by Ranolf made,
And turned to Maori to assay

His skill, and see how far would reach
Or be constrained, the native speech;
When sport was slack one summer day,
As ambushed in tall reeds he lay,
Just in the wary wild duck's way—
While thinking by what wonder it befel,
And with what natural supernatural aid—
The mighty Stream—the fluent race of Man,
Since first its mystic course began,
Even while in foam and turbulence it ran
Adown those ancient faintly-glimmering slopes
The shadowy-lit Himálayas of old Time,
Had still been fed from age to age
With springs of Spiritual Truth sublime;
Rillets and runnels of immortal Hopes:
Some crystal Soul of saint or sage
For the great River timeously supplied;
Slipping, as 'twere, from any side,
Into its clouded and tumultuous tide:—
And how above, around us, and below
Those myriad-branching rivulets may flow
Capriciously, it seems, yet ever feeding
The heart of Man when most 'tis needing:—
Then all the evil that proceeds
From dams and dykes of narrow Creeds;—
Last how to enter that coy shadowy ground,
And the pure runnel's bright arrival wait;
Or in what spirit penetrate
Up to the airhung crevices of snow,
Or thicket-stifled gorges, dense, profound,
Where those divinest Wellsprings may abound.—

Well, but this Song, a glimpse, a hint,
An impress from Reflection's mint
Struck faintly of a theme so vast—
Of a wide bee-eyed truth one tiny facet
With nothing but simplicity to grace it—
The fancy of the native girls had caught
(Who only of its literal meaning thought)
And Amohia's self had reached at last.

IV.

But that slight gesture of the Maid
Which tossed the calabash away,
Renewed the fears her song allayed ;
No gift had bribed the Child to stay.
To Ranolf's side he scampered back
Aghast, agape with fright—Alack !
There was a Spirit at the well,
A *Pátu-páere ! he* could tell—
That voice so sweet—that form so fair,
Those eyes, with such a dancing glare !—
Rebuked, cross-questioned, coaxed or jeered,
Still to his tale the lad adhered.
So Ranolf, as he could not sleep,
And must perforce a vigil keep,
Strolled to the Spring himself to see
What might this wondrous Spirit be.

CANTO THE THIRTEENTH.

I.

"SPIRITS—still Spirits!—strange that every race
Of Man," thought Ranolf as he went,
"Still on that fixed idea is bent,
That in some fashion, form or place,
Spirit without Matter can and does exist:
Yet to its source whene'er we trace
Some record of its presence, sent
Without a bodily environment,
The 'proof' (so-called) is always missed.
What then?—Is Matter's self much better off?
Prove *its* appearance unallied
With Spirit, if you can. Sure, Reason's pride
Should spurn the refuge of a scoff,
When Matter's very being is denied,
And bring us proof. Probe Matter to the last,
Nothing but active Spirit will be found:
Aye, all we see and hear, the glorious round
Of our sensations has no other *ground;*
Only their *sequence* stands so fixed and fast;
In such unchanged alliance are they passed
Before us by the Master-Showman's hand.—
All Ghosts and Apparitions here we stand!

And for your vulgar 'ghosts,' indeed
'Tis breach of sequence only that we need
Produce—no more; prove shadows may succeed
Each other in a series yet to law
Unknown; find but a single certain flaw
Or falter in the dream-procession grand.
An easy task 'twould seem! And yet 'tis true
'Tis that—that merely—we can never do!

And yet, since Man *will* have his Ghost
Whate'er his race—not as a thing to boast
Or glory in; no fancy bright and wild
Of one by his self-love beguiled,
No whim by fond ambition feigned or fed,
Or vulgar 'medium' by imposture bred;
But as a terror, a revolting dread,
Which his repugnant Will had gladly fled;
What can be thought, when all is said,
But that about this notion there must be
Some still unravelled mystery,
Some germ of purposed certainty."

II.

So Ranolf sauntered down the hill,
And now had reached the trickling rill.
There, all save its low plash was still;
Only a movement caught his eye
Scarce visible, as he drew nigh
The thicket dense that grew thereby;
Only a bough's-top in the brake
Did for a single moment shake.
He pushed straight towards it through the broom;

But finding nothing in the gloom,
Came out upon the open Lake.

Still all was lonely—silent—bright ;
Only himself and living light !—
He followed where the pathway wound
Beneath the cliffs, with many a turn
Round buttressed steep, projecting mound,
And waterscarped low spur tree-crowned,
Or rocky—bare of bush or fern.

One of these last he just had passed :—
Beyond it lay in deepest shade
A dense ravine's mouth, which had made
With clustered shrubs a safe retreat
For foeman of pursuit afraid.
He paused :—could mark no trace of feet,
No sign of life—before—around ;
Saw nothing move—heard not a sound—
But keenly gazed into the gloom profound.

No sound, indeed, no motion. All in tune
With speaking Silence. Even the Moon
Lulled in the lap of Heaven serene
Lay back—albeit with watchful mien.
Transfigured by her flooding rays
To airy cloud, the Mountains blue
Up to their floating goddess threw
A rapt and meditative gaze.

Upon the moonlit fractured rock beside him,
With not a rustle that the ear would strike,
A rapid-wriggling Lizard lightning-like

Leapt into stoniest stillness. In the dark,
Only a steady diamond spark
Told where it watching stood and sidelong eyed him.

"How well," he thought, "these creatures suit,
How well uphold their ill-repute;
By all these natives held in dread,
Because informed by Spirits of the dead."

In the full stream of light,
Close to his cheek, projecting on his right,
His glance was resting on a bright green sprig
Of broom-like myrtle.—As he looked, it grew
To something that was watching too.
A span-long Phasmid then he knew,
Stretching its forelimbs like a branching twig
In air, and motionless as death—
Save that it swayed its frail form to and fro
Gently, as in a soft wind's dying breath,
And then subsided slow
To rigid stillness. There,
Its forelimbs still outstretched in air,
With startling faith in its weird wondrous trick
Of aping lower life, the animated Stick
In watchful mood
Close to his cheek unmoving stood.

Suspense how fixed and strange—
Dumb witchery of magic change!
Swift spritelike life to seeming death—and seeming
Inanimate life to deathlike animation—
The real and seeming seemed to waver, reel, and mingle!
One of those flashes for a moment gleaming,

When o'er the Soul the thought will pass,
'Is it illusion then, this whole Creation,
This outward Universe, a breath on glass?'—
One of those pauses in the rush
Of Life's phantasmagoric dreaming,
When in the hush,
The Spiritual speaks in vivid hints that tingle
Through our material framework, listening vigilant;
And as the deep-sea plummet, Consciousness,
Strikes soundings on the eternal adamant
Beneath the visionary Ocean
Whereon our frail barks ever forward press,
And rock and nod
With such unquiet motion—
Lo! the revealing veil of God
Called Nature—as transpierced by darkling light
Divine—imprisoned splendour—on the fret
To escape for all her cunning might,
Emits keen sparkles in her own despite;
And seems one moment almost to forget
Her tantalizing trust, her mystic high vocation;
Seems for a thrilling moment, just about
To turn transparent wholly, and to let
Her awful Secret out.

The conscious Silence seemed to win
Its way across the fleshly bar,
To some responsive sense akin
His own deep soul within;
As in the shadowy river pool
Below the rapids, still and full,
Two floating globules nearing run
Together into one.

And now a little breath of air,
That had, it seemed, been lurking there,
Itself the moonlit calm enjoying,
Along the white bright-shadowy cliffs behind him,
Stealing, as if glad to find him,
Came creeping through his hair and with its clusters toying;
Then passed—and left the lonely shore,
Hushed and breathless as before.

Again the haunting shy mistrust
Of Nature's simplest doings thrust
Its coy suggestive self between
The sensuous impress on his brain
And the conclusion, else so plain,
Of what it was, might be or mean.
Almost he could have held it true,
That fancy of the land he knew,
The creeping breeze must be a spirit too.
He dallied with the whim awhile—
Then with a musing smile,
His idle quest renounced as vain,
Turned his cottage to regain.

III.

"What *is* there," he thought, "in the scene, in the hour,
The moonlight—the silence—that tempts us to dower
All Nature thus with spiritual power?
Can it be that their magical influence
But awakes in ourselves a keener sense
Of some mysterious manifold chain—
The myriad channels that may knit
Magnetic currents of the brain,

Or subtler filaments more fit,
Along which Thought and Feeling flit,
To those that permeate Air and Earth
And all things that from these have birth?
Linking in one consentient whole
All Nature to each living Soul;
And opening for each Soul again
Subtle ways of intercourse
With every other, near, aloof;
An infinite web of spiritual force,
An universal warp-and-woof
Of Sympathy—though yet but rare
The minds whereby, the moments when,
The mystic threads and what they bear
(Like gossamers fine in autumn air
That softly undulate, float, and run,
Viewless but where they catch the sun)
Are brought within the conscious ken?"

IV.

Slowly, and with looks downbent,
On such wayward thoughts intent,
By the rocky path he went.
Suddenly a hand is thrown
Lightly, softly on his own.
Lightly as rosy apple-bloom
Comes twirling to the orchard-grass,
When April winds that gaily pass
Kiss it away to its sunny doom.
So softly o'er his fingers flew
That timid playful pressure too—
The velvet plumage, all aglow
With jetty black and violet blue,

Of the crimson-billed porphyrio,
That jerking struts among the cool
Thick rushes by their rust-red pool—
Felt never more soft, more downy-smooth.
Quickly turned the startled youth,
And the sight that met his eyes
Brightened them with glad surprise.

There was a deeply-scooped recess
In the rock-side's ruggedness,
Hollow and arching: you discern
Through the moon-illumined gloom,
Mantling it above, below.
Wondrous work of Nature's loom,
Delicate broidry like a bride's—
Traceried wealth of many a fern.
Some are filmy-fine and soaking wet,
By the ever-oozing lymph
Matted to its dripping sides;
Some are thatch-like thick-layered—some plume-like and free;
Some like fingers outspread, that caressing and fond
Would clutch at all comers whoever they be;
Some soft, silver-woven, down-pointing and broad,
Like Seraphims' wings when their eyes they would shade
From the shock of that Robe-Skirt's ineffable load
Of splendour that else the high heavens dismayed!
But finger-like, feather-like, wing-like—each frond
(As by daylight the curious eye might see!)
Bedropt and bestudded and thickly beset
With intricate, daintiest fancy-freaks
Of golden spots and russet streaks.
More gracefully draperied niche never yet

Enshrined the pure graces of goddess or nymph ;
And rarely has Goddess or Wood-nymph been
With statelier graces endued than were seen
In the Maiden who stood in that alcove so green !

CANTO THE FOURTEENTH.

I.

In days when Nature—ere discharmed,
Undeified by Science—swarmed
With bright Divinities akin
To the forces that within
Her outward phases lurked terrific,
Or in genial ferment bland
Slumbered in her blissful breast,
In daimoniac delitescence;
Till with fervour too intense,
They would quicken and condense
And kindle into visible presence
And vitality specific,
Glowing on the too imprest
Keen sense in Shapes, appalling, grand
Grotesque or graceful—Phantoms haunting
And to human beauty moulding,
For quick-fancied Faith's beholding,
(Till all Earth was holy ground)
All the still-eyed Soul that broods
In wide wind-whispering solitudes—
Each cloudchase chequering hill and plain—
Moon-shadows—sunny silences—

Lone mists on fire in glens profound—
Old half-lit trunks of twisted trees—
And stealthy gleams in gloomy woods;—
In those old days what dearer dreaming
Than the Vision such deep feeling,
Instantaneously revealing
Traits of rare resemblance, fashioned
Out of things so diverse-seeming,
Ocean-foam and Love impassioned,—
As it flashed in pictured splendour
On the fine Ephesian brain?—
Will devotion true and tender
Ever at that shrine be wanting?
Ever poet's heart refrain
From a chance to touch again
That wan sweet faith and form enchanting—
Sweetest myth of all the train?
Of all the mystic Shapes and mighty,
Sovran, while Love's passionate pain
Can the senses charm and chain—
That dream divine of Aphrodite
Freshly risen from the main?

Lo! upon the amber sands,
Brilliant throbbing Apparition—
As if poised in air she stands!
Proudly conscious, frankly smiling,
Sure of homage, love, submission;
Mostly triumph—some surprise,
In the dangerous innocent eyes,
Where, what witchery world-beguiling
Lies in childlike archness hid!
Where the sense grows faint to mark

How the purple depths that glow
Like the velvet-petalled pansy, show
Dark—almost too lovely-dark—
Too like a stain almost,—amid
All that gleam of snowy brightness,
All her form's effulgent whiteness :
While the dazzling flood of tresses
Ripples like gold lines of light
In a hanging waterfall,
When you look from the curved rock-wall
Behind it, through its crystal pall ;
Wavy sunbeams whence she presses
With those rosy-tipped fair fingers
Every diamond-drop that lingers
Lovingly in their bright recesses.
So was seen the Foam-born standing—
So for ever standeth she
In enamoured memory—
Darling Anadyomene !
While the leopard-sleek and fawning Sea
Round her plays caressingly,
Plays in many a broad festoon
Of foam-flowers—many a sliding sheet
Lovely-creaming, long-expanding,
Then dying off in a luxurious swoon ;—
As if Poseidon love-beguiled,
To beguile, attract, adore her,
Ere he stood confest before her,
Mocked the playful gambols mild
Of some creature of the wild ;
And one sweet look to deserve,
But one glance so killing-sweet,
Kept the simple wile repeating,

Stealing swiftly, curve on curve,
Bounding forward and retreating,
Cowering, crouching at her feet.

II.

Like and unlike—such counterpart
And contrast to that deathless dream of Art,
As gay glad Sunrise when it breaks
In splendour-smitten mist and sparkling dew,
To all the deep-impurpled tenderness
Of soft-illumined Sunset makes,
Though both impress
Their varying glories on the self-same view:
So like and so unlike—the Vision seemed
That on our Wanderer now in beauty beamed.

There, as the shy white crane, so rarely seen,
Stands proudly gentle and reserved,
Erect, but with her neck back-curved
Her breast's light-waving snow to preen—
There Amohia stood. Although downcast the rays
Of her clear-shining eyes—and on her cheek
The rosy flushings momently that broke
Through the clear olive, some distress bespoke—
Yet grandly winning and queenly-meek,
Erect the Maiden stood. About her all
Her affluent hair, unstirred by any breeze
Fell sheltering—a sable silky pall.
How like a strong ebullient swarm
Of hive-o'erflowing honey-bees
Forth issuing black and glad a hundred ways,
Still soaking wet and dripping yet,
The tendrilled tresses spread and ran and clung

To all the balanced beauties of her form;
And sinuously streaming
Adown her polished shoulder palely gleaming,
And rippling ebon-soft over her rounded arm,
A natural drapery hung.

The moonlight's vague unsteady brightness
And depth of mellow shade,
Bewilderingly beauteous made
(So half-concealed and half-displayed)
The graces of a Form wherein it seemed
A bounding spirit of young elastic Life essayed,
In conscious exultation,
To float and flow and wind and wander
And on itself return in many a coy meander
And subtle undulation;
And yet—as all perfection blends
Harmonious opposites for happiest ends—
Seemed ever in its wild luxuriance chained
And by a stronger spirit of proud reserve restrained,
Upholding the fine form in wingëd lightness—
As ivory serpents, held in graceful bond
Would twine of old about a silver Hermes-wand.

III.

So Amohia stood—nor longer sported;
Quite serious now, perhaps a little trembling;
Yet, though her bosom's quickened rise
And fall betrayed the anxious breathing,
By clear unconscious innocence supported,
And that sweet might of Nature when it knows
Few laws conventional that teach dissembling;

So that true Love in loving act o'erflows
As truly, artlessly, in loveliest guise,
As from the bud's moss-browned and tender sheathing,
When Spring has swollen its crumpled tissues
And filled them with its genial influence, issues
That crimson apparition—the young rose.

" Stranger—from far realms that lie
Beyond the steep slope of the sky,
Hapless Amohia, see,
Chieftain's daughter though she be,
Gives her love, her life to thee.
Amohia throws aside
Rank and chieftainship and pride ;
For the lonely Stranger's sake
Every tie has dared to break ;
Dared desert, with him to roam,
Father, Mother, friends and home ;
All the Atuas' wrath to brave,
But to be the Stranger's slave.—
Take her—teach her—till she be
Worthy thy great race and thee ! "

" Dearest—loveliest—bravest Maid,
Your true love shall be well repaid !
But whence, and how, my grand Wildflower,
Came you—and thus—at such an hour ? "

" I swam the Lake—was almost gone—
Reached land and hither stole alone."

Surprise a moment held him dumb—
And why set down the words he spoke—

Disjoined and crowded as the sum
Of mingled feelings that within him woke ?—
What speech has Passion's mastering moods ? what speech
Is possible to *any* Ecstasy ?
Can finite words an infinite feeling reach,
Or the mere bounded Intellect express
The Soul's emotions in their boundlessness ?
No ! as the sky-drawn moisture that distils
Down from the sky-aspiring hills,
A sea-side valley slowly fills—
But, if some milder earthquake's pant
Have slightly changed its downward slant,
Suddenly bursts the marsh below
And seaward rushes in mad overflow,
Bearing before it to the mighty Main
The wrecked and flowery richness of the plain,
Till all the calm eternal blue,
About the outlet of the river new,
Is strewn with floating fragments—little isles
Where still the clinging flax-flower smiles,
Minute azolla-stains of ruddiest hue,
And many a water-loving bloom that grew
Luxuriant while the swamp its moisture could sustain :—
So Speech and all the forms of Thought,
Yea, every medium Intellect supplies,
Are shattered and distraught,
Whene'er the o'er-informing Soul doth rise
And swell and sweep in native might
On to its kindred Infinite—
And broken words and images essay
In vain the abounding current to convey,
In vain to express the inexpressible ;

While blissful moans and happy murmurs tell,—
And only they,—
How the Eternal that within us sleeps,
Stirred to its inmost mystic deeps,
Is welling forth its own imperial way—
Bursting the crust where Custom's weeds are growing,
And its material marge triumphantly o'erflowing!

IV.

What wonder therefore if our youth's emotion,
With no coherent flow of phrases fair,
Could answer that devotion?
If, while beneath the showering night
Of gleaming hair, dark eyes all light
Burned on him—speaking speechless tendernesses—
He could but answer, warm and wild,
With many a fervent deep ejaculation
Of pity, love and admiration;
With broken words and tones endearing,
Soothing, comforting and cheering;
And the soul-converse was sustained
With the only eloquence of passionate caresses,
Kissed eyes and lips, and fluttering breath and fondled tresses,
And throbbing hearts together strained:
Till with his cloak around her thrown
He led her to his dwelling lone;
By all the law the land supplied
So wedded and so made his bride:
And as they went in rapturous tone
Loving and low, half murmured and half sung
A playful tender ditty in her native tongue:

"*Praise her—bless her—O caress her! lavish glorious gifts upon her:*
Piles of woven wealth to dress her—glossy-rippling robes of honour!
O our Pride, the peerless, single—many-vassaled Chiefs' descendant—
Flax o' the finest, silky-tasselled—breadth o'er breadth of costly chequer,
Choicest broidries shall bedeck her! all to grace that form divinest,
And its buoyant blithe uprightness, and its lithe and sinuous lightness,
Rapture-fraught for souls supinest—proudly, peerlessly array.—
Range for birds of beauteous feather, marsh and mountain, dell and dingle—
Stock-doves on whose necks resplendent rich reflections melt and mingle;
Black Sultana-birds blue-breasted as deep Ocean in blue weather;
Cuckoos, many a shy Sea-comer with its green dusk-golden glimmer,
Lackey of the golden Summer, Sun-attendant:—and scarce dimmer
Than that wanderer alien-nested, paraquitos crimson-crested,
Like Spring's emerald verdure vested;—parrots dyed like dying day.
Weave their downy hues together—weave, relieve each tint transcendent;
And the mantle bride-beseeming, fair as fairy gifts in dreaming,

Round her shoulders shapely-showing, wrap it fondly—fold the flowing
Feathery softness, beaming, glowing, with the rainbow's radiance gay.
From her rounded neck dependent—where it curves so proud and stately,
Where her buoyant bosom heaves in tranquil triumph how sedately,
Precious trinkets, famous, greatly-storied from old days or lately,
Lucid as transparent leaves in sunshine, shall their green display.
For her tresses—massy-streaming—floods of glittering gloom and brightness—
Black as pine-trunks burnt and gleaming, charred and sunlit boles and bosses!
Heron-plumes of snowy whiteness—down of sea-pure albatrosses—
Like foam-flakes on torrents raving through swart chasms night-encaving—
O'er those ebon wavelets waving,—shall the Chieftainess betray.

Then caress her—praise her—bless her; load her with delight and honour;
Let no evil thing distress her; lavish all your love upon her!"

CANTO THE FIFTEENTH.

I.

The dawn, faint-tinted as a yellow rose,
Peeped behind mountains purple-black as sloes ;
O'er these—a tuft of thick short shreds (not rays)
Of brilliancy, the Morning Star ablaze
On the funereal darkness seemed to gaze,—
Awe-struck forerunner of the Sun beneath,—
Checked at his sudden entrance on a scene
Solemn with all the sable pomp of death,
The thousand lights still burning for the Queen
Laid out in state—the just departed Night.—
Then Amo, starting from her brief repose,
Urged upon Ranolf their immediate flight ;
For fly they must from that dread Priest she said,
Or even her Father by his counsels led.
Vain Ranolf's reasoned wish to try his skill
Upon her sire, and bend perchance his will
Into approval of their love.—" Nay—nay—
Fly—fly !" she prayed, and he of course gave way :
A power there's no resisting or ignoring,—
A loving, loved and lovely one imploring !
True, the romance of her proposal charmed ;
As o'er its possibilities he ran,

Visions of risks defied his fancy warmed:
To steal by night through unsuspecting foes,
Or baffle them suspecting, was a plan
At which his buoyancy of spirit rose.
His followers therefore quickly paid—dismissed—
Were Northward with his light effects sent back.
One lad of Amo's tribe would still insist
(Te Manu 'twas, who brought the fish that day,
And served him since for pleasure and some pay)
Out of new love for him and old for her—
He should not from their side be forced to stir;
Pleading his usefulness—to bear a pack,
Cook—work—provide such comforts they would lack
Nay, to their safety sometimes minister.
So be it then. What needs is promptly done;
Revolver trim and double-barrell'd gun,
Powder and shot and fish-hooks not a few,
And axe, and matches, most essential too,
Some extra mats for tent-roofs against rain,
And—better currency than minted gold,
A savage's best treasures to unfold—
Allowance good of treacle-smelling cakes
Of jammed tobacco-plaits; with odds and ends,
The boy at cost of carrying would retain
Of fancied value to himself or friends—
Light shoulder-burdens—he or Ranolf takes.

Prosaic details, truly! Lady mine—
Who hold etherial Love a power divine;
O let it not your fervid faith displease,
Romance so realistic stoops to these!
Love is the prime of Gods—O clearly!
A Thaumaturge and Master-mage is he;

Let all confess him as puissant—(nearly)—
  As he conceits himself to be!
Yes! yes! we know, and none deny,
All risks, all ventures, He will try,
All checks and chances, dare—defy!
To his great heart and hope elate
What are the threats of adverse Fate!
How fade the frowns of Circumstance
Before his forward-leaping glance!
His course that ever forth and far
Seems trained by some triumphant Star
Shall rivers bound, shall mountains bar?—
One look, and lo! from mouth to fountain
Uprising from its gravelly bed,
Each river, shrunk to a silver thread
Floats gossamer-like across the lea;
One waive or nod of hand or head,
And every forest-puckered mountain
Rocked from its base uneasily
Goes crab-like lumbering to the Sea!—
Shall not the Ocean heave up pearls
To deck one Beauty's golden curls?
Shall not the Stars come trickling down
If one dear brow demand a crown?—
Yes, fair ones! so shall you decree,
And youthful hearts shall all agree
In LOVE's divine supremacy!
Though duller Deities the while
May at his proud pretensions smile;
Bid Cold and gaunt-eyed Hunger clip
The splendour of his purple wings;
And from his graceful shoulders strip
The golden bow, the ivory quiver,

Unless across them too he flings
The wallet vile and vulgar scrip,
Replete with gross substantial things ;
Nay, make the beauteous stripling shiver
Unless to some frieze cloak he clings ;
Nor, jealous, let the bright Joy-Giver
From Psyche's mouth the honey sip,
And purse and press her sweet lips out
To semblance of a tempting pout,
Or round them bud-like for the bliss
Of a playful passionate kiss,
Till with his own he first have blown
Each rosy frozen finger-tip.
Ah sad ! this glowing glorious God to see,
And think what paltry hests and heeds may be
Importunate, imperative as he !

II.

So to the forests on Taupiri's face
O'er the low cliffs at first the three retreat ;
There they can find a handy hiding-place,
And Amohia rest through noonday heat.
At nightfall they retrace their steps at first
Uncertain—guided by immediate need
Of shelter—and resolve their course to shape
By Amo's counsel for the land that nursed
Her mother, whose great brother ruled indeed
O'er all the tribes about the earliest Cape
The Sun salutes when his resplendent hair
Shakes off the foam-flakes of his Ocean-lair ;
There she was well-beloved ; and both might there,
She for her mother's, he for her sake, share
The nigh-related Chief's protecting care,

Secure alike from rescue and pursuit
With one so potent of such good repute.
So North of Roto-iti, East away,
And for the seaside by the Bounteous Bay,
Though from the route direct still given to stray,
They travel; resting in the woods by day
When needful, and by villages at night
Passing with cautious speed; and none the less
On Ranolf's part, with undisguised delight
At all the shifts, suspenses, and success
And stealthy freedom of their dexterous flight.

III.

And thus o'er many a mountain wood-entangled,
And stony plain of stunted fern that hides
The bright-green oily anise; and hill-sides
And valleys, where its dense luxuriance balks
With interclinging fronds and tough red stalks
The traveller's hard-fought path—they took their way.
Sometimes they traversed, half the dreary day,
A deep-glenned wilderness all dark and dank
With trees, whence tattered and dishevelled dangled
Pale streaming strips of mosses long and lank;
Where at each second step of tedious toil
On perfect forms of fallen trunks they tread,
And ankle-deep sink in their yielding bed—
Moss-covered rottenness long turned to soil:—
Until, ascending ever in the drear
Dumb gloom forlorn, a sudden rushing sound
Of pattering rain strikes freshly on the ear—
'Tis but the breeze that up so high has found
Amid the rattling leaves a free career!
To the soft, mighty, sea-like roar they list:—

Or else 'tis calm ; the gloom itself is gone ;
And all is airiness and light-filled mist,
As on the open mountain-side, so lone
And lofty, freely breathing they emerge.
And sometimes through a league-long swamp they urge
Slow progress, dragging through foot-sucking slush
Their weary limbs, red-painted to the knees
In pap rust-stained by iron or seeding rush ;
But soon through limpid brilliant streams that travel
With murmuring, momentary-gleaming foam
That flits and flashes over sun-warmed gravel
They wade, and laughing wash that unctuous loam
Off blood-stained limbs now clean beyond all cavil
And start refreshed new road-knots to unravel.
And what delight, at length, that glimpse instils,
That wedge-shaped opening in the wooded hills,
Which, like a cup, the far-off Ocean fills !—
Anon they skirt the winding wild sea-shore ;
From woody crag or ferny bluff admiring
The dim-bright beautiful blue bloom it wore—
That still Immensity—that placid Ocean—
With all its thousand leagues of level calm,
Tremendously serene ; he, fancying more
Than feeling, for tired Spirits peace-desiring,
With the world-fret and life's low fever sore—
Weary and worn with turmoil and emotion—
The soothing might of its majestic balm.
Or to the beach descending, with joined hands
They pace the firm tide-saturated sands
Whitening beneath their footpress as they pass ;
And from that fresh and tender marble floor
So glossy-shining in the morning sun,
Watch the broad billows at their chase untiring—

How they come rolling on, in rougher weather—
How in long lines they swell and link together,
Till, as their watery walls they grandly lift,
Their level crests extending sideways, swift
Shoot over into headlong roofs of glass
Cylindric—thundering as they curl and run
And close, down-rushing to a weltering dance
Of foam that slides along the smooth expanse,
Nor seldom, in a streaked and creamy sheet
Comes unexpected hissing round their feet,
While with great leaps and hurry-skurry fleet,
His louder laughter mixed with her's so sweet,
Each tries to stop the other's quick retreat.
Or else on sands that, white and loose, give way
At every step, they toil; till labor-sped
Their limbs in the noon-loneliness they lay
On that hot, soft, yet unelastic bed,
With brittle seaweed, pink and black o'erstrewn,
And wrecks of many a forest-growth upthrown,
Bare stem and barkless branches, clean, sea-bleached,
Milk-white—or stringy logs deep-red as wine,
Their ends ground smooth against a thousand rocks,
Dead-heavy, soaked with penetrating brine;
Or bolted fragment of some Ship storm-breached
And shattered—all with barnacles o'ergrown,
Grey-crusted thick with hollow-coned small shells—
So silent in the sunshine still and lone,
So reticent of what it sadly tells;
Which Ranolf then imagines till he shocks
Quick-sympathising Amo with a tale
Of brave men lost, and haply lovers gone
For ever—never heard of nor forgot;
And so beguiles the bright one of her tears,

Which, while he kisses the wet cheek so pale
He charms away, and the sweet mourner cheers,
Hinting the contrast of their happier lot:
Then turns to livelier sights the scene supplied;
And near some river-mouth—shoal—marshy-wide—
Would mark the swarming sea-birds o'er the waste
Tremble across the air in glimmering flocks;
Or how, long-legged with little steps they plied
Their yellow webs, in such high-shouldered haste
Pattering along the cockle-filled sandbanks,
Some refuse dainty of the Sea to taste;
Or standing stupefied in huddled ranks
Still rounded up by the advancing tide—
White glittering squadrons on the level mud
Dressing their lines before the enclosing flood;
Or what strange instinct guided them so well,
Posed by their mollusk, up in air to start,
And soaring, on the rocks let fall the shell
Whose stubborn valves they could not force apart.
And once, hard by a gloomy forest-side,
How Amo clapped her hands in pure delight
At Ranolf's puzzled wonder when he spied
What seemed so surely—for 'twas clear in sight—
Some furry three-legged thing without a head,
Fixed to the ground—a tripòd!—how amazed
Was he to find when serpent-like it raised
Long neck and bill, and swiftly running fled,
'Twas nothing but that wing-less, tail-less bird
Boring for worms—less feathered too than furred—
The *kiwi*—strange brown-speckled would-be beast,
Which the pair hunted half the day at least,
While needful look-out young Te Manu kept.
Or else the lovers, tired or cautious, stepped

From the chalk-bouldered, pumice-crumbling strand
On to black broken-edged o'erlapping land,
And o'er the flax-swamped rushy level then
Betook themselves to some inviting wood
Just at the black-green opening of a glen
Where mighty trunks like shadowy columns stood,
Solemn, expectant—promising so meet
A shelter for their day or night retreat;
Shore-loving vine-trees, *púriri*, they were
The enormous mounds that with such swelling state
Arose—in masses so consolidate
And caked, the light-green foliage, here and there,
Seemed cracking only from its very weight.

—How free—how free it was! nothing it seemed,
Between themselves and God! so Ranolf felt;—
That world of Man, how oft it seemed to melt
Wholly away! his Soul in contact brought
With Nature's nakedness, exulting teemed
With raptures Life refined had never bought;
Proud vigor from her vivid touches caught;
And from the exhilarating hale embrace
Drew hardier, wilder will to set at nought
All risks—and dauntless every danger face!—
Yet little this was needed now—although
Amo could not her anxious fears forego;
For dread of all that Priest might prompt destroyed
Half of the pleasure she had else enjoyed.

IV.

Now, through some dim white days of ceaseless rain,
They waited till the sky should clear again,

Roofed by a hut no woodman would demur
To call a palace for a forester.
Amid the trees—where loftiest towering grew
Some spiny-leaved *totáras* like the yew,
Root-buttressed, forty yards or so in height,—
They—ere the mist first gathering blanched the blue,
Though many a sign that threatened rain they knew,—
Had built a hasty homestead snug and tight.
Some of these trees, notch-circled near the ground,
That for such end their bark might well be dried,
Or trunks be seasoned for canoes, they found;
Their stringy coats were easily off-stripped,
In stripes, long, broad and heavy, upward ripped;
These, fastened on a frame of poles flax-tied,
Slant roof and walls against the windward side—
Made such a pleasant dwelling in three hours
As had withstood a month of drenching showers;
Thick fern and broom were fragrant floor and couch;
And to the sweet clean roof and walls upslung,
Guns, shot-belt, matches, flints and powder-pouch
And change of raiment, dry and safely hung.

In this retreat three quiet days they passed
In perfect shelter; and the time flew fast,
Though to the hut they mostly were confined,
And spite of care that lurked in Amo's mind.
Love wrapped in sunshine that rain-beaten bower,
Made prisoned solitude and silence dear;
Her care diverted, half-assuaged her fear;
Surcharged e'en trivial chat with eloquent power;
To slight details of daily intercourse
Gave magic sweetness and electric force;
Nay, lent to weeping Nature's gloomier hour

A gentle charm they ne'er before descried
When bathed in brilliant light her features smiled :
So Ranolf felt when over wood and wild
That quiet sadness first began to creep ;
And sheltered safe within their mountain-nook
On his fern-pillow he could lie and look
Past forest tree-tops surging down the steep,
With rocks out-slanting bold, dark-red and grey—
Through the glen's mouth, o'er yellow plains outside,
Mixed with the skies, it seemed, so high and wide—
Melting to misty dimness far away ;—
Look—but to feel with more supreme content
That luxury of loneliness profound—
No human soul but theirs for miles around !
Feel how serenely, pensively forlorn
The tender silence of the tearful Morn ;
Of those unmoving trees as still as thought,
And leaves imbibing in their happy sleep
Rich greenness ever more refreshed and deep ;
Each branch with bright drops hung that would not fall
The faint blue haze upon the grass ; while nought
But the slight tremble, shimmering on the shade
So glowing dark about their stems, betrayed
The fine soft rain's inaudible descent.
Then, as the thickening weather with its pall
Of gloom shut out the distant hills and sky,
How pleasant there to lounge secure and mark
Emerging from the mists in forests high
Black jutting trees to shadows turn, and fade,
Where sullen, ragged, smothering vapors weighed
Upon the nearer summits ; or when wind
Arose, and hurried up the storm, behind
Their hill-protected hut and roof of bark—

To mark each sudden, snowy, crooked skein
With fibres opening here and there, appear
Along the sloping hollows—all pure green
But now—inlaid between round knolls, and seen
White through thin clouds of level-driving rain.
And then within their wildwood home, what cheer—
What manifold amusements might be found!
What pleasure in the necessary round
Of primitive provisions for so rude
A life—whose mere privations still endued
The hours that flew so fast, with fleeter wings;
The merry makeshifts, and the thousand things
To tax contrivance, whence ingenious tact
A double comfort from discomfort wrings;
Scant implements still put to novel use;
Forced partnership in many a little act
For which e'en Love had else scarce found excuse.
Then Ranolf had in note-book to record
Brief hints of many an incident or word
That might the vivid memory reproduce
Of these bright scenes far hence when they should be
Forgotten into freshness. Or he made
Upon the inside smoothness of a square
Of that stripped bark, with pistol-barrel ruled,
Draft-chequers—clipping flat for draftsmen rare
Hard violet drupes of the great laurel-tree
And gold karaka-dates—and soon had schooled
His quick companion in the game they played
For kisses like Campaspe! though, he said,
Amo from Cupid had not cared to win
Cheek-bloom—lips bow-curved—tender turn of chin—
Hers sweeter far already! Or he strove
With taste, and skill—but not in like degree—

Still quickened, still impeded by his love—
Sketchbook on knee, to reproduce, though slight,
Some glimpses of the spirit-winning light
That danced in dazzling depths of Amo's eyes—
Some of her shape's enchanting symmetries ;
While she, with wondering bright compliance bore
The frequent interruptions and delay
To the immediate work she had in hand,
As he so oft entreated her to stay
In that position just one moment more—
Just to continue so to kneel or stand—
Reach up—bend over—let him seize the charm
Of some fine posture, planted foot, or arm
Upraised, that any Sculptor's heart might warm.
And truly, every instant she displayed
A look or attitude that would have made
A Phidias turn admiring, though intent
On one fastidious finishing touch, the last—
One pumice-polish, warm wax-stain, that lent
Perfection to some wonder, now complete,
Some marble miracle or famous feat
Chryselephantine, all the world to beat,
And stamp his own surpassing self surpassed—
Though on his ears, already charmed, he felt
Aspasia's clear Milesian accents melt
In critic subtleties of praise that seize
The heart of his conception, and excite
The stoic soul of stately Pericles
Into confest emotions of delight :
For, as the busy Maid would oft look round
With brows and high-upcurling lashes raised,
And such a glance, what Ranolf wished, to ask—
Bright glance of innocent enquiry, sweet

Alert attention ; or would leave her task,
And throw herself beside him on the ground
To see *what 'twas* that he would sometimes look
Half-pleased with, proud of, in the fast-leaved book
Where he "wrote images"—then with such heat
Would "pish" and "pshaw" at, as on her he gazed,
Abused the work so much—the model praised—
There, as she watched him, toying all the while
With those light locks she loved so, with a smile
Where such a depth of playful fondness shone ;
Might not her aspect then almost have fired
Some later living Phidias of our own,
Some Foley, with such fancies as inspired
His Ino, feeding her maternal joy
On purple temptings of her grape-fed boy?
Almost have made his great compeer conceive
An added loveliness for listening Eve?—
And could wise Nature's so conspicuous Art,—
Lavish of might divinest to unfold
The linkèd glory of mere human limbs
Which all beside of form and hue bedims,—
If ever, fail with this susceptive heart
And fiery Sense, in her design to raise
That fervid admiration, uncontrolled
And uncontrollable, she *must* intend
Should ne'er be foiled for fairest moral end?—
No! well might that pure form, as he surveys
Its rich proportions cast in such a mould—
The perfect mould of Beauty, that combines
Rare lightness with luxuriance, and displays
What subtle joy can lurk in sinuous lines
That in their delicate winding wavure seem
Self-singing of their fine felicities

Like musical meanderings of a stream—
Well might its melodies of movement thrill
His soul with rapture—dash his baffled skill
With blank despair—so distanced in the chase,
The fond attempt to seize on and pourtray
Some one perfection from the plastic play
Of flitting statue-pictures that displace
Each other—and successive charms efface
In ever new varieties of grace!

V.

So in the glen three days had well-nigh passed;
The pelting rain seemed holding up at last.
Ranolf and Amo in their bark-built tent
Were busy; she, in sylvan arts adept,
With scraps of fern drybrown from where they slept,
And moss from underneath thick boughs, in spite
Of damp, preparing her quick fire to light;
But with grave brow half-puzzled how to glean
A savory meal from viands well-nigh spent:
And he, in prospect of the brightening weather,
Intent, but leisurely, with loitering mien,
On ferreting with purple-glossed green feather—
The wild-duck's, moistened with its searching oil—
Into the fastenings of his rifle's lock,
The shining intricacies rust would spoil;
Still pausing in his task, with banter fond
Her over-anxious care for him to mock,
To which, no whit disturbed, she would respond
Her fixed conviction what to him was due;
Or, if a longer silence intervened
Wondering what strange wild tameness towards him drew
The large red-breasted robin—kinsman true

Of England's delicate highbred bird of home,—
So fine-limbed, full of spirit !—how 'twould come
After a little startled flight or two
And perch upon the very gun he cleaned.—
'Twas then, Te Manu—who, sent off to scout,
A cloak of perfect thatch about him thrown,
Had fetched a wary compass wide about
To a far village off their route—prepared
With preconcerted tale—was seen alone
Returning from the journey safely dared,
O'er the dim plain—a shadow : till as near
He drew, the triumph on his face was clear :
Laden he came—though nought for loads he cared
When self-imposed by fancy for good cheer—
Cray-fish—plump pigeons in their fat preserved,
Neat-packed in pottles of dark wood, adorned
With carvings arabesque so quaintly curved—
Store of that tiny fish like whitebait, dried
In sunshine on hot stones—with scraps beside
Of native dainties nowise to be scorned ;—
And when his shoulders from the pack were freed,
With joyous face he told them news indeed :
How he had met a traveller newly come
From Rotorua, and from him had learnt the sum
Of all that there had happened ; how at first
When missing Amohia's clothes were found
Upon the shore, all had believed her drowned :
Then what a wailing had ensued—a burst
Of genuine grief—no counterfeiting show—
What gashing of the breast with shells, and flow
Of blood had marked the matrons' gory woe ;
How Tangimoana had torn his hair
And curst his gods in frenzy of despair,

And raved against the Priest whose scheming greed
His own too ready confidence had wronged,
And driven his darling to the desperate deed—
(From Miroa was that certain fact derived);
Then what a coolness rose between the two:
And how when Ranolf's absence so prolonged,
Begun that very day, had roused more true
Suspicions, fresh inquiry set on foot
Led to the knowledge that the pair had been
By accident upon their journey seen:
And then the Priest so hotly urged pursuit
His obvious spite provoked a new dispute;
For Tangi's heart such great revulsion swelled
Of rapture that his dearest Child survived,
It found no room for thoughts of hate and rage,
And all the vengeful Priest's advice repelled
Almost with scorn; whereat the other turned
Livid with sulky wrath that inly burned,
And no amends of Tangi's could assuage;
At which all wondered; (here in Amo's breast
An undivulged remembrance more than guessed
The jealous fury that his heart possessed:)
And how the Priest soon from the Island went,
None knew when, whither, or with what intent—
Went mutely maddening with his fancied wrong
Though muttering vengeance and return erelong;
At which in hardy confidence so strong
Stout Tangi only laughed; and longed to see
His hoary age's pride again, and press
Her brow against his own in fond caress;
Yearned for her home—companioned should she be
By husband, fair or tawny—what cared he!—

VI.

'But what of Miroa?' Amo asked—'her friend?'—
Ah! there too he had tidings somewhat strange,
He answered, with a shrewd and prying glance
Eyeing the beauteous questioner askance:
"O'er Miroa there had come a curious change
Since Amo left, which none could comprehend
At first; for she—that merry maid—had grown
Sad, absent, sullen-seeming; given up all
Her favourite haunts and friends to muse alone;
Thrown all the sports and frolic games aside
Of which she was the leader, life, and pride;
The lively matches with the dangling ball
Struck at each other by the seated band;
The hunted pebble passed from hand to hand;
'*Káhu*' the 'hawk' of rushes she could weave
And coax with scarce-seen string to soar so high
That all the children said it must deceive
The living hawks they saw beside it fly;
The *háka*-dances where she shone supreme,
For gayer postures who could shape or dream?
With half her archness give each new grimace
Or shake the quivering hands with saucier grace?
The skipping-rope she never had to hold,
For who could ever trip her nimble feet?
Maui, the string she could dispart and fold
With dextrous fingers into forms complete
Of all things 'twas your fancy to behold—
Canoes, men, houses, wonders new and old—
Great Mother Night producing all her train
Of Gods—or cutting with swift snap in twain

Even Maui's self—inventor of the game,
For daring to invade that darksome dame:
All these poor Miroa had discarded now
And moped and slunk about with moody brow.

"Well, all believed it was for Amo's loss
The shadow lay upon the damsel's heart;
Till recently they saw her one fine day
Alert and brisk, preparing for a start,
It seemed, to visit some one far away:
For she was with a studied neatness drest,
Her curling locks smoothed to their brightest gloss—
And striving spite of grief to look her best;
A light food-kit was o'er her shoulders slung:—
When questioned, she declared she meant to make
Her way to Roto Aira's distant Lake,
Where welcome she could always find among
Near relatives that loved her; and you know
Where'er she pleased the Maid could always go—
For who would check her movements—interfere
With one that Amohia held so dear?
But she by accident was overheard
That morning when she thought none near her stirred,
Plaintively crooning o'er an artless song
(While to and fro her form impatient swayed),
That told what secret on her spirit weighed;
The more, that from her bosom she was seen
To draw some finery—woven flowers or braid—
That there it seemed she must have cherished long,
And press them to her brow with passionate mien
And many tears—redoubled as she gazed
Awhile upon these tokens of desire
How vain! then flung them on her matin fire:

But when they quickly shrivelled up and blazed,
Gone like her dream for ever! she arose
Passing her slender hands with gesture swift
Across her brows and sweeping back the drift
Of streaming tresses, as she waved her head
And tossed her arms out wearily once—like those
Who brush aside a troublous dream :—so she
Seemed in that act to shake herself quite free
From that entangling coil of memory.
Then started on her journey as I said.
But these proceedings and the song combined,
And most that wreath—the withered flowery string,
Red feathers from the parrot's under-wing,
And scarlet band—that shining foreign thing—
Told them 'twas for the Stranger that she pined."

Scarce had the word been uttered, ere with eyes
That flashed a sudden fire, fair Amo threw
Her arm round Ranolf as if danger near
Were threatening to despoil her of her prize,
Her heart's whole treasure—then withdrew it too
As swiftly—blushing at her foolish fear,
And asked, her bright confusion to disguise,
More than from any wish the lay to hear,
What song it was made Miroa's love so clear?—
"'*E tangi—e—te ihu*'—what comes next
I'm sure I quite forget, although I heard ;
At *waiatas* * I always was a dunce.
'Twas all about a girl or some one—vexed
At scandal—full of wants and whims absurd.'
But Amo recognised the words at once,

* Waiatas—Songs.

And knew the song of course ; and at request
Of Ranolf, with an accent that expressed
Compassion mixed with somewhat of disdain,
Recited in sweet tones the childish strain,
Whose meaning this loose version may explain :

1.

" Alas, and well-a-day ! they are talking of me still :
By the tingling of my nostril, I fear they are talking ill ;
Poor hapless I—poor little I—so many mouths to fill
And all for this strange feeling, O this sad sweet pain !

2.

O senseless heart—O simple ! to yearn so and to pine
For one so far above me, confest o'er all to shine—
For one a hundred dote upon, who never can be mine !
O 'tis a foolish feeling—all this fond sweet pain !

3.

When I was quite a child—not so many moons ago—
A happy little maiden—O then it was not so ;
Like a sunny-dancing wavelet then I sparkled to and fro ;
And I never had this feeling, O this sad sweet pain !

4.

I think it must be owing to the idle life I lead
In the dreamy house for ever that this new bosom-weed
Has sprouted up and spread its shoots till it troubles me indeed
With a restless weary feeling—such a sad sweet pain !

5.

So in this pleasant islet, O no longer will I stay—
And the shadowy summer-dwelling, I will leave this very day;
On Arapá I'll launch my skiff and soon be borne away
From all that feeds this feeling, O this fond sweet pain!

6.

I'll go and see dear Rima—she'll welcome me I know,
And a flaxen cloak, her gayest—o'er my weary shoulders throw,
With purfle red and points so free—O quite a lovely show—
To charm away this feeling—O this sad sweet pain!

7.

Two feathers I will borrow, and so gracefully I'll wear,
Two feathers soft and snowy for my long black lustrous hair;
Of the Albatross's down they'll be—O how charming they'll look there—
All to chase away this feeling—O this fond sweet pain!

8.

Then the lads will flock around me with flattering talk all day—
And with anxious little pinches sly hints of love convey;
And I shall blush with happy pride to hear them . . . . I daresay . . .
And quite forget this feeling, O this sad sweet pain!"

VII.

So with much grief for Miroa's fond distress,
The pair recalled full many a sign that might
Have helped them read her simple heart aright,

Had both not been too much pre-occupied
With fancies of their own at hers to guess:
And they remembered with what eyes—how wide—
Of eager wondering gladness she had seemed
To feed and fasten on all Ranolf's ways
And looks and movements, when, those two first days,
They met at Rotorua; how they beamed
When with such giggling blushes of delight
She bent her head as carelessly he tied
The ribbon round it he declared less fair
And tasteful than the wreath already there,
Of crimson feathers and the snowy rays
Of clematis—while all might see she deemed
The present of less value than the praise.
And then it flashed on Amo's mind, as sped
Her memory back, with such a cue supplied,
How artfully and oft the Maid would guide
Their talk the way that to the Stranger led;
And when that theme was reached, how glibly ran
Her tongue, unceasing when it once began
In Ranolf's favour mostly, or would raise
Some point against him—find some fault—aver
Some blemish—that she, Amo, might demur
More warmly—more unguardedly be brought
To sound his dear deserts for whom she fought,
And his light-jesting enemy upbraid:
All which the unsuspecting Amo thought
She did to humour, not herself but her—
The foolish Mistress, not the foolish Maid;
(With an arch glance at Ranolf this was said)
And then she recollected once, when turning
Suddenly, with what surprise she caught
Poor Miroa's bloodshot eyes fixed on her, burning

With envy, almost hate; with what swift check
She changed that look to one of passionate yearning,
And wildly flung her arms round Amo's neck
And burst into a flood of tears, and cried:
"My good, good Mistress—O how good and kind
And always dear—O do not mark or mind
The passion of your worthless slave—too bad
For such a mistress—O too false and mad!
Kill, kill me if you will—you should—you may—
But tear this blackness from my breast away!"—
"And then she lavished on me little acts
Of kindness and attention all that day.
And I, still blind to these so patent facts,
Thought 'twas the memory of her home afar
And friends, from whom long years ago in war
She had been torn, a captive, that oppressed
Her fancy then, with fond regrets distressed;
Although I rather wondered she was moved
By that so deeply—scarcely could ascribe
Such passion to such cause; for she had known
Nothing but kindness, since, so terrified
That day she came she shuffled to my side,
And I scarce older, set her numbed limbs free
From bonds, and said she should belong to me.
But since that day so merry had she grown—
She, sprung too from a chief of good degree—
That all our people looked upon and loved
The Child as a true daughter of the tribe,
I always as a sister of my own."

VIII.

Well, so they grieved for Miroa: yet no less
Perhaps, and shall we blame her if 'twere so?

This very feeling for poor Miroa's woe,
Though Amo's love for her was true indeed,
In her unconscious heart could not but breed
A secret feeling she would not confess
Of greater joy in her own happiness.
And cheering up, she said—"You may depend
On this—from what Te Manu says, our friend
Has overcome and shaken off her pain ;
That song would tell it—but still more the power
To burn the keepsake—what was it? the flower
Or ribbon you bestowed in luckless hour.
And she has lovers, O in plenty—she!
And there was one on whom she always smiled,
I thought ; a lad who lives or I mistake,
A fine good lad, beside that very Lake
And near the friends she must have gone to see ;
She will be happy soon—dear merry Child!
Though how she could get o'er such love"—the rest
Was hidden with her face on Ranolf's breast.

IX.

Then, as they marked the sky still growing bright ;
The distant mountains visible once more,
Black-blue, with smothering fleeces flattened o'er
Their ridges—sprawling harpies snowy white
With claws that clutched their summits hid from sight ;
Or like a sudden foam-sea, o'er each brow
Arrested in its branching overflow ;
The pair made ready for a happier start,
Free to obey each prompting of the heart,
Go where they list—all apprehension flown—
And give themselves to Love and Joy alone.

CANTO THE SIXTEENTH.

I.

A King—a God—a little Child
Your happy Lover is; a Saint
With all the Eternal Powers at one—
Serene—confiding—reconciled:
He thinks no ill—believes in none;
There is for him no sin, no taint,
No room for doubt, disgust, complaint,
Misgiving or despondence faint:
Life's mystery flies, her secret won,
Like morning frost before the sun;
How should its cobweb ties arrest
The triumph of his bounding breast!
How should *he* feel, with actual heaven
In measureless fruition given,
The mounting spirit's mortal load?
Feel, steeped in empyrean day
And rapture without stint bestowed,
The Mind too big for its abode,
The Soul's discomfort in its clay?
Why look to some seraphic sphere
For light, for love, so lavish here?
In this our gorgeous Paradise
Why bend to grief—why stoop to vice—

Ah why distrest and sorrow-prest—
Why not be right and brave and blest?
How easy, in a world so bright
To be, to live, blest, brave and right!—
He breathes Elysium—walks on wings;
His own unbounded bliss he flings
O'er all deformed, unhappy things:
Transfigured are they—glorified;
Or vanish and cannot abide
The flood of splendor, the full tide
Of joy that from his heart so wide
Wells over all the world beside.
O Melodist unequalled—Pride
Of Nature's self-taught songsters he!
Inspired—unconscious—mute too soon—
Who sets and sings his lyric Life-song free
To glad Creation's high triumphant tune!

So for herself and most for her beloved
All anxious cares and fears removed,
So upon Amohia now, unclouded beams—
In rounded fulness of possession streams
Once more, the dream of dreams—
The dear divine delirium! say
Once to all by fate allowed;
Though from its shy crescent small,
That finest silver eyelash, fall
Only its earliest rising ray—
Clothing them ever with a luminous cloud
Wherein they may a sweet while stray,
In the thronging whisper-play
Of Angel-wings, on life's highway,
Monomaniacs, in the charge

Of Beauty—blissfully at large
'Mid the sadly saner crowd.

—But we pause—we pale before it,
Fairest reader—that soft splendor!
And your pardon we implore it,
If in sight of scene so tender
Heart and voice we haply harden,
And with faltering step pass o'er it,
That sequestered Eden-garden;
Painting in evasive fashion
Two young lovers, wildly loving,
Through a lovely region roving,
Free as Nature—free as birds are,
Free as infants' thoughts and words are!
Ah! too rich for our rude treating,
Too exalted for our story
That intense absorbing passion—
That fine fever of young Love;
Which though cheating, swiftly fleeting,
Oft it seem to mock and flout us,
Comes, so innocent, undesigning,
Comes into our darkness shining,
Comes and wraps the mystic glory
Of the golden Heavens about us!
And though pining or declining,
Buried—pent here—without vent here—
Lone—a stranger, wild, erratic;
Soon returning to the burning
Blisses of its home above—
Leaves a bud elsewhere to blossom,
Leaves a light in every bosom;—
Just revealing ere off-stealing,

One brief glimpse of soul-enjoyment,
To endure a memory sure—
Pure—a secret life-refiner
And great lure to realms diviner,
Where abandonment ecstatic
To the infinite of feeling—
Loftier love than aught existent,
Ever by indulgence growing
Deeper, fonder, and more glowing—
Tide at flooding still new flowing,
Flower fresh-budding while full-blowing—
Is consistent—is persistent,
Is our normal, true employment!

II.

Amo and Ranolf slowly journeying home,
Had to a pleasant place for camping come
Inside a glorious forest; and although
  The atmosphere was still aglow
  With heat—the Sun still shining high,
Resolved that day they would no further go:
  Why should they haste—what seek or fly?
  Each rocky niche or woody nook
  Of most retired romantic look,
  There they could make their home, their rest,
  And choose next day as fair a nest:—
  'Twas such a joy to journey so,
  How could their journey be too slow!
  So long as not compelled to sever,
  They cared not should it last for ever.

  The youth, with hands beneath his head,
  Against a great *titóki's* base,

Where, less compact and tangled, spread
The underbrush a little space,
Lay watching, now the forest scene,
Now Amo, as with accents gay
And lovely looks and lively mien,
Directions to the lad she gave
How best and where the stones to lay
When heated well—and neatly pave
The little hollow cleared away
To make his oven in, and cook—
In leaves close-folded, lightly sprinkled
With water from the fretting brook
O'er rocky bed that near them tinkled—
The savory palm-tree's pithy heart,
By Ranolf just cut down—but not,
Be sure, without a little smart—
(Though many grew about the spot)
Some slight compunction, for a meal
To strike with his destructive steel,
A thing so fair, a woodland treasure
You could not look at without pleasure;
A slim smooth pillar, ribbed and round,
With drooping crimson chaplet crowned;
O'er that, erect, symmetric, chaste,
A green Greek vase of perfect taste,
With narrow neck and swelling side,
Smooth-shining, sinuous; whence in pride
Of beauty issued, spreading wide,
A fan-like tuft of feathers free—
All in artistic harmony!
Nor this alone employed the lad;
Intent upon a forest feast,
A more attractive task he had—

To raise and fix his three forked sticks,
The little iron pot to sling
He *would* on that excursion bring:
Its use, of all the white man's ways
Had won his most decided praise;
In Ranolf's service he at least
Had learnt what pleasant things were made
With its inestimable aid;
And now with ducks and pigeons shot
By Ranolf, he designed a stew,
Should all his former stews outdo,
Since he had shared a traveller's lot.

III.

But watching thus the wood, or these,
As Ranolf lay, his facile eye
Ran o'er the shapes of plants and trees
Exuberant round him, known or new;
And while once more, as oft before,
He marked with pleasure deep and true,
What varied charms in form and hue
Dear Nature's forest-children wore,
It so did chance his curious glance
Fell on a slender shrub hard by,
All trace-work of transparent gold,
Or gold and emerald blended—neither,
Yet far more beautiful than either!
Against a ground of shadow, black
And soft as velvet, at its back—
So delicately pencilled in green splendor,
Stem branch and twig and leaflet tender
So saturate with sunshine, such a flood
Of light—the exquisite creation stood!—

Then out at once at that sweet sight,
Outbroke in words his pure delight
And admiration uncontrolled:

"*O the ineffable loveliness*
Of the green works of God!—how strange
Their perfect power to mock each one some dress
  Our many-masquing Spirits wear;
Mute, yet expert, like Music, to express
In forms as it in sounds what mood soe'er
The Soul may take through feeling's varied range!
Look at that star-crowned beauty how she stoops,
With what meek pride her plumy crest is bent!
See that fair wanton's figure forward leant
With open arms and every spreading spray
In trustful, loving, frank abandoment;
What shrinking tenderness does one display,
Another languidly despondent droops!
Here, some advanced in bold defiance stand,
While others crouch in shy reserve behind;
There innocent grace, or full contentment bland,
Or swelling pomp their fit exponents find:
And see! how that dismantled forest-king
Does his contorted silver branches fling,
  All bare to heaven, in wild despair,
Or writhing agony of speechless prayer!
Surely some Spirit kindred to our own
Must lurk within these woodland shapes, unknown
Since every image they excite in us,
With feelings so like ours is coupled thus;
Why Soul's effects on forms should they so well
Exhibit, if no Soul within them dwell?—
But O their rich luxuriance! what a load

That sturdy giant lifts in air!
His mighty arms are strong and broad,
But all with alien growths are furred,
A shaggy hide of creepers rare;
Their forks are all blocked up and blurred
With tufts of clogging parasites
That crowd till not a spot left bare
Might offer footing for a bird!—
And such her boundless vigour, see,
Above, below, and everywhere,
Exulting Nature so delights,
So riots in profusion, she
Twice over does her work for glee!
A tangled intricacy first she weaves,
Under and upper growth of bush and tree
In rampant wrestle for ascendancy;
Then round it all a richer overflow
Of reckless vegetation flings,
That here, close-moulding on the shrubs below
A matted coat of delicate leaves,
Mantles the muffled life whereon it clings
Into a solid mass of greenery;
There, mounting to the tree-tops, down again
Comes wildly wantoning in a perfect rain
Of trailers—self-encircling living strings
Unravellable! see how all about
The hundred-stranded creeper-cordage swings!
And when the breeze, so loud without,
Now tamed and awe-struck, gliding in, has found
Amid the stately trees a stealthy way—
How gently to-and-fro just o'er the ground
The low-depending woody ringlets sway,
Like panting creatures on the watch for play!"

IV.

"Why, Rano," with her cheerful smile
Said Amo, at her wifely tasks the while;
"If you were Tanë's self indeed,
The Atua and the Father of the trees,
You could not of their ways take greater heed."

The fancy seemed his mood to please:
"Hurrah!" he cried, and following her lead
Went on, as with mock-solemn triumph fired,
Half to himself, and half to her, as whim
To speech or thought unspoken guided him,
To dally with the notion she inspired:

I.

"I am TANE—the Tree-God!
Mine are forests not a few—
Forests, and I love them greatly,
Moss-encrusted, ancient, stately—
Lusty, lightly-clad, and new.
Mottled lights and chequered changes,
Mid all these my roam and range is;
Shadowy aisle and avenue;
Creeper-girdled column too:
In the mystic mid-day night,
Many-mullioned openings bright;
Solemn tracery far aloof
Letting trefoiled radiance through!
Many a splintered sun-shaft leaning
Staff-like straight against the roof
Of black alcoves, overspread,

Arched, with foliage—intervening,
Layer on layer in verdurous heaps,—
'Twixt that blackness and the sun ;
With a tiny gap, but one,
Light-admitting ; brilliance-proof,
Day-defying, all unriven
Elsewhere—all beside offscreening
Of the grand wide glow of Heaven !
Or, where thinner the green woof
Veils the vault of outer blue,
Many a branch that upward creeps,
Wandering darkly overhead
Under luminous leafy deeps,
Which an emerald splendour steeps,
From the noon that o'er them sleeps !—
O I tend them, love, defend them,
And all kindly influence lend them ;
For my worship all are suited,
If, but, in the firm earth rooted,
By the living air recruited,
They, ere it grow withered, dull—
Their green mantle beautiful,
Still repair, revive, renew."

(Then to himself, more musingly :)

"*Many creeds, and sects and churches,—hopeful each its own way going;*
Bigots, sceptics, saints and sinners—precious to the Power all-knowing.
So they keep absorbing ever more of Truth, the ever-growing."

(*This*, by the way, because he could not smother
That inveterate tendency
To find in all things symbols of each other.)

2.

"I am Tanë—the Tree-God!
My sons are a million;
In every region,
Their name it is legion;
And they build a pavilion
My glory to hold.
Which shall my favourites be?
Which are most pleasing to me,
Of their shapes and their qualities manifold?—
The gigantic parasite-myrtle
That over its victims piles up
Great domes of pure vermilion
Filling the black defiles up:
The King-Pine that grandly towers:—
The fuschia-tree with its flowers,
Poor rustics that timidly ape
Their sisters of daintier shape
With their delicate bells downhung,
And their waxen filaments flung
So jauntily out in the air,
Like girls in short crimson kirtle
That spins in the wind as they whirl
A-tiptoe one pointed foot,
And one horizontal outshoot:—
The clematis-garlands that curl
And their graceful wreaths unfurl
From many a monstrous withe;
Snowy-starred serpents and lithe

That in subtle contortions writhe,
Till Fancy could almost declare
That great Ophiucus, down-hurled
From his throne in the skiey star-world,
Had been caught with his glittering gems
'Mid those giant entangling stems
Which he deemed but a dwarfish copse,
So was struggling and surging in vain
To rear his vast coils o'er their tops
And his gleaming lair regain !—
Then the limber-limbed tree that will shower its
Corollas—a saffrony sleet,
Till Taupo's soft sappharine face is
Illumined for wonderful spaces
With a matting of floating flowerets—
Drift-bloom and a watersward meet
For a watersprite's fairy feet ;
'Tis the *kowhai*, that spendthrift so golden :
But its kinsman to Nature beholden
For raiment its beauty to fold in
Deep-dyed as of trogon or lory,
How with parrot-bill fringes 'tis burning,
One blood-red mound of glory !
Then the pallid eurybia turning
　　The vernal hill-slopes hoary
With its feathers so faintly sweet
And its under-leaves white as a sheet ;—
　All of them, all—both the lofty and lowly,
　Equally love I and wholly ;
So that each take form and feature
After its genuine law and nature.
　Its true and peculiar plan ;
So that each, with live sap flowing,

Keep on growing, upward growing,
As high from the earth as it can!

"*Many creatures—varied features—dark and bright still onward moving;*
Tyrants—tumblers—boors and beauties, kings and clowns alike approving,
To them ALL *the Gods are gracious—to them all the Gods are loving.*

3.

"I am Tanë the Tree-God.
What will you bring to me?
Fruits of all kinds will I take
So ripe, true fruits they be!
Melting pulp—juicy flake—
Sweet kernel or bitter
None are better—none fitter—
All are grateful to me.
But your shell with no lining
Though splendidly shining;
But your husk with a varnish
That nought seems to tarnish—
If any of these I espy,
Empty and hard and dry,
That serve but for clamour and clatter
Or the genuine fruit to belie;
These cheats will I shiver and shatter
And their fragments scornfully scatter,
O none of them bring to me!

"*Pains and passions—deeds and duties—virtues, vices—gifts and graces—*
Have not all, their value, uses—in their various fitting places—
So they be not false pretences, mocking masks for natural faces?—

"'There, my sweet one, that is what,
Were I Tanë (which, thank God, *I'm not*,
Seeing mine's a happier lot)
That is about what I should say,
Had I my own, my wondrous way."

V.

And Amo coming to his side amused,
Her smiling eyes with tender love suffused,
"How fond, O Rano mine," said she,
"Of these dumb things you seem to be;
I shall be jealous soon, I think,
And wish myself a Tree!"

"A tree, my Amo! but I wonder which?
O which so fair that we might link
Such loveliness in fancy with its form?
Which should be haven for a heart so warm,
So sweet a Spirit's dwelling-place?
The Rata-myrtle for its bloom so rich—
Or Tree-fern for its perfect grace?
Its slender stem I would embrace
How fondly!—nay, but that would never do—
That limbless tree-fern never should be you
With nothing but a stem and plumy crest!
Ah no! the glorious Rata-tree were best,
With blooming arms that spread around—above;

That should be you, my sole delight,
My darling bliss! that so I might
Embosomed in embowering beauty rest,
And nestle in the branches of my love!"

"Nay—but I would not be," said Amo—"I,
That Rata—if the change I had to try;
Rather the snowy Clematis, to twine
About the tree I loved; or rather yet
That creeper Fern, with little roots so fine
Along its running cords, it seems to get
For its gay leaves with golden spots beset,
Its dearest nurture from the bark whereto
It clings so close; as if its life it drew,
Drew all its loving life from that alone—
As I from thee, Ranoro, all my own!"
She paused a tender moment—then resumed:
"Nay, *not* the Rata! howsoe'er it bloomed,
Paling the crimson sunset; for you know,
Its twining arms and shoots together grow
Around the trunk it clasps, conjoining slow
Till they become consolidate, and show
An ever-thickening sheath that kills at last
The helpless tree round which it clings so fast.
Rather, O how much rather than destroy
The thing I loved, the source of all my joy,
Would I, my Rano, share the piteous fate
The Rata's poor companion must await—
Were you the clasper, I the tree that died,
That you might flourish in full strength and pride!"

"Nay—nay—my Amo! were't to be my doom
To clasp you till you perished in your bloom,

Neither to misery should be left behind—
Together would we be to death consigned—
In death, as all through life, in love entwined.
But now, my lovely Clematis, be gay!—
Though never shall I see that Rata bright,
In murderous fondness, fastening round its prey
The serpent-folds that hug the friend they slay,
Without a sigh for the poor victim's plight;
Without a wish to cut and cleave away
The monster throttling what has been his stay;
Without some wonder why the Power divine
Includes such pictures in his world's design,
And even in lovely vegetable life
Leaves startling models of unnatural strife."

VI.

Thus they two in their dream. But Evening now
Steals, like a serious thought o'er joyous face,
Its cooling veil o'er the warm Earth to throw.
The hawk no longer soars in pride of place,
Stiff-wheeling with bent head in circles slow;
The teal and wild-duck leave the floating weed
And open pool, for sheltering rush and reed;
And home with outstretched necks the cormorants fly
In strings—each train dark-lettering the sky,
Now V exact, now lengthening into Y—
As arrow-like direct their course they steer
To haunts afar, unseen, but somewhere near
Those mountain-summits carpeted and black
With forests dense without a break or track,
Whence smooth and ferny spurs in golden dun
Of solemn sunlight undulating run

Down to dim bases lost in shadows blue
That blot the intervening gullies too—
Encroaching darkness creeping upward still
O'er chequered black-and-gold of dell and hill.

"How pleasant is the life those birds must lead—
About the sea all day to sport and feed,
  Where'er they will, with little heed;
And flee away at night with aim so sure
Striking across the sky, so eager each
His inaccessible far roost to reach—
So secret, solitary and secure
In solitude. And is not ours like theirs—
As free, as lonely sweet, as void of cares!"
Said Ranolf, as beside him closer drew
Fair Amo: "Yes, my wildwood dove,
What have we else to do but live and love!"—
And she, her native tongue, no doubt, too weak
The fond delight that filled her heart to speak,
Replied in one more rich, she felt, though new,
That foreign language of a fervid kiss;
Shaping her smiling lips as if they might
Unlearnedly perform the mystic rite,
Some feature of its due observance miss.
"But see," she hints, "Te Manu comes to say
The *kúkupas** are done he takes such pride
In cooking."—As she spoke the youngster gay
Came running up and grinning cried:
"*Ranoro, come! come, Amo, quickly—do!*
Ka rawe! 'tis a glorious stew!"

* Kúkupas (coo-coo-pas)—wood-pigeons.

CANTO THE SEVENTEENTH.

I.

"*How beautiful! how wonderful! how strange!*"—

Such words, less thought than mere emotion, well
Might Ranolf with abated breath, in tone
That wonder-stricken to a whisper fell,
For Amo's looks of triumph now exchange:
So fair a vision charmed our loiterers lone,
As at the closing of a sultry day,
  In search of some good camping-ground
  They paddled, up Mahána's Lake,
  A small canoe by chance they found
  (And Amo settled they might take)
  With little care half-hid in sedge
  Flax-fastened to the water's edge—
  Its owners clearly far away.

From the low sky-line of the hilly range
Before them, sweeping down its dark-green face
Into the lake that slumbered at its base,
  A mighty Cataract—so it seemed—
Over a hundred steps of marble streamed

And gushed, or fell in dripping overflow—
Flat steps, in flights half-circled—row o'er row,
Irregularly mingling side by side ;
They and the torrent-curtain wide,
All rosy-hued, it seemed, with sunset's glow.—
—But what is this !—no roar, no sound,
Disturbs that torrent's hush profound !
The wanderers near and nearer come—
Still is the mighty Cataract dumb !
A thousand fairy lights may shimmer
With tender sheen, with glossy glimmer,
O'er curve advanced and salient edge
Of many a luminous water-ledge ;
A thousand slanting shadows pale
May fling their thin transparent veil
O'er deep recess and shallow dent
In many a watery stair's descent :
Yet, mellow-bright, or mildly dim,
Both lights and shades—both dent and rim—
Each wavy streak, each warm snow-tress—
Stand rigid, mute and motionless !
No faintest murmur—not a sound—
Relieves that Cataract's hush profound ;
No tiniest bubble, not a flake
Of floating foam is seen to break
The smoothness where it meets the Lake :
Along that shining surface move
No ripples ; not the slightest swell
Rolls o'er the mirror darkly green,
Where, every feature limned so well—
Pale, silent, and serene as death—
The cataract's image hangs beneath
The cataract—but not more serene,

More phantom-silent than is seen
The white rose-hued reality above.

They paddle past--for on the right
Another Cataract comes in sight;
Another broader, grander flight
Of steps—all stainless, snowy-bright!
They land—their curious way they track
Near thickets made by contrast black;
And then that wonder seems to be
A Cataract carved in Parian stone,
Or any purer substance known—
Agate or milk-chalcedony!
Its showering snow-cascades appear
Long ranges bright of stalactite,
And sparry frets and fringes white,
Thick-falling, plenteous, tier o'er tier;
Its crowding stairs, in bold ascent
Piled up that silvery-glimmering height.
Are layers, they know—accretions slow
Of hard silicious sediment:
For as they gain a rugged road,
And cautious climb the solid rime,
Each step becomes a terrace broad—
Each terrace a wide basin brimmed
With water, brilliant, yet in hue
The tenderest delicate harebell-blue
Deepening to violet! Slowly climb
The twain, and turn from time to time
To mark the hundred baths in view—
Crystalline azure, snowy-rimmed—
The marge of every beauteous pond
Curve after curve—each lower beyond

The higher—outsweeping white and wide,
Like snowy lines of foam that glide
O'er level seasands lightly skimmed
By thin sheets of the glistening tide.
They climb those milk-white flats incrusted
And netted o'er with wavy ropes
Of wrinkled silica. At last—
Each basin's heat increasing fast—
The topmost step the pair surmount,
And lo, the cause of all! Around,
The circling cliffs a crater bound—
Cliffs damp with dark-green moss—their slopes
All crimson-stained with blots and streaks—
White-mottled and vermilion-rusted;
And in the midst, beneath a cloud
That ever upward rolls and reeks
And hides the sky with its dim shroud,
Look where upshoots a fuming fount—
Up through a blue and boiling pool
Perennial—a great sapphire steaming,
In that coralline crater gleaming.
Upwelling ever, amethystal,
Ebullient comes the bubbling crystal!
Still growing cooler and more cool
As down the porcelain stairway slips
The fluid flint, and slowly drips,
And hangs each basin's curling lips
With crusted fringe each year increases,
Thicker than shear-forgotten fleeces;
More close and regular than rows,
Long rows of snowy trumpet-flowers
Some day to hang in garden-bowers,
When strangers shall these wilds enclose.

But see ! in all that lively spread
Of blue and white and vermeil red,
How dark with growths of greenest gloss,
Just at the edge of that first ledge,
A little rocky islet peeps
Into the crater-caldron's deeps.
Along the ledge they lightly cross,
And from that place of vantage gaze
O'er all the scene—and every phase
The current takes as down it strays :
They note where'er, by step or stair,
By brimming bath, on hollow reef
Or hoary plain, its magic rain
Can reach a branch, a flower, a leaf—
The branching spray, leaf, blossom gay,
Are blanched and stiffened into stone !
So round about lurks tracery strewn
Of daintiest-moulded porcelain-ware,
Or coral wreaths and clusters rare,
A white flint-foliage !—rather say
Such fairy-work as frost alone
Were equal to, could it o'erlay
With tender crust of crystals fair,—
Fine spikes so delicately piled—
Not wintry trees, leafstripped and bare,
But summer's vegetation, rich and wild.

II.

But while all this they watch, lo, still and grand,
The enormous Moon !—how, like
A great gold cymbal on its edge upright,
Upon the mountain's ridge it takes its stand

So close—there balanced broad and steady,
To bathe in dreamily-magical light
What seemed a magical dream already,
Twice beautify the beautiful, and strike
Transcended sense dead-mute with admiration!—
And who could mark, with wondering soul-elation,
That revel of redundant loveliness,
Nor some such truth as Ranolf felt confess:

"*O these charms of great Nature!* who ever has seen them
In their glory as these are, nor owned that the notion
They force on the thinker, is true, not illusive—
That our senses and they, so composed as between them
To awake in the mind such delightful emotion,
Are proofs self-attested, as logic conclusive,
Of Benevolence *somewhere*, in what has created
And keeps them to act and react on each other:
A sentiment this, that no Science can smother.
Nor condemn it as anthropomorphical folly—
Since a cause they *must* have, one intelligent wholly—
To hold that the Cause of these marvels must mean them
To display that Benevolence—mutely reveal it
In delight to the creature most fitted to feel it!
—Aye truly! and though by stern reasoning's parity
You maintain that in Nature, the baleful, disgusting
Should be proof in its Cause of defect of such charity—
That if Beauty be vaunted as sign of Benevolence,
Deformity equally argues Malevolence,—
Yet the first so outsplendours the last—so exceeds it—
And the last has such uses, Mankind almost needs it—
'Tis hard not to side with the hopeful and trusting!
Yes, cavil and carp, the nice balance adjusting,

Yet is Beauty in literal truth, nothing less
Than a Gospel—an embassy mute yet express
From some Power imperial, of friendliness felt
For mankind—say of Love! one that never will cease
To diffuse its serene revelations of peace;
Bright dawns and rich sunsets its eloquent books;
And the broad laugh of flowers, and the soft-chiming brook's
Secret murmurs of joy, and the rapture of birds,
Its angelical whispers,—accredited words:
But holiest Woman's affectionate looks,
Most thrillingly potent to move and to melt,
Are the pages where clearest its plenary power
Of divine Inspiration for ever has dwelt!
And he who has basked but one bliss-giving hour
In their sunshine and solace, like me must avow,
With the loveliest lessons of Love, it is thou
O God-ordained Beauty, the Spirit canst fill!
Aye, 'tis Thou, in all shapes, of celestial good-will,
Art the sweetest, most suasive Evangelist still!"—

III.

Content that night no more to see,
The wanderers push off merrily
To what that night their home shall be:
A little rugged isle (another
Beside it standing, its twin-brother
In conformation strange) that lifts
Its verdurous tufts o'er tortuous rifts
Misshapen—many a dip and rent
In rock that—ever bathed, besprent
With oozy hotspring, fervid play
Of steam that finds a viewless vent—
Is softening slow to pallid clay.

By isles—mere knots of waving grass,
By thin-spread rush and reed they pass;
And fright a thousand birds that rise
From bubbling channel, heated marsh;
And flee in flocks away, with cries
Now plaintive, wild—now hoarse and harsh;
Coot, teal and that rich gallinule
Of velvet violet plumage proud;
That, night and day, each open pool
Or warm and watery covert crowd,
And stalk and strut and peer and pry
With jerking tail and searching eye;
Or plash and paddle, duck and dive,
And through green bills quick-gargling drive
The scooped-up Lake's clear lymph. And see,
Pink-legged, snow-white or sable-pied,
Those strangers from far Ocean's side;
Slim oyster-catcher, avocet,
And tripping beach-birds, seldom met
Elsewhere—come hither, not for food,
But on this warm delight to brood,
This tepid inland luxury.

The pair have left the light canoe
And cross the soil with cautious tread,
Whose treacherous crust they scarce can trust—
Each step, it seems, may break it through.
With springy swelling moss 'tis spread,
An emerald, warm, and soaking sod,
In places; then their way they track
Through little thickets, very black
In shade against the tumbled blocks—
The steaming, white and moonlit rocks—

But cherished there to richness rare
Of fragrant broom and ferny plume
And winding woven lychopod
Close-creeping—all luxuriant, lush,
In that pervading vapour-gush.
Then on a grassy spot the brake
Left free—just large enough to make
A couch for two, fenced all around
With aromatic leptosperm—
A soft green gapless wall—they heap
Elastic fern and broom to keep
Down to a pleasant warmth the heat
The ground gives out ; where they may sleep—
Could Love desire a bower more sweet ?—
Secure no noxious reptiles creep
Throughout the land—evenomed worm,
Or poison-snake you dread to meet ;
And lulled by that low changeless churme,
The hissing, simmering, seething sound
That sings and murmurs all the while
And ever round that mystic isle—
May sleep a blissful sleep profound,
Plunged in the calm unconscious heaven
To youth and health out-wearied given.

IV.

Soon as the Morn from curtain-folds of grey
  Peeped out with smile so grave and tender,
Like a young Queen upon her crowning-day
  Blushing to put on all that gold and splendour—
    Up rose the lovers to survey
The marvels yet unseen that round them lay.

Baths beauteous, statelier than of old
Rome's silken Emperors ever planned,
Of every nice degree of heat and cold,
Are ready crystal-filled at hand:
No need have they of fuel or fire
To cook their morning meal to their desire;
'Tis but to scrape a primrose-tinted seam,
Some sulphur-crusted fissure dry
That runs through fern and grass hard by—
Up comes the hot and fizzing steam,
Wherein—or plunged in water boiling blue
The food suspended, is, without ado,
In style as wholesome quickly drest
As Savarin's choicest, Soyer's best.

V.

Forthwith their gladsome way they take
To all the marvels of the Lake.
To Wáta-poho's endless wail
They list—the groans its tortures wrest
From its hard agonising breast,
So hollow, inward-deep and fierce,
As upward shoot its showers intense,
Cramming the narrow shaft they pierce
Through shuddering rocks blanched ashy-pale;
Hot water, steam and sulphur-smoke
Commingling in one column dense
Of white terrific turbulence!
But other gentler feelings woke
Its sister fountain welling nigh,
Whose bursts of grief for moments brief
Long-intervalled, in streams out-broke,
And then would sink away and die

With such soft moan relapsing slow—
Such long-drawn breath of utter woe—
It well became its mournful name,
'Kó-ingo—Love's desponding Sigh.'
They visit then that narrow glen,
Where at the foot of hills forlorn,
Silicious slabs of spar flood borne,
Like cakes of ice when Spring is young,
Burst up by freshets wild, are flung:
And slow they pick their cautious way
By liquid beds of creamy clay,
Where large white nipples rise and sink,
And lazy bubbles break and fume,
Up to a small square tarn pea-green—
As green and bright as malachite,
Beneath a crimson cliff in part
White-mottled, and along the brink
Of that clear water's grass-hued sheen—
Where azure dragon-flies will dart
A moment—feathered rich and dark
With mánuka, like fragrant broom.
And near the valley's mouth they mark,
Where thickets dense scarce leave a track,
A boiling mud-pool sputtering black
And baleful;—mark, above its gloom
What weird wild shapes the rocks assume!
Here, worn by water's sapping might,
Time-crennelled turrets half o'erthrown;
There, idols blurred by ages' flight
To shapes of unconjectured stone;
Now on the hill's low brow upright,
Like men who walk in dreams by night,
Dumbfounded, tottering—lost and lone;

Now, muffled forms their faces shrouding
Opprest with some unheard-of doom ;
Or woe-struck up the hillside crowding—
Funereal mourners round a tomb :—
Grotesque and ominous and grim,
As Doré's wonder-teeming whim
E'er forged and fixed in stony trance
Of subtle-shaped significance.

And next across the Lake they steer
To see that fair cascaded stair
That yester-eve they passed so near—
'The Fountain of the Clouded Sky,'
Tu-kápua-rangi—fitly styled,
It flings its steam so wide and high.
'Tis *rosy* rime they climb this time ;
For floors and fringes, terrace piled
O'er terrace, glow with faint carmine
As fashioned of carnelian fine ;
As if, continuous, full, from heaven
Some wide white avalanche downward driven
Came pouring out of Sunset, stained
With sanguine hues it still retained.
But at the topmost terrace—lo,
A vision like a lovely dream !—
A basin large, its further marge
And all its surface hid in steam
That thinly driving o'er it flies,
Spreads, level with the level plain
Of smoothest milk-white marble grain :
And all around its nearer brink
A border broad of delicate pink
That melts to lemon-yellow, dyes

That whiteness, and with even hues
Fair as a rainbow laid on snow,
Its wavy outline still pursues.
But through the driving vapour, see,
Translucent depths of azure, bright
And soft as heaven's divinest blue—
A gulf profound of liquid light!
And from those depths, uprising through
That azure light—yet all beneath
The steaming surface—still as death,
In snowy mute solemnity,
A mighty forward-bending peak
Of marble bows; shaped like a *paw*,
Say, some enormous polar bear's—
Thick-set with many a flattened claw,
All one way level-pointing—scale
O'er scale like th' Indian pangolin's mail—
All snowiest alabaster!—Weak,
Too weak, were any words to speak
The hushed mysterious charm it wears,
That ghostly-lovely miracle,
Whose sides of snow far down below
In boiling light that round them lies,
Fade where the clear cerulean glow
Of that unfathomed fervent well,
In tenderest turquoise dimness dies!
O well may Ranolf for a while
Enthusiast-like, sit rapt before
That heaven-blue gulf and rock snow-white,
Unconscious even of Amo's smile,
Unconscious of her joyous eyes,
And loving arms he scarce could feel
That softly *would* around him steal

As silent by his side she lay
On that pure speckless snowy floor
With pink and saffron purfle gay.

Thus all the varied fountains found
Among the ferny hills that bound
Mahana, and a mile around—
Of every flow and hue and sound
They visit ;—tall columnar mound
And diamond-cone, and haycock heap
Of boiling snow, and springs that leap
And languish, spurting fitful spray,
And cloud-crowned stems of steam that spout
At seasons, or shoot up alway ;
Hid white about this verdurous waste
Like statues in proud gardens placed :
And one large font whose hollow bed
With branching emerald coral spread,
Through brilliant boiling crystal shows,
Fine as the daintiest moss that grows !—
And sights as dread they meet throughout,
As wild Imagination's worst
Of black hell-broths and witches' bowls
Infernal—Dante-pits accurst,
Here realised in cankerous holes
And sloughs of mud as red as blood,
Pitch-black, or viscid yellow-drab,
Or pap of clay light-bluish gray,
Or sulphurous gruel thick and slab :
Each sputtering, hot, commixture dire,
Earth mineral-stuffed, and flood and fire,
Together pashed and pent-up make,
And fuse in sluggish fever nought can slake.

So passed the day ; and swiftly sped
Mid scenes where marvels ever varying rise ;
The wanderers' eyes with wonder ever fed—
Bright with continual flashes of surprise.

VI.

Late after noon it was, when tired the pair
Returning to their starting point, once more
  Beside the mighty geyser stood
That flings a panting column high in air—
'Ohápu'—'Fountain of the dreadful Roar.'

Their fancy sated with the sight of fear,
  They sate upon the hill above
That cauldron, in the shade of rocky wood
  By bursting spring and boiling flood
Distorted—sate in lounging mood
In careless converse, to themselves how dear !
(Is any talk too trifling for true love ?)
Where still the geysers' raging they could hear.

—"This loitering through the land on foot,
Now slow, now faster, as may suit
One's humour best, I do enjoy
So thoroughly—did always from a boy !"—
Said Ranolf, as himself he threw
Upon the stunted fern—"Do you ?"

"On foot !" said Amo, "how else *could* you go ?
Though in your land, I've heard, indeed,
That travellers sometimes go at greater speed
In strangest style—I ne'er believed it, though."

"What did you hear, my Amo?"

"It was he
E Ruka, who had sailed beyond the sea;
But he so many monstrous stories told
With face so true, by young and old
'*Kai-tito-nui*' he was named,
'The big lie-swallower;' 'pumpkin-headed' too,
To take whate'er he heard for true—
They called him. I should be ashamed
His silly solemn stories to repeat."

"But let me hear about the travelling, sweet!"

"Well, promise not to laugh—at least, not laugh
Too much at me. I did not credit half
The story, mind. He said, your people use
To travel in, great land-canoes,
Dragged by enormous dogs as tall
As men, or taller; nay, more strange—
A thing that had to do with travel,
Though *how*, I could not quite unravel—
That beasts about your country range
To which the mighty Moas were small
Our songs make mention of; that these
Gigantic monsters, each and all
Have double heads and shoulders double,
Six legs or so; and therefore go
Swift as the wind; then without trouble
Can split in two whene'er they please,
And both the fragments when they sever,
Can run about as well as ever!—

Nay, now, but I will hold your lips—
You are not to laugh so—understand ;
I will not take away my hand,
Kiss as you may my finger-tips."

The fact explained to her well nigh
As wondrous as the fiction seemed :
What ! get astride those beasts and fly !
'Twas like what Maui did or schemed,
Who fished the Isles up—almost hitched
The Sun into his noose, and then
Had freed the happy sons of men
From Night—Death—every denizen
Of Darkness—all the evil crew
Of powers bewitching or bewitched.

"My Child—but these are trifles to
The wondrous things our people do.—"
He pointed toward the place where bellowing, crashing,
That fierce terrific Hotspring raged ;
With monstrous head in furious foam upsoaring,
And boiling billows round the crater dashing—
Its crusted soot-brown sides, like demons lashing ;
Or if a moment from its maddest mood
The lapsing Geyser seemed to sink assuaged,
Mounting again amid the ceaseless roaring,
Like hissing Cobra with inflated hood
Upswelling swift—its reeking rush renewing,
With force and frenzy evermore accruing !

"You hear," he said, "that hell-pool dread :
What would you think if I should say

My people have the skill to yoke
The fiercest whirls of steam that ever broke
From that tremendous pit of wrath, and tether
As many moving houses gay
Behind it as would all your tribe contain;
Then make it whisk them o'er the plain,
Aye! all your Tribe at once together,
As smoothly, rapidly as flew
The Kingfisher the other day
With chestnut breast and back so blue
That round our heads came swooping, screaming,
Because we chanced to saunter near
The barkless twisted tree-trunk (gleaming
In sunshine silver-sharp and clear
Against far purple hills) that hid
The nest wherein his young ones lay?"

"Well, but if such a word you spoke
I could but think, I could but say,
'Twas my Ranoro's whim to joke;
And on her fond reliance play
Who takes and trusts his every word,
As if an Atua's voice she heard."

"Nay; pretty one! 'tis simple fact—
No silly jest, but truth exact."

"Well then, my Chief, my Master dear
Shall do as I, his handmaid, bid,
And let me all the wonder hear."

"Your language has no words, I fear—"

"Ah, we poor Maori! worthless still,
In deeds and words, no power, no skill!—
But tell me—that tremendous flying
Is it not something dreadful, frightful
Your people tremble at, while trying?"

"Not dreadful, dearest, but delightful—"
And then with her request complying,
"See—" he went on, as best he could, constraining
Strange words and strange ideas to fit—
Though all the interruptions we omit
Where foreign thought or phrase required explaining:—
"See! all in order ranged at hand
The moving houses ready stand;
Your tribe all ranged in order too,
Inside them sit—imagine how;
We take our places, I and you—"
("Yes—were I close to you as now!"—)
"Impatient frets the giant, Steam,—
You hear his wild complaining scream;
You hear him hissing ere he start
Like pinned-down Snake that strives to dart;
Then off at once! in perfect row
Swift as a lance your warriors throw,
Men, houses, all, away we go!—
Give place! give place! in silent race
The distant woods each other chase!
Trees, hedges, hamlets—far and wide,
They reel and spin, they shift and slide!
The dim horizon all alive—
Hills, plains and forests, how they drive!
Determined to keep up and see
They shoot ahead as fast as we;

But nearer objects, soon as spied,
Detach themselves and backward glide ;
Behind us drifting one by one,
Wink past the others and are gone !
See ! parallel field-furrows broad,
That lie right-angled to the road,
Like swiftly-turning wheel-spokes play—
Turn—open—float and flit away !
　More speed—more speed ! and shriller cries !
The panting road begins to rise,
And like a whirling grindstone flies !
The fields close by can scarce be seen,
A swift continuous stream of green !—
—But fix upon the scene around
A steadier glance—in how profound
A stillness seems that hamlet bound :
How solemn, in secluded meadows
Those oak trees standing on their shadows ;
That church-tower wrapt in ivy-fleece,
How sacred its inviolate peace !
The riot of our wild career
Seems rushing through a land asleep
Where all things rapt—entranced, appear,
Or if they move, can only creep ;
The lightest car, the heaviest wain—
(Those land-canoes, you know, we use)
And walking men whose figures plain
A moment on the eye remain,
Seem toiling backwards, all in vain !—
Then sudden—close—ere you can think,
The blackest blinding midnight seems
To make your very eyeballs shrink ;
The air is dank—a hollow roar

And deeper, harsher than before
Is mingled with the Giant's screams,
As—all the houses in a row—
Right through a Mountain's heart we go !
But swiftly from the jaws of night
Emerging, screeching with delight,
Outcomes with unabated might
The Monster and pursues his flight !
In sable stream thick issuing flies
His furious breath across the skies :
Each laborer as the ponderous whirr,
The hammer-beats, incessant, strong
And fast as flap of flying bird,
The monster's eager pulse, are heard,
Suspends the busy fork or prong
And turns to look, but scarce can see
The phantom, ere the rush and stir,
Men, monster, long-linked houses, we—
All smoothly thundering, tearing on,
A human hurricane—are gone !"—

She listened with rapt lips asunder,
And rounded eyes of brilliant wonder :
Love lent her Faith—nor could she draw
Distinctions nice between what broke
Or did not break, the natural law ;
But could she, 'twould have been the same ;
Not what was said, but he who spoke,
Made what she heard as what she saw.
That cloudy madness chained and curbed—
And all her Tribe turned undisturbed
Into a screeching bird that flew
Unchecked the yielding Mountains through !—

What myth could daunt her after that?
What miracle could Superstition name
Were not beside it commonplace and flat—
To stagger her belief, too tame?—
"These foreigners," she smiled, "'tis true,
Whate'er they wish, their Atuas do!"

"An Atua—yes! divine not dread—"
(But this was rather thought than said)
"Could I but make her understand
How this benignant Genie grand,
In form so fierce, in deeds so bland,
Is toiling still o'er sea and land
With might unwearied and unworn
By slow degrees to raise Mankind;
Bestowing god-like powers, designed
For mightier millions yet unborn,
To wrest her plenteous treasure-horn
From Nature's wise reluctant hand;
Consigning so to second place
The Body's too absorbing claims;
Clearing the ground for higher aims;
Wiping the tears from Man's sad face;
Amalgamating every race—
Creating Time—destroying Space."

VII.

Now to the Fountain Stair beside the pass,
The great white Fount, the pair their footsteps turning
Paused to admire the baths, whose sheets of glass,
Warm azure, with the blushing west were burning;
And Amo when her simple phrase had told
The simple triumph that illumed

Her features at her friend's delight
Which seemed to say her country had one sight
At least, as lovely, it must be avowed,
As any in his native land so proud—
The talk where it had broken off resumed:

"Atuas or not—you must be wise and bold
To work the wonders you unfold;
Too ignorant, alas! or dull
Am I, O friend, to comprehend
Such things, I fear. But let me hear—"
She said, in somewhat faltering tone
As shy, lest what she asked make known
More feelings than she cared to own:
"Are not your Maidens beautiful?"

"More so than well my tongue can tell."

"But not more beautiful than you—"

"Than I!" with laughter loud, he cried:
"As much more as the graceful crane
In dainty plumes without a stain
Than her brown-mottled brother harsh,
The booming bittern of the marsh;
As much more as the fragrant strings
Of milky stars I've seen you tear
From some great forest-galaxy
With their sweet snows to double-dye
The sable splendour of your hair,
Than that vile twine of prickles fine
Which if it touch you cuts and clings
Whene'er you push through briar and bush."

"But O, describe them, dearest, do!"

"Nay, how pourtray, how paint or say
What deep enchantment round them lies—
Great Nature's last felicities,
Her happiest strokes of genius! some of whom—
Heart, mind and body, in the May
And melody of perfect bloom,
The coldest sceptic must assume
The mighty Master fashioned to display
In one consummate work how he
Could make its outward form a shrine,
A visible symbol and a sign
Of what was throned within—divine!
Aye! spite of Man's idolatry,
For ever pardonably prone
To worship more the shrine than Saint,
And feel from love of that alone
His beauty-burdened Spirit grow
With too much adoration faint—
Resolved in that rare Form to show
For what the rarer Soul was given—
To be to Man a living light
And lure of spiritual beauty bright,
To lead him on from height to height
Of self-denying Love to heaven!—
But who that outward Shrine can paint,
Whose mortal scarce can its immortal shroud!
What lofty-passioned words and tones
Can picture forth those loveliest ones!
So blossom-cheeked, so heavenly-browed,
With dowery of divinest eyes,
Twin fragments of the azure skies

Beaming celestial blessing through
Pure chastened lids whose perfect white,
And the transparent temples too,
Are stained with streaks of delicate blue
As tender as thick-fallen snow
Deep down in crack and crevice makes
With its own shadow, when the weight
Of piled-up frail congealment breaks.—
Their hair! O take when Morning wakes
Her beams and twine them! pleach and plait
The Moon-sparks shrinking, leaping, linking,
On yonder Lake at midnight—spin them
With all the liquid gold within them
Into fine skeins of splendour! so
You best may guess how tress on tress
In long luxuriant glossiness
Its gleaming undulations flow!—
But you should see—I cannot tell—
What they resemble who so well
Attest what truth of fancy nurst
Your native myth how Woman first
Was fashioned from comminglings sweet
Of brilliant tremors of the noontide heat
  That shimmering near you, still retreat,
  And airy Echoes, sprites so shy
  Yet quick with answering sympathy,
  That ever haunting, ever hide
  Near cliff abrupt and mountain-side;—
  With just enough of added Earth
To temper charms of such etherial birth,
  Which else e'en Rapture's self would miss,
  Which else its fond embrace would fly—
To something lovelier it can clasp and kiss!"—

"And have they flaxen mantles fair
As this—with broidered border rare?
And do their greenest jewels shine
Like this pellucid jade of mine?"

"For dress they rob the sunset—take
Its gorgeous glisterings from the Lake,
Or swathe their forms in gauzy mist
The Moon might envy them at night,
Pavilioned with pure amethyst,
In pearliest virgin vesture dight!
And as for gems!—they wreathe about
Their arms that dazzle you without,
And necks, that when your eyes you shut,
Leave shapes of sinuous snowy bloom
In vivid loveliness clear-cut
And floating on the purple gloom—
Such trails of richest radiance set
In linked array of flower and fret,
As if they strung the beaded clusters,
The little lamping flame-hued lustres,
Sapphires winking, rubies blinking,
Trembling emerald-sparks, adorning
The mist-besilvered meads of morning
When first the Sun new-fires them! Aye
And always had that Sun hard by
To keep them, as his only duty,
Still bristling with all hues of beauty!"—

VIII.

But while he spoke there stole unseen
O'er Amohia's frank bright face

A shadow—as a slow white cloud
Grows over all the blue sky-space
Left by an opening in the green
O'er-roofing forest thick-emboughed,
And sheds soft gloom where light but now was shining.
He marked the mournful drooping head,
The cheek where sadly-pensive spread
The long-curled lashes low-declining :
"Yet," said he quickly, "few of those
Have such a faultless form as you,
Whose every facile movement shows
What perfect grace on perfect limbs
The perfect freedom from restraint bestows ;
Few such a blithe bright bearing ; few
Could bound as is your wont
Up the great mountain-side and chase
The shadow of the cloud that skims
Scarce fleeter in its flying race ;
Or at the summit could confront
The bland magnificence of Nature's brow
With such superb and regal innocence
And look and mien so kindred ! few have eyes
Of such a brilliant power
They take away your breath and burn
Right through your heart whene'er they turn
Their melting flashes on you ! few could shower
Such silky breadths of darkness down as now
I hold between me and their gaze,
To see if still their brightness will
Come breaking through in spurry rays
Like evening sunbeams through a thicket dense !
Yes ! howsoe'er those beings fair
With Art to aid and Culture's care

From human almost to divine may rise.
For charms like these, not many there
Could with my Wonder of the Wilds compare!"

The sunny look at once returned,
And through the clear warm brown discerned,
The blush of artless triumph burned.
Then round his neck her arms she threw
And gazed, with love how fond and true
As upon something to adore,
Upon the face above her—in that vein
When parted lips and anxious sigh confess
Content is at its highest, and the excess
Of pleasure trembles on the brink of pain;
With simplest admiration too
Reading his features o'er and o'er,
As if her eyes could never feed
Enough, nor sate her heart's impassioned greed
For what to her was beautiful indeed:
'*Kai-máta*'—'face-devouring gaze'
Her country's own poetic phrase
Had called the glance that so much love displays.
But how conceive her feeling? how
The picture fond her fancy drew,
The halo round his form she threw!
To that enamoured fancy, quite
Unused to the fair-tinted faces
Of our Caucasian northern races,
This Stranger, with his eyes of sparkling blue
That shone through shadows of a thoughtful brow
Embossed with Intellect, and full and white,
With clustered gold about it curled,
Seemed some high Being from another World!

August and beautiful and bright
To her he well might seem,
As you perchance would deem
Some Phidian Temple must have looked of old;
Where architrave and pediment arise,
With metope-squares of dauntless proud emprise,
And friezes full of life !—serenely bold
Broadly confronting the broad skies,
And throwing deep majestic shade
(As human brow o'er human eyes)
Into the interspaces made
By many a stately colonnade ;—
As such a Temple must have looked when bare
Its snowy grace and lovely grandeur first
Upon the shouting people burst !
Its solemn charm that would have awed, almost
In the mere splendor of material lost ;
Because so brilliant fresh and new,
So delicately tinted here and there
With rainbow colours pure and fair,
The sculptured Marvel stood in view ;
The matchless groups around it rife
In stirring trance of pomp or strife,
Sharp from some famous chisel, every one ;
The marble dust of recent working
In glittering specks about them lurking—
All just uncovered to the morning Sun !

IX.

But fair as Phidian Temple tinged so purely,
That pure untinged white-terraced Fount corálline
Showed, with its baths cerulean and crystálline,
Whereon they gazed when not upon each other

Their lover-gaze delightedly was dwelling;
When looks, where Love was seated so securely,
To answering looks ceased passionately telling
The tide of tenderness each bosom swelling:
Then, as they watched the huge Steam-cloud that whitely
O'er the main pool, like some nest-brooding mother,
Spread swanlike wings the brilliant water shading—
Enveloped and imparadised more brightly
In a Love-cloud as fervid and unfading,
They saw how richly, though from surface duller,
That still, suspended Mist reflected duly
The bubbling basin's amethystine colour;
Returning tint for lovely tint as truly
As in their mirrored eyes, fond, deep, untroubled,
They marked, upwelling ever freshly, newly,
Their mutual Love reflected and redoubled!

Then to the glen that fronts the islets twain
  And to their isle itself they come—
That ever-singing isle—through all the train
Of water-birds that swarm the simmering plain,
  Thick as the sower's air-scattered grain;
  And then their bower of mánuka they gain
  Already soothing with a sense of home;
  The grateful viands follow, fountain-drest;
  And then that churme monotonous, ne'er represt,
Lulls them again entranced to Love's Elysian rest.

CANTO THE EIGHTEENTH.

I.

"*Shall we run into the cloudlet, love, so luminous and white*
That is crouching, up in sunshine there, on yonder lofty height?
We could step out of the splendour all at once into the mist—
Such a sunny snowy bower where a maiden might be kissed!
From the woody lower terrace we could climb the russet steep
Near that chasm gorged with tree-tops still in shadow dewy-deep,
Where another slip of vapour, see! against the purple black,
Set on fire by the sunbeam which has caught it there alone,
Like a warrior-chief inciting his adherents to attack,
Has upreared itself upright with one imperious arm out-thrown!
Up that slope so smooth and ruddy we could clamber to the crags
To the jutting rim of granite where the crouching cloudlet lags:
In and out the bright suffusion up above there in the skies,
I would follow my fleet darling by the flashing of her eyes,
O'er that lofty level summit, as they vanished vapour-veiled,

Or would glitter out rekindling and then glance away to seek,
Like swift meteors seen a moment, for some other silver streak—
Now bedimmed and now bedazzling till each dodge and double failed,
And I caught her—O would clasp her! such delicious vengeance wreak
On those eyes—the glad, the grand ones! on that laughter-dimpled cheek,
Till with merciless caresses the fine damask flushed and paled,
And half-quenched in burning kisses those bewitching lustres quailed!"

"*Nay, but Rano, my adored one—O my heart and soul's delight!*
Scarce with all your love to lead me—fold me round from all affright—
Would I dare ascend that Mountain! woody cleft and fissure brown
Are so thick with evil spirits—it has such a dread renown!
Such a hideous Lizard-Monster in its gloomy shades it screens,
That as rugged as the rocks are, winds along the close ravines—
E'en asleep lies with them sinuous like a worm in twisted shell—
And has eaten up more people in old days than I can tell!
Would you go and wake that Taniwha! O not at least to-day:
Look how lovely calm the Lake is!—'twill be sweeter far to stray

In the blue hot brilliant noon-tide to each secret shadowy bay,
And afloat on liquid crystal pass the happy time away!"—

So he, who when he had his will,
For pleasure always went *up* hill,
So Ranolf spoke; and so replied
His wildwood bride, the diamond-eyed,
When morning's beam began to burn,
Up-springing from their couch of fern
By charming Tára-wéra's side.
A little plot of smooth green grass—
By tapering trees thick-set and tall
Beneath grey rocks that rose o'er all,
Shut in behind—a verdurous wall
Circling that lawny flat so small
Down to the very water's edge,
That spread in front its liquid glass;—
Not far from where, 'mid reed and sedge
The warm Mahana's rapid tide,
A mile-long stream scarce six feet wide,
Comes rushing through the open pass—
As seeks a hot and fevered child
Its Mother's bosom cool and mild—
To Tára-wéras' ample Lake;
This shallow niche, tree-girt and green,
With nought its still sweet charm to break,
The lovers' lonely bower had been.

II.

In sunshine stretching lightly o'er
The Lake's far end from shore to shore,

Long stripes of gauze-like awning lay—
In stripes serene and white as they,
Repeated on its bright blue floor:
And many a rocky rugged bluff,
With crimson-blossoming boscage rough,
O'er beetling crest and crevice flung;—
White cliff or dark-green hill afar
With patches bleached of scarp and scar—
Stood boldly forward sunrise-fired,
Or back in sun-filled mist retired.
Untrembling, round the glistering rim
Of that expanse of blooming blue,
From headland bright or inlet's brim,
Long fringes of reflection hung.
Its ramparts stretched along the sky,
One mighty Mountain reared on high
Far o'er the rest a level crest,
With jutting rounded parapet
And rude rock-corbels rough-beset,
Half-blurred by time and tempest's fret;
While smooth its slopes came sweeping down
From that abraded cornice brown.
The mountain this, the ruddy steep,
That Ranolf, sun-awaked from sleep,
So longed to scale; and high in air
In glad imagination share
Its sky-possessing majesty
Of haughty isolation!—there
Into each dark recess to pry
And every sight and secret see
Its lofty level might reveal,
Or those grim fissures' depths conceal,
That split the Mountain into three.

About the heights, soft clouds, a few,
Clung here and there like floating flue ;
Like helpless sea-birds breeze-bereft,
Unmoving spread their pinions white—
From jutting crag, deep-bathed in light,
To slip away in snowy flight ;
Or closely crouched in shadowy cleft,
Like lambing ewes the flock has left.
Below, o'erjoyed at darkness fleeing,
Reviving Nature woke again
To all the exceeding bliss of being !
The minnows leapt the liquid plain
In shoals—each silvery-shivering train,
A sudden dash of sprinkled rain !
The wild-ducks' black and tiny fleet
Shot in-and-out their shy retreat ;
The cormorant left his crowded tree
And stretched his tinselled neck for sea ;
All Nature's feathered favourites poured
To their adored undoubted Lord
Of light and heat, accordance sweet
Of pure impassioned revelry ;
And honey-bird and mocking-bird
And he of clearest melody,
The blossom-loving bell-bird—each
Delicious-throated devotee
In happy ignorance framed to be
Content with rapture—longing-free
For life or love they cannot reach—
Like chimes rich-tuned, to heaven preferred
The praise of their mellifluous glee ;
Each lurking lyrist of the grove
With all his might sung all his love ;

Till every foliage-filled ravine
And bower of amaranthine green
Rang persevering ecstasy.

III.

With free elastic hearts that shone
In joy as fresh as morning's own—
Each seated in a light canoe,
The kind Lake-villagers supplied—
Amo's the lighter—gayer too,
With snowy tufts of feathers tied
In rows along each ruddy side—
The pair went paddling, fancy-led;
For here no wondrous sights of dread
Or beauty lurked to guide their guest
As at Mahana—nothing strange,
Or out of Nature's wonted range:
Yet Ranolf marked with lively zest
What charms the changeful scene possest:
The billowy-tumbling hills—the crags—
The smooth green slopes fern-carpeted;
Low cliffs with feathery foliage graced;
Rock-palisades emerging pale
And grey; and precipices faced
With headstones—close-set armour-scale
Of gothic-pointed bristling flags;
Flat islets crowned with wood—cliff-bound;
And lake-side bowers and canopies;
And caves and grottos within these;
And lichened rocks that singly stand
Detached from green umbrageous land,
Mere pedestals for single trees;
Or, jutting out with jagged arms

All plumed and fair with greenery, bear
Into the Lake the forest's charms;
And with the bank that proudly swells—
A wooded wall without a strand—
Make niches, nooks, and liquid cells,
With interlacing boughs o'erspanned.

IV.

The mists were gone—the sun rode high;
On went they paddling merrily,
Each bay and cove and nook to try;
In loving converse sauntering slow
Or darting swiftly to and fro,
Except for pleasure, purposeless
As minnow-crowds whose sinuous stream
Meandering through the azure gleam
Darkened the watery depths below.
It chanced the boats a moment lay
With prows that pointed both one way,
Amo's ahead a little space:
A sudden whim lit up her face;
Then, as a challenge for a race,
She chaunted, ere away she sped,
With laughing frowns of loving spite,
Set teeth and sideways-shaken head,
Mock words of bitter-sweet delight:

"I am Hatu! I'm Hatu! poor boy of the glen
Whom the wicked witch-giantess hid in her den!
And you are the Giantess hoarding her prize
With her terrible claws—O such hideous eyes!
But I've fled from caresses I . . . hate, O so much!
Escaped from her loathsome, her horrible touch—

From her dreadful . . dear ! . . clutches escaped to the plain,
And I dare, I defy her, to catch me again ! "—

Then paddling off with all her might,
Away across the lake she flew,
And left a wake of foam snow-bright,
And broadening ripple glassy-blue ;
While, dashing after, less expert
Soon Ranolf finds he must exert
His utmost skill to catch her, too.
But when, though less by skill than strength,
He nears her flying skiff at length—
With nimble paddle, dodging back
She slips off on another tack,
With swiftly-flitting noiseless ease ;
As—when some fisher thinks to seize
With gently-dropped and stealthy spear
A flounder, down in shallows clear,
'Mid mottling tufts of dusky weeds
And white sand-patches where it feeds—
The trembling shadow shifts away
Through faintly-shimmering water grey—
'Tis there—and gone—his would-be prey !
So, hovering round with wistful eyes,
While many a feint, to cheat, surprise,
That merry mocker, Ranolf tries,
She, at a little distance staying,
And watchful, with the paddle playing,
No move of his, no glance to miss—
Now darts alert that way, now this ;
And at each foiled attempt again
Provokes him in alluring strain :

"Look! I'm one of those divine ones—joy and love of all beholders,
Who had pinions, O such fine ones! growing from their stately shoulders;
Not that fond one too confiding—so in vain your bright eyes watch me—
He, the last on earth residing . . . Ah! you need not think to catch me! . . .
Who, beside his loved-one lying, let the Maid while he was sleeping,
Press his wings off, spoil his flying—lest he e'er should leave her weeping!"—

Then off she skims in circuit wide,
Resolved another plan to try.
Again with paddles swiftly plied,
Again across the lake they fly;
And as her little bark he nears,
A new defiance Ranolf hears:

"I'm Wakatau, he—
That Child of the Sea!
And my dearest delight
Is flying my kite.
Down beneath, on the sand,
With the string in my hand,
Under water I stand;
Or the kite in the air,
Like the day-moon up there,
Like an albatross strong,
Draws me swiftly along
As I float to and fro
On the green sea below.—

Apakúra, my mother,
Can catch me, none other;
From the quickest alive,
Down—down—would I dive!—
Whoever you be—
Though fonder, though dearer,
You, you are not she,
Apakúra, O no!—
So if you come nearer,
See—down I must go!"

Scarce on the gunwale had he laid
His hand, and scarce the words were said,
Ere, slipping from her loosened dress,
Her simple kilt and cloak of flax—
Just as a chestnut you may press
With careful foot ere ripened well,
Shoots from its green and prickly shell,
With tender rind so tawny-clean
And dainty-pure and smooth as wax—
She shot into the blue serene—
A moment gleamed, then out of sight,
Swift as a falling flash of light!
All round he seeks with anxious mien
The Naiad—nowhere to be seen:
A fearful time he seems to spy—
His heart beats quick—when lo, hard by,
A mermaid! risen on the rocks,
Whose diamond glances archly play
Through shaken clouds of glittering locks,
And glancing showers of diamond-spray:
"*You are not Apakúra! O, no, no, not you!*"
She cries—and dives beneath the blue.

He follows, watching where she glides
Beneath a drooping pall profound
Of boughs, that all the water hides.
Into the gloom he pushes : sound
Or sight of her is none around.
But hark !—'twas somewhere near the bank
That sudden plash ! it takes his ear
As startlingly as sometimes, near
A stream where June's hot grass is rank,
You hear the coiled-up water-snake
Your unsuspecting footsteps wake,
Flap down upon the wave below,
And wabbling through the water go.
Again to the mid lake she hies ;
In swift pursuit again he flies :
And see ! she waits with face, how meek !
Till he can touch and almost clasp,
The shining shoulders, laughing cheek ;
Then, diving swift, eludes his grasp :
Just as, with quick astonished eye,
A wild-duck waits, until well-nigh
The ruddy-curled retriever's snap
Is gently closing like a trap
On its poor neck and broken wing,
Before with sudden jerk she dips,
Beneath the ripple vanishing.
From Ranolf so the Maiden slips—
And when, the chase renewed, he nears
The spot where next she reappears,
Look ! floating on the glass she lies
With close-sealed lips and fast-shut eyes,
Still as a Saint in marble bloom
Carved snowy-dead upon a tomb.

Close to her side his skiff he steers :
"O Swallow of the waters fleet,
O wild lake-bird ! my Swift, my sweet,
My lovely-crested grebe ! at last,
I catch, I kiss, I hold you fast !"
He takes that slender hand of hers ;
She answers not—nor looks—nor stirs ;
Surprised, her listless arm he shakes—
She neither stirs—looks up—nor wakes.
"Speak, speak, my Amo ! what is this !
Do you not feel my clasp, my kiss ?
Do you not hear my voice ?"—Ah no !
That low sad moan no answer gives :
She breathes—but heavy, stertorous, slow ;
That breathing barely shows she lives.
He felt her heart—it faintly pulsed ;
At times she shudders as convulsed ;
"Yes, it must be ! the hot, high sun
Has struck her, dear one ; too opprest,
With such exertions quite o'erdone !"
Alarmed—reflecting what were best,
He soon resolves, and does it too.
Beneath each arm with tenderest care,
He twines a tress of streaming hair,
And knots them both with double turn,
Rich-volumed to his own canoe—
The open carved work of the stern :
Then tows her senseless till they reach
The nearest stripe of sandy beach :
There leaps ashore—seeks—breaks in half,
A cockle-shell—'twill answer well :
Then finds and feels the corded vein
That crosses with its azure stain

The tender hollow of her arm,
And soon will wake the life-tide warm.
But ere the shell's sharp point can wound—
Just ere it pricks her—from the ground,
Upleaping with a silvery laugh,
The cheat confessed, she darts away,
(Snatching her mantle up that lay
In Ranolf's boat, which he had thrown
Into it as she left her own)
And to a thicket near has flown—
Swift—sudden-glancing as a bird
The loud flirt of whose wing is heard
A moment, on the hot wood-side,
As, brushing out and in again,
A scarlet gleam, you see him glide,
Lancing his dodging flight; even so
Does Amo still the chase maintain;
And Ranolf follows, with mock-angry show
Of mirthful vengeance, fondly-threatening cries,
And chastisements that are caresses in disguise.

V.

Thus ever and anon, this buoyant Child,
Free as the winds and as the waters wild,
With wayward whims the time beguiled:
Thus would the tranquil tenor of her joy
Still quicken into rapids of delight;
And break meandering into branches bright
Of manifold emotions that would rove
Diversely, but to give redoubled force
And sweet variety to one sure course—
Spreading and sparkling only to unite
In one broad current of unfailing Love.

Such simple arts would she employ
To tamper with, and tease, and toy
With her content, its depth to prove,
With sportive sallies—sly disguises,
Arch mockeries—mimicries—surprises;
So on her heart impress a sense
More varied, vivid, and intense,
Of bliss all golden-pure without alloy,
And Love no time could cool, no fond fruition cloy!

VI.

'Tis burning Noon: from heat and glare
How sweet the bower the lovers share!
A Lakeside cleft—a rock-recess
Of soft sun-chequered quietness,
A nook for lovers made express.
Like birds in some umbrageous tree
Girt round with leaves they seemed to be,
A hollow globe of greenery:
For twisting, arching, overhead
Dark serpentining stems were spread;
And arching, twisting, down below,
Stems serpentining seemed to grow;
While on a plane of light between,
Suspended lay those skiffs serene.
Sunbathed arose the dome-like roof
A strangely-splendid wondrous woof;
Whose dark-green glistening foliage seemed
Thick over-showered with shining snow,
Except where blood-red masses gleamed—
Such luminous crimson—all aglow!
White buds and opening leaves the first,
With silvery-sheening velvet lined;

The last, rich-tufted bloom that burst
Bright-bristling, with the sun behind;
As if whole trees, 'mid heaped snow-showers
Were turning into burning flowers!
Below, the pair as thus in air
Upbuoyed, a sight as fair enjoyed;
The hollow shadowy floor, o'erlaid,
Beneath the clear transparent void,
With silvery-crimson soft brocade,
To that above in shape and hue
So like, the seeming from the true
By its inversion best they knew.
It was the 'downy ironheart'
That from the cliffs o'erhanging grew,
And o'er the alcove, every part,
Such beauteous leaves and blossoms threw,
And made this cool sequestered nest
For silent, lone and loving rest.

Then for refreshment in the noontide heat,
With mockery of much ado,
And lips comprest and pursed-up too,
And little nods of playful pride,
And self-complacent confidence to win
Applause at fine arrangements so complete—
As who should say: 'Now open wide
Your eyes and see how *I* provide!—
Fair Amo with arch mimic pomp outdrew
A platted basket hid in her canoe,
Cool-packed with leaves and lightly tied—
A flax-green basket autumn-piled; wherein
Date-like karakas made a golden show
Quince-coloured and quince-smelling; faintly sweet

Soft aromatic pepper-spikes were seen ;
Potato-apples of the poro-poro tall
Rich-mellowing from their crude lip-burning green :
And, bounteous 'mid these wood-gifts wild and small,
Ripe, slippery-seeded and of juiciest flow,
Great water-melons melting crisp with crimson snow.

Nor was there lack of more substantial food,
Leaf-hidden in a smaller green flax-hamper ;
Choice too, for appetites so young and good—
As roasted wild duck, red-gray parrot stewed,
And bread in its primeval form of 'damper'—
Unleavened cakes of palatable maize
Well pounded by Te Manu, and well kneaded
By Amo, and in hot wood-ashes clean
Well baked—or rather in oven of simpler sort
Than most remote 'Stone-period' could report—
Mere flagstones laid and heated without trouble
Upon a quenchless fountain's boiling bubble ;
Flat cakes that dish and platter superseded ;
And used instead, recalled in this far scene
A moment's memory of old school-boy days
To Ranolf—that crab-apple-feasted crew
Of Ocean-wanderers, wearily reposing
In maple shadows on green sunny slopes,
And watching with dim eyes and fading hopes.
The sparkle of the sea-waves summer-beaded ;
Then fair Ascanius luckily disclosing
The prophecy's fulfilment, else unheeded,
"What ! must we eat our very tables too !"—
Nay, one more luxury swelled the savoury list—
That dainty by our daintiest humourist

So prized—roast sucking-pig ! for two of these
Nimble Te Manu had contrived to seize,
Cut off by clever doubles yesternight
From a long train that scampered after
Their grunting dam, and, driven from her track
Could not escape the youngster's clutches, though
They dodged him, as disabled half by laughter,
He obstinately chased them to and fro
An hour at least, imprisoned as they were
Between a shrunken river, and cliff chalk-white
    That wall-like rising at their back
    From the broad gravelbed upright
    Without a blade of verdure, bright and bare,
Made the small runaways look doubly black,
Doubly conspicuous in the sunset's glare.

VII.

So each as in a floating nest,
Moored side by side the lovers rest,
And catch veiled glimpses as they lie
Of splendour-flooded azure sky.
The birds that sung those matins sweet
Are silent now in slumberous heat.
In dreamy-lighted luxury
Lies Ranolf musing—marking well
Each charm of water, rock and tree
About that shadowy glimmering cell ;
The low grey cliffs with stains imbued
Of lichens white and saffron-hued,
Flat crumpled—or blue hairy moss ;
All doubled in the shimmering gloss :
Sometimes a loose-furred hawkmoth, see !
At those rich blossoms restlessly

Fumbles to suck their anthers sweet:
Sometimes, invading that retreat
Great black white-banded dragon-flies—
With green and gold-shot globuled eyes
On either side projecting wide
Like swift coach-lamps—on quivering wings
Of glittering gauze dart all about;
With tinier ones of richer dyes,
That hover—dodge aside—and fix
Themselves with those bent-elbowed legs,
And heads so loose, endlong to sticks
And twigs, and hold as straight as pegs
Their blue or scarlet bodies out;
Just as a tumbler, mid his tricks
Seizes an upright pole and flings
His particoloured legs in air,
And holds them horizontal there—
So proud to ape a finger-post.
"They were revolting, hideous things,"
Thought Ranolf, "but at least could boast
A faith that made them leave in time—
Come shouldering up through mud and slime
With horny eyes and dull surprize,
Out of the clogging element
Where their first grovelling life they spent!"—
—Meanwhile unseen cicadas fill
The air with obstinate rapture shrill—
A wide-fermenting restless hiss
Proclaiming their persistent bliss;
As if the very sunshine found
A joyous voice—and all around,
While woods and rocks and valleys rung,
In brilliant exultation sung.

And Ranolf loved—could not but prize
That tiny classic Cymbalist,
So graced with old Greek memories ;
The rapture-brimmed, rich-burnished one—
His bright green corselet streaked with jet,
His brow with ruby brilliants set—
That, undisturbed, would ne'er desist
From clicking, clattering in the sun
His strident plates—at every trill
Jerking with stiffly quivering thrill
His glassy-roofing wings ; as gay
As when two thousand years ago—
Where—through thin morning vapour gray,
With snowy marble gleams between
Blue-shadowy clefts of fragrant gloom,
Melodious ever and alive
With immemorial bees that hive
In honied thickets, lilac-green
With sage and thyme in deathless bloom—
Bare old Hymettus looked serene
O'er silvery glimpses far below
Of pure Ilyssus in swift flow
Through plains—one revel of renown ;—
The hyacinth-curled bronzed Attic boy,—
As fond of sunshine, full of joy,
In some hot mead where violets hid
Blue round the well's white time-worn trunk
Of hollow marble slightly sunk
In grass about the spring that slid
Slow-steeping crystal all the year—
Would pause beneath the olive shade
In loitering chat with one so dear,

That slim slip of a Greek-limbed Maid,
Who looks so sweetly grave upon
Sad news about their neighbour's son
Killed—since they met, at . . . Marathon !—
—Pause, in the act of sucking down
The fig she brings him—bursting-ripe,
Plump, melting-skinned, and purple-brown,
To mark their little gay compeer,
As hand in hand they draw too near,
Abruptly stilling his sweet shrilling,
And edging round his olive branch,
Backing and sidling out of sight
Of eager eyes, that gleam gray-bright,
As one fond wish the Boy expresses,
That chirper were but turned to gold
To stick in Myrrhin's golden tresses !
While not his wildest dream had told
The lad, how many an age to come,
In what far regions all unknown,
His race's merry earthborn type
Would still be singing blithe and stanch,
After its own grand Muse was dumb,
Its noisy greeds and glories gone !

So Ranolf's musing fancy strung
Together olden scenes and new ;
Or on more dubious ventures flew,
If e'er as to some bough it clung
The songster's pupa-case was seen,
Whence from his base life subterrene
He made escape in wingëd shape—
The bright transparent brittle sheath
Wherein he slept his life-in-death.

A suit of perfect armour, where
He left it Ranolf notes it still;
An open crack across the back,
And lobster-claws thrown by because
Superfluous found, his labour crowned;
The forelegs raised—'not as in prayer.'
Thinks he—"but work; for he too, mark!
Was forced to dig with strength and skill
His stout way from his dungeon dark
Up to his heaven of sunshine! Thus
From clogged and cramped existence fleeing,
He tries a second state of being
In the sphere that holds but one for us:
But both his lives to us seem one
Who see the changes undergone:
So this life and another too,
Nay, lives on lives, perhaps, of ours,
May seem but one to wider view
And keenlier-gifted loftier powers;
The subtle links *we* lose pursued,
The metamorphose understood.
But with what pitying smile must they
Look on, when with such sad array
The human insects hide away
Some care-worn soul-case out of sight—
And weep because they cannot stay
The freshwinged Soul's unfettered flight
To wider spheres and new delight!—

* * * *

"That *was* the way those types to read—
A fine old cheery way indeed.
Will Science say remorseless?—'Nay,
You must not read them so to-day.

The actual metamorphoses
Foreshadowed by—akin to these,
Are antenatal in mankind,
Gone through already. One surmise
From lingering traces undesigned
Of transformations some low grade
Of life sustained, ere birth displayed
In nascent undeveloped Man,
Might be by strictest reasoning made:
That if organic Being rise
Elsewhere upon the selfsame plan—
Continue so ascending—there
Some glorious creature might be found
Of frame more complex, powers more rare,
In whom Man's perfect mould would be
But one in its imperfect round
Of embryotic stages. Try
What help, what hope therein may lie!'—
Well, then, methinks, that surging sea
Of resonant shrill melody
Rings out a thoughtless answer free,
Whence one may frame a thoughtful plea:
'O human Insect! sad Truth-seeker—
Which of us two is wiser—weaker?
Your senses—those deep reasoning powers
You *will* within their bounds compress,
May take a wider range than ours,
How vastly wider! none the less
They both are dwarfed, unspeakably
Fall short of, and are distanced by
The infinite Reality:
And all beyond their feeble reach
Will doubtless seem and *be* for each

A blank—a void—mere nothingness!
Think you the mighty gains you boast,
The ever deepening, widening host
Of wonders Science as she presses
Into the Mystery's first recesses,
Works out, worms into, proves or guesses:—
—Creation, like a firework splendid
Ever exploding, unexpended;
As endlessly it whirls and flies
Still breaking into brilliancies
Of stranger gleam and lovelier guise:—
—Organic Nature, in its flow
By inorganic guided, so
Divinely from its hidden fount;
Germs, gemmules, cells, life-struggles dense—
And Circumstance turned God at least,
Combining, with intelligence
So matchless, to evolve and mould
Life's plastic structures manifold
To perfect tree, man, insect, beast;
With agents—climate, fire and frost,
Food, famine—skilled to crush, uphold,
Choose what had best survive or perish—
The lower to check, the higher to cherish—
Make progress sure at any cost:—
—Then all those correlated forces,
All Motion's masquerading courses;
And passing far all puny count
Of million million 'powers of horses,'
Dynamic energies immense,
At work, asleep, alike intense;
Evasive, latent—never lost—
That utterly from sight and sense

Can vanish, *imperceptible*
As any disembodied Soul,
Yet all the while about you dwell;
Until, a hundred ages hence,
Their cycle—seeming proved so well—
Of dark annihilation finished,
They reappear, alive and whole
With force and fervour undiminished!—
Think you all this, so far beyond
Our powers perceptive, would not seem
To us a blank your fancy fond
Filled with a visionary dream
As vain and baseless as you deem
All in the blank beyond your own?—
O human Insect! wiser—weaker—
O suicidal secret-seeker,
What if you left your 'types' alone
And joined our reckless rapturous Pæan
Of clear confiding trustfulness,
That once so charmed the jovial Teian,
Whose loves and lyre and brimming beaker
Were all o'erthrown by one grape-stone
That choked his life out, just as you
Your life of life by laying stress
On doubts perhaps as trivial too—
Wresting despair with so much pain
Out of a scheme not your poor brain
Nor ours can compass or contain,
Exhaust, unravel, or explain!'"—

VIII.

Still side by side the lovers rest
Afloat in that sequestered nest.

As close to Ranolf's, Amo's head
Reclined,—her silky tresses spread
Beneath, beyond his own—unrolled
In black abundance uncontrolled,
To the warm and moisture-drinking air—
A splintered sunbeam lighting there,
Upon his locks of amber gleamed,
Which so contrasted—cushioned—seemed
A moon where sable soft cloud streamed,
Or golden lustrous coronet
On funeral pall of velvet set.
O'er rocks and trees, through light and shade
His curious eyes unresting strayed;
But hers were fixed upon his face,
Their choicest, dearest resting-place!
"O Rano—" such appeared to be
The train of feelings half expressed
In murmuring words that filled her breast:
"Great is indeed my love for thee!
It seems almost a dream, even now,
These lips—these eyes—this noble brow,
These locks that like the day-break shine,
Are mine, O mine—all—only mine!
How *can* I make you know and feel
How much I love you! how reveal
My thirst for what my heart adores,
The longing of my soul for yours!—
O best I love to lie awake,
A lonely tender watch to keep
Over my trusting own one's sleep,
And think, how *can* my love be shown!—
What can I ever do to make
Myself more worthy of his own?

And almost wish your welfare less
That more might be the chance for me
To make or mend the happiness,
Health, comfort, I would have depend
On me, your dearest, only friend!
To do some little more of good
Than just preparing clothes or food;—
And I at times would almost flee
Your dear caress and company,
E'en when I know no need to go,
Just to contrive—consider—do
Some thing—some active thing for you;
As if the care itself were dear
As him I cared for!—all the same
It is my joy to trust—revere—
Look up to—as my ruler claim
And sole protector, guide and guard,—
Him o'er whose weal I watch and ward.
So would I, with the parent's love
The cherished child's affection prove;
So be the mother-bird to hold
The young one in her fond wing's fold,
Yet nestle like the fledgeling too
Beneath the breast so sheltering, true:
As if—my love, my lord, my life,
It were not all to be your wife!—
But I can never, never have
Enough of that sweet love I crave;
Can never find or feign or steal
Sufficient outlet to reveal
The burning boundless love I *feel!*
So could I anger—give you pain,
To soothe, coax, comfort you again;

Would have you sick, to nurse and tend,
And deeper love that way expend
Upon you ; have you cruel, sweet !
So might I down before you throw
Myself in self-abandonment
More utter—not to frustrate so
The working of your full intent,
But to cling to you and entreat
And clasp your knees and kiss your feet
And mercy with hot tears implore,
Only to feel myself the more
Your own—all yours—life—body—soul—
On whom no shadow of control
Shall check your power at any hour
To wreak your wildest whim or will—
To ban—to bless—to save or kill !
So would I tend—implore—offend—
Do *anything* your thoughts to fill,
Share each emotion, every thrill,
And bear an all-absorbing part
In all the beatings of your heart !
So should my Soul live, drink, and feed
On yours—its ardour-kindling spring !
For are you not—indeed—indeed—
The gulf into whose depths I fling
My all of being ; plunged and tost
In fathomless sweet fires, and lost
In this immeasurable abyss
And whirl of overwhelming bliss !
Yes, yes ! you know that you are this,
My soul-devouring, lordly bird
Of beauty ! O, with plumes so fair,
Such stately step, commanding air

And eyes so proud and free ! O whence,
Whence shall I seek new life to drain,
Win some existence back again,
But from this heart of yours alone
Which so consumes—absorbs my own !—

* * * *

So dearest, you conceive how thence
My foolish fancy, my pretence
Of drowning came ; 'twas but to hear
Your love in your lamenting—cheer
My heart with your despair and feel
The sweet sensations o'er me steal
Of your fond efforts to restore
And bring me back to life once more !—
But had I really died to-day
Think not, dear friend ! my Soul set free—
This 'Wairua'—could have fled away
To any realm where Spirits stray,
Could ever have abandoned thee !
I know, I know ! distressed, forlorn,
It could not from thy side be torn—
Would long for—linger—only rest
Near what in life it loved the best !"

IX.

"You *know* it, dearest ! and just now,
To see you looking forth and far,
As bright, soft, bold and beautiful
As some outstanding steady Star,
With full assurance so serene,
Such radiant love upon your brow—
Might make the wretch most doubting, dull,
Catch confidence from yours, my queen !"

"Nay, surely 'twere a little thing,
My soul to yours should choose to cling;
Not stay to vex, as others do,
Poor wretches who may break taboo——"

"So then you think, if this sweet breath
Were stopped—these kindling eyes were closed—
These lovely living limbs reposed
In rigid, stirless, icy death,
My loving Amo would not be
Gone—perished—done with utterly!"

"Nay, what have these to do with me—
With *me* who speak to—love you so?
How strange a fancy!—tell me then
For you know all things, you white men,
What course my Spirit, down below,
If to that land before your own
It chanced to go (I know, behind
It could not, would not stay alone!)
Should take with least delay to find
And fly to your dear heart, and show
The deep and deathless love, I know,
It would be burning to bestow?"—

"What can *I* tell you! you know more,
Dearest, yourself—as much at least;
Do you remember, once before
I told you, love, I was no priest,
No learned Tóhunga—not I——"

"But tell me what your wise men say,
And all about us when we die;
You laughed at us, I know, that day,
Too proud to give a true reply!"

"Our wise men, Amo!—sooth to say, the most
Of these, just now seem doing as one day
A great white War-chief did to find a way
O'er shallow sea-flats when the ford was lost.
Straight through the rising tide his band he sent
In all directions radiating round,
Resolved to follow him who furthest went,
And footing most secure the longest found.
So seem our Sages wandering, all and each.
Some struggle through the weltering waves and sink,
Still panting for the shore they never reach;
Some plod along complacently and think
Already they enjoy the wished-for beach;
Some crouch upon a rock-reef close at hand
Whence leads no path, and swear the vaunted land
Is but a film that dims the seeker's eye,
A passing cloud that mocks the groping band;
Content to perish where gulf-girt they stand
They hug their barren rock with dreary cheer—
Confess to no confinement—vow they hear
No wanderer's wail—no plaintive breeze's sigh,
No moanings of the melancholy main:
Life after death—that any Spirit can
Exist apart from Matter—God or Man—
To them a dream, how visionary—vain!
What their minute sensorium may contain,
What they could touch, taste, smell or hear or see,
Is all that in the Universe can be!

Did ever brain conceive an idler notion !—
Might they not just as well—these hardy men—
Strive to compress the blue tremendous Ocean
In all its dim far-sparkling boundlessness
Into yon yellow calabash ! And when
They failed—declare with confidence no less,
With self-complacent doggedness insist,
That all it would not hold did ne'er exist :
That no reflections on its outer side,
No dancing day-gleams from the waters wide,
Are any signs that Seas or Oceans roll
Beyond the circlet of that narrow bowl ?"

"Well, that I cannot understand, you know ;
But tell me what you think yourself is true ;
That I am certain must be right—and so
Will I believe, and only trust in you."

"In me, dear Child !—but that indeed
Were trusting to a broken reed !"

"That reed no whit the less shall be
A staff of trust and truth for me !"

"Well then, suppose your eyes you close,
And on my shoulder rest your head,
While lasts, my sweet ! this noontide heat,
And that shrill music sunshine-bred ;
And try to sleep while I devise
Some answer wondrous deep and wise
To my fond querist, little dreaming
What mysteries questions may comprise
To her so plain and simple-seeming."

"There—then ; I will be still as death—"
And soon the soft-recurring breath
Long-drawn, and breast that gently heaves,
Tell how the life that gushed and glanced
So brightly, lies in sleep entranced—
Sleep, placid, light and infantine—
Serene as those green-imaged leaves
That up through crystal pointing shine.

CANTO THE NINETEENTH.

I.

And what reflections took their way
Through Ranolf's mind as thus he lay
Pondering on Amo's questions, while the Maid
So lightly slumbered, lulled in noontide rest
So still, the golden spots that flecked its shade
Moved only with her moving half-hid breast?

"What must I teach her? how impress
This pliant Spirit's willingness?
On this unlettered Soul so white
What characters am I to write?
What truths in sooth have I to tell
To one whose native instincts might,
For aught I know, teach me as well?—
Where am I? let me run again
O'er facts indubitable and plain.
With nothing else have I to do
But what I know or feel is true.—

II.

"Behind this Universe—this train
Of grandest beauties, on the brain

Painted in such mysterious wise
How much is real none know—there lies
The unknown region undenied
Where (but in their effects descried)
Efficient Causes all reside.
But if all subtlest Forces—those
Perception grasps and Science knows,
That work in Nature's myriad shows,
All tend to one, and one alone—
A truth that each day clearer grows ;
Must not the mystic Fountain, whence
That one proceeds, transcending Sense,
The primal Source of power, unknown
And unperceived—be One as well,
Though nought can yet its nature tell ?

"Say you, there is no proof nor need
Of Cause—that 'tis a dream indeed
Begot by habit—but a vain
Conception of the human brain !—
'Tis answered—the idea of Cause
Is based on fundamental laws
Of human thought—with all that live
The notion is intuitive.

"You say—we can no more conceive
A thing that no beginning knew,
But has from all eternity
Existed—than a thing that grew
Or sprang from Nothing !—Well—'tis true,
Both inconceivable must be :
Yet I, for my part, must believe—

Most surely feel—while by the first
Our purest reason at the worst
Is merely overwhelmed—surpassed—
'Tis jarred—revolted by the last.

§ III.

"One cause we are conscious of—must own
Can to no Matter be assigned,—
The Will, that in our human Mind
Sets Thought in motion when we please.
Be it to demonstration shown
That Thought, once set in motion, works
Through molecules no sight can seize—
Changes in brain material—still,
That motive force, say what you will,
That primal Impulse we can lend
To subtlest matter every hour—
Deep in the Unapparent lurks,
Does our acutest sense transcend,
Yet somehow lies within our power.

"Is it so senseless then, to hold,
This Will may some faint hint unfold,
Of what in its unboundedness
Is different still beyond all guess—
The Infinite Force—unknown—untold
That still creating, still o'erseeing,
Still sets the glories we behold
For ever whirling into Being—
The Will Divine—First Cause of All,
Which GOD we in our ignorance call?—

IV.

" Be all that as it may—for me
I hold the mind so made, of course
It *must* assume the primal Force
That causes Mind, must mental be!
And does not one strange fact proclaim
The power that framed the mighty plan
Of Mind and Universe the same?
Nay, prove this bounded Mind of Man
In close accordance made, or grown,
With that all-boundless Mind unknown—
Faint spark from its omnific Flame?—
A thousand years that human Mind
Its subtle sciences designed
Of numbers—angles—ratios—lines—
Complex ingenious symbol-signs—
Pure brainwork as the wildest dream!
Then, when the long research of Time,
For Man's rapt gaze withdraws the veil
That hides the Universe sublime,
To his amazement, lo! the scheme
Of the majestic fabric stands
Before him, fitting to the Scale
So long prepared by his own hands;
In strictest keeping ranged and wrought
With fine gradations, ratios, rules,
Spun out of his unaided Thought
So many an age before, and taught
As abstract Science in his schools.
'Tis as if God himself blazed out
A moment there! beyond all doubt
Perceived—the still small voice profound
Speaking for once with trumpet-sound!

V.

"One boundless Mind first Cause of All—
That mighty fact not Physics—no,
Nor Metaphysics can o'erthrow;
Our subtlest faculties impress
Our Reason favours it, no less.
So far seems plain. But must we call
That Cause all good—that infinite Will
Omnipotent? with Evil still
So rampant? even the babe unborn
By reckless Sires' diseases torn?
The God-made cat before your hearth
Torturing the God-made mouse for mirth?

"Well, these things outrage all our sense
Of Justice—Love—Benevolence
Or Veneration; moral powers
That most exalt this soul of ours
In Being's scale; the organs, these
High sentiments, whereby alone
Perhaps 'twas meant that we should seize,
Become impressed by—apprehend
As much as need be dimly known
Of Essences that Sense transcend;
These instincts—surely in us made
Ere birth in every varying grade—
Joined to man's structure from the first
(That brain, which they so shape and mould—
By *them*, not *they* by *it*, controlled)
Surely as hunger is or thirst—
These instincts, so God-made, we say—

Make what allowances you list
For Evil's uses, ends, excuses—
Are jarred, revolted every way
That *any* Evil should exist!

"What then! why should the Power that gave
To man that *mental* standard, found
As true, complete, as wish could crave
To gauge the sensuous Universe
As its majestic shows unfurled—
Be deemed to mock, as stinted, bound
By some defect, some flaw unsound,
Man's dearer need with any worse
A standard of his *moral* World?
Our Love, distinctly his own dower
As is that calculating power—
As surely our one gauge, the best—
His spiritual Creation's test;
Why should *it* be less true, complete?
Why should *it* only prove a cheat?

VI.

"Again—the Will Divine must be
Denoted by some power at least
Of overmastering energy,
Throughout the Universe we see
Or that we see not; one whose sway
Is active—in the ascendant—free—
Ever increasing and increased;
Not one that flourish how it may—
Is worsted—weaker—giving way.
In the material World, we know,

Though Action and Re-action show
Equal and needed both ; although
Both motion and inertness seem
Balanced—essential to the scheme ;
Yet so-called Matter, in the last
Result of that harmonious strife,
Is whirled into victorious life ;
Resistance in the glorious sum
Of things, is overborne, surpassed—
If still renewed, is still o'ercome.
Well, what results is what is willed—
The intended—that which is fulfilled.
So in the moral World—the Good
Is counteracted and withstood
By Evil ; yet this last, 'tis clear
(The matter of the moral sphere)
Is found, as the long centuries roll,
Still more and more subdued—outdone ;
Of those two forces, on the whole
The losing and the lessening one.
Although the contest ceases never,
Though nothing may the two dissever,
Though Evil may the stuff supply
Good works on—*here* has being by ;
Yet, as Time flies, who can deny,
For guerdon of the World's endeavour,
Good triumphs—there is Progress ever !—
No doubt, the single Will Divine
Decrees and works both powers ; as, when
A rower directs a pair of sculls,
With one hand backs, the other pulls—
Both acts are caused by one design.
So Evil seconds Good ; but then

The most triumphant element,
The victor principle, must best
That Universal Will suggest,
Best argue the Supreme Intent.

"So even in the World we see,
Good grows—and grows unceasingly:
This Will must therefore be confessed—
As far as our Experience shows,
Or finite faculties disclose
Its working—on the whole to tend
Triumphantly to some great end
In harmony with that high test
Itself first planted in Man's breast,
With this intent among the rest.

VII.

"But why, because that mighty Will
Cannot be said, within the bound
Of our perceptions to fulfil
All that the test, so true and sound,
Demands—insists on; why declare
Its wondrous working ceases where
Our poor perceptions do?—why fear
To say that what it breaks off here
It perfects in some other sphere?
Why carry through all Time and Space
The flaw we only *know* has place
Within the narrow field we trace?
Why this avowed, yet finite Wrong,
Into the Infinite prolong?—
More true to Reason 'tis, to trust
That standard of the Good and Just

And Loving—trust its dictates too.
If *this* world wrongs that standard true,
It wrongs *God's* Love, *God's* Right no less;
That wrong his justice *must* redress:
And how? but by some other state
Where compensation must await
All wrongs endured by small or great;
All Love's requirements be supplied—
The God-given standard justified?

VIII.

"Aye truly! and as when by mere appliance
Of that brain-fashioned scale of Abstract Science
To the Star-worlds on high, diviners bold
Have sometimes found a gap—declared a flaw
In our serenest dance of sister spheres;
And with a god-like confidence foretold
The missing Planet needed by their law:
And when the optic tube, redoubling sight,
Comes in the course of long-revolving years
To test the startling prophecy aright—
Lo! there the cinders of the crumbled World,
Of proper weight, in fitting orbit hurled!
Or down in some obscure recess of Space,
Lo! there the lurking lost one they will trace,
And in some shining crowd you least suspect,
The furtive golden fugitive detect!—
Even so—when Love, that test diviner far,
Finds mightier flaws the moral fabric mar,
With full assurance may he not foretell
Some compensating cure must somewhere dwell—
Some good that shall the sense of wrong dispel?

And if immortal Life and nothing less
Be needed that deficience to redress,
Is it a splendour of too vast an orb,
Too bright for those whose gloom it should absorb—
Too grand a boon by Man to be enjoyed,
With his material kinship to the clod?—
Nay—'tis a speck to Him who left the void;
A World to *us*—a tiny Asteroid
To the infinite Munificence of God!

"Well then—through all that glittering mystery
Man sees that each demand brings its supply;
Responsive forces each stray force correct,
All waste restored, all aberrations checked;
Till perfect in all parts before him stands
The mighty structure from the Master's hands.
With no harsh note—no inharmonious noise,
Vast Worlds in myriads wing their flight sublime;
Their balanced whirl no chance, no change destroys;
But every pebble finds its counterpoise,
And every Star comes rounding up to time!—
So were the Spirit-World found perfect too
Could we its whole completed cycle view;
No wrong its neutralizing right would miss;
No sorrow some equivalent of bliss;
And every Soul whate'er its make or mood,
Though long or short the circuit it pursued,
Come brightening back at last to happiness and good!

—"Enough—enough! I feel, I see
The Cheerful still the True must be!
Look up, my love! nor longer keep
That sweet pretence of trustful sleep:

I know beneath each full-orbed lid,
The coiled-up living lustre hid,
Lurks ready for an innocent dart,
Not aimed at, sure to hit, the heart;
And round the placid lips the while,
Dawns the faint twilight of a smile.
Then listen, love! and let me try
To queries wide some weak reply!"

IX.

So then he told her of one Spirit for ever
Unknown; invisible—intangible—
Inaudible; whose nature none can tell;
Subtler than Thought in essence; and yet never
To be disproved—discarded—disavowed;
Educing Good with infinite endeavour
From Evil for some mystic end allowed;
Whose work, Mankind, would be a cheat detected,
A palpable abortion and confusion
(Truly an inconceivable conclusion!)
If not in some serener Sphere perfected:
For He was good—all Life and Time proclaimed it,
Where good was ever in the slow ascendant;
And that blind bias—Conscience, as we named it—
Towards what seems good and better—though dependent
On other powers, for knowledge, be it granted,
Of what *is* good and better—was implanted
Within our brain at first, and could not be
Belied or outraged by Himself who framed it;
So must the Evil and the wrong be righted
In some great World of bliss we could not see,
Where suffering innocence would be requited,
And ties of rent affections reunited.

And this, which Reason pleaded for—the best
And brightest of that Spirit's emanations—
Souls in their very structure, revelations
Of his high nature on their own impressed,
Had felt and died for; on the facts insisting
Their souls were forced and fashioned to attest—
The certain Life immortal, to remove
And remedy all mortal woes existing—
And that supreme predominance of Love!
And therefore they who most their Souls may nourish
On Love, and hearken to his high decreeing—
Doing all right and every wrong repressing,
With pure self-sacrifice for others' blessing—
Must be the least unlike that Power supernal—
Most with that Will in their poor way agreeing;
Must be the fittest to survive and flourish
In that transcendant Sphere of Life eternal—
Of ever blest and beatific Being.

X.

Poor, vague, and disappointing merely
These reasonings to the listening Maid appeared;
Scarce lighting up that shadowy Life more clearly
Than the rude faith wherein she had been reared.
Some simple tale of pathos and pure wonder,
The founts divine of pity and awe unsealing,
With death's great mystery mystically dealing,
Her mental clouds had sooner rent asunder—
More strongly stirred her fancy and her feeling.
But all was Gospel from his lips that fell;
His tongue more gifted than with Prophet's spell;
And what *he* felt might well for her suffice,
Who, free from anxious fear too curious, nice,

Held this no theme to handle too austerely,
Wholly absorb, or trouble her too nearly!
Her lovelit bosom knew no listless pining
For future worlds or lives beyond divining,
With so much glory in the present shining:
And Ranolf had no taste for doubts intrusive,
Nor chafed too much at reasons inconclusive.
The mystery of the mighty Universe
He loved to play with as a subtle jest,
As children with conundrums—none the worse
Because the answer could not soon be guessed.
While its reality was a pure joy
That well might heart and life and love employ—
A bliss no doubt, no mystery could destroy.

And though he showed himself content no more
Even now than in old student-days of yore
To practise and abide by what he saw
Even then might be for Man a settled Law;
He could not, while he reasoned, quite forget
The possible truth so long before descried,
Which of itself had made him feel as yet
How slight his power to be that Maiden's guide—
That time-developed secret of the soul,
How the conviction of its glorious goal
And ultimate high destiny divine,
Is haply not designed to be the dower
Of any play of intellectual power—
No cold deduction Logic's subtlest line
Could dimly draw from shadowy postulate,
Mental or moral axiom overfine,
Admitted or disputed, as innate
Or for purblind Experience to acquire;

No theme to wrangle on with wordy strife:
But down—far down—in gulfs of Spirit profound,
Which action and keen passion only sound—
Lies, a pure gem for purified desire;
But rather, perfect gold by patience won,
Must by severer Alchemy be run
Out of each Soul plunged in the actual fire,
And smelted in the crucible of Life.

No! he could not forget that Truths like these
May lurk secreted for the Soul to seize
Out of the chaos of her own emotions—
Heights of celestial rapture—depths like Ocean's
Of sacred sorrow; mystic yearnings speech
Is speechless for, no intellect can reach;
Divinely-darkling inmost sympathies,
Dimly discerned—awakened—half-exprest,
Haply by the blind might of Music best,
Echoing Infinitude; 'strange melodies'
That lustrous Song-Child languished to impart,
Breathing his boundless Love through boundless Art—
Impassioned Seraph from his mint of gold
By our full-handed Master-Maker flung;
By him whose lays, like eagles, still upwheeling
To that shy Empyrean of high feeling,
Float steadiest in the luminous fold on fold
Of wonder-cloud around its sun-depths rolled.
Whether he paint, all patience and pure snow,
Pompilia's fluttering innocence unsoiled;—
In verse, though fresh as dew, one lava-flow
In fervour—with rich Titian-dyes aglow—
Paint Paracelsus to grand frenzy stung,
Quixotic dreams and fiery quackeries foiled;—

Or—of Sordello's delicate Spirit unstrung
For action, in its vast Ideal's glare
Blasting the Real to its own dumb despair,—
On that Venetian water-lapped stair-flight,
In words condensed to diamond, indite
A lay dark-splendid as star-spangled Night:—
Still—though the pulses of the world-wide throng
He wields, with racy life blood beat so strong—
Subtlest Assertor of the Soul in song!—
—No! with that possible Soul-truth full in sight,
'Twas little disappointment, less surprise,
To Ranolf that he read in Amo's eyes
Not all the satisfaction and delight
She looked for when the queries first she pressed
Which he with more delight and greater zest
Would doubtless, if he *could*, have set at rest.

But all these things apart—to *them* the Real
The Present seemed so rapturous an Ideal,
It seemed almost a sin to speculate
Or spend a thought upon another state;
Seemed flat ingratitude to Him who spread
A banquet so superb his guests before,
To ask, when on its dainties they had fed,
What his great bounty had provided more?
While sitting at his luxury-laden board,
To guess what fair festivities the Lord
Of the redundant feast had yet in store,
Music or dance to follow when 'twas o'er.

XI.

And so to lighter themes they gaily turn;
And "Rano! when shall I begin to learn"—

Said then the lively girl, "the white man's art
Of seeing talk—and sending, word for word,
To distant eyes unspoken speech unheard?"—
And Ranolf straightway hastened to impart
A first fond lesson in the mystery deep
Of letters—guiding that confiding hand
To trace huge characters on marbled sand,
Or clean smooth claystone of some yellow steep;
With many a toying frolicsome reproof,
And merry chiding, when the stalk of fern
And taper fingers seemed resolved to turn
Some curve from what was aimed at far aloof;
And both would join in joyous outcry wild
At each great blunder of the Woman-Child;
With childlike guerdon of a kiss no less
Rewarded at each wonderful success.
But such a keen and kindling sympathy
Between their hearts and minds electric played,
Both Taught and Teacher could delighted see
How swiftly and how sweetly, so conveyed,
The pupil would imbibe that mystery;
How soon that lovely Learner would o'ercome
The task of noting down in symbols dumb
The speech the learner with her loving smile
Was teaching to the Teacher all the while.

XII.

And now, upon a knoll beside the Lake,
Embowered with trees their resting-place they make;
The savoury light repast was over, won
By Manu's indefatigable gun,
Whose echo through the day they oft had caught
Faint from the glens or o'er the waters brought.

Their young elastic spirits they resigned
To the soft hour's delicious influence,
And the full consciousness of all the bliss
Of love like theirs in such a life as this;
As sweet and free to their enamoured sense
As the pure air without a sound or sigh
They breathed in its sunlit serenity.
The solitude—the stillness so intense—
The blue ethereal lake—the liquid sky—
The silent banks and bluffs that watched around;—
The silent beams that broadly visible streamed
Through limpid veils of atmosphere, and gleamed
Along the silent hills that looked, spell-bound,
As if they felt the shadows o'er them grow,
From every fold and crevice creeping slow
And linking to exclude each slanting ray
That slumberous on their burnished shoulders lay;—
Or where those faint cliffs seemed in fading day
Refining to a vision far away—
Soft tints aërial—tender streaks of shade,
Or mottling stains their painted verdure made;—
All was so rapt and mute and motionless—
The pictured dream of lonely loveliness
Diffused o'er hearts that needed no such balm
The soft contagion of its soothing calm!
Twin hearts—mere atoms in the wide expanse—
They seemed absorbed in its voluptuous trance;
Yet 'twas the rapturous love that through them thrilled
That rather into Nature's frame instilled
Their own impassioned warmth, until it glowed
As fit for spirits in bliss some high divine abode!

Now Sunset's hushed and awful Splendour fills
The solemn scene ;—transfigures heaven and earth
With luminous glory as in strange new-birth ;
Clothes with vermilion woods the Eastern hills ;
And where the Lake should spread its glassy length
Leaves a great hollow of one hue—blood-red
As the mysterious garments round Him rolled
Who travelling in the greatness of his strength,
In glory of apparel unalloyed,
Though stained like one who doth the winepress tread,
From Edom and from Bozrah came of old.
A single bar of light, a silver thread—
Stretched o'er the incarnadined and hollow void—
Betrays the viewless surface. On each hand
See how the headlands glow in solid gold !
See in the midst that mighty Mountain stand
One ruby !—deepening off through bluer shade
And bluer, towards the North the hills and sky
Lose more and more of that ensanguined dye—
Through all the purples of the pansy fade ;
And in their darkest, most impressive gloom,
Rival the richest violet's loveliest bloom.

And Amo felt the evening ;—felt
The solemn tenderness that dwelt
In all that gorgeous flood of pride
And splendour, spreading far and wide
Into her kindred spirit melt :
And nestling close to Ranolf's side
As half in sport and half in fear—
"Hush !"—whispered she, quite serious-eyed—
"Some awful Spirit must be near !—

What is it else that from the deep
Abyss o'erhead, seems so to creep
And creep—and ever nearer steal,
As though the heavens above us bending
Were closing round us—slow descending !—
Not evil though, that Spirit, I feel !
But like some gentle boundless arm
Encircling us—in shelter warm
Infolding us from hurt or harm ;
Close to us, yet unheard, unseen :
Just as I felt you bending down
One morn above our couch of fern,
Which you had left so soon, to learn
What bird it was whose strange new cry
('Twas that blue crane with bristly crown—
You recollect ?) we heard so nigh ;
And I, unknowing your return
Lay half-awake nor wooing sleep ;
With eyes just lightly shut to keep
Your image there with clearer glow,
And play with it in fancy so ;
In dreamy bliss—such full content—
Somehow as calm and innocent,
It seemed, as when in infant days
Upon a mother's breast I leant ;
So loath was I my lids to raise ;
Or my fantastic joy resign
Till I should be no more alone !—
But you had stol'n towards me unknown ;
And though I neither saw nor heard,
I felt your face approach my own :
Your lips were almost touching mine,
But did not—and no limb you stirred ;

I neither heard nor felt your breath,
For you were silent—still as death ;
And yet I knew your presence dear,
I knew that it was *you* so near,
Pausing before you would impress
To wake me quite, some light caress
Of fond and playful tenderness.
But that was Love—made me so wise,
To see without the use of eyes ;
And know who 'twas did by me stand,
Without the aid of ear or hand :
No tongue to speak—no limb to move,
Was needed for my heart to prove
That near approach of Love to Love !"—

"Yes—that was Love ! and this, as well,
This solemn, sweet, absorbing spell,
This charm diffused o'er heaven and earth,
In Love may have its hidden birth !
For all that Reason—Science—guess,
It stands a mystery, none the less ;—
A symbol, why not so designed
To do just what we find it do ?
Impress upon the human Mind
A soothing sense of Love as true,
As warm and true as mine and thine,
But infinite—and *all* divine !—

XIII.

"But see ! how through the floating, thin,
And tender purple gloom, one star
Is wildly throbbing—faint and far !
And lost in liquid twilight, look,

Where others lurk its depths within !—
Come, dearest, then ! in yonder nook
See how, from its sun-smitten slopes
The snowy-crimson trees outthrow
Their sturdy stems that downward grow,
All firmly laced, securely braced
And cabled to the rocks with ropes
Of their own branches, backward bent
Along each coalescing trunk,
Half in its rugged column sunk
As up to roots again they run,
Stem, branch, and root, distinct yet one !
As if they saw and would prevent,
With conscious aim intelligent,
The great tree's risk so imminent
Of slipping down the steep descent.
But does the risk produce the aim ?—
On level ground no cables sprout :
Or if in some rare case thrown out—
Perchance where casual winds create
A partial risk, but not the same—
The listless cable seems to fall
Unreaching earth ; its would-be roots,
A tuft of red abortive shoots.
Adaptive Nature's powers are great ;
And her organic products mate
And match each shifting change and chance
Of inorganic Circumstance ;
Set each to each in ordered dance,
With a discriminating might
Of blindness keener than all sight ;
And kindling here, and quenching there
At random—but with luck so rare

And mutual, ever full and fair
The cycle of Existence leave.
The trees that could their cable weave
Might stand—and those that could not—fall ;
I wonder what the cause they call,
Gave this and not some other tree
That cunning first propensity
For veering cables out at all !
No matter, sweet, since there at last,
The pendent trees are anchored fast.
Suppose a fern-filled mat we sling
To one, up high, of those that fling
Their branches out most straight and stout ;
So fine the night we need devise
No roof against those loving skies !
How pleasant there to lie awake
And try if any glimmering sheen
Or shimmer of the sleeping Lake
So far beneath—through all the green,
The latticed screen of boughs between,
A leafy labyrinth—could be seen !
How sweet to lie up there so high,
And half asleep, so drowsily,
To all the faint night-noises hark
That make the hush more deep ; and mark,
Watching the dim o'erbrooding sky,
How one by one and two by two
The moving stars come blinking through
The unmoving leaves—chink after chink—
Slow-pacing !—or if you should sleep
I might alone a vigil keep
Sometimes for mere delight ; and think
What mighty Suns we use to link

Our tiny memories with ; and how
Keen Sirius and red-flashing fierce
Aldebaran that deep Space may pierce,
And have no other end just now
For me, but with familiar rays
To call back far-off scenes and days :
How the faint Pleiads are less clear
Than fond regards they bring—so dear !
And old Orion upside down,
Mythic Bœotian huntsman brown—
Though here such different names he own,
Shines grand as his antique renown ;
And flings abroad his giant limbs
In daring splendour nothing dims !
Although head foremost towards the sea
In all his glittering panoply
He plunges, eager to return
To those dear glorious lands below,
Far down below, where long ago
I first beheld his ardours burn !—
And we will settle, nestling there
Which way to-morrow we shall fare ;
If back to strange Orákei's stream
Whose dark-green banks are chequered bright
With many a gaudy scar and seam
Sulphureous yellow—red and white,
Where over crusted strata grey
A hundred hot-springs steam and play :
Or shall we to the Lake hard by
Of woody Oka-réka hie,
That mocks you with deceitful mien,
By loving cliffs encompassed round—
Fair captive, so resigned, serene,

Lulled in a seeming sleep profound;
Yet all the while slips off unseen
In secret diving underground;
And bursts out into open day
A beautiful Cascade, they say,
All flash and foam, a mile away!
A sudden startling change, complete
From mimic death to leaping life,
As yours, my wily, winsome cheat,
This morn when starting to your feet
At touch of that rude ready knife!"

What answer? but a laugh of fond assent
From her whose head upon his shoulder leant;
As, gaily springing up, the Maid addrest
Herself to that delightful task—to aid
In building birdlike such a pendulous nest
Mid twisted stems over the waters thrown,
As charmed with thoughts of airy rest
Lightly leaf-canopied and star-inrayed;
Toyed with by tender touches of the Moon;
Bare to each influence of the fine-flecked skies;
And yet secure as ever flung the boon
Of sweet unconsciousness o'er lovers' eyes—
Yet in secluded luxury uplaid
As ever rest enjoyed by lovers lone
In any green serenity of shade.

* * * * * *

XIV.

So through the fervid Autumn's lingering glow
But Life and Love's young Spring-time; revelling so

In Eden-scenes as lovely-strange
As to the lover's power to change
All scenes to Edens, ever yet displayed
An Eden ready-made:
So, custom-licensed to be blest and bless
In luxury of lawful lawlessness,
Did our unbridled bridal pair
Pass their wild-honeymoon no moon
Restricted—and, arriving all too soon,
Homeward to Roturua slowly strayed.

CANTO THE TWENTIETH.

I.

I.

THE clashing of Tempests!
The tumult of Tempests!
To the West and the North
On their terrible path
They are rioting forth;
And they crash altogether in a whirlwind of wrath
Against the high fortress that bristles and towers
In the midst of the torn Rotorua. How cowers
The scared Lake!—how it shrieks—do you hear it?
As the lightnings spear it,
And savagely chase
In the race
Of affright
The mad-fleeing flakes of the wind-levelled spray;
Or shrivel, in flame-sheets how blindingly bright,
Black tangible night
To blue hideous day!—
O the clashing, the flashing, the tumult, the jar,
Of the gathered confederate tempests of War
Over Mókoi-ahía!

2.

See, see you the glare,
O Riri, the glare?—
How the flames leap in air,
Bloodstaining the leaden-hued murkiness scowling
O'er the high Western hills where the tempests are howling,
Paparáta, Wainúku, with thunderclouds growling?—
—No fire, no flashes,
Erelong shall be there,
No life-spark or love-light on mountain—in vale;
Not a sound of despair,
Sorrow-breath,
Sob of wail—
But the blackness of ashes,
The silence of Death,
Over Mókoi-ahía.

3.

Come forth, my Canoe,
My glorious Canoe!—
Right over the war-boats of Tangi,
Right over their gunwales though fiercely they strive,
Thou shalt drive, thou shalt drive,
While the paddle-beat foam-waves enwreathe us, ha! ha!—
Resistless—remorseless—right onward—no check—
Thou shalt tread down and trample each plunging wreck!
Thou shall ride
In thy pride
O'er its hollow inside,
While the hissing wave fills it beneath us, ha! ha!—
O my tearing, all-daring, unsparing Canoe—

O the might,
The delight
Of your conquering crew !—
What a tustle shall wait them,
A triumph elate them,
A blood-revel sate them,
At Mókoi-ahía !

4.

Weave the great Chain—
The great living Chain !—
Over hill, over plain,
Round and round, high and low,
It shall go, it shall go,
The beleaguering Chain round the Fort of the foe !—
I-ará ! I-ará !—
Firm shoulder to shoulder, every inch of the ground—
Strongly woven—well-knit—all the links true and sound—
Around and around shall the great Chain be wound !
High and low
It shall go
Round the fear-smitten foe !—
Soft-stealing — close-hemming — all-stemming — death-dealing—
O the leaguer of heroes
At Mókoi-ahía !

5.

How fretful the cries,
The plaintive wild cries
Of crimson-billed terns when in bright azure weather
They flock wheeling in from all parts of the skies,
Confusedly fluttering and huddling together

To dabble and scramble for food in the water!—
Rotorua's proud islet shall see such a muster;
From the regions all round so our victims shall cluster!
So shall they
On that day
Crowd in helpless array,
So be gathered at once all together for slaughter!
Wild-crying—no flying—all dying—no trace
Of their race
Shall be left on earth's face!—
Thus our foes shall be crushed
And the battle-roar hushed
Over Mókoi-ahía!—

Such was the purport of the measured roar,
A warrior-crowd by Rotorua's shore
From time to time across its waters flung,
Their wild excitement growing as they sung.
The song foreshadowed vengeance long-desired;
Visions of victory hate and hope inspired—
But vengeance doubtful—victory yet to win.
One singer fierce in savage solo first,
Within the space the circling throng left clear,
Darting about with madly brandished spear,
The ranting wild war-ditty would begin;
Then as they all struck in, the chorus strong,
Now full and furious, with a sea-like burst
Of guttural thunder grandly rolled along;
Now at the war-chaunt's pauses, interspersed
Its short harsh sighs of deep-lunged expiration,
Such as a pavier in a London street
Gives when his ponderous hammer strikes the stones;—
All panting forth in unison complete

Hoarse harmony of heartfelt execration!
Crash after crash of deep earthshaking groans,
Whose echoes through the folded mountains tore—
Escaping monsters, plunging on to hide
In their recesses; nor even then forbore
But far and farther off faint bellowings plied.

II.

This storm of war by Kangapo was brewed:
'Twas he had roused this raging multitude
Of Uri-wéra, Nati-pórou—all
The restless spirits turbulent and rude
Amid the neighbouring tribes, South, East or West
He found, or made, obedient to his call:
For stung by Tangi's cool disdain—his breast
Black with foul bile that Amo could arrest
His schemes by flight; and worst, that such a prize
Should by this chance-sent Stranger be possessed—
One whom he would so heartily despise,
But that he hated him so much, and feared,—
Aye, feared!—he could no more endure those eyes
That met his own so calmly and appeared
To look right through his soul and life of lies,
So high and safe above his sorceries—
More than the hound the Moon's unmoving gaze
Fixed on him mutely till he howls—and feels,
How through his canine consciousness it steals—
The fascination of those searching rays,
That read his inmost thoughts, know all his ways,
And fix him all the more, the more he bays:—
Stung with such rabid jealousy and pain,
Less for his own loss than the other's gain:—

For he was of a nature Hate could move
More deeply even than successful love ;
And even his Love burnt livid, like the flames
Of liquids lit for joy in Christmas games,
With bitter selfishness 'twas so imbued ;
While Hate that could through Love's triumphant mood
Survive, on baffled Love would surely prey
And batten into boundless life and play :—
With all these feelings fuming thus, the Priest
Had sought out Tangi's many secret foes
And hollow friends ; these—most in peace retained
By dread of Tangi, and as great at least
Of powers himself from his dark Atuas gained—
Were prompt to seize whatever chance arose,
That seemed to promise surety of success
Against a Chief, whose frank blunt haughtiness
Left many a rankling grudge, in hearts that owned
His chieftainship while backed by strength ; and more
In neighbours not dependent ; most of whom
Could always point, besides, to some heirloom
Of injury—ancient grievance safe in store
Kept to produce, parade as unatoned,
Harangue on and grow wild about, whene'er
Interest might prove a breach was worth their care.
And now that Priest's defection—proffered aid
To Tangi's foes, such tempting juncture made !
That sorcerer's help, to warn, foresee, foretell,
And ever keep at hand, whate'er befel,
The fresh reserve of some religious spell
The fiercest Atua's favour to compel—
With such ally what could against them be
The force or fortune of the "Wailing Sea"?—
And readier even than these for reckless raid

Was many a youth with jealous fury fired,
Who, when that liquid landslip set her free
From bonds the "tapu" had around her knit,
To Amo's hand had fruitlessly aspired.
So, mustering quick in arms—sharp lances fit
For thrust or whirl; flat spears with cleaving blade
Of iron-hard wood; smooth clublets of green jade
Whale's bone or black obsidian: and, though few,
The white man's lightning weapons dearly prized
For such death-dealing powers, swift, safe, and true
As made all slaughter's ruder tools despised:—
—Bearing of berries dried sufficient store,
Hinau—karaka, sun-cured fish and maize—
Their siege-provisions for not many days,
As trusting to catch Tangi unprepared
And take his fortress by surprise before
His distant friends could to the rescue pour:—
—Dragging—(by dint of desperate labour, shared
Among thick-crowding, oft-renewed relays—
A hundred straining limbs and voices timed
As one, by that wild chaunt in chorus chimed)—
Or carrying bodily—their big canoes,
O'er hill and dale, with fierce incessant toil,
And frantic ardour nothing could infuse
But rampant greed secure of blood and spoil:—
—Leaving the friends of Tangi as they passed—
Too weak alone, each hamlet, to withstand
The headlong progress of so large a band,—
Within their palisadoes shut up fast:—
Thus had the host with hopes of victory flushed,
Through Tangi's country unimpeded rushed;
And now were camped by Rotorua's Lake
In swarms resolved his island-fort to take,

Under the leadership of one, by far
The boldest, vainest that had joined the war—
And "WHETU-RIRI" named—"The Angry Star."

III.

Nor deem that Priest had wholly laid aside
The object of his passion and his pride
So long—his native tribe's success and power.
Incensed to be so baffled and defied,
His aim in giving Tangi's foes their hour
Of partial triumph, was but to reduce
The Chieftain's haughtiness till he should be
More pliant to his own ascendancy.
These crowds were tools and creatures for his use;
For well he knew whenever he might please,
He could the tumult he had raised appease;
Upon their superstitious fears could play,
And fright his new adherents from the fray
With well-invented omens of dismay.
This crooked course to so concealed an end,
Did to his mind his project recommend;
'Twas doubly dear to him to win his will
By secret exercise of sinuous skill;
The consciousness of cunning mastery made
A guerdon of success almost as dear
As aught for which his cunning schemes were laid.
Yet would he not even then, with insight clear,
Deliberate purpose to himself confess,
With cool deceptive art to forge or feign
Omens and signs sinistrous, to restrain
The assailants at the height of their success;
But he had taught himself to think and feel
The Atuas ever favoured his appeal—

Could with a little management be brought
To give him mystic aid whenever sought.
And at the outset, glad was he to find,
Tangi's own acts to aid his plans inclined ;
For the old Chief was so devoid of fear,
When rumours of invasion reached his ear
By foemen such as these, the thought he spurned,
A notion too absurd to entertain ;
And still refused, when surer news he learned,
With obstinate and absolute disdain,
To sanction against danger threatening thence,
Any unwonted measures of defence.
So when the storm broke o'er him, and he found
The tide of War advancing all around,
He gathered hastily a sturdy band
Of staunch adherents readiest to his hand :
And on that island hill-cone, girt and swathed
In tiers, with terrace, ditch and smooth-scarped bank,
Where'er its natural slope less steeply sank ;
Each terrace a successive fighting stage ;
Behind each fosse, a bristling palisade
Of posts with carved and monstrous heads arrayed,
Red-ochred, grim, and grinning scorn and rage ;—
There they ensconced themselves to wait unscathed
Till succours should be hurried up by sure
And faithful emissaries swift despatched ;
There, in their fortress, as they felt, secure—
Withdrawing from each ditch its wooden bridge,
Lifting each terrace-ladder o'er its ridge,
Each gate closed fast—there scornfully they watched,
Behind the walls, each movement of the foe ;—
Or frantically darting in and out
The palisades, kept rushing to and fro

With wild-tossed limbs and yell and taunting shout ;
Or wasting at long range a charge or two
Of precious ammunition, if it chanced,
Prowling about, a prying war-canoe
Close to the isle too temptingly advanced ;
Or some marauding, reconnoitring band
Upon the garden-level dared to land.—
Thus, keeping ever at the boiling fret
The fury that could find scant outlet yet,
Thus did they shout, from morn to even close,
Or dance defiance of their swarming foes.

IV.

Twice had the foe made fierce attack ;
With slaughter twice been beaten back ;
For Tangi's staunch and stalwart band—
The skill and valour far-renowned
That marked the veteran's cool command—
The lines that wound that hill around—
And last, not least, unknown before,
The dreaded weapon Ranolf bore
That through the press could swiftly hurl
A shower of deaths at every whirl—
All these together made a sum
Of tough impediments no rush
Of Uri-wéra's hosts could crush,
Or arts, so far essayed, o'ercome.
Yet for a fresh assault, one more
Ere they should give the contest o'er,
They roused, revived their flagging force
And spirit dashed by ill-success ;
Revolving every rude resource
Of savage war's ingeniousness ;

Each tried, untried, expedient
Old lore could teach, new craft invent;
And plying all the wild man's ways
Their forced factitious wrath to raise
And blow their fury to a blaze.

V.

—But who can dwell with much delight
On details bare of barbarous fight?
War stripped of that superb disguise
Of splendour which to youthful eyes
Gives Terror more than Beauty's charms,
And o'er Death's revel scatters rife
Stern raptures of sublimest Life?
The marshalled ranks—far-glittering lines;
And square on square compact and dense—
Each layer-like slab of life intense
That firm as bristling rampart shines
In such high-drilled magnificence!
The single tramp and serried arms
Of myriads moved like one together!
The bayonet-blades—each row of steel
Soft waving like a brilliant feather,
As in broad lines the regiments wheel—
How in the sun they flash and quiver!
The ponderous flying guns that cling,
Like savage birds of heavy wing,
And clutch at every vantage ground,
And with volcano smoke and sound
Exulting boom and blaze away;
Or flit when they no more may stay,
As vultures lagging leave their prey!

Then Music's thrilling witchery,
From Matter's gross enthralment ever
Potent the spirit to deliver,
Fans all the Soul to fever-heat ;
The big drum's distant windy beat,
Tumultuous-heaving stormy sea,
Over whose plunging waves alway
The fife's light notes dance up like spray !
And trumpet's soar and bugles call ;
Or, loud in fits far rattling, comes
The glorious long-resounding shiver
Of those impatient kettle-drums !—
—But more than Music—more than all
Imperial pomps and prides that shine
To make Destruction's Art divine,
Is that display, the grandest still
To any human lot can fall,
When Genius with consummate skill
Wields the ennobling sword it draws
Resistless in a righteous cause :
Such as our wondrous Warrior drew,
To Duty God had set him to,
Ever like an Archangel true !
Whose Soul to that unsetting Sun—
The denselier rolled the storm-clouds dun
Of Fate—still soared on steadier wings ;
A soul, a mien—godlike—serene—
'Mid tumbling thrones and trembling kings !
—Or that high-passioned One—our loved
Sea-King—whose frail war-shattered frame
Seems, like the Sun's disc in its flame,
Lost in his Spirit's blaze of Fame ;
That fiery soft great heart sublime,

Who with his stately white-winged crowd
Of lightning-bearing Sea-Swans, moved
Majestical from clime to clime,
And, wrapped in one sky-reaching shroud
Of dense white level-jetted cloud,
With grand sea-thunders swept away
His country's foes where'er they rose ;—
Who, with such cool and crushing ease
Like chessmen used to place and play
His crowded floating fortresses ;—
Who like a rushing Comet, prest
Across the World from East to West
And back, in that gigantic race
Of Warfleets o'er the Atlantic Main ;
When wondering Europe saw him chase
Like doubling hares that scud in vain,
The navies of proud France and Spain !—
—Or He, whose dazzling deeds make pale
(As well says one who paints the fray)
Old marvellous times of casque and mail—
Dense arrow-flights through thronging knights
At Agincourt's and Cressy's fights ;
Whose might on great Meánee's day
Wiped out again the Cábul stain
That red retreat—one slaughter ! he
Who that audacious victory
With his heroic handful tore
From twice as many thousand foes
As he had hundreds ; so, dispersed
The hovering hundred thousand more
Of ruffian-hordes with razor-swords
Keen-panting on their prey to close ;
Flung to the winds the sway accurst,

And rooted up no more to rise
The regal stews and robber sties
Of those Emeers whose quaking fears
Erelong through Asia's wide heart ran:
Till every turbaned Tyrant there
And bloodstained bandit in his lair
Shook at his very name—unscreened
Though wastes and mountains intervened,
Though round him raged a ruthless clan,
Against this terrible true MAN,
This justice-wreaking holy fiend,
This demon 'brother of Shay-tan'
Fighting God's battles!—Ay, indeed!
These men were the right genuine stuff
To rule a World—a hero-breed—
High minds, such as by instinct feed
On mighty tasks—Souls large enough
For Empire! not the creeping crew
Whose rule our England yet may rue;
Whose huckstering God is only Gold—
That 'cheaply bought' be 'dearly sold,'
Their sordid creed and single heed;
Whose grovelling zeal—their Altar still
The counter, and their Ark the till—
At that base shrine would sacrifice
Power, honour, Empire!—all the ties
That keep us one; whatever wakes
The patriot glow, the pride of race;—
All that, with love of Order, makes
A people of a populace,
And *any* people great! whate'er
Of quick and kindling sympathy
With England's children everywhere—

Our common claim to one great name,
One heritage of storied Fame,
It was our boast, our strength to share ;—
That conscious thrill of kindred blood
Which false refinement feigns to raise,
Evaporating all its good,
Into a fine and feeble phase
Of vague and vain philanthropy;
But kept within true range of kin,
The more it can inspire, expand,
So much more glorious, powerful, grand,
Becomes each human brotherhood ;
And ever, just as each has grown
To greatness or remained unknown,
Did each this genial warmth possess
Defective or in bright excess—
The savage, for his tribe alone,
The Roman for a World—*his own !*
But these cold-hearted theorists cower
At Empire thrust upon them—slink
From their compatriots in the hour
Of danger ; nay, that moment seize
With peevish pettiness to rail
At all the points (and numerous these)
Where those who seek their succour fail—
Not aid them first, in such a case
As men had done in their high place
Who nobly ruled a noble race !
Aye, noble still ! *not* apt to shrink
From that '*self-help*' these selfish lords,
Unhelping, save with worthless words,
Consign them to with shameless taunt :
Let that plain fact, no idle vaunt,

Their deaths, those gallant ones ! attest,
So oft struck down in wretched war
By savage pride upon us prest :—
Attest it *his*, among the rest—
(Be thus much said for kinship's sake)
Who sleeps the sleep no more to wake
On earth, 'mid loveliest scenes afar
Where Tonga-riro's snows disgorge
Their flames by blue Te Aira's lake—
Young, kindly, chivalrous St. George !
Whose honour-fired aspiring brain
Before that instant-blighting ball
Flashed into darkness without pain,
As in his wonted "dashing style"
(His comrades said) his men he led
Against the palisadoed wall
Of that last prophet-cannibal
Whose torturing tastes—impostures vile—
Our rulers' sympathies beguile !
So swiftly his bold course was run—
That ardent spirit's duties done,
To whom the night and day were one,
As through dense forest-glooms he crashed,
Through flooded rivers dauntless dashed,
Or galloped past thick fern, close by
Where murderous scouts would lurking lie—
To keep our friends in heart, disclose
The machinations of our foes ;
With cool, clear-sighted, fiery zeal
Unceasing !—ah, too soon the seal
Was set upon that life unknown,
That bud of promise nipt unblown !
The making of a hero marred,

If ever, then, when evil-starred
That young career by death was barred!
—But not in vain! no, though our bane,
These rulers, should renounce the power
For good such deaths are dared to dower
Their weakness with; though they, the same,
New conquests should alike disclaim,
And old assured dominion—nay,
Should fling away the world-wide Lands,
For ends that own God's clear commands
Entrusted to their trembling hands—
Birthright of England's swarming sons,
Won by her mighty deathless dead,
Her heroes' blood like water shed!—
But let such soulless puppet-play
Of rabble-rid mock-rule endure,
Such crawling creeds thy councils sway
Unchecked—unchanged—O then be sure,
England, my Country! nought avails
Thy wealth, thy commerce; he who runs
May read upon thy whited wall,
The 'Mene, Tekel' of thy fall!
Then hide thy head for shame—then say
And sigh—thy soaring Sun has past
Its zenith; own thyself at last—
Weighed in the fitting trader-scales,
Found wanting; then confess thy day
Of greatness done—thy glory gone—
Thy peddling kingdom passing fast away!——

These thoughts in loyal hearts are rife—
But let not here their shadows dark
Intrude—where need was but to mark

How poor a thing is human strife
Deprived of aids that seem designed
To make even War a Worship—make
Its mad turmoil the aspect take
Of some ennobling rite where Mind
Lords it o'er Matter—Soul o'er clay—
With absolute predominance
And solemn deep significance;
Until the very Battlefield
Becomes a Temple for display
Of spirit-proving deeds death-sealed
Of high Self-sacrifice, sublime
Devotion; and the bloody sod
Grows eloquent of something more
Than Duty—something beyond Time—
In recompense of Life and Soul
Flung freely down, unstinted, whole,
To magnify, uphold, restore
The cause of Good—and therefore God!

But War in this stark savage way
Looked too much like mere lust to slay:
Of its majestic mask laid bare
The face of naked Murder seemed to wear;
Its hateful visage tempered by no glance
Of lofty purpose or superb Romance.

VI.

Well—all the warrior-speeches had been made;
Now, with a coarsely classic dignity
Of grave debate and stern; and full parade
Of flowing dog-furred mantle, and blunt spear
With head tongue-shaped and feathery-ruffed, inlaid

With glistening shelly eyelets pearly-clear ;
Now in rank virulence of savagery
Complete—each naked speaker as he shrieked
In hoarse harsh tones of mad complaint and rage,
Impatient, like a wild-beast in its cage,
To and fro fretting at a short quick run,
With which each fragmentary fierce appeal,
Each furious burst was ended and begun ;
And every time he turned his angry heel
Slapping his tattoed thigh ; until he reeked
And foamed ; and breathless, voiceless, faint,
Was forced at last to yield the task, to paint
And passionate his griefs, to younger tongues,
Less wearied limbs and unexhausted lungs.
And then they danced their last war-dance to gain
The physical fever of the blood and brain
That might their dashed and drooping spirit sustain,
Nor let their flagging courage fail or flinch.
Then formal frenzy in full play was seen ;
The dancers seemed a mob of maniacs, swayed
By one insane volition, all obeyed,
Their mad gesticulations to enact
With frantic uniformity, exact
As some innumerably-limbed machine,
With rows of corresponding joints compact
All one way working from a single winch :
The leaping, dense, conglomerate mass of men
Now all together off the ground—in air—
Like some vast bird a moment's space—and then
Down, with a single ponderous shock, again
Down thundering on the groaning, trembling plain !
And every gesture fury could devise
And practice regulate, was rampant there ;

The loud slaps sounding on five hundred thighs ;
Five hundred hideous faces drawn aside,
Distorted with one paroxysm wide ;
Five hundred tongues like one, protruding red,
Thrust straining out to taunt, defy, deride ;
And the cold glitter of a thousand eyes
Upturning white far back into the head ;
The heads from side to side with scorn all jerking
And demon-spite, as if the wearers tried
To jerk them off those frantic bodies working
With such convulsive energy the while !
—Thus—and with grinding gnashing teeth, and fierce
Explosions deep in oft narrated style,
Those vollied pants of heartfelt execration ;
Or showers of shuddering hissing groans that pierce
The air with harsh accordance, like the crash
When regiments their returning ramrods dash
Sharp down the barrel-grooves with quivering clang
In myriad-ringing unison—they lash
Their maddened Souls to madder desperation !—
Thus all the day their fury hissed and rang ;
So groaned, leapt, foamed, grimaced they o'er and o'er ;
Till all were burning, ere the Sun should soar,
Against that stubborn Fort to fling themselves once more.

CANTO THE TWENTY-FIRST.

I.

Before the faint wide smile of dawn, so wan
And grey, to steal up Night's sad face began,
Crammed in canoes bold Whetu-riri's host
With favouring breeze had to Mokoia crossed.
With hearts high-beating to the strand they spring,
Each band behind its Chief; without a check
Hasten through grove and garden—many a bed,
That late in such luxuriant neatness spread,
Of melons, maize and taro—now a wreck.
  The outer palisades the foremost reach;
Take the positions prearranged for each;
And close around the Fort, a swarming ring:—
Then—as no challenge came—no warrior stirred,
And not a sound about the Fort was heard;
At once, like *one*—six hundred throats or more
Sent thundering skyward such a sea-like roar
As old Mokoia never heard before:

"How long, how long
Will your courage sleep?
When will it wake from its slumber deep,
When will your fury be fierce and strong?—

O but the tide it murmurs low,
Low and slow
Beginning to creep;
'Twill be long
'Twill be long
Ere it roar on the shore
In the strength of its flow

Take with spirits heavy-laden,
Take your leave of wife and maiden;
Press, ha! press in last embraces
To your own their weeping faces!
Press them paling,
Weeping, wailing—
All your efforts unavailing!
For see, for see,
The brave and the strong
At your gateways throng!
See, see, how advancing in lines victorious,
All your efforts scouting, scorning,
To the fort you lurk dismayed in,
Brave and strong
We tramp along!
Ha! we come! exulting, glorious
As those mountain-summits hoary!
Proud as mountain-peaks arrayed in
The magnificence of Morning
We come for glory—glory—glory!
We come! we come!—"

Stern—silent—in determined mood
Within those loop-holed walls of wood,
Alert, be sure, old Tangi stood;

He and his stalwart warriors true,
Alert, well-armed and watchful too!
Each short sharp-edged batoon of stone
Grass-green, or white of polished bone,—
That from the hand no foe might wring
The weapon at close grips—was bound
With thongs each sinewy wrist around;
But loose the long-armed axe was left,
Both hardwood blade and pointed heft—
A dagger, or an axe to swing,
Just as the warrior thrust or cleft.
The precious muskets, rude and few,
Their blunted flints well-chipped anew,
All primed and cocked, were pointing through
The palisades, behind whose breast
Keen, eager, fierce, the clansmen pressed,
Like wild-beasts waiting for a spring.
But yet no tongue the stillness broke,
No shout of wild defiance woke;
For to that threatening, thundering strain,
The sole reply the Chief would deign
Was one brief proverb, as his hand
Waved silence to his eager band;
And that firm lip, comprest before,
A haughty smile contemptuous wore;
"*Ay, come!*" he growled—"*come on to shell*
Cockles on Kátikáti's shore!"—
That long-disputed dangerous land,
As every Maori knew so well,
Fit for no tool but spear and brand;
On whose contested sands and rocks,
Who came got nothing but hard knocks;
For, plucked from that long home of strife

A limpet might have cost a life!
Hence grown a gibe for all who set
Their hearts on gain they ne'er would get.

But soon as Tangi's taunt was flung,
And while the roar redoubled rung,
The assailing ranks disparting wide,—
There forward rushed—a gloomy wood,
In doubtful light the dawning gave,
It seemed, or some great tidal wave!
A hundred of the bravest brave
Swept darkling up in order good;
Each in his left hand holding high
A bundle huge of brushwood dry
And withered fern that hid him quite—
Him and the fire-brand in his right.
Against the fort their heaps they piled,
And soon the flames were raging wild;
For still the breeze that brought them o'er
Blew freshly from the further shore.
It lighted up, that sudden glare,
The fort—the shore—the swarming, bold,
Blue, ghastly faces writhing there
With wrath and frenzy uncontrolled!
The fern became a mass of fire,
A brilliant yeast of surging gold;
And whirling darkly from the pyre
The smoke in russet volumes rolled,
With showers of sparks and frond and spray
Red-hot, or floating filmy-grey.
Old Tangi, Ranolf, and his train
Of warriors strove, and strove in vain

To heave the blazing heaps aside ;
No naked limbs or clothed could bide
That heat—no lungs could long sustain
The smoke that, blinding, stifling, dense,
Drove ever thicker through the fence.
So forced from that first outwork, they
With teeth that gnashed in scornful rage,
And shouts of fury, burst away
Leaping and clambering up to wage
The fight upon a higher stage ;
Headlong as alligators bounce
With water-snakes and bull-frogs harsh,
Out of some rank rush-covered marsh,
In river-depths to plunge and flounce—
In Hayti or the Isle made glad
With springs perennial crystal-fed—
When some crab-hunting negro-lad
Has fired their reedy crackling bed.

II.

Then wild with joy the 'Angry Star,'
At this success—the first the war
Vouchsafed his arms—let loose again
His rampant pride, his boastful vein.
By fear, by prudence undebarred,
Up to the fence, black, tottering, charred
(His feet,—with green flax-sandals shod
Prepared for this, the reeking sod
And glowing embers safely trod)
He bounded ; took his dauntless stand
With granite-headed axe in hand
Beneath it, and began to rain
A shower of blows with might and main,

As each had been his last for life,
On crumbling post and crashing stake,
Broad entrance for his band to make.
There—bellowing loud his battle-song,
His favourite song in such a strife ;
While all the less adventurous throng,
Save six or eight who lent their aid,
Until the breach might be essayed,
A more respectful distance kept ;—
Less man than frenzied fiend of hell,
He raved and roared and danced and leapt
And right and left his weapon swept—
A blow at every leap and yell—
Against that smoking citadel :

"Hit out, hit out
My battle-axe stout!
Ha, ha! you should tell
The sound of it well,
  How it played
  Long ago
On your crashing stockade!
  Do you know,
  Do you know
Who your foe may be?
Prick your ears up and hark
  Or come if you dare,
  I-ará! if you dare
  Come out and see!
  WHETURIRI!—'tis he,
  Whose eyeballs glare
  Red stars in the dark!
  'Tis he! 'tis he!—

Hit away—hit away,
My battle-axe gay!
Hit out—hit out,
My warriors stout!
The dastards rout
And Victory shout—
I-ará! I-ará!"—

Now all upon that windward side
The fallen fence left passage wide,
And Wheturiri's raging host
The ditch and barrier swiftly crossed;
While Tangi's men retreating, threw
Themselves inside the rampart new;
And as the palisades they passed
Made every sliding panel fast,
Till round the fort the assailant horde
Upon the second platform poured.
Then out—unable to restrain
His pent-up wrath, his fierce disdain,
Or patient wait his foes' attack;
With all his bravest at his back,—
Just as the glorious Sun again
Slipped silvery from the mountains black
With panting disc upfloating free—
Out rushed at last the 'Wailing Sea'
In wild ferocious majesty,
His battle-cry resounding loud
Above the tumult of the crowd!
"*Now, forward, now, my Sons with me—*
Now forward to the Land of Death!—"
That shout o'er all the hubbub swelled

Of casual shots and bulwarks felled,
And stakes that crashed and fiends that yelled,
Distinct, as from the midnight's core,
Where leaps the blue sheet-lightning's blaze
And hissing rains in torrents pour,
The dread Caffrarian lion's roar,
That shakes the earth to which he lays
His head and thunders—rises o'er
And deeper-volumed rolls beneath
The angry bellowings that disclose
Where stamp, upstarting from repose
Whole herds of snorting buffaloes!
Where'er that Chieftain charged, dismayed
His foes fell back like huddling sheep
The wild-dog drives into a heap;
Or brief the fight the brave essayed:
So deadly swept on as he rushed
His ponderous battle-axe's blade;
Each chief who his encounter stayed
Just met him, and with right arm crushed
Disabled from the contest slunk;
Or down at once scarce groaning sunk
With cloven skull and quivering trunk.
—The Angry Star, for all his boast,
Not yet the veteran's path had crossed,
But, as it seemed, preferred to close
With less renowned, less dangerous foes;
Or had a craftier game to play
More sure than such a doubtful fray.
So still resistless through the fight
Old Tangi raged; still rose on high
O'er all the noise that battle-cry,
"*Now forward to the realms of Night!*"—

Yet still, for numbers beaten back
Fresh numbers pressed the fierce attack ;
The platform mounted—haply dared
To charge the very gates, across
The bridges left upon the fosse
By Tangi, for retreat prepared.
But vain their toil—their fury vain ;
No hold, no entrance could they gain—
Resisted all—repulsed or slain.

III.

Meanwhile upon another side
Young Ranolf with a trusty band
Had sallied,—when his anxious bride
Fair Amo,—who whate'er her fears
Gave no weak way to sighs and tears
But o'er her heart kept brave command,
Had to her serious brow and breast
Her hero—husband—lover prest ;
And prayed him, only for her sake
Be careful, or her heart would break !
But he, although his own beat fast
With strange excitement at this new
Experience, reassuring smiled
On the devoted desert-child ;
And with that confidence, the glow
Of burning blood, and nerves high-strung
And braced by hardy life, bestow
On those born brave, in health, and young—
Till death, disaster, they contemn
As things not meant, not made for them !
And hold their fortune, fate so high,
All danger they may well defy—

He bade her, laughingly, rely
Upon his luck, too good by far
For *him* to fall in such a war!
Then sallied with his friends, where they
As older warriors, led the way.
With no ferocious wish to slay,
No savage thirst for blood, at first
Our generous youngster only chose
To use his deadlier weapon more
To save his friends than harm his foes.
And when increased the wild uproar,
And more intense the tustle grew,
Himself with wild delight he threw
Into the press as it had been
Some headlong, jovial, schoolboy scene,
'King-seal-ye!'—football—any game
Might more than usual daring claim.

While thus engaged, it chanced the youth
Full upon Wheturiri came;
And with a moment's shock, in truth,
That back his blood's quick current sent,
Found his revolver's barrels spent!
Himself, in fact, unarmed, before
The Chief who down upon him bore,
But paused until he joyful saw
The pistol never raised to fire;
Then out his tongue was thrust—his jaw
Aside—his eyes turned back—his face
Distorted with the grim grimace,
His sign of hate, defiance, ire;
High whirled his axe for one sure blow
To lay his helpless victim low.

But Ranolf rallying swift as light
Or lightning, leaping forward, dashed
(Before the axe could downward sweep)
His clenched right hand with all his might
And the momentum of his leap,
Full into that grimacing grin;
And made the astonished savage spin,—
While fast his rolling eyeballs flashed
With other gleams than fury lent—
Clean o'er the ditch's sheer descent
Amid the smouldering stakes that crashed
Beneath him as he headlong went,
Wondering what demon could assist
The weight of that hard English fist.—
"*Kapai! ka* NUI *pai!—Well done!*
O right well done!" a hoarse voice cried—
Old Tangi's—at his topmost run
As rushing round the palisade
That brief encounter he espied,
And hastened to the young man's aid.
—A griesly sight in sooth was he
That huge exulting Chief to see,
As there with lowered axe he stood
And Whetu's smashing fall surveyed!
From his broad axe-blade dripped and drained
The blood; and all with hostile blood
His hoary hair and beard were stained;
With drops of fierce exertion rained
His brow; his chest—so rugged, vast,
And muscle-woven like the twist
Of cable-cords some olive rears,
Some mighty trunk eight hundred years
Have seen in rocky strength resist

Their rending frost and raging heat ;—
Like some great engine working fast,
That knotty chest quick-heaving beat :
So stood the Giant in his glee
In friendly hideous ecstasy !
But scarce could toil or triumph check
His course an instant ; on he went
(As Ranolf leaving clear his road
Back to the barrier stepped to load)
On towards his prostrate breathless prey,—
That fallen Star,—with fell intent
To dash his life out where he lay.
But ere he reached him, to his feet
Up sprung Te Whetu, bold, erect—
Though still his blue-lined face streamed red
With that well-planted blow's effect ;
At first prepared his foe to meet ;
But seemed an instant to reflect ;
That tough encounter seemed to dread ;
Then shouting bade his men retreat,
And o'er the flat, deliberate, fled.
Swift passed the word from man to man
And swiftly leaping down they ran
On all sides from the leaguered fort.
Three steps to follow, Tangi took,
With glad but half-astonished look ;
And then in full career stopped short ;
Smiled sternly with disdainful lip ;
And pulling with his finger-tip
His under-eyelid down in scorn
"*Is this your mutton-fish ! Am I
Your greenhorn !*" was his haughty cry ;
For all the plan was patent then,

To draw him to the open plain,
Where his slight force though stanch and good,
No chance against their numbers stood.
So, with the crowd though onward borne
A moment, back he forced his men ;
Bade them for very shame restrain
Their shouts of 'Victory,' yet to gain ;
And soon had all except the slain
Safe in the fort, to counsel there
How best they might the wall repair—
How best to meet—forestall—defeat,
The next assault their foes might dare.

IV.

Short breathing time the Angry Star
Gave Tangi, nor retreated far.
Soon as he saw his feint to draw
The veteran from his Fort had failed,
Again he marshalled all his band
Upon the flat beside the shore.
Then with a new device though planned
Before, with hearts and hopes new-fanned,
And by the cunning Priest beguiled
With omens sure and safe, once more
The stubborn stronghold they assailed.
With songs and yells and gestures wild
In swarms across the ditch they swept ;
In swarms the broken barrier leapt ;
Once more by casual shots annoyed
Around the platform swift deployed.
Again—scarce waiting their attack—
The fiery Chief, whom neither age

Nor odds, nor toil made slow or slack,
Had sallied forth to force them back,
Or hand-to-hand at least engage
The first who scaled that fighting-stage.
So all the terrace circling round
The ramparts, as before, was crowned
With thronging men in deadly broil
O'erthrown—o'erthrowing ; a dark coil
Convulsive, fluctuating, dense,
Of agonising forms confused,
In every violent posture used
In mad attack or tough defence !
A mass of spears and clubs that crossed
And clashed, and limbs that twined and tossed,
As leathery links of seaweed lithe
At ebbing tide on rock-reefs writhe :
And all the forms and limbs exact
In statuesque proportions cast—
Dark symmetry of strength compact ;
Where working muscles rose and fell
With shifting undulations, fast
As poppling wavelets when the breeze
The tiderip grates in narrow seas !
Till all that ring of wrestlings rife,
Continuous knots of naked strife,
Had seemed, to looker-on at ease,
Some crowded Phigaleian frieze,
Or Parthenaic miracle
Of Art, awaked to sudden life—
Or worked in terra-cotta, say,
Brown Lapithæ in deadly fray ;
Large-limbed Theseian heroes old,
But darkly dyed, of kindred race,

Whose naked forms of classic mould
In one wide-raging death-embrace
Their naked struggling foes enfold.

But when the fight was at its height
His new device Te Whetu tried.
Up-rushed a shouting band outside
The black-charred fence before laid low.
In order good, a double row
They came; each warrior of the first
Poising a platted green-flax sling
Well wetted in the nearest spring;
And in the sling a red-hot stone,
Which, high above the ramparts thrown
Should soon make such a blaze outburst
From walls of rush and roofs of thatch
As might the whole defences catch,
And force the stifled foe to fly
The Fort he held so stubbornly.
The second rank bore, close behind,
In baskets green with earth safe-lined,
Of heated stones a fresh supply.
Then, at a signal given they hurl
A burning volley, thick and hot
As soft red lumps of scoria whirl,
In showers from dark abysses shot
By old Vesuvius in his play,
His common freaks of every day,
When all his lava floods repose:
Or such as o'er his creviced snows
The grander Tongaríro throws—
While dread reverberations round
His sulphurous crater-depths resound—

When all the solemn midnight skies
With that red beacon of surprise
He startles—seeming from afar,
Though low upon the horizon's bound,
Sole object in the vault profound !
So baleful glares its fiery shine,
To all the tribes an ominous sign
Of death and wide disastrous war.
—Now, now, alert and active be,
Ye children of the 'Wailing Sea !'
Your shifty foes will else make good
The threats erelong that boastful song
Sent echoing late o'er vale and wood !—
Not wholly unprepared they speed
To baulk and baffle, if they may
Their fierce assailant's fresh essay.
For they had seen above the green
The smoke of fires lit up when need
Was none of fires for warmth or food ;
And soon the project understood.
So all the gourds they could provide
Were ready, every house beside ;
And even a large canoe to be
Their tank in this extremity
Hauled up and fitly placed ;—all filled
With water from a well, supplied
Itself by channels issuing through
The rock upon the Lake, below
Its surface cut ; their outlet so
From keenest-eyed besiegers' view
Well-hidden by its waters blue.
And when that shower of firestones red
Came whirling, whizzing overhead,

For this vocation primed and drilled,
All those whom duty did not call
To watch the gates, defend the wall—
The old by age outworn, the young
With sinews yet for fight unstrung—
And young or old, the women too,
With Amohia first of all,—
Quick to the calabashes flew
Or tottered as they best could do.
And when the slightest whiff of smoke
From any roof or rush-wall broke,
Some hand was prompt the place to drench
And ere it spread, the burning quench.
But Amo, first among the crowd,
With cheery accents, low not loud,
As if at once their hearts to warm
To effort, yet repress alarm—
With smiles upon her face—howe'er
Her heart might throb with secret care—
Seemed ever everywhere at hand,
To guide, encourage, cheer, command!
And once when fire broke out indeed
And none just then appeared to heed,
Nor quick enough the water came—
Up to the roof she leapt, she sprung,
And o'er the thatch her mantle flung,
And trampled out the mounting flame.—
With arms and that firm bosom bare,
In skirt of glossy flax, as there
Aloft in such excited mood
Hurrying her hastening handmaids, stood
The dauntless Girl—she looked as rare
For spirit, grace, commanding mien,

As loveliest Amazonian Queen
In those surpassing friezes seen!

V.

But while this passed upon the hill
The fight below was raging still;
And that resistless 'Wailing Sea'
At last had met the enemy
Whose death the most, of all the heap
Of slaughter his remorseless blade
That day, a bloody harvest, made,
The haughty Veteran cared to reap.
With satisfaction stern and deep
To feel his foe within his power,
He hurled—through clenching teeth that ground,
As if with grim resolve that hour
Should be the last of both or one,
And see the hateful contest done—
Defiance at "the slave—the hound!"
Then rushed upon him with a shower
Of blows of such terrific power
And weight and swiftness, left and right—
The Angry Star, who tried in vain
The pelting tempest to sustain,
Was backward borne in self-despite,
Parrying the blows as best he might;
Ducking his head from side to side
Like tortured tree that scarce can bide
The beating of a gusty gale.
But Tangi's breath begins to fail,
The driving blows at length relax;
Less swiftly whirls his battle-axe;
And Whetu in his turn attacks;

But stalking round and round his foe
And watching where a blow to plant,
As runs a Tiger crouching low
Around some wary Elephant,
For chance, with viewless lightning-spring,
His weight to launch upon the haunch
Of the dread monster, and escape
The white destruction that in shape
Of those impaling tusks still gleams
Before him—still to face him seems
Turn where his eyes' green lustres may!
So watched Te Whetu when to fling
Himself upon that warrior grey;
So round him plied his swinging stride;
Then flew at him with yell, and blow
'Twas well for Tangi, eye and hand
Were quick enough to slant aside—
And tough enough his battle-brand
Its sweeping fury to withstand.
Then such a whirling maze began
Of clattering weapons—stroke and guard
And feint and parry, thrust and ward,
As up and down the axes ran
Together, that no sharpest eye
Could follow their rapidity!
But Tangi, see! has clutched at last
Te Whetu by a necklace fast
The boastful savage ever wore
Of warriors' teeth, a ghastly wreath—
And twists it hard his foe to choke,
And shortens for a final stroke
His axe's hold—but fails once more—
The treacherous chain beneath the strain

Breaks, scattering wide the hideous beads.
Back springs Te Whetu—free again,
The deadly strife may still maintain:
Close follows Tangi; mad to be
Baulked of so sure a victory,
The road beneath him little heeds:
His step upon a spot is set
Where the hard clay is slippery wet
With gore; he slips—he stumbles o'er
A wounded wretch unseen who lies
Right in his path, on crimsoned stones
And dust that chokes a ruddy rill
Slow-creeping but increasing still—
Lies in the pathway there—with eyes
That anguished roll, heartrending groans,
And writhings like a centipede's
Caught in a burning log—and bleeds.
Down, down the Giant goes before
His Foe, who now began to rave
With joy at this unwonted run
Of luck his favouring Atuas gave!
Ere Tangi—old—with toil o'erdone—
Could raise him from his heavy fall,
He whirled his poleaxe high to end
Him and his triumphs, once for all.—
The blow was never to descend;
For at that instant at full speed
Up Ranolf ran to save his friend:
There was no time for thought, nor need:
Three balls in swift succession sent
Through Whetu's body crashing went:
Down drops his axe—his arms upthrown—
His eyes a moment wildly glare,

Then glaze with fixed and ghastly stare;
His staggering knees give way,—and there
He lies a corpse without a groan!
A pang smote Ranolf—though he knew
There was nought else for him to do.
Slowly rose Tangi; dauntless still;
And half-disposed to take it ill
That Ranolf's shot *his* debt should pay
And from his clutches snatch his prey.

VI.

But when Te Whetu's men beheld
Their Angry Star, their hero, slain;
And Tangi up again, unquelled,
With such triumphant fierce disdain
Looking where next to dash among
The thickest of the wavering throng;—
Beheld that Stranger's bearing bold,
And in his firm determined hold
His life-devouring weapon raised;
A terror seized the nearest band—
Who since the duel first began
Had breathless stood on either hand,
Inactive; wondering, half-amazed
What would the conflict's issue be
'Twixt 'Angry Star' and 'Wailing Sea.'—
Through all the host the panic ran:
Down from the platform headlong leapt
The foremost fighting-men, and swept
Along with them the slingers too
And all the pebble-carrying crew!
Then Tangi, for he saw the rout

Was real this time, began to shout
To all his clansmen to come out,
Pursue and press the flying foe,
And smite and spare not high or low—
No glut of dear revenge forego!
But short his course—his triumph short;
For as he turned him—and addrest
To those behind a brief behest
That some should stay to guard the fort,
A bullet pierced his rugged breast,
Out of a near plantation fired
By some obscure assailant, hid
Behind a fence—ensconced amid
The rattling stems of withered maize—
A parting gift ere he retired;
'Twas Márupo, so named to mark
His ways—the 'Striker in the Dark.'—
Down sinks the Chieftain—to the ground
Bowed down by that slight-seeming wound;
Yet makes fierce efforts still to raise
The fainting form one elbow stays:
Still keeps erect that dizzying head,
And lifts the arm that weighs like lead,
And feebly cries a battle-cry
Of Vengeance and of Victory:
Still cheers with broken words and brief
His men, with horror struck and grief
To see, thus fall'n, their honoured Chief;
But most exhausts his gasping breath
In bidding them avenge his death
By such a havoc of his foes
As shall illume where'er it goes
The tale of his inglorious close.

His life-blood ebbing, thus he steeled
His old brave heart, nor yet would yield
To be transported from the field ;
Less heeding death than this disgrace
To fall by hand obscure or base ;
Cursing the coward tools that gave
Such easy power to every slave
To slay the foe he durst not face !—
But while the most his hest obeyed,
With Ranolf some about him stayed ;
And with their sturdy tender aid,
The Chief whom nothing could persuade,
But senseless could resist no more,
Into the nearest house he bore.

VII.

Meantime among the host that fled
And few that followed, quickly spread
The rumour Tangi too was dead ;
And of the fugitives ahead
The foremost and least scared began
To make their comrades as they ran
Note their pursuers—far and few—
Their own o'erwhelming numbers too.
They pause—they turn ; collect in knots
About the ruined garden-plots ;
Not unobserved of him, in place
Of Tangi now who led the chase,
A wary warrior 'Máwai' named ;—
'Máwai—the Gourd'—because far-famed
For many a crafty deep design
By sap and trench and secret mine

For creeping into forts—unstayed
By tallest post and palisade;
As sure, though unperceived and slow,
As over fences high or low
That creeping climbing gourd will grow;—
Máwai amid the shrubs and trees
The foe in clusters rallying sees:
So shouts the danger out to all
His headlong comrades within call;
Rates—reasons—threats—entreats and makes
All whom his step or voice o'ertakes
Keep more together—rest content
Just now at least with what was done,
The vengeance taken—victory won.
And thus, with caution, by degrees,
And often turning as they went
As if to ferret out and slay
Chance fugitives that hiding lay—
So that a front they still present
To that recovering enemy
In crowds tumultuous hovering nigh.
And make him doubt their true intent—
The scanty band of victors back
To their intrenchments take their way—
Their fort, unconquered still, though black
And reeking from the late attack.

CANTO THE TWENTY-SECOND.

I.

But ere with Tangi Ranolf reached
The Fort, the anxious Amo came—
With more than one deep-wrinkled dame
Of reputation unimpeached
For skill medicinal—supplied
With best resources from their store
Kept ready and prepared before—
Lint, splints and bands and simples dried—
Came hasting to her Father's side.
Soon as his dangerous state appears,
She dashes off the starting tears ;
And sets to work the whimpering crones,
And checks their loud untimely moans.
Thus schooled, with old experienced eye
And gentle hand, the nurses pry
Into the wound, and probe, and try
With styptic herbs well understood
To check and stanch the oozing blood ;
With many a mild restorative
And crooning incantation, strive
His pausing pulses to revive ;

And back the flitting life allure
With all they know to charm and cure!
With anodynes they soothe his pains;
And many a cooling drink restrains
The fever in his feeble veins.
By Amo's self, sad loving Child,
The thick elastic mats are piled
Whereon the helpless Chief they lay;
By Amo's hands are softly spread
The silkiest, for that poor grand head!
Her tender hands alone essay
To wash the battle-stains away;
And smooth and comb with fondest care,
His snowy beard and matted hair:
While from her heart to those still skies,
Sincere and fervent yearnings rise
For aid, where'er it lives or lies,
With any pitying deities!—
For she to Ranolf's Gods will pray—
Her father's—*any* Gods that may
Save that dear life, that pain allay!
And must not heartfelt wishes pure,
Deep-breathings of a daughter's love,
Be grateful to the Powers above,
And of benignant hearing sure,
As any prayers howe'er exprest,
And to whate'er enlightened, best
Ideal of Infinite God addrest?—

And Ranolf, wondering, watched her glide—
Mid all that carnage sanguine-dyed,
And brutal savage homicide,
And murderous passions raging wide—

A Seraph of bright tenderness,
A healing Angel, in distress
Sent down to soothe—console and bless!
And felt, to see her there and thus,—
"How sad and beautiful a thing,
How sordid, sad, and glorious,
This human Nature *is!* where spring
Out of each other, linked by fate,
Such heavenly love, such hellish hate;
What bred this vermin Hate?—Love's rose!
Now, Love in Hate's vile hotbed blows!—
If Evil root itself in Good,
And Good must be evolved from Ill,
Must not the Author of the Good
Be Author of the Evil still?
And we, to work his ends, must *we*
For love of Good, the Evil flee,
That without which it could not be?—
Aye truly! if to be the seed
Of Good, is Evil's end decreed,
Enough, be sure, will still remain
To raise the plant, howe'er we strain
The seed's destruction to attain.
Say, by the great Soul-Shaper's plan
(Not quite a maze, not wholly dim)
'Tis Evil, tried and conquered, can
Alone exalt ascending Man;—
That just to win his way therein
Unsoiled, unquelled, is asked of him:
The very power, from this life freed,
In loftier life he most may need!
Then Evil's gauntlet he must run—
Be plunged o'erhead in it, as one

In water who would learn to swim ;
And stumbling often—oft o'erthrown
Must risk it, as the Child ungrown
Must risk the fall to go alone ;
Held ever by its Mother's hand,
How should it learn to walk or stand ?
''Twere better it were born complete,
Set up at once on steady feet,'
Say you—' could walk, swim, run at first—
No need to have those weak limbs nurst !'
Nay, then the holiest ties that bless
Our Nature, you remove, repress—
The Infant's love and soft caress,
The Mother's depth of tenderness.
So haply through all Being's round
To this condition Good is bound,
Evil in this alliance found ;
That each must to the other lead,
And from the other each proceed.
And are they then each other's dower,
Two opposite forces of one Power,
Indifferent, central ? must we give
Credence to that about the poles
The positive and negative ?
While to their union would we mount
The ever mystic marvellous Fount
Of Good and Evil, where they live
In unimagined Essence bright
Of Perfect, Necessary, Right,
We come but to the Soul of Souls
Unknowable, for aye unknown
The Centre—God ? whence issuing, still
Is issuing into Good and Ill ?—

Who knows? but one thing might be shown:
Some Evil there must be where'er
Is Imperfection, foul or fair:
Perfection by a hairbreadth missed
Is Imperfection; you *must* say
The One Allperfect every way
Is God alone—what else but He?—
It follows—Evil must exist
Or God's the sole Existence be.
But say the Imperfect might be made
Complete within its bounds—its grade-
From every possible degree
Of Evil done or suffered free—
(Which none can prove)—with no desire
As no conception of the higher:
Would *that* a loftier lot have been?
To rest, a faultless mere machine
Bound down to automatic bliss
Of stagnant Being—that, or *this*
Which works through Darkness to the Light,
Still struggling towards the highest height
Perhaps in progress infinite?—
Pooh—pooh!" within himself he said
Breaking the speculative thread
Short off;—for that tumultuous fight,
His own exertions—and the sight
Of Amo by her father's bed
Working in strong affection's might
To soothe and cheer his evil plight—
Most keenly made him feel how vain,
How sickly all the skeptic train
Of thoughts on God, Man's doom or chance,
And Nature's mystic governance:

How true is Goethe's word—'the cure
For Doubt is Action;' not indeed
As making speculation sure—
As solving any special doubt,
Or settling any special creed,
But making Doubt itself appear
A thing impertinent and out
Of place in this bright work-day sphere;
And all that Speculation seem
The maundering of a feverish dream;
An idle growth, deficient both
In fragrant flower and wholesome fruit;
Like some white straggling ivy-sprout,
Or sickly honeysuckle-shoot,
That thrusts a pale and feeble trail
Inside a darksome building's wall;
But kept without, in light and heat,
Had spread a green and graceful pall
With feathery blossoms luscious-sweet
O'er many a dreary blank or stain
And blotch that else the eye would pain—
Nor should have been allowed to crawl
Into the inner dark at all.

II.

Crest-fallen—sullen at their ill-success,
Across the Lake the sad assailants go;
With murmurs, not even fear can quite suppress,
Against the Priest—for omens so belied—
And each against the other, as the first
Who after such defeats new hopes had nursed,
And on such omens would fresh faith bestow.
With smooth cajolings Kangapo replied,

Though deep chagrin and rage he scarce could hide;
Showed how, the Fort half-burnt and Tangi killed,
His prophecies had been wellnigh fulfilled;
And if at last on any point they failed
'Twas that the white man's Atuas had prevailed
O'er his—who shameless had their cause betrayed
But there were stronger Spirits to his aid
He might have summoned had he been so willed;
Had not too great contempt his bosom swayed
For those strange Gods, and want of caution bred
In one those Gods should yet be taught to dread!
Thus much he owned; but this would soon repair;
Only let not his faithful sons despair:
By mightier Powers they soon should see o'erthrown
His foes in spirit, and in flesh their own.
But with his Atuas let him work alone
That night;—when daybreak glimmered should be shown
What they must do: how best this juncture meet,
And make their partial victory complete.

So urged the glozing Priest, his only aim
To gain more time to patch his tattered Fame;
Or find an opportunity to leave
Those he scarce hoped much longer to deceive.
They seemed to listen—feigned their fear dispelled;
Then their own agitated councils held;
Some to contrive new measures to achieve
The Priest's designs and their defeat retrieve;
Most to devise safe means without delay
To get themselves and their canoes away
From the increasing dangers of their stay.

III.

That eve a thought struck Ranolf, as he stood
Watching the foe retreat in sullen mood—
Brown barebacked bending crowds, and each canoe
Its ruddy sides white-spotted with a row
Of tufted feathers, paddling, silent, slow,
With wake wide-rippling, o'er the Lake—light-blue
As silver-shining skin of fish new-caught—
Towards hills, of burnished copper cauldron's hue
With the departing sunset; landing then,
How, like dispirited, distracted men,
In huddling knots they flocked and flitted—used
Gesticulations, violent confused,
Conflicting, undetermined; while alone
The Priest to his secluded cot had gone,
How meditative, silent!—then a thought
Struck Ranolf, of a deed that might be done
Would yield rich harvest with the morning sun.

Oft through the pocket spy-glass thrown ashore
When he was wrecked and which just now he wore,
He from the island had observed before,
How Kangapo from motives quickly guessed
Had made his temporary place of rest
Apart from all the crowd and tumult; screened,
By the low spur of hill that intervened,
From that familiarity which breeds
Contempt—(for hollow-glittering men and deeds!)
And knowing well their superstitious fear
From friends or foes would keep him safe and clear.
Thus by the waterside alone he dwelt,
Nor any fear of their annoyance felt.

IV.

'Twas dead of night; the stars with clouds were blurred:
Within the fort the wearied warriors lay
And slept or still discussed the deadly fray.
As noiselessly as Sunbeams on the plain,
That shine and shift and fade and shine again,
Bright Amo tended Tangi's fevered pain.
Solemn and deep—distinct in every word,
The intermittent watch-song might be heard
O'er the monotonous, moaning, plaintive strain
Of women wailing for their kinsmen slain,
In groups, with heads down-bent upon their knees—
A musical low tremulous hum like bees—
Or swelling high like far-off murmuring seas;
But o'er it rose the watch-song clear and plain:
For even the sentinels as round and round
With frequent pause they paced the higher ground,
Had many a chaunt and metaphoric snatch
Of verse, to while the tedium of their watch;
(Say ye, the wise, O worthy of all praise,
Who toil, with tokens from forgotten days
The veil from that grand mystery to raise
The origin of Man and all his ways—
Say through what inborn need, what instinct strong,
These savage races are such slaves to Song!)
But these, the watchers round Mokoia's fort
Were sounding through the gloom, in phrases short,
By snatches given, a song against surprise,—
Half chaunt—half shouts, deep melancholy cries,
Whose purport, feebler paraphrase alone
Can give—the sense that to themselves it gave;
For the simplicity of that rude stave

Was so severe, its literal words made known,
Were almost gibberish in their brevity:
Only dilution can lend any zest,
Or nutriment a stranger could digest,
To song in short-hand, verse so cramped—comprest,
The very pemmican of poetry:

"Be wakeful — O be watchful! men at every post around;
Lest on a barren rock hemmed in at morning ye be found!

Hemmed in — blocked up — cut off, by the advancing tide;—
O watchful, wakeful be — sharp-eared and lightning-eyed!

By Hari-hari's shore the beetling cliffs (O wakeful be!)
Are at all times and tides beset by the beleaguering Sea.

O watchful, wakeful be! when women wail for warriors lost,
'Tis like the high-complaining surf on Mokau's sounding coast,—

Ay me! Ay me! still creeping nigher—still swarming up and trying
Each ledge where seamews light—where'er their young ones nestle, prying!—

Not so—not so, on us the foe shall steal—yet wakeful be—
O watchful, wakeful till the Sun spring glorious from the Sea!"—

So rolled the solemn Song the darkness through,
As Ranolf with two lads—his trustiest two,
Whose faith was greatest in himself, he knew;
From all the rest dissembling his design
Nor letting even these two its end divine,
Stole from the fort and launched a light canoe;
Then softly paddled o'er the Lake until
They dimly could discern the looming hill
Where Kangapo resided; there they paused
Intently listening—paddled on once more—
(A low wind sighing scarce a ripple caused)
Then cautiously approached the darksome shore,
Some distance from the glen; the keelless prore
Slid smoothly up the pumice-sandy marge:
Then out stepped Ranolf, giving strictest charge
The two should wait there till his quick return,
When they the object of their voyage should learn.

So Ranolf stepped upon the strand;
His foot scarce craunched the gritty sand;
A flax-rope wound his waist around—
Revolver ready in his hand.
With eye and ear alert, and keen
For dimmest sight or faintest sound,
In that lone, dark and silent scene,
His stealthy way he quickly found:
That way he oft before had been;
That cottage lone had been his own:

Each woody rolling spur and dell,
And wavy cliff to which they fell,
Cut off below,—he knew full well.
With noiseless pace he neared the place—
Behind some bushes listening stood.
No sign of life he saw or heard,
But distant murmurs; nothing stirred.
On tiptoe to the hut he went;
Close to the wall his ear he leant,
And while his own light-breathing ceased
Could hear the breathing of the Priest;
Could hear his sighs—his mutterings low
And restless shiftings to and fro.—
"Awake, then—and too dark 'twould be
Inside for me my work to see!"
Thought Ranolf—"how to bring him out?
The foe so near, their noise I hear;
He must be left no time to shout."
A rustling noise along the thatch
Like stealthy rats that creep and scratch,
He made—"his ear 'twill surely catch!
With sounds like these along the wall
The Atuas come at priestly call."—
Small notice seemed the Priest to take:—
The muttering voice a moment dropped;
The train of sad reflections stopped;
He listened—then the gloomy train
Of muttered thoughts began again;
More certain sign the Gods must make
Their votary's dull regard to wake!
His pistol stuck in that rope-belt,—
Then Ranolf lifted up with care
A heavy cooking-stone he felt

About his feet—left always there—
And pitched it full upon the roof;
The stealthy rustling noise renewed;
His pistol drew, and ready stood.
"Against a summons so divine,
Of present Gods so sure a sign,
His priestly ear will ne'er be proof!—"
—Bewildered—wondering—all subdued
By strange and superstitious fright,
Out rushed the Priest into the night—
Rushed into Ranolf's gripe that clutched
About his throat his mat so tight,
While his scared brow the pistol touched—
Of Ranolf's threat was little need:
"Hist, wretch! the pistol's at your head—
The slightest noise—and you are dead!"
He could not speak, scarce breathe indeed,
Till from that rivet somewhat freed.
Thus grappled, to the beach below,
Till out of hearing of the foe,
Ranolf his cowering captive led;
Then on a sudden, turning round,
Tripped up and threw him on the ground;
While the poor Sorcerer, sore dismayed,
Believing his last moment come,
For life, for mercy, whimpering prayed.
Nought answered Ranolf; stern and dumb,
His knee upon his chest he placed;
Unwound the cord about his waist;
And quick the Sorcerer's mantle rolled,
Leaving enough for breathing loose,
About his head and frightened face:
Then, from his sea-experience old,

Expert at every tie and noose,
In briefest space contrived to lace
And truss his victim up, from nape
Of neck to sole of foot, compact;
Till chance was none of his escape.
"There, friend! for that kind trick you played
Me once, I think you're well repaid."—
Then to the hut again he tracked
His hasty steps; against the door
A sketch-book-leaf prepared before
He stuck, with this inscription fit,
In letters large in Maori writ:
"*Kua kawakína—e—te Tōhunga;*
Kia túpato apópo, mo te há—te há!"
"YOUR SORCERER FROM YOUR SIDE IS TORN;
BEWARE, BEWARE TO-MORROW MORN!"
Beneath was sketched for signature
The dreaded pistol—token sure
To all the foe, if none could read,
Whence came the message—whose the deed.
Then back to where his helpless prey
With muffled moanings writhing lay,
Just like a chrysalis that works
Its head and tail with useless jerks,
Cramped by the sheath wherein it lurks—
He sped; hailed softly through the dark
The lads expectant with their bark;
And helped by these, who little knew
Their gruesome captive, packed him safe,
Nor daring now to moan or chafe
Beneath the thwarts of the canoe;
And to the isle, all danger past,
In triumph soon was paddling fast.

But when with quickened stroke they strove,
And up the beach the vessel drove
With many a cheer—they just could hear
On high, the sentries' livelier lay
Begin to greet the breaking day :

"Stars are fleeting ;
Night retreating—
Yellow-stealing Dawn begun !
Slowly, mark !
Uplifts the dark—
See, there a spark—then all the Sun !
Birds are singing,
Forests ringing,
Hark, O hark !
Danger flies with daylight springing ;
O rejoice—your watch is done !"—

But when the invading host next day
Found their great bulwark, guide and stay
Borne off in this mysterious way,
A panic seized them, one and all !
No further councils would they call ;
Their planned retreat became a flight,
And all had disappeared ere night.

V.

Much trouble it cost Ranolf when 'twas known
What captive thus into their hands was thrown,
To save his forfeit life ; for Tangi's ire
Against the scheming traitor burnt like fire.
But generous still, and holding hardly worth
His vengeance, one, who never from his birth

Had been a warrior, he at last gave way,
Much wondering at the Stranger's strange desire
To save the victim he had power to slay.
So, hiding all his hatred, much increased
By Ranolf's kindly act, the dangerous Priest,
Scarce seeming sullen, spiteful or morose,
Was for the present kept a prisoner close.

VI.

Wasting and weakening ever, day by day,
The 'Wailing Sea,' deep-wounded, lingering lay;
Or heavily dragged about his gaunt great frame,
With hollowing cheeks, and eyes that yet would flame
When news about his late assailants came,
And how his gallant clansmen on all hands
Made deadly havoc of their scattered bands.
The fatal ball that pierced his massive chest
Had torn an opening to his lungs their art
Could never close, although it healed in part;
So that whene'er the gasping Chieftain drew
A labouring breath, the air came hissing through:
At which in pure self-scorn he oft would jest,
Laugh a faint echo of his old great laugh,
And say he was already more than half
A ghost, and talked the language of the dead,
The whistling tones of spirits that have fled;
And Kangapo had best beware, or he
Would worry him, for all his witchery!
—But most he loved to spend his scanty breath
In urging all who stood his couch beside
To hold their own, whatever might betide;
Whate'er the odds, the arms, the Chiefs renowned
Assailed them, still unblenched to keep their ground,
And never, never yield—but fight till death!

And, when too weak to rise, his race nigh run,—
He made them lift him out into the sun:
Had all his favourite weapons round him laid—
The weapons of his glory, youth, and pride;
And these, while memory with old visions played
Of many a furious fight and famous raid,
He feebly handled—proudly, fondly eyed:
That heavy batlet bright of nephrite pure,
Green, smooth and oval as a cactus leaf—
'How heavy!' sighed he with a moment's grief;
But then what blows it dealt, how deadly sure—
Its fame and his for ever must endure!
And that great battleaxe, from many a field
Notched, hacked and stained, he could no longer wield,
How many a warrior's fate that blade had sealed!—
The others to his kinsmen he bequeathed,
But these he could not part with while he breathed.
Then all the musquets he could boast—but few—
And even his powder-kegs were set in view;
These were the Gods on whom he placed his trust
To guard and keep his tribe when he was dust;
These were the sacred symbols—holy books—
Whereon for comfort dwelt his dying looks.
—Thus, all his Soul, in gesture, word and thought,
One blaze of high defiance of the power
Of Death to quell or quench it—thus he fought
The griesly Tyrant to his latest hour;
As Tongariro's fires flare upward red
And fierce, against the blackest clouds that shed
Their stormy torrents on his shrouded head!—
The Priest, in place of Kangapo supplied,
Sung ceaseless incantations at his side;
On him or them but little he relied.
And when the inevitable talons fast

Clutched his old heathen hero-heart at last;
When life's large flame slow-flickering fell and rose,
Death's shadows flapping closer and more close,
Still his unconquered Spirit strove to wave
Its fluttering standard of defiance high;
And "*Kia tóa—kia tóa!* O be brave,
Be brave, my Sons!"—he gasped with broken cry!
Then as the rattling throat and back-turned eye
Told his last moment come, the restless Priest,
With zeal to frenzy at the sight increased,
Seizing his shoulders, shook him to set free
His Spirit in its parting agony;
And bending o'er that dying head down-bowed,
Into its heedless ear kept shouting loud:
"Now, now, be one with the wide Light, the Sun!
With Night and Darkness, O be one, be one!"—
Then rushed the men about with furious yells;
Then clubs were brandished—every musket fired;
The women shrilled, and as stern use required
Their bosoms gashed with sharpened flints and shells;
Dogs barked and howled, the more the warriors leapt;
The Priest, like one madraving or inspired,
Still shouting his viaticum untired!
So while both men and women, old and young
Seemed by some demon to distraction stung—
Though Amo, better taught by Ranolf, kept
More self-command and only moaned and wept,—
So while this stormy hubbub round him swept,
The mighty Chief—the 'Wailing Sea,' expired.

Thus Tangi died;—not vastly grieved or vexed
To leave this world—or grave about the next.
He had his Heaven, be sure; where warriors brave
Found all the luxuries their rude tastes would crave:

Transparent greenstone glorious, in excess,
And lovelier-streaked than language could express;
Fairtinted feathercrests of stateliest plume;
Rare flaxen robes of silkiest glossiness;
Roots of the richest succulence, perfume,
And flavour, more than famine could consume;
And beauteous women of unwithering bloom!
All this would lure them, lapt in skies, serene
As on the long sweet summer-days are seen
When silver-cradled clouds soft-piled upturn
Their innocent white faces to the Sun;
Or spread o'er all the abyss of light a screen
Snowy and delicate and overrun
With little cracks, unequal network fine,
Like those through which the firelogs' red hearts shine
While at the surface ashenwhite they burn.—
Of Paradise no lofty notion this—
Yet their ideal no less, of perfect bliss.
And whose is more?—Of all the heavens divulged,
Is there not still one staple, worst and best?
Sense, mental powers or moral, all indulged
And exercised with mightier sway and zest:
On infinite Perfection, say, entranced
In rapturous rest to dwell; or work its will,
With nobler strengths, aims evermore advanced:—
'Tis but your highest bliss you look for still!
You wish for the best state you can conceive,
Or something better which to God you leave;
To self-denying selfishness hold fast—
Denying Self as best for Self at last:
Who so unselfish as consent to fall
At last to lower life or none at all?
So 'tis for Happiness you press and pray—
The state most blest, define it how you may.

Are then your motives less by interest marred—
Your self-devotion greater, self-regard
Much less than *his*—the heathen's—who so true,
So stanch and faithful to his simple creed
Of Courage for his Tribe's well-being, threw
His life away to win it, nor would deign
To waste a sigh upon his loss or pain ;
And self-forgetful still, no more would heed
His gain—his not exceeding great reward,
That heaven of sweet potatoes ?—yet confess
The merit greater as the meed was less.
Nor haply should his 'trust in God' be scorned,
Because, not naming Him whom none can name,
It was but Confidence, upheld the same,
By praises, prayers, professions unadorned,
In what was Right, his Duty, so he felt ;
Because in that unconsciousness he dwelt
Much more upon the Duty to be done
To win it, than the guerdon to be won ;
So *did* the Duty ; cared for nought beside ;
And let his Gods for all the rest provide.

Two days in state the Chieftain's body lay,
In arms, mats, feathers, all his best array ;
And women wailed and musquet-volleys rung
And funeral dirges were in chorus sung,
Which likened him to things below—above—
Best worth their admiration, pride and love ;
Most precious trinkets of the greenstone jade—
Canoe-prows carved with most elaborate blade
And trees of stateliest height—most sheltering shade ;—
Bade fiery mountains open to admit
Their hero to the Reinga's gloomy pit ;—

Made breezes sigh and boiling geysers groan
In cavernous depths for their great Warrior gone ;
Bade Tu, the God of War, look favouring down ;
And all the mighty Shades of old renown
Welcome a Spirit who among them came
Proud as themselves, and of congenial fame !
Then to some secret cave and catacomb,
Of all their nobly born the ancient tomb,
In long procession slow, with chaplets crowned
Of fresh-plucked leaves, their dirge-timed way they wound :
There left the dead Form couched in lonely state,
The annual-rounding Sun's return to wait ;
Then to be taken out with reverent care,
And the dry bones, corruption-clogged—laid bare—
With songs and savage rites and dances wild,
Cleansed from all fleshly fragments of decay ;
And 'mid white skulls and skeletons up-piled,
In that most dreaded Sanctuary laid away.

CANTO THE TWENTY-THIRD.

I.

ALAS! that human Happiness should never
Like those fair-flowing snowy fringes be,
That down Mahana's geyser-terraced hill,
Grow into permanence as they distil;
In loveliness of marble mimicry
There, in the act of falling, fixed for ever!—
    Alas! that Love's best transports may—
    Like rills that dance and gleam and glance,
    In loveliest forms of foam and spray
    Down common cataracts every day—
    So swiftly cease their sparkling play;
    Though Love—the River's self—below
    As deep or deeper still may flow!

The days rolled on—as dark or bright they will;
And found those lovers fondly loving still.
Could chance or change or circumstance destroy
Fair Amo's fondness for her bright Sea-boy?
Hers was a love exhaustless as the Ocean;
Her heart unwearied—as his waves with motion—
With restless play of passionate devotion.

Her pure profound Affection could outpour
Its tender tributes from an endless store,
With lavish waste diminishing no more,
Than *his* with rolling snow-wreaths on the shore.
Enraptured in the presence of the Lord
And Idol of her young imagination,
Her Soul seemed always in the act to bless—
Her Spirit in a posture that adored ;
Each look seemed love—each gesture a caress ;
And every breath a yearning aspiration !
Though half the gems with which her Idol glowed
And won her worship, she herself bestowed—
Her heart was an unworked Golconda-mine,
Unconscious as 'twas careless, what a dower—
As a volcano might its scoria-shower—
It flung of diamond-fancies on the shrine
And round the Deity it made divine.
The knowledge—courage—courtesy—whate'er
In mind or body might be found, of fair
Intelligent or brave in him she loved,
By her fresh bosom's fond illusive pride,
Were all sublimed, transfigured, glorified ;
Beyond the reach of her and hers removed—
As are some landscapes' beauties you survey
With head downbent, and such new charms diffuse,
That woods and plains are in transcendant hues
Of tenderest richness floated far away.

II.

Was she not happy then?—what shadow stole
Over her full contentedness of soul?—
It was that as the days less swiftly flew
A weariness o'er Ranolf's spirit grew ;

Not of her charms or her—for none the less
He loved his Wonder of the Wilderness.
But that the Life he led of savage ease
The more it was prolonged, seemed less to please.
Perhaps his love of roving was too strong,
Too deep-engrained to be quiescent long:
But this was not a conscious need, nor would
Have been the parent of his present mood:
It was the crave for intellectual food,
For which a young enthusiast Thinker pines,
Who daringly has tasted of the Tree,
Forbidden still, of Knowledge of a Good
Beyond the actual still to be pursued
In all things to all ends; an Evil still
To be assailed by Reason still more free,
By wider Love and more exalted Will.
It was the crave for Books—the mighty mines
Where all the extinguished forests of mankind
In diamond-thoughts lie crystallised—enshrined:
And 'twas the haply sadder doom to be
Excluded from the guidance—sympathy—
The fellowship or presence of the prime
Of men who towards the Light the highest climb:
And head the onslaught of the human Mind
Against the strongholds of dim Destiny.
Ambition—progress—all the hope and pride
Of true Existence seemed to him denied.
That land so rich in Beauty's sensuous smile,
Seemed for the Soul, only a desert Isle.
If ever chance-sent rumours reached his ear
Of the great Nations in their grand career,
They seemed dim records of aërial hosts
Who struggled in the heavens—or shadowy ghosts.

All the loud wonder-throes of peace or war
Seemed melted to a murmur faint and far!
What marvel if a feeling would intrude
Of something wanting in this solitude?—
Was it a treason to almighty Love
This sense of unfulfilled desire to prove?
Could any Love in any Paradise,
Howe'er impassioned, mutual, melting, true—
Alone for any lovers long suffice?—
Not poets' dreams can make it ever new—
Not even a bustling dove can *always* coo!

And anxious Amo could not but perceive
His thoughts were often wandering far away;
Her keen-eyed love would note, and inly grieve,
The shadow on his features once so gay.
The very love that, to her faithful breast,
So magnified the merits he possessed;
On which to dwell and feel them all her own
Were highest bliss to be conceived or known:
Made her inclined to rate herself too low;
With timid doubt it could indeed be so,
That such a treasure was reserved for her!
And often to her memory would recur,
With what a glow he answered her demand
To paint the Beauties of his native Land.
And when her fond eye marked—more frequent now,
His sad abstracted air and troubled brow,
She could not check the thought, how full of woe,
"Ah! he is pining for those charms, I know,
Those lovely beings all of light and snow!
O my o'erweening pride to think that he
The glorious one, could be content with me!—"

Then would she seek the saddened heart to ease,
And ply with simple craft her arts to please ;
With skilful change her finest mantles choose
Of broadest purfle and the fairest hues ;
Their folds around her shapely shoulders place
Or dainty waist, in each remembered way
He most had praised for piquancy and grace :
Or the soft glitter of her lustrous hair—
So glossy black, the lights thrown off would play
In sharp metallic gleams of bluish gray—
In crimson flowers he loved her so to wear,
Or wax-white creeper-wreaths, she would array,
With chance-taught Taste so sure—such careless Care !
Or she would set herself a serious task,
Through tangled woods and thickets dense to range
In search of plants and insects—else despised—
Because he took in them an interest strange,
She knew not why and scarcely cared to ask,
Since 'twas enough they were by Ranolf prized.
Or she would summon all her Damsels gay,
To lively dance or sportive game, that best
Would dexterous skill or native grace display :
Or send them on a harvest-gathering quest
Of clustering purple-fringes whence they squeeze
Sweet jellies ruby-clear ; because the sight
Once seemed his fancy so to strike and please
Of these wild Wood-nymphs trooping through the trees
Back with their mirth-lit eyes—teeth glittering white
With laughter—tresses floating on the breeze,
And cheeks and foreheads in their reckless mood
All dashed and splashed with crimson berry-blood ;
Like nymphs that frolic reeled in Bacchic dance
In Nature's golden-aged exuberance,

Or with goat-borne Silenus loved to romp
In grape-empurpled grace and tipsy pomp!
And Ranolf would her loving purpose guess;
And chide himself that he could not repress
The weary longing that would o'er him steal;
And force a gaiety he could not feel;
And show her deeper love and double tenderness.
But how should this content her? whose sole aim
Was to light up the old gladness in his eyes;
And little cared what of herself became,
Were that secured at any sacrifice;
But gained from true love far too keen a glance
To be deceived by any simulance
Of feeling, or affectionate pretence;—
Is not true Love the Mesmerizer true—
Beyond material Nature and above;
Clear-seeing, with its supernatural sense
The sympathetic object through and through?
Into its inmost being swift to dart,
In strange emotion take magnetic part,
And throb with beatings of the loved one's heart?—
So Ranolf fondly sought—but sought in vain
From those fond eyes to hide his inward pain.

III.

What *could* be done? could he then bear her hence,
A wondering Wilding to his native land,
A savage wife! Ah what a startling shock
To prejudices like a wall of rock
Sense-based or senseless—piled on every hand!
Could *he* find fortitude or impudence
The ridicule and censure to withstand
Wisdom and folly would alike dispense?

Could he endure to be the mark or mock
For open pity—secret insolence?
To friends and kindred such a stumbling-block
Of deep and irremediable offence?
Ah could he brave all this?—But graver care
It was, how Amo such a change could bear?
Could this bright Child of woods and waters thrive
In the hot crowding of our social hive—
Though not like its mere honey-workers tasked,
Though only for such lightsome labour asked,
Such sweet monotony of toil as there
The partner of his moderate means must share?—
This life, self-guided by her will or whim—
Could she resign it for confinement dim,
Cooped round with indoor comfort—too secure?
Give up bright careless ease and breathing pure
In azure liberty of Sun and Air,
To choke in some fine atmosphere, of nice
Punctilios and proprieties precise?
Be drilled into the trite and tedious round
Of petty duties, poor amusements, found
In formal life by strict conventions bound?—
Or could it flourish, this wild-flowering Tree,
Transparent with the sunbeams flowing free
Through its white cloud of blossom—nailed and trained
Espalier-wise against the rigid Wall
Of civilised existence—shorn of all
Its shoots of natural beauty—every spray
Checked in its impulses of artless play—
And all its waving wanton boughs constrained
And tortured into stiff and starch array,
In straightened uniformity controlled,
Like iron grate-bars regular and cold?—

Or could the Tree transplanted long endure
The chill and rigour of a rougher sky?
The beautiful Exotic would be sure
In such ungenial clime to droop and die!
Nay (for this minor matter too deserves
A moment's thought) what sacrilege 'twould seem
To bolster out, disfigure and compress
That realization of a sculptor's dream
Of pure proportion—sinuous symmetry—
So simply clad in classic drapery—
That hit the happy and harmonious mean
Between the ripe and rich voluptuousness
Of lovely Aphrodite—soft and warm—
And beauty bright with a severer charm,
The light strong grace of active Artemis:—
Ah! what a sin to screw a shape like this
Into some flaunting wire-and-whalebone screen
Of beauty-blighting frippery, that combines
In dull extravagance discordant lines—
Sharp angles—shooting arcs and cutting curves—
Each form fantastic from true taste that swerves
In hideous freaks of fashionable dress!
No! whether for her mind's or body's weal
He most was anxious—most was bound to feel—
Whichever way he looked, it seemed too plain,
He must this longing for his home restrain.

IV.

So with factitious fervour—wearied zeal
As if to banish thought and deaden pain
He takes to his boar-hunting toils again;
While native mongrels, bad or good, replace
His first stanch sturdy comrade in the chase;

But none he loved so—none that so loved him—
As that good-tempered wriggling tiger—Nim!
And many a day and sometimes nights he passed
Amid the forests on the Mountains vast;
While Amo, loving still and lonely grieved,
By his affected interest undeceived
In these pursuits; and with increased distress,
Saw the sad struggle she so well could guess—
The discontent of forced contentedness.
Though he was kind—aye kinder than before,
'Twas not for kindness that she yearned alone,
But love—glad glowing love like that of yore,
Impetuous and impassioned as her own!
That kindness might be pity—nay, it must!
What else could be more likely—natural—just!
What else could one of such exalted sphere
Her fancy lifted to a realm so clear
And high above her, from his glorious place
Feel towards a being of inferior race,
Such as her love still made herself appear?
"Did he not come, a wonder and a prize
From some far Clime mysterious as the Skies—
Stoop in his flight to steep me in excess
Of too delightful, fleeting happiness—
My lowly life with strange wild joys to crown,
As Hapae in the legend once came down,
The white-winged Wanderer from blue haunts above—
And on Tawhaki lavished all that love?
Ah! what am I, or what my claim or right
To keep all to myself a thing so bright?—"
And then her anguish took another turn;
With the old pride at moments would she burn:
"Am I not something too! through all the land

Where'er on great or small the Sun would shine
What Maid could boast superior birth to mine?
Could I help hearing how on every hand
They said—not men, even women—far and wide
For beauty none with Amohia vied;
None in the dance such wavy grace displayed;
Such fair designs for rich-wrought purfles made—
Like her could tell a legend—turn a song?—
Was it all flattery then—delusive—wrong?
Is she—through her whole life so praised—so prized,
Doomed to be now neglected and despised?"—
In her distraction then how would she try
To hate the cause of all this agony;
Half curse him in her impotent distress—
Aye—curse him with a passion that—would bless!
The mere conception of harsh words of hate
Such instant fond revulsion would create,
The ire wrung out by woe, in utterance choked,
Itself a gush of boundless love provoked—
The rage ran off in tears of tenderness:
"Too mad! too mad!—too horrible to curse
One so beloved—so beautiful—O worse
Than Rona cursing the full Moon for light!
Is it *his* blame he shines at such a height?
Ah, miserable me! who can but find
Food for a curse in what I am too blind—
No—not too blind! I cannot, ne'er could be
So blind, that dear, dear glory, not to see!
And seeing it and him—to think it strange
If love like mine he only could bestow
On beings like himself in fair exchange—
Bright beings—ah—those Maids he talked of so—
All golden light and sunset-tinted snow!

In beauty, knowledge—all attractions fine
Such as perchance I never could divine,
Would they not dim these poor dark charms of mine
As he does all our native youths outshine!
But could they love like me? Ah were they here
To show which held the dearest one most dear!
Would they were here! if deadly danger prest
His life, he soon would learn who loved him best!
Would they, like me (O would I might!) to save
Him sinking, rush into the flooded wave
And all the terrors of the torrent brave?
Would they, like me, dash into the thickest fight,
Cling to his conquering foe, about to smite
And take the blow—Ah me! with what delight,
Aimed at that head so beautiful—so bright!
Then, then—those Wonders—none he soon would see
Could worship—doat on—die for him like me!
Ah, why can men love nothing but the skin,
So little care for all that glows within—
All that should lure their love—their praises win?
Ah, why was I not made as wise, as fair—
Why should those Gods or Atuas—whatsoe'er
They be—have left me of these gifts so bare,
And grudged me all but misery and despair?
And yet he said—for I remember well
When of those wondrous beauties he would tell
The greatest merit could be had or known
Was for another's good to give your own;
And those grand Creatures, born to light and bliss,
Good in so much besides, were best in this.
But there at least I am their equal—I;
O could I not the best of them defy
To give all *I* would give his good to buy?

None—none of them like me, without a sigh,
To give him joy, a thousand times would die:
O that the chance would rise—howe'er it came
That I might prove, and he might learn, the same!"

And so the days slid heavily for both—
Each grief grew daily with the other's growth;
And from the woods upon his sad return
The sadness in her eyes he would discern,
And try to cheer her, O, with words too drear—
Words meaning much—but sounding little—cheer.
And then it was *her* turn sad joy to feign,
Which, pressing hard her heart to check its pain
She feigned—with stiffening lips that twitched in vain;
Thinking—with anguish smiling for his sake—
"O misery! my heart will break, will break!"

V.

So matters stood. And now the Autumn's fruits—
Karaka—taro—kumera—berries, roots—
Had all been harvested with merry lays
And rites of solemn gladness; choral praise
And pure religious feeling—grateful—true;
Though rude, benighted if you will, the due
Of the great bounteous Spirit unknown or known
Of Nature; due in every clime or zone;
They called it 'Rongo'—God of fruits and peace;
What matter, so the gratitude was given
To Spirit—call it Nature, God or Heaven?—
The worst was, almost ere the songs could cease,
With idiot inconsistency, like—men,
The very life-preserving gifts that then

They thanked their God for, they would straight employ
As means, almost incentives, to destroy;
And seize the occasion of abundant food
As fittest for the work of war and blood.

'Twas then, that tidings of invasion, planned
By far more dangerous foes, against their land,
Reached Rotorua's people; how in brief
That mighty tribe, of all the tribes the chief,
Far in the North, whom not their neighbours dread
Not even the great Waikato could withstand—
Such wealth of guns and powder could they boast,
(For with the white man's ships they trafficked most)
Were coming, an innumerable host
'Twas rumoured, by the famous Chieftain led
With whom the marriage treaty was begun
Which Amo when she swam the Lake had fled;
So much the picture of her beauty brought
By Kangapo had on his fancy wrought;
Such power had recently that rabid Priest—
(By careless Ranolf in contempt released
When after Tangi's death the warfare ceased)—
O'er the excited haughty Chieftain won;
And, mad with rancour and revengeful spite
He could not wreak on Ranolf, nor requite
That spurner of his supernatural might
Who laughed at necromantic spells and charms,
Except by tearing Amo from his arms—
Had roused the Chief's too ready sense of slight,
By representing Tangi in the light
Of an abettor of his daughter's flight;
And acquiescent in the wrong his pride
Endured from those who sought—then set aside—

The great alliance they would now deride.
So all this storm was brewing, it was plain,
And soon would ruin and destruction rain
Upon their tribe, one special end to gain,—
To force surrender of the proffered bride,
And vengeance on the Stranger so obtain.

Before the tidings well were told, which filled
The eager-listening crowd with blank dismay,
The prescient heart of Amohia chilled;
And through her brain there shot a gloomy ray.
That Message seemed her secret Soul to seek;
Seemed to her inner consciousness to speak
Doomlike, before the story was got through;
Almost before she heard the half, she knew
Her hour was come, and all she had to do.
To foes like these, resistance would be vain,
She would be captured, Ranolf would be slain.
This was the chance that she had prayed for still;
This was the moment when her heart should thrill
With joy, not terror, for the hope it gave—
Nay, all the certainty her heart could crave—
To prove her love and her adored one save!
Yes; she, ere it burst forth, that storm would stay,
Anticipate—prevent that dreadful day
And turn its terrors from *one* head away!
To save that dear one, she would go alone
And give herself to that resistless Chief;
The wrong, if done by Ranolf, so atone
And buy his life, O more than with her own!—
Her life were little—better could she bear
To give a thousand lives than seem to share

Another's love ; that was the pain, the smart,
That was the sacrifice that wrung her heart ;
Yet, worse than death, to make his life secure
This outrage to her love would she endure !
Yet life would still be given—for O with grief
She soon would die, and death would be relief !
Or if it came not of itself—and here
Pale grew her solemn brow and more severe
Her eyes and firm prest lips—herself would rend
The life away that misery would not end.
But Ranolf would be saved—O he would know
How matchless, boundless was her love—and woe ;
And feel, the best of those he vaunted so
Could not outdare her in devotion—make
Such sacrifice of self for his dear sake !
Then would he long for her again—and weep
Her loss, and ever in his bosom deep
His poor wild maiden's memory fondly keep !

But Ranolf, whose own cares too deeply weighed,
Not much attention to these tidings paid :
" It was their greed for marvels—nothing more ;
Or if that doughty Chieftain and his men
Were bent upon invading them—what then ?
They would be *threshed* as Whetu was before."
So he continued listless to explore
The forests for the footprints of the boar.
And Amo thought, " He does not know their power,
Nor half their evil deeds in victory's hour "—
And all the more determined it was right
Herself should save him in his own despite.

VI.

And often had she fixed the day to start,
Yet could not bear from all life's light to part;
The project oft deferred, was still renewed,
Whenever Ranolf's restlessness she viewed;
Until one night arrived for her and him,
That filled their cup of misery to the brim.
That day a precious letter from his home—
With slanting oval postmarks blue and red,
And scrawls "Try here—try there" all overspread—
Had (passed from tribe to tribe) to Ranolf come;
And with it, news that all the Chiefs who shared
The great prop sed invasion were prepared
With countless guns and piles of packed-up food
And war-canoes and crowds of warriors good
To start in sanguinary, sanguine mood.—
And Amo all that eve had sate and gazed
With tearful looks, how fond! on Ranolf's face
And eyes, so seldom from the letter raised,
Or fixed in sad abstraction far away,
While on his knees the fatal missive lay;
And fancied all his thoughts she well could trace—
With maddening hopelessness how they would run
Upon the Sister—Mother—long unseen;
And what a roar of Ocean—vast—unknown—
And obstacles far greater, stood between
Those loved ones and the Brother and lost Son;
And some sweet phantom Shape still dearer, she
Would fancy in his picture there must be!—
'Twas then, and there, with burning—bursting heart
And choking throat— she bound herself, alone
Come what come might—next morning to depart.

So, when day broke, while Ranolf, half the night
Awake, was sleeping sadly by her side,
She rose up—from her prostrate grief upright—
To take a last long gaze—heart-broken bride—
Upon that sleeping face—her life—her pride!
Then, in an agony of tenderness
With those fair golden curls she toyed awhile
That seemed to mock her with their sunny smile;
And lavished many a bitter-sweet caress
Upon the brow and cheeks and fast-closed eyes
She loved so—more than ever seemed to prize,
And thought more beautiful in this distress;
And hid at last her face upon his breast,
And wept a passionate flood of bitter tears—
"O could she there end all—joys, woes and fears—
Dead—dead at once—for ever there to rest!"—
And when at those fond touches Ranolf woke,
And saw her grief, and words of comfort spoke,
Returning her caress, and sought to know
What sudden sorrow caused these tears to flow;
With quick-recovered firmness she replied—
"Twas nothing—he was not to mind her—she
Was foolish—was '*porangi*'—and would be
Better directly—" and her tears she dried
And smiled in utter misery—and tried
Her deep despairing eyes from his to hide;
The while with more than usual busy zeal,
It seemed, she went about the morning meal;
Then set it quietly before him—made
Some light excuse why he could not persuade
Herself to touch it—quietly received
His last caress, as, bidding her be cheered,

"For he would soon return, she might be sure!"—
And kissing her, he stroked her tresses black,
And with his dogs and gun, and heart sore-grieved
Off to the hills, by her calm looks deceived,
As usual went; while she, with bosom seared,
And brain that whirled confused upon a rack
Of thoughts and feelings she could scarce endure,
Till all that she was seeing, hearing—seemed
Something she heard not—saw not—only dreamed,
She stood there watching till he disappeared;—
Then flung herself upon her couch, and there
Gave full, wild vent to sobbings of despair.

Soon with set teeth she rises; from her eyes
Brushes the blinding tears that *will* arise;
And snatching up a small supply of food—
For life must last to make her purpose good—
Still in the clutch of that wild passion held,
That from her tight grief-strangled bosom swelled
Up to her throbbing brow—as if compelled
By outward force—she keeps her frenzied thought
As well as her despairing fevered glance,
From resting on a single circumstance
Of past or recent happiness, or aught
About that dim—loved—lost—and torturing scene—
The hut—the room where she so blest had been!
But staggering as beneath a heavy load,
Rushes straight forward on her blighted road.

CANTO THE TWENTY-FOURTH.

I.

So all that day, as by a dream possessed—
On—on—by one idea absorbed, opprest—
For many a mile, as if herself she fled,
Shunning all human sight the Wanderer sped:
'To save *him!*' the one hope, one lure to guide
Her course—all goading sharp despair beside.

But when exhausted nature *would* have rest,
And, reckless where, she sank upon the ground,
She was upon the very spot, she found,
Where Ranolf and herself, by rain delayed,
On that first blessed journey once had stayed.
And at a little distance she espied
The cave itself where they had made their nest,—
Laughing, their happy nest!—a yellow cave
Of clayey sandstone scooped out smooth and round
By some long-vanished immemorial wave;
One of a row that undermined the base
Of the steep hill-side green with tangled fern—
Only a few feet high and deep—a place
Just large enough for those two lovers fond,
And over-draped with drooping bough and frond.

There lay the flattened fern-couch—brown and dry ;
The impress of two forms she could descry,
Still undisturbed by winds or passers-by.
Then did the conquering tenderness return ;
And she resolved (for, but a little space,
The circuit her arrival would delay
At her sad journey's end) she would repair
Once more to those dear Lakes ; the district fair
Where all the bliss of her life's little day
Lay like a vanished treasure ; stored up there—
Quite lost to her—gone—lost and laid away !

II.

Dim skies and heavy rain !—
And by Mahana's Lake she roams again ;
Nursing her agony with insensate care,
And pampering her despair :
Has sought out every scene
Where she and Ranolf had together been :
On every sight
Of wonder once and such delight
Again has dwelt :
And in their presence felt—
Delight? Ah no ! increased distress—
No wonder—worse than weariness.

The clouds were dark and low ;
Rain falling, soft and slow ;
Day closing on her woe ;
As, little heeding where she went,
With trouble more than travel spent,
She wandered reckless near the weird ravine
That leads up to the Lake of waters green,

Through spectral shapes forlorn
Of rocks all torn and weather-worn:
More gaunt, distorted, grim,
Thus shadowy seen through vapours dim.
Then at the entrance of that dismal vale,
Where dense broom-thickets hide
Mud-pools that boil on every side,
And pit the crust, that anywhere might fail
The footstep, with foul cauldrons deep and wide;—
There, she—with hands upon her knees that hid
Her face, unmoving sat.
And though the rain had soaked her flaxen mat,
And slowly down the silken tresses slid,
That fell neglected on the ground;
Though in the silence as they slipped,
The unkindly drops of dew
Audibly dripped and dripped—
She felt it not, nor knew.
The only sight or sound
She saw or heard around,
Was that lost voice, that vanished face
That once had glorified the place;
And now, in such a torturing maze
Of tender recollections, wound
Her burning brain, her breaking heart;
The past to life appeared to start
In vivid hues too beautiful to bear!
Her vanished Bliss seemed over her to glare,
A deadly-terrible Angel lovely-bright,
With outspread wings ablaze
Above her hung;—till blasted by its light
Down—down—she cowered—she sank—in misery's blackest night.

How the gleam iridescent and shapeless—that lies
Like the Wreck of a Rainbow flung crushed on the skies
In the rack of the tempest, low down where it flies,
With its hues dimly blurred;—to the mariner drear,
How forlornly it bids the fair vision appear
Of the Arch all resplendent! the luminous Bow
In the glory of orange and purple aglow;
On the thick of the violet shadow behind
In rounded perfection so sharply defined;
So airily tender—transparently mild,
Yet so firmly enthroned o'er the elements wild;
So softly aspiring, so gracefully grand,
On the air, like a rock, it has taken its stand,
And lords it serenely o'er ocean and land!—
Even so—as she lay overwhelmed by despair
Wan, weary and haggard—crushed, cowering there,
Even so—and so sadly! her woe-begone mien
Might have roused the remembrance of what she had been
When the Maid in the maddening days that had flown
In the bloom and the pride of her happiness shone!

III.

A hand upon her shoulder laid,
With sudden startling pressure stayed
Her anguish in its mid career;
Though not the slightest sound betrayed
A human being's presence near.
'Twas Kangapo! who silent crept
Upon her, thinking that she slept;
Till as he neared the weeping maid,
Her heart-wrung moans the truth conveyed.

To aid the northern Chief's designs, and make
The conquest sure which his revenge would slake;
To spy into the schemes the people planned
To meet the invaders of their threatened land;
But most, with well-feigned tale and crafty lie
To lull them into false security;
The wily Priest had ventured back once more—
Safe in the sorcerer's dread repute he bore—
To prowl about the country, gather news,
And disaffection, where he could, diffuse;
Hiding the while, and less from need than taste,
In many a well-known haunt of wood and waste.

When Amo raised in wild surprise
Her tear-bedabbled face and eyes,
And saw whose form above her hung;
Whose spiteful, cool, triumphant leer
Into her grief would pry and peer,
Indignant to her feet she sprung:
"You, Kangapo! and wherefore here?"
"Nay, rather—" was the answering sneer,
"Say what has brought to such disgrace,
Such evil plight, so lone a place,
The Stranger's Love—the white man's bride!
Has he, whose pale and girlish face
Could win, despite her birth and race,
Her tribe's renown—her father's pride,
The Maori maiden to his side—
Has he turned false, or fled—or died?"

"Ask nought of him; no mate of thine;
Thy course pursue—leave me to mine!"

"Nay—listen, Amo! let me tell—"

"Away! I know thy wiles too well!"—

No longer now his darkening brow
And coldly-glittering eye instilled
The terror that, whene'er he willed
Had once the Maiden's bosom chilled.
The might of one supreme despair
Would let no lesser passion share
That bosom; one absorbing care
Had left no room for terror there.
She sought not to upbraid, reply;
Too sad for scorn, she turned to fly.
He saw his words their purpose missed,
Yet would not from his aim desist;
"Not listen! so resolved to go!—
Think not you shall escape me so;—
Think not I've no assistance nigh!—"
With sudden grasp he seized her wrist
And shouted. Then once more her eye
Shot forth its proud indignant light;
Her form expanded to full height;
She looked almost as when she stood
A captive bound beside the wood
When first she dazzled Ranolf's sight;—
Yet now so haggard, wan and worn,
By grief of so much beauty shorn,
Not much more like that Vision bright
Of anger-flashing loveliness,
Than some too early perished Tree,
A silver skeleton pourtrayed
Against the mountain's violet shade,

Like its own former self would be.
In luxury clad of leafy dress :—
In sunlit symmetry of frame,
And every sinuous branch the same ;
But all the wealth wherewith it shone
Of blossom gay and verdure—gone !—
The wrist he held—she wrenched it free,
And flung him off with all her might :
He reeled—he stumbled—staggered back ;
Nor had he seen how near he stood,
To that fierce cauldron, sputtering black
And baleful—ever-boiling mud—
Beneath the phantom-shapes of rock
That seemed to gibber, jeer and mock :
The treacherous bank began to crack—
Gave way—and with a sullen plash
He plumped into the viscous mash ;
The sable filth upspurted high—
Foul steam in thicker volumes gushed ;
Then back the burning batter rushed
And closed o'er that despairing face
Upturned in blue-lined agony,
Those writhing limbs—that stifled cry !
Then heavily swelled into a cone,
Sunk down ; and ring on ring a space
In sluggish undulations rolled ;
And thicklier rising crowds alone
Of bubbles, of that horror told ;
Though just as lazily they burst,
And not more poisonous than at first
Their old sulphureous stench dispersed.

Shocked, horrified, at sight so dread
Swift through the thicket Amo sped:
So rapidly had all occurred,
Well might what she had seen and heard—
That Sorcerer's apparition—then
And there—in that secluded glen,
And his swift disappearance, seem
Illusions of a hideous dream.

IV

Again her journey she pursues.
Her thoughts come back to their accustomed train:
"Only to save him—only make him know,
Although her joy—her life—her love she lose—
No other Maid could love him so!"—
Still fell the sad, slow, melancholy rain;
And though the white mist hid sky, mountain, plain,
Yet somehow seemed it, on her weary brain
The sunshine of that awful morn
When Ranolf last she saw and left—
Still lay—a solemn sombre light forlorn;—
Ever she seemed to wander woebegone
Through endless mazes of a forest lone
All stripped and bare, of every leaf bereft;
While far above her, through the treetops high
That, leafless, yet shut out the sky,
A loud monotonous wind for ever roared,
And those strange, dreary, sombre sunbeams poured;
While in the foreground only could be seen
The lover and the love-joy that had been!
And every actual outward sight and sound,
Men, women, places, voices all around,

Came faintly breaking through this muffling screen,
This sad bright curtain that would intervene;
And only for a moment, face or speech
Importunate of others, could emerge
Through that drear desolate light and murmur loud,
As through an ever-circling shroud—
And her preoccupied perception reach
And on her absent mind their presence urge.

On—on! for days as by a dream oppressed—
Still on—by one idea absorbed—possessed!—
Directly in her way
A broad and swollen river lay:
Her road led through the shallows by its bank,
Where yellow waters eddying swirled
Through flax-tufts waving green and tall and rank;
But in the midst the raging torrent hurled
Its waters swift, direct, and deep,
Where often some uprooted tree would sweep—
A great black trunk unwieldy—hastening down
The flood surcharged with clayey silt;
And dip and heave and plunge and tilt
Half buried in the wavelets brown.
She paused—but something in her breast
Still urged her on:—she could not rest:
And then those friends whom Kangapo addrest—
Might they not still her course arrest?
What if they still should be upon her track—
Would they not meet her if she ventured back?—
She tore her mantle off in haste,
And rolled it up, and tightly tied
With flax, and slung it round her waist;

Then wading, struggled through the high sword-grass
And streambowed tortured blades—a tangled mass,
And struck into the torrent fierce and wide !

Alas ! no strength of limb or will,
No stoutest heart, no swimmer's skill
Could long withstand the headlong weight and force
Of that wild tide in its tumultuous course !—
Soon was she swept away—whirled o'er and o'er—
And hurried out of conscious life
Almost without a sense of pain or strife.

* * * * * *

V.

And if that self-forgetting Life was passed,
To peace, it seemed, it had been lulled at last.
For one who by the river's side
Far lower down, that day by chance descried
A floating form he could not aid,
Glide swiftly by, soon after said
The Maiden lay, as past she hied,
Upon her back as on a quiet bed.
Her eyes were closed—the lashes long and sleek,
Reposing on the placid cheek ;
Along the yellow waters wild
Her jet-black tresses softly streamed ;
And though careworn, just then it seemed,
Her face was so serene and mild,
So mournful, yet with meek content so deep,—
She looked an innocent Child,
Laid on its couch asleep.

And that informant told them how they found,
Cast on the gravel by the riverside,
The body of the Maiden drowned.

Alas, for Ranolf! in his passionate pain
That image ever was before his brain
In terrible distinctness night and day!
With pertinacious torture self-applied
How would he conjure up to his despair,
And paint with accurate anguish-seeking care
Its harrowing details o'er and o'er again!
How, while the river ran its calm career,
From the spent freshet's fury once more clear;
All heartless Nature, bright, alive and gay
With its accustomed, gentle, joyous stir—
How then they found—O say not *her!*
She could not be the form that lay
So stilly—half above and half beneath
The shallow, bright, transparent stream,
Upon the clean smooth gravel bank
From which it slowly shrank:
Such mournful meek content upon the face
That you could think it for a little space
Lit by some sadly-pleasing dream;
But then so marble-like and motionless—
Persistent in intensest quietness—
Too soon the moulded lineaments you know
Fixed in the dread serenity of death.
One quiet arm the peaceful head below—
While ever in its flow
The eddying current would come up and play
With the long tresses—as to coax away

And lure the floating tangles to and fro;
While others, in the sunshine dried,
The idle breeze at times would lift aside
Gently— then leave at rest,
Where curling they caressed
The cold unheaving breast;
Or revelled in the gloss and gleam of life,
As if in mockery spread
Along the form that lay as still and dead
As any of the logs of driftwood rife,
By the decreasing tide
Left near it as it fled.—
But piteous—O how piteous! there to see
The wavelets in their sunny chase
In that deserted place—
Upon the bank exposed and lone,
With such an inward-happy sound,
Familiarly and carelessly
Gurgling against and rippling round
The sad and sacred human face,
As if it were a stone.

And had he any comfort in the thought,
The sight his fancy clung to might have brought
To one who could more calmly think?—
"That sad—sad face! as there it lay
Beside the river's brink,
So calm, neglected—helpless—meek—
Would not its silence seem to speak—
In mournful whispers seem to say,
For such a heart, for such a soul,
This cannot be the end— the whole!—

"But O! great God of heaven!
If in the poor dead face of one
Slight savage girl who thus has given
Her life's light for another's good in vain—
All her high hopes and generous aims undone!
If in its stony stillness and fixed woe,
All the more harrowing for the mournful show
Of sad resigned repose on mouth and brow—
If from that face, in very deed,
Such obstacle and protest and disdain
Arise against the desolating creed
Of soul-annihilation in the disarray
And dissolution of our worthless clay—
O what a vast Himmálayan pinnacle-chain
Of insurmountable obstruction Thou
Hast thrown in the pale spectral Conqueror's way;
And what a boundless protest has been wrung—
(Although to absolute Love's all-pitying eyes
The humblest instance would the whole comprise)
A protest myriad-voiced as Ocean's roar,
Compelled to just Omnipotence to soar,—
In all the baffled lives and labours flung
Ungrudgingly thy great White Throne before—
The death-requited sacrifices through all time
Made in thy cause by hero-hearts sublime!

"Yet what a thought it is, O God! that we
But by the incredible cruelty of Fate
Ordained by Thee,
Are by a strong revulsion forced to flee
To Reason's refuge in her grief,
The astounding beautiful belief

In Death reviving to some glorious state
Which all that cruelty shall compensate !—
Say, that it is so, and must ever be,
By Nature's strong necessity ;—
As air plunged deep in water still must rise,
So, plunged in Life, the Soul to the Eternal flies !—
And if it be denied
That Nature—which is Thou !
Does that necessity provide,
Even Doubt must still avow
It *should* be so provided—must and should—
If Thou art what Thyself hast made us to call good.
Or if at last Doubt *will* remain
What more ? but it is plain,
Faith has to be created—self-resigning Trust
In Thee—the all-generous and just ;
And Trust like that, for aught we know,
Can but in the absence of Assurance grow ;
Can but be strengthened to the due degree
By actual plunging in the furnace-glow
And wavering flames of forced Uncertainty :
The Soul can but be fashioned *so*,
Into the shape of Beauty, and substance clear
Of crystal Confidence sincere—
The form and fineness its high fates require :
As the glass-worker whirls and moulds
Into a graceful vase, the glass he holds
Molten in jets intense of fierce white fire."

VI.

Ah no ! but no such speculation now
Could smooth the agony on Ranolf's brow.

And so he may depart,
And bind up as he can his bleeding heart ;
And moan his lovely wild-flower reft away,
With unresigning anguish night and day ;
And gnash his teeth and tear his hair,
Untaught to bear !
And for a time his faith in joy forswear ;
And feel how vain
Is poor Philosophy to stifle pain ;
How impotent against the ready sting
Of every trivial and inanimate thing,
That seems to start up eloquent everywhere,
More poignant memories of the Lost to bring—
All leagued with Love to drive him to despair !
Not only the brief words she left to tell
The motive and the purpose of her flight,
Scratched upon shining flax-blades with a shell,
And laid to meet—but not too soon—his sight ;—
Ah ! how it tore his heart—that simple scrawl—
Pothooks and hangers painfully produced—
Disjointed—childlike ! yet a wonder all,
In one to symbolled language so unused,
And with such marvellous aptitude acquired ;
The tenfold talent by the heart inspired ;
Docility no school but one e'er knew—
Whose teacher Love, has Love for learner too !
Not these alone—but every object round
Had silent power and pungency to wound :
The withered wreaths of flowers hung up with care
Which for his pleasure she so loved to wear ;
The span-board mirror on the reeded wall
That oft had imaged such a happy smile,
And so much beauty, on its surface small ;

The broidry-staves her tedium to beguile—
Rude with still-dangling vary-coloured strands ;—
Half-charred mid ashes white, the very brands
Left lying where her loving busy hands
Had laid them on that latest fire extinct—
Ah, with what torturing memories were they linked !
Ah, those dumb things—how deeply did he feel
The maddening pathos of their mute appeal !

Yes ! let him wrestle with distress ;
And feel how grief grown languid, though not less,
In the exhaustion of mere weariness,
Renews itself from its excess ;—
Learn how the heart bereft of one beloved,
Will, self-upbraiding, self-reproved,
In bitterest grief feel bitter grief,
Because its grief seems all too slight and brief ;
Because it cannot grieve enough—nor feed
The ravenous appetite for woe the sense
Of its immeasurable loss will breed—
Thirsting for grief more crushing—more intense ;
Recoiling from the hateful thought, that e'er
The time should come when it may bear
To think upon such loss, and *not* despair !

VII.

Yet should he long endure
Such pangs and pains, be sure
He must escape them—being left alive ;
For the old joyous temper *must* revive.
The clouds of Anguish o'er the blue would drive
And hide—but not annihilate the Sun :
Grief has a work to do—which must be done.

Though o'er his Soul the waves of Sorrow surge,
That buoyant joyous Nature *must* emerge
By animal force into a realm more bright;
And that reflective tendency would urge
His Soul—long after—into peaceful light.
And he would first experience—and then know,
How great a purger of the Soul is Woe;
A fine manipulator skilled to drain
The Spirit of the grosser atmosphere
Which can alone give life to and sustain
Prides—lusts—ambitions—passions fierce and vain:
Until the heart is a receiver clear,
Exhausted of the elements they need,
And wanting which, they droop and disappear.

Aye! he would prove, by God's great scheme the seed
Of Soul best in the soil of Sorrow grows;
And that such pangs and tortures are indeed
Sharp chisel-strokes and heavy mallet-blows
Wherewith the grand Soul-Sculptor cleaves and chips
His native marble into nobler shapes:
And as the mallet swings and chisel trips,—
Out from the sluggish cold chaotic heap
Wherein as possibilities they sleep,
Out come, emerging from their long eclipse
Into vitality that, kindling, glows
Ever more clear, significant and deep—
Heroic white Existences, serene
And lovely, which the divine Artist drapes
With qualities his great Idea must mean
Should make his glorious marbles fit to be
Shrined in high temples of Eternity.

And he would learn, when calmly could be viewed
What sad results from simple love ensued,
How foresight—prudence—cold considerate powers
We need for guidance of this life of ours:
To follow instincts—doing ill to none—
Nay—loving everything beneath the sun—
This will not do—it seems!
Alas!—for *such* the World with misery teems.

But this—all this would be for Time to teach;
A goal his fortitude not yet may reach.
All he has now to do is to depart
And bind up as he may his bleeding heart.

CANTO THE TWENTY-FIFTH.

I.

DEPART then, Ranolf! leave to Grief and Time
The task to cleave out, in some other clime
Less fraught with frenzied thoughts, their ends sublime!
Even Sorrow could not here its fruits mature—
Not here—nor now; for Change and Time, be sure,
Are needed to assist it in its Art
Of Soul-Tuition. This by theory too,
Though spurning now the power of both, he knew;
And felt his only course was to depart.
The land seemed loathsome to his laden heart;
Sick—sick he was; aweary of the skies:
The Mountains seemed to look him in the face—
Cold—calm and sullen, conscious of his woe;
Each shrub and tree that once had charmed him so,
Turned wormwood with the thoughts it bade him trace:
And every River rolled before his eyes,
A Mara-flood of bitterest memories.

When the first shock of Amo's death was o'er,
And he could rouse himself to act once more,
With but one lad his light effects to bear,
He started for some Northwest harbour, where
Vessels that haunt these latitudes repair.

A Ship he sought; but cared not whence it came,
Or whither bound: to him it was the same,
So that away, far distant, he were borne:
All lands seemed now of all attractions shorn!
Perhaps, as most deserted and forlorn,
The barren, dreary, ever-restless Sea,
Would to his desolate Soul most soothing be.

His road was nearly that which Amo chose,
In search self-ruinous of ruthless foes;
Not that he sought with conscious aim the more
To take that path because 'twas her's before:
His unresigning anguish could not crave
To see, or seek for solace at her grave;
Herself—herself! the vain demand—nought less—
His greedy grief insatiable would press;
Not any maddening circumstance or scene
To rouse remembrances of what had been—
Too prompt already, manifold and keen!
Yet haply he was guided on the whole,
By that attraction of his secret soul;
A bias, though unconsciously, obeyed,
Towards even the shadow of that loved one's shade—
Towards any place her sweetest presence still
With haunting fondness sadly seemed to fill.

When near the coast, they told him of a Ship
Whose Master would ere long his anchor trip;
For three years' chase of his gigantic game,
Run down o'er boundless Ocean hunting-grounds,
With hardy boats'-crews for his well-trained hounds—
In that most venturous, gravest, grandest Sport
Which makes all others seem contracted—tame—

Had now his Ship with ample produce stored.
And so he was about to leave the Port—
Wood—water—fresh provisions all on board—
And cut his boisterous crew's rude revels short.

II.

Sad, weary, listless, and alone—
For nought companionship had cheered—
'Twas Ranolf's habit through the day
To take his solitary way,
Letting Te Manu choose his own.
Before him now the Port appeared:
There—with dim spire of masts and shrouds,
And yards across like streaky clouds,—
The Ship he sought at anchor lay.
Crowning a cliff that overstooped
The sea—whence trees o'erhanging drooped,
The village stood the Wanderer neared.
With rows of posts, unequal, high,—
That level crest against the sky
Was bristling; and within them grouped,
Thick thatch-roofs nestled peacefully.

Woeworn and weary, then he went
Thoughtfully up the steep ascent;
And passed the log, rough-hewn and laid
For bridge across the empty fosse;
And paused before the opening made
For entrance in the palisade.
He looked around; upon the spot
He saw no living being stirred:
Fast-closed was every silent cot;
The sun was shining, high and hot—

A lingering summer afternoon;
Faint insects hummed a drowsy tune
At times—no other sound was heard.

In doubt what course he should pursue,
On sad and gloomy thoughts intent,
With folded arms and head downbent,
Against an entrance-post he leant.
Not far below, there hung in view
That immemorial red-blue gleam
Of world-embracing Ocean-fame—
The flag that long shall float supreme,
Let all of English blood and name
Be to each other staunch and true!
Ah, with what sense of proud delight,
So long unseen, a short time back
That flag had flashed upon his sight!
But now it bade his memory track
The train of evils that had come
Out of that longing for his home.
Well might his heart so busied, feed
On bitter anguish; well might bleed
Remembering why he shunned to share
That home with *her!* He could not bear
Nor blink the truth, the cause, to-day—
Contemptible and coward care
Of what 'the World' might think or say—
That blatant—brainless—soul-less World!
Ah with what scorn he would have hurled
Such pitiful respect away,
Had one more chance been given to prove
How much he prized that priceless love!

O but one chance—giv'n then and there
The 'World' and all its slaves to dare!
With measureless defiance brave
Its worthless worst rebukes, and save
A heart, so simply grand, beside
Its poor conventions, paltry pride;
Refined frivolities—and cant,
The natural course, or worse, the want
Of real emotions, framed to hide!—
Aye! but too late that wisdom came;
The shame, too late, of that mean shame;
Remorse, and withering self-disdain,
Too late and impotent and vain!
There was nought left him but to rave
With voiceless, useless, inward pain.
His trust in higher things was gone—
His 'Power Divine'—his 'God of good,'
What faith in Him could he retain!
It seemed to his despairing mood,
Faith could not, should not, live alone
When Hope and happiness had flown.

On such distressful thoughts intent,
Against that entrance-post he leant.
Forlorn alike to eye and ear
Seemed time and place and atmosphere!
With wearying, bright unchanging glow,
The calm, regardless sunbeams shone;
With wearying faintly-changeful flow
The insects' tune went murmuring on;
No sign of living thing beside;
Not even a dog's out-wearied howl;—
Yes—once his listless eye espied

Scarce noting it, a sleepy fowl
Ruffling its feathers in the dust ;
Companionless—the moping bird,
Stalking and pecking leisurely
Beneath a cottage wall, went by ;
No longer were its mutterings heard.
Yes—once a rat, in open day
Stole forth, and crossed at easy pace
The silent solitary place ;
Stopped often, shewing no distrust
Nor any haste to slink away.
It too had vanished. Still fast-shut,
In sunshine stood each silent hut :
And dark, distinct, beside it lay
Its shadow still—no cloudlet slow
Passing, to make it come or go—
Unfading—seeming changeless too
As if it neither moved nor grew,
That lingering, loitering afternoon.
Then even the murmuring, dreamy tune,
That now would swell and now subside,
Awhile in utter silence died.

* * * * *
* * * *

Fair Reader ! have you ever been
Sauntering in meditative mood,
In some sequestered sunny scene,
Some perfect solitude serene,
Where tenantless a building stood—
Old ruined Castle, if you will—
Neglected Hall of recent days,

Though fit for habitation still,
Long empty ;—any place almost
Where human beings once have dwelt
And ceased to dwell ;—but if your gaze,
On such deserted Mansion lone
Were fixed awhile, will you not own
How strong a fancy you have felt,
That some still human visage—ghost
Or not—through one blank window, less
Observed—or loophole's high recess—
With eyes in vague abstraction lost,
Not marking, minding you at all—
Was looking out ?—Did you not feel
As if you saw or soon would see,
A lonely Figure, silently,
With features, haply, undiscerned
Because its back towards you was turned,
Across some empty courtyard steal—
Or glide beneath some ruined wall ?—

* * * * *
* * * *

As Ranolf leant there so distrest,
Once, with a writhe of ill-represt
Impatient anguish, at the tide
Of keen regrets which o'er his breast—
Remorseful, merciless, upheld
By that full moon of memory, swelled—
As wearily his head he raised,
His glance unconscious chanced to rest
Upon a distant cot—whose side
Of close-packed wisps of bulrush dried.

Stood half in brightness—half in gloom ;
The sunbeam's glow still bright below—
Its upper part, in clear deep shade,
Beneath some palm-trees' tufts of bloom,
With a square opening in it, made
For light—a window though unglazed ;
And suddenly he seemed aware
A wan pale face—how wan and fair,
Was in the square of blackness there,
With eyes unmoving—eyes all light—
So preternaturally bright—
Haggardly beautiful !—Amazed,
His very heart turned sick and faint ;
Almost he could have fallen with fear—
That Spirit from the Dead—so near !
He rallied quickly ; for he knew
How fancy can send back again,
Some image from the heated brain,
And on the retina repaint
Such apparitions, till they seem
External, actual, and no dream.
He passed his hand across his eyes ;
Sprang forward ; shook himself to free
His fancy from such phantasies,
His brain from this delusion. There,
Framed in the blackness of that square,
Still shewed the visage, haggard, fair,
And would not vanish into air !—
And then it changed before his sight ;
A sudden gleam of wild delight
Illumed it ; the next moment checked,
As from the Vision seemed to come
A shriek that died off in a moan—

Painful, unnatural—as the tone
Wrung from the wretched deaf and dumb
Whom sudden pangs of passion stir.
Then to the hut—for nought he recked—
"What *could* it be?" he thought, "but *her!*"
He would have rushed; but yet once more
Those earnest gestures—looks—deter;
So vehemently they implore,
So unmistakably entreat
Silence—and that he should not greet—
Heed—recognise the vision then.
For the same moment might be seen
Behind him, close upon the fence,
What stifled as it rose, that keen
Great cry of joy or pain intense;—
The inmates of the village—men
And women and a merry crowd
Of children; all with laughter loud
Returning from the plot where they
Within the woods not far away
Had been at pleasant work all day.

III.

With lips comprest—clenched hand—knit brow—
By violent effort he restrained
Emotions nigh o'ermastering now.
He turned—accosted them—explained
In terms he scarce knew what, but brief,
To one who seemed to be their Chief
Why he had come to that seaport.
At once they knew their guest unknown
Must be, from bearing, mien and tone,

Though roughly drest and travel-stained,
A "Rangatira"*—of the sort
Who paid for all attentions shewn:
So to his use a cot assigned;
Brought food; and as he seemed inclined
For little converse, or to care
About themselves or ways; or share
The interest newer comers take
In all that might the curious wake
To wonder; but appeared to be
Absorbed in troubles of his own;
They soon with truest courtesy
Left him to his reflections lone.

And all that evening, in a maze
He seemed: a sort of luminous haze
Of anxious, wondering, strange delight
Moved with him, move where'er he might:
Nor could he lie, or sit, or stand,
Or many moments keep at rest,
Howe'er he strove at self-command.
He closed his eyes—his temples pressed;—
That light, for all his efforts vain
Still hovered o'er his haunted brain:
And once, in this his feverish fret,
He checked himself in looking round
As half expectant he would yet
See, though long since the sun had set,
His shadow fall upon the ground.
And oft he tried if he could still
By strong exertion of the will

* 'Chief or Gentleman.'

Make that fair, haggard vision rise
Again, and stand before his eyes
With such a sharp external show
Of life, and every feature, so
Distinct in joy, surprise, or woe!
That face, so sweet, though so careworn,
And of its brilliant beauty shorn;
The hollow cheek; the shrunken hand;
And the too delicate finger laid
Upon the faded lips; and grand
All wonder, joy, or woe above—
That deep unfathomable love
In eyes whose brightness *could* not fade!
Yes! he could shape them in his mind;
But overjoyed was he to find
No yearning made the illusion dear
As real or outward reappear.

IV.

Night came at last; at last ev'n midnight came.
How wearily the hours for Ranolf passed—
On tenterhooks of expectation cast—
Such incomplete and tantalising joy!
But even the noisy natives sunk at last
To rest—the earlier for their day's employ.
The flittings to and fro, from hut to hut,
Ceased by degrees, and every door was shut;
The laughter loud and lazy chat were o'er;
The smouldering firesticks on each earthen floor
Had for the last time been together raked,
And blown with lips far-pouted, to a flame;
The last pipe smoked; and the consuming thirst
For gossip haply for the moment slaked.

The large-limbed lounging men upon the ground,
Naked whene'er the heat too great was found ;
And every active, restless, wrinkled dame,—
Crowded in some convenient house at first,
Had to their separate homes retired to sleep ;
And all the 'pah' was wrapt in silence deep.

Then Ranolf, with a quicker-throbbing heart,
Watched in the cot consigned to him apart ;
With door ajar, and sharp attentive ear
Watched—listened for the faint delicious sound—
The footstep that he felt must now be near.
—A rustle . . . No ?—'twas fancy !—then more clear
Another !—'Tis herself ! with that wan face,
Locked in his almost fiercely fond embrace !—
Yes, 'tis herself ! and never, come what may,
Shall she be torn from that fond heart away !
And She—into his arms herself she flung
With what a burst of passionate sobs ! and hung
Upon his neck with moans of happiness ;
And felt once more his vehement caress,
With what an ecstacy of soothing tears !
And revelled in the burning kiss on kiss,
With such intense relief from doubts and fears ;
Such sense of infinite agony supprest,
Swallowed, like night in lightning-sheets—in this,
This full fruition of exceeding bliss—
As if upon the heaven of that breast
Her soul had reached its everlasting rest !

But when the Sea of their emotions ran
In less tumultuous billows, and began
In gentler agitation to subside,

So that clear Thought and Speech articulate
  Above the tide unwrecked could ride ;
Then Ranolf, holding at arms' length awhile
His new-found treasure, his recovered bride,
Gazes with mournful gladness in his smile—
Gazes with fond and pitying tenderness—
At those thin pallid features, which the weight
And anguish of despair no more depress—
Into those eyes which happy tears beteem—
As to make sure it was not all a dream !

  "No Spirit then !—my own
 Own Amo, loving and alive again !
 O God ! can such delight indeed be mine !"—

 "No Spirit—no—nor dead ; but with the pain
 To lose thy love ; and thought of that alone
 Would kill me any time—"

                "Then never think
 The thought ; the thing itself, my dearest, best,
  Shall never be a grief of thine !"

 "What ! you will never be distrest
 For want of all that sunset-tinted snow
 And hair, such as the moonbeams link . . .
 What was it ?"

              "Amo !—"

                "Nay, then nay—
 Not that upbraiding look to-day !
See ! o'er these dear, dear features, worn with care,

See, see! my murmuring lips must stray
With flying faint half-kisses, so
To brush all that reproach away!
No, I will never doubt again—
Do not these features, pale with grief,
Do they not say my Stranger-Chief
My lord, my life, will never choose
His poor wild maiden's love to lose?—
But how then could you be so sad
When I was with you?"

"I was mad—
An idiot, dearest! just to shun
A small misfortune, so to run
The risk of that o'erwhelming one
By which I were indeed undone!—
But small and great shall soon be o'er,
And neither shall afflict us more,
If you will leave this land with me,
And dare to cross yon starlit sea!"

"What is to me land, sea, or sky
So that with you, I live and die!"—

Then soon a plan for their escape
Was moulded into practicable shape:
Only the pressing, first, immediate need
Was that before these natives they should be
Absolute strangers, nor each other heed.
This need did Amo when she first caught sight
Of Ranolf, feel—this, somehow could foresee;
And this perception made her first wild cry,

That sudden cry of wonder and delight
Die off in such a strange unmeaning moan.

V.

But she had told ere this, the how and why
She had been saved, and now was here alone;
How it was true, by that wild freshet's force
She was whirled down till consciousness was gone;
And soon upon a gravel-bank was thrown.
How a chance Traveller saw the seeming corse;
Apprised these natives; and observed them bear
The breathless body home with sorrowing care,
Home to their huts hard-by; then went his way,
Thinking her dead; that nought required his stay;
And anxious by no loss of time to lose
The importance, well he knew, none would refuse
To the first bearer of such startling news.
But those good Women, in the senseless Form
They carried, saw or felt there yet might lurk
Some faintest spark of life; so set to work
Its embers to re-waken and re-warm;
Made fires; applied hot stones, and rubbed her feet
And hands and heart with toil incessant; poured
Down her unconscious throat for greater heat
Some of the white man's liquid fire; implored
With moaned and murmured incantations meet
The Water-God and Storm-God; till at length
Her feeble fluttering pulse began to beat;
And that suspended current in her veins
To run, and rack her, as it gathered strength,
And prick with tingling tortures, pangs and pains,
Far worse than any she in drowning felt.
So with their patient patiently they dealt,

And charmed and chafed her till to life restored.
But with her life her first resolve returned ;
And in her recklessness she let them know
The scheme which to accomplish still she burned,
To yield herself, ere he could strike a blow,
To save her people, to her people's foe.
How she repented soon that she had told
Her secret : for the Chief, of no great name
Or note, and doubtless of as little worth,
Who ruled this petty village, stood,
With that marauding magnate of the North,—
Though some remote connexion he could claim,
So she was told, by marriage or by blood—
On terms of doubtful amity ; and hence
The crafty schemer was too glad to seize
An opportunity like this to please
The mightier potentate ; so forthwith hatched
A plan—to feign he could not trust her tale ;
And hold her captive, on the false pretence
He did so to secure her without fail
For the great Chief, until the last could say
What was his will about her : then dispatched
A trusty messenger that will to learn ;
And issued strict commands, till his return
Her every movement should be closely watched,
Nor she permitted from the pah to stray.
And thus the great man's favour would be won ;
Besides that, for such shining service done,
A splendid claim, he reckoned, would arise
For '*utu*'—compensation or reward,
The other could not fail to recognise.
But she, determined not to be debarred
From fully working out her first intent,

To put both Chief and people off their guard,
Affected in this plan to acquiesce;
Resolved whene'er their watchfulness grew less,
As finding 'twas but trouble vainly spent,
She would escape; her lonely road resume;
Self-guided seek her self-inflicted doom;
The merit of her sacrifice retain,
And greater power o'er proud Pomarë gain.
So at the village patiently she stayed;
Till all their first suspicions were allayed;
About her ways it seemed they little cared;
And she had everything for flight prepared:
Nay, would that very night, unseen, unknown,
Upon her errand of despair have flown;
Rushed on the fate she loathed, yet would have braved
Had she not been, by gift of all she craved,
This blest return of his affection, saved.

VI.

So, parting ere the dawn, with life renewed,
The plan concerted, calmly they pursued.
Two days they passed, eventless and serene,
Each by the other seemingly unseen;
Or in what intercourse they chanced to hold
Making a mock indifference, forced and cold,
Their fervid interest in each other screen.
In sad regards dissembling deep delight,
Impassioned, with how passionless a mien,
They crossed each other's path! with loving slight,
Hidden half-glances of such dear deceit—
Unrecognising recognition sly and sweet!

Then Ranolf to his hosts kind farewell bade ;
Much to their grief—so handsomely he paid ;
Nor seemed to notice Amo was not there
Just at the instant that farewell to share :
Then went on board ; and found the busy Ship
With cheery noise of near departure gay ;
Sails shaken loose and anchor now atrip,
Waiting the evening hour of ebbing tide ;
Worked by the steadiest of the men—a few
Exceptions to the riot-wearied crew—
Who jaded with rude revel, listless lay,
Nor longer to evade their duty tried,
Content at last, or glad, to get away.

Then down the harbour she was seen to glide,
Past the bare windy outer heads sunbright,
The glossy yellowish bluffs—into the blue ;
There on the dim expanse, she lingering lay
With slowly changing attitudes, in sight,
As if her stately beauty to display ;
Then, dwindling ever in the fading light,
Looked, now a column sloping softly white,
Now ruddy, blushing in the sunset's ray ;
Till silently absorbed in growing grey
She vanished—wrapt in close-encircling Night.

* * * * * *

VII.

These moving moveless Mountains and still Main,
Had nearly in their unfelt flight again
Slipped from beneath the funnel of deep shade,
For ever shot from our Sun-circling ball,

Through which we peer into Infinity ;—
Those four grand worlds tremendous which we call
A Cross—and their immensity invade
With faiths and fancies of our tiny Star,
Seemed to have turned them in their watch on high,
And changed the side from which to gaze afar
On the dark Pole—the seeming vacant Throne
Of One that Warder bright adored alone !
As in blue Syrian midnights long bygone,
Some jewel-armoured Satrap Damascene,
More from the fevered restlessness inspired
By Love, than with his tedious vigil tired,
Might oft have changed the spot where he would lean
And keep his fierce enamoured glances, keen
And glittering as his falchion, rapt and fast
Upon the lattice-screen, whereat at last
His maddening matchless quest—some miracle-Queen,
In loveliness and learnedness and loftiness
Of spirit, perfect as that Palmyrene—
But one ecstatic moment might appear,
Zenobia-like—too dazzlingly severe—
And frown a sunrise on the love's excess
Its glory could reward but not repress !—
Beneath the myriad eyes of that still Sky
Cowering, the conscious Ocean seemed to lie,
With faint soft murmuring, finely-wrinkled swell ;
As if it scarcely dared to heave or sigh
Beneath the fascination of their spell ;—
In brief, dear tortured Reader—it was near
The dawn ; and Sea and Sky were calm and clear.

Not far below the Port the Ship had left,
The hills into a little cove were cleft ;

The stony faces of the cliffs thus rent
Showed twisted strata, strangely earthquake-bent,
Running on each side circularly up—
A great grey hollow like a broken cup!
From crest and crevice, tortuously flung
Those monstrous iron-hearted myrtles hung—
Stiff snaky writhing trunks, and roots that clave
And crawled to any hold the ramparts gave.
Below, the level floor of sea-smoothed stone
Was all scooped out and scored by wear and tear
Of tides into round baths, and channels—bare
Or with sea-windflowers, scarlet-ringed, o'ergrown:
And big clay-coloured rocks and boulders, dropt
From mouldlike hollows in the cliffs above,
Where others like them sticking still, outcropped,
Lay scattered round the margin of the cove.

Look! in the starlit stillness, there and then,
A boat emerging from the gloom appears;
Rowed by four stalwart, darkling, silent, men,
With muffled oars and faintest plash scarce heard;
No sound beside, but the rare muttered word
Of brief command from him who mutely steers
And keenly round him through the darkness peers.
How cautiously her channelled way she feels,
And towards the rocks above the tideline steals!
There with suspended oars the boatmen wait,
Careful lest even their drip be heard; the Chief
Steps out and listens on the lonely reef;
No sight—no sound of anything that lives—
A 'cooey!' low and cautious, then he gives.
See! one of those clay-coloured rocks, descried
Dimly from where, with boathook held, the skiff,

Lies gently tilting with the lapping tide,
Seems, 'mid its dumb companions 'neath the cliff
With life and motion suddenly endowed!
It rises—swiftly running—leaping o'er
The stony-ribbed and channel-furrowed floor;
See! 'tis a female form—a graceful shape
Not even the clay-hued mats that thickly drape
The head and shoulders, all the figure shroud—
Can wholly hide; and see! as it draws near
And Ranolf ('twas none other) runs to meet
And with glad gesture greet the vision dear,
Beneath the hood—*this* time no doubtful dream—
Two great delighted sparkling eyes appear—
A wan glad face appears, so wan and sweet,
And kindling with triumphant love supreme!

An ardent pressure of the hand (before
That crew) a whisper of fond cheer—no more;
And in the boat he makes her take her seat;—
"Push off, my lads—look sharp!"—and from the shore
They steal; while she, her trustful heart at last
At peace, albeit from apprehension past
Still fluttering with a somewhat quicker beat,
Crouches by that loved form; and by degrees
With his rude comrades learns to feel at ease,
Confiding in the rough respect she sees
They pay to his sea-knowledge—ready hand—
Firm lip—and eye accustomed to command.
The men 'give way' with vigorous strokes, nor fear
Nor care, who now may see the boat or hear;
With hoisted sail to catch what airs there be,
She soon is gently trampling through the sea.

The Ship that in the offing, out of sight
Had with scarce flapping canvas hung all night
Becalmed, now as the breeze begins to rise
With topsails backed and filled alternate, lies
About one spot, till o'er the clearing main
The boat returning is descried again;
Then, with her yards braced round, and fair inclined,
She lets them curve out boldly to the wind,
Tacks towards the boat, and soon receives on board
The wondering Maid, to life and love restored!

How all this had been planned need we describe?
That night when Ranolf found the drowned alive;
How he had won, and hardly had to bribe
The bluff Ship-Master's soon-accorded aid;
How, unobserved, while for the Ship he stayed,
The neighbouring coast he carefully surveyed
And found a cove whence they could well embark;
How 'twas agreed that Amo should contrive
After the Ship's departure, in the dark,
When towards the morning all were sunk in sleep,
Out of the village secretly to creep,
And to the spot he pointed out repair;
There wait until she saw his boat arrive;
And do the same, as he would—'twas agreed—
If obstacles were met with, and need were—
Night after night, until they should succeed.

VIII.

Then, as some choice and cherished plant, erewhile
A thousand-blossomed wonder and a show—
Camellia or Azalea—one great pile
Of rounded knots of lovely-moulded snow,

Starring the glistening gloom of dark-green leaves
With such luxuriance in simplicity,
A purity so lavish and so free ;—
Or one unbroken broad diaphanous flush
Of delicate flow'rets, luminous and lush
As they were fashioned of the finest blush
Of light, the heart's core of soft summer-eves,
The tenderest recess of sunset, weaves ;—
As such a Plant—if set in hard-bound soil,
Where cutting winds could wither and despoil,
Till cankered leaves and scanty blooms declared
How ill in such environment it fared ;
But then again transferred from clay and cold,
To some warm nook of mellow-crumbling mould ;
Reviving and re-blooming, would outburst
In all the glory it could boast at first :—
Even thus did Amo, and in days as few
As this in months, her fairest charms renew ;
Thus, rooted in the soil of rich Content,
And breathing Love's serenest element,
Recovered fast, elastic and erect—
The sprightliness of form by sorrow checked ;
Once more, its supple roundness, sinuous grace,
With slim and slender vigour chastely vied ;
Her eyes regained their dancing lights—her face
Its winning frankness—sweet and sunny pride ;
Thus did she, brilliant as again a bride,
The shape and hues of happy health resume,
And all her wild magnificence of bloom !

So, with its loving freight, to scenes untold—
As daybreak wrapt her in its rosy fold,

So—down and down, beneath the horizon's brink—
Hull—sails—and masts—did that lone Vessel sink,
And melt into the flood of morning gold.
The Husband-lover and the lover-Wife
Dipped down into the chequered deep of Life!
So vanished—gliding down the blue hill-slope
Of Ocean into an abyss of Hope;
Plunged deep and deeper, every day that flew
In golden gulfs of bright Expectance—new
Experience—all of glad and glowing True
Or glorious Seeming, that can soothe and bless
Youth, Fancy, fondest Love, with dreams of Happiness!

* * * * * * *

IX.

Well then—for this time—Ranolf has escaped
The threatened doom, the shattering blow that might
By that Soul-Sculptor's hammer have been dealt.
Perhaps—who knows?—there was no need to smite:
Perhaps the marble could, with blow more slight
Or shadow of that heavy one, be shaped:
For he was of a nature that delight
Could sooner than despair, refine and melt.
Yet—never doubt it—Life and Time will teach
Him too what they enforce on all and each;
That for all Souls, however richly dowered
With amplest gifts by fate or fortune showered,
Something, where to the full they seem possest,
Will surely seem deficient in the best;
Or those that seem complete, will flit or fade
Long ere the thirst they cause can be allayed;

As if their only end, undoubted, clear,
Was to make one, old, world-wide Truth appear—
Man ne'er shall find full satisfaction here ;
To teach him—bound upon this earthly ball,
The power and practice to renounce them all.

Yes ! doubt it not ; he too in time will glean
A glimpse so far into the mighty Plan,
Into the working of this strange Machine
The Universe ; and what mysterious ways
  The Wonder-worker takes to solve
The problem he has set himself ; to make
His glorious World in one rich round revolve
Of beauty and attractiveness ; yet wean
By Good disguised as Evil—helpless Man
  Her nursling, from her lovely breast
  And bid him from the sleep awake
Wherein contented else he would for ever rest.

* * * * * *

X.

Now of his feelings in the after-day,
Of all his findings by Life's varied way,
But little further—little fuller—may
This realistic record sing or say.

First—for the tasks of Life ;—whate'er the sphere
Wherein his fleeting forces may be spent
Will he not learn, herein too, Life was lent
But as one stage for our development?—
    God's studio is this Earth,

And we, his pupils, for instruction sent,
Are pottering at our work of little worth
But to attain to faculties that here
Reach no perfection, or at least complete
No works that seem for such perfection meet.
How oft does mastery, even the most assured,
Moral or mental, seem in vain secured !
Our poets—artists—heroes—those
Whose ripening powers or ripened *could* not fail,
Their transient tools and organs lose,
Oft when their Souls seem fittest to prevail—
Most apt for thoughts or deeds sublime !
As if their lives were but a blossoming time ;
They students—and the works they leave,
So far beneath what they conceive,
But tyros' crude essays to what in vain
Their growing Souls may long indeed
In this life—but in this life are in train
Only in larger—loftier to achieve ;
Essaying here, but elsewhere to succeed.
Till not alone the buds of beauty left
By Nature's younger darlings, soon bereft
Of life and lyre—too soon !—a Shelley made
All spirit—nay—frail spirit-tortured flesh,
Self-fevering through false theories, griefs and heats
And phantasms, to pure Spirit ; or a Keats,
In senses for a human Soul too fresh
And keen and fine, too dangerously arrayed—
Our young-eyed Cherubim, who like poor bees
Over a citron-blossom lifeless curled,
Not half their honey gathered for the world,
Died at their sweet vocation—O not these—
Nor the rathe buds of amaranth they seize—

But roses fully blown; the gorgeous train
Of bright humanities a Shakspeare's brain
Bids into being, deathless and intense,
  With hue for hue, and gleam for gleam
Reflecting God's creations till they seem
The double Rainbow's second Arch, in stripe
And stain as lovely as its archetype!—
Even these, to his great Spirit, taken hence
  Seem left but like the drooping coronet
Of threaded anthers hanging still around
Some tiny nectarine-fruit, green, newly-set;
The poor triumphant relic that once crowned
Its flowering-time incipient, immature;
Just dropping from the fruit that must expand
To golden richness in the radiance pure
Of wider Skies and some diviner Land!

XI.

And as the Will Supreme intends
Life's highest work as means, not ends:
Its joys and pleasures, coarse—refined—
Alike to be renounced—resigned;
Will he not feel at last, and see
The more for every misery,
The rolling seasons as they flee,
To *him* too, as to all mankind
Full surely will dispense—decree—
That Life itself is meant to be
Held loosely—lightly?—as one day
When he with Amohia gay
Roamed in that earliest bliss of love,
He held upon his open palm
A slender beetle, silver-bright

Beneath, all pure grass-green above;
And bade her come and look how fair
The dainty creature, 'lighted there,
And running to his finger-tip
To gain a vantage-ground, to slip
Off into air, its native balm;
"So should we hold this Life" he thought,
So watch with interest, deep delight,
The flitting thing with beauty fraught,
Long as it lingers in our sight;—
So let it take, nor e'er repine,
When go it must, its mystic flight,
Into the limitless Divine!"

And he will feel—for such as he,
Of healthy frame and reason free,
Are more than most, secure to feel,
As straight he steers through rocks and shoals,
What haven rests for noble souls!
Yes, he will feel through woe and weal,
The power of Time to soothe and heal;
And tune the Soul to full concent
With its surrounding element.
The wear and tear of right and wrong
Less injure than befriend, the strong,
And cheerful heart and chastened will
Uplift them; and Experience still
Maturing, lends a master's skill,
Life's rich Harmonium-reeds to sound,
Once dumb, or so discordant found;
With easy stop some pain prevent;
With facile touches, lightly thrown,
Give simpler pleasures fuller tone

And from the ebon-ivory range
Of chequered days and chance and change,
Draw symphonies serene and strange,
Melodious Music of Content.
They gain, like fruits, as ripe they grow,
More sweetness, with a sunnier glow;
Till, mellowing ever, they begin
The faith as very truth to hold—
The best of worlds is that wherein
Is much of Evil, so-called 'Sin';
With active wish and earnestness
To make that 'Sin' and Evil less.
So by degrees to Fate they mould
The Will that seemed so uncontrolled;
And patience comes—and passions cool;
And where they once were ruled, they rule:
Love's wing grows wider—Thought's more bold!
The iron bonds are turned to gold;
The chafing and restraint are past;
And what were chains at first, are ornaments at last.

XII.

And what if he one day shall see, nor dream—
Though from the Soul's own intimate emotions
It be conceded the profoundest notions
Of the unfathomable unison
Between it and the Universe be won—
What if it grow with gathering years more plain,
That the divine Developer's Life-Scheme
Might yet by Science in her own domain,
The Positive—that euphrasy and rhue,
The mental vision from the mists to purge
Of Speculation beyond Reason's verge—

Be caught a glimpse of; with no logic-strain,
Transcendent or empiric, or the twain
United, over-subtle for sound brain;
But patient observation, record true
Of all the agencies clear sight may trace
Of Circumstance, beyond its own control
That make and mould each individual Soul
Of myriad myriads of the human race;—
Of all the hints and seeming accidents,
Felicitous and opportune events,
Though slight, so often from without supplied,
The balanced Will that seems so free, to guide;
And be the fountains of a cataract wide
Involving the whole being in its tide;
All that strange Loom of Life that round us plays,
That made the grand old Greek, beyond all praise,
The wisest, bravest, best, of Ancient Days,
Paint it a guardian Angel by his side—
His prescient Diotima piteous-eyed;
All this shall make at last a Science grand
Of Circumstance—no sceptic shall withstand,
Wherein shall be perceived a law and laws,
Not to be gathered from a single mind,
But myriad inner histories combined;
And in the laws, clear purpose, conscious Cause.
What! shall the very Winds of heaven that rise
And sink and run their seeming reckless round,
Like Tartar cavalry scouring the wide skies,
Intractable and trackless! shall all these
And every Storm that tears the limitless seas,
Ranging the Ocean's amplitude—be found—
Obedient to fixed Law—to Order bound?—
Shall all that shifting swift Aurora-dance,

Those phantom revels round the secret Poles,
Be set to God-made music that controls
And bids each brilliant spasm up-leap and glance
By happy rule—harmonious governance?
Yet this—Humanity's abounding Mould,
The ever-active matrix manifold
Of Spirit, restless round Earth's millions rolled,
This vast Machinery for making Souls,
Be but chaotic Force—the child of Chance?—
A vain surmise!—but as that Law of Storms
Cannot be gathered from a single breeze
Or local gale; so must a myriad forms
Of lives and their environments be learned
And disentangled ere can be discerned
The law that flows round each, unguessed, unseen,
Like fluid wool that through the ribbed machine
Which looks so bare, so finely runs and fast
O'er whirling cylinders, a viewless stream,
Till in a visible flue scraped off at last:—
Even so, the presence of a Power supreme
Shall be detected as its subtle way
It works throughout the infinite whirl and play
Of ever-rolling restless Circumstance;
So from a million inmost beings scanned
With cool and scrutinising vigilance
That marks each motive whencesoever brought,
Each faintest impulse from without them caught;
So may at last material pure be won
Whence ductile threads of reasoning may be spun,
Which all the strain of logic shall withstand;
And such a radiant raiment woven alone
By Intellect, as—warmly, widely thrown
About the shivering Soul—shall make it feel
Aglow with full assurance of eternal weal!

XIII.

But still will he—the thoughtful—sanguine-hearted
With greater zeal by Time and Life imparted
Swear fearless fealty, in age as youth,
To highest Reason and all-questioning Truth !
That Reason which must own
Inferior truths alone
Are yet within the range of proof,
As wholly to be sifted, fathomed, known :
While to some glimpses of the higher,
That wake most wise desire,
Soar as they may above us and aloof,
Through Feeling checked by Reason we may still aspire !
And still will he exclaim,
With thought as daring, earnestness the same :
" O heat of loving Heart ! O Light of chainless Mind !
When will conviction flash on dull mankind,
That you are One and True ; to doubt you, false and blind !
And O, thou *One Ineffable !* O Being
In infinite ubiquitous persistence
By our conceptions inconceivable—to all our seeing
Invisible ! yet forced upon us as unknown Existence
By all Existence known ! O Thou
The source of Soul and Nature, Man and Brute
Whom in this sensuous deep thou dost immerse—
Thou hast ordained *that* deep shall still avow
Thyself—some shadow of Thyself reveal—
Potent o'er inmost consciousness to steal ;
A conscious brooding PRESENCE—through thy Universe
For ever everywhere intrusive—
For ever everywhere elusive—
Resistlessly suggestive, yet inexorably mute !—

Thou, in the very strangeness of the Mystery
Of everything that *is*—this actual Here and Now—
A mystery impenetrable—from the highest cope
Of heaven with Astral Systems flung along its slope
To the minutest microscopic spark
Or speck of life obscure in air or earth or sea—
Some viewless animalcule—such a vivid shield
Of trembling rings of iridescent splendour
The very Rainbow by its side would yield
The palm—has no such glory to attend her
As we are startled to find there, unseen
By unassisted sense; a glow
Of Beauty and Power divine that, from below
Rising to meet the Power and Beauty above
That through those star-worlds limitless expand—
Floods all the Universe with boundless Love!
Until we feel, we darkling men—
So darkling in our nook of narrow days
And cramping thoughts and creeping ways—
As in the midst, stark-blind with light, between
That Infinitesimal and Infinite we stand—
Feel wholly plunged, enveloped in the blaze
Of the abounding Presence then
Of that creative Beauty and Power divine—
Say rather, O UNNAMEABLE, of Thine!—
Yes! in this Mystery, though dark as night
Yet beautiful and wonderful beyond the scope
Of utmost admiration; yet a joy to mark
And marvel at, exhaustless by all thirst
For joy Thyself didst plant within us first;
Thou hast therein writ thy decree
It shall for Man for ever be
Inevitable to conclude Thee good and just;

Most rational to hold a boundless Hope;
Most tenderly ennobling utterly to trust
In the Omnipotence of Love and Thee!
Therefore we thank Thee! therefore boldly say:
'O Man! thou momentary ray
Shot from the hidden Splendour far away—
Sheet-lightning gleam of a perceptive power
Taking wide Nature's surface for its dower;
O phantom-puppet of miraculous clay!
Thou that art launched into the infinite void
Upon thy sparkling bubble-world upbuoyed;
And—as an Insect on a floating leaf
Runs to and fro, incapable of flight,
And works and waves in air its horns so slight—
Dost ever, on thy voyage brief,
Keep stretching towards some unimagined goal
Hid in the blank abyss of Light
The feeble feelers of thy Soul!
Poor Atom on the Ocean of the All—
Hold bravely onward! faint not yet nor fall—
Some day shall come full answer to thy call!'"

* * * * * *

Enough—the homely reel of Life we hold—
Of Amo's life and Ranolf's is unrolled;
She and her thoughtful thoughtless Wanderer bold,
Slight subjects of a lingering theme,
Faint visions of a too protracted dream,
Sink down—and like the ghosts of every-day,
The solid real flesh-phantoms—fade away!

NOTES.

PRONUNCIATION OF NATIVE WORDS.

NATIVE words occurring in the foregoing poem, should be pronounced like Italian ; the double letter "ng" as the softer sound of the same letters in English. So "*Maori*" is pronounced "*Mowree*" (so as to rhyme with "*dowry*"—with an indication, however, of both the *a* and the *o*) ; and the nasal letters in "*Tangi*," precisely as in "*slangy*" (if there be such a word in English) with no separate sound of the *g*. The diphthong "*ai*" is sounded like long *i* or *y*. The emphasised syllables are mostly in the text marked with accents, though none are used in the written language.

To avoid what Mr. Rossetti happily calls, "tripping up the reader and sending him to the bottom of the page" with continual references to explanatory notes, all such references have been omitted, with one or two exceptions, in the text, in the hope that the latter may be found sufficiently intelligible without them. Where for any reason notes appear to be desirable, they are inserted below, in the order in which the subjects they refer to occur in the book.

I.—MISCELLANEOUS NOTES.

Pages 1 and 2.—"Rata root" and "koromiko"; see note below on "Natural Objects."

Page 5.—"Keen Searcher of the Seas": "Acerrimus Oceani Investigator."—See Capt. Cook's epitaph in St. Paul's.

Page 5.—The legend of MAUI, chief of Polynesian hero-gods, and his fishing up the islands, is found with variations in the Tongan, Samoan, Tahitian, and Sandwich-Island groups as well as in New Zealand.

Page 7.—"Asphodel" and "Tree-fern," note below, "Natural Objects," where the scientific names of other plants or animals alluded to will be found.

Page 11.—Seizure of Amohia. That this incident is sufficiently in accordance with Maori usages will appear from the following extract of an official letter received by the author in the colony :—

"*Ranganui, Waikato, 4th October,* 1869.

"SIR,—Last June I petitioned H. E. the Governor relative to certain lands in right of my wife, who is a native of the Whakatane district, who was *stolen* with her mother by Potatau" (since the so-called *Maori king*) "taken as slaves and removed to the Waikato, where they were forced to remain," &c.

In the petition the writer says, "She belonged to a tribe having large possessions in her original district ; having been twice married (to Europeans), has been the mother of nineteen children, of whom fourteen are now alive, and twelve of whom reside near the Waikato River." A list of the family accompanying the petition showed that her three elder daughters have respectively six, six, and five children—again by Europeans. A fact for the Anthropologists.

Page 16.—"A parrot for a pet." "Possessing excellent powers of mimicry, and useful to the natives as a decoy-bird, the *Kaka* (parrot) is much sought after, and almost every native village has its '*mokai.*'" —*History of the Birds of New Zealand*, by Dr. Buller.

Page 17.—"*Haere atu*, Go your way." Common form of words used by the Maori to persons taking leave of them.

Page 26.—"Ahuramasda," "Living I Am." See Professor Max Müller's *Chips from a German Workshop.* So with respect to Buddha. (See below.)

Page 26.—"Egg of Order." By the Egg of Ormusd (Ahuramasda) the old Magians typified the moral and physical order of his work, the

Universe; pierced by Ahriman with Evil, of which he was the origin and author. See Gibbon's *Decline and Fall*, ch. 8, &c.

Page 27.—"Jamaica" means "Isle of Springs;" see Bryan Edwards's *West Indies.*

Page 31.—"What other just conclusion, &c." I cannot help venturing to think, in spite of the high authority of Mr. Grote (*Plato and other Companions of Socrates*), that Socrates must have held the opinions here attributed to him; because it is difficult to conceive, that with the general notions of the Gods or God, the learned historian himself describes as those of Socrates, the latter could have arrived at the conclusions Mr. Grote, discarding the evidence of Plato, conceives him to have come to.

Page 31.—"Bullwise"—"ἀλλ' ὥς περ εἰώθει ταυρηδὸν ὑποβλέψας," κ.τ.λ.—*Phædo.* Though directed towards the gaoler, was not the expression of the look of Socrates caused as supposed in the text?

Page 35.—*Kapila's "Perfect Wisdom."* Kapila, founder of the Sankhya system; one of the systems of Brahmann philosophy prior to Buddhism, though the Kapila *Sutras* ("Aphorisms or Precepts of Kapila") are subsequent. Kapila gives his philosophy in the book he styles "Pragnaparamita," or "Perfect Wisdom." Both Hindu and Buddhist philosophers deny the reality of the objective world. See Essays of Professor H. H. Wilson, and Professor Max Müller's *Chips*, &c., above cited.

Page 35.—Sakya Muni or Guatama, the Buddha, founder of Buddhism, lived about 500 B.C. A Buddha ("the enlightened one") was a human being, who had attained, by the practice of virtue through millions of ages and many transformations, to that highest state of perfection.

Page 35.—"Its founder's self, made God, &c." "Buddha being supreme, worship of gods was superfluous; but the mass of mankind needing sensible objects of worship, Buddha came to be substituted for the gods. In course of time other inconsistent gods were added. . . Belief in a supreme Being, Creator, and Ruler of the Universe is a modern graft upon the unqualified atheism of Sakya Muni."—*Essays* by H. H. Wilson, Boden Professor of Sanskrit, Oxford. Vol. 4.

Page 35.—"Night of non-existence." "Utter extinction, as the great end and object of life, was a fundamental feature of Buddhism; 'Nirvana,' a 'blowing out' as of a candle—annihilation."—*Ibid.* It seems doubtful (according to Professor Müller) whether this last doctrine was really that of Sakya, or only of Kasyapa, and other followers.

Page 35.—"High-moralled faith." "This moral code, one of the most perfect the world has ever known."—Max Müller's *Chips*, &c.

Page 36.—"Basket." The earliest Buddhist canon is called the "Tripitaka," or "The Three Baskets;" the 1st, contains the Sutras or discourses of Buddha, written by Ananda. 2nd, Vinaya, his code of morality, by Upali. 3rd, Abhidarma, his system of metaphysics, by Kasyapa. All the writers, pupils and friends of Sakya Muni.—*Ibid.*

Page 39.—"No vision of the City, &c." "Hast thou not considered how thy Lord dealt with Ad, the people of Irem, adorned with lofty buildings, the like whereof hath not been erected in the land?"—*Koran*, ch. 98, Sale's Translation. In a note, Sale says the passage refers to the "sumptuous palace and delightful gardens built and made in the deserts of Aden in imitation of the celestial paradise," by Sheddad, son of Ad, the king and founder of "a potent tribe destroyed for their infidelity. When finished, he set out with a great attendance to take a view of it, but within a day's journey of it they were all destroyed by a terrible noise from heaven. *Al Beidawi* adds, that one *Abdallah Ebn Kelabah* accidentally hit on this wonderful place as he was seeking a camel."—Sale's *Koran*, vol. ii. p. 484.

Page 40.—"Three-tongued wedge-rows." Cuneiform inscriptions in Assyrian, Persian, and Tahtar.

Page 41.—"Portico," and "Academe." See the magnificent picture of Fichte by the great portrait-painter of the age. "The cold, colossal, adamantine Spirit, standing erect and clear like a Cato Major among men; fit to have been the teacher of the Stoa, and to have discoursed of beauty and virtue in the groves of Academe, &c."—

"State of German Literature," in *Essays and Miscellanies*, by Thomas Carlyle.

Page 42.—"Healthier dreams." "Exemption from being born again, the *summum bonum*. The Brahmins think this, but effect it by spiritual absorption either into the universal spirit or into an all-comprehending divine spirit; but the Buddhists recognize no such recipient for the liberated soul."—Wilson's *Essays*, &c. The heterodox Buddhists, in Thibet, Ceylon, and Burmah, probably all but the learned everywhere, —seem to have relapsed into the old Hindu doctrine. "The modern Buddhists of Burmah hold *Nirvana* (their *Nigban*) simply to be freedom from old age, disease, and death. . . Buddha, who denied the existence, or at least the divine nature of the gods worshipped by the Brahmans, was made a deity by some of his followers as early as the age of Clemens of Alexandria; and we need not wonder if his Nirvana was gradually changed into an Elysian field."—Müller's *Chips*, &c.

Page 42.—"Red robes," &c. Worn in heterodox Tartary and Thibet; the priests in Ceylon, Ava, and Siam adhering to the more orthodox fashion of yellow robes, with shaven heads.—Wilson's *Essays*.

Page 42.—"Gem in the Lotus-flower, Amen." "The sacred formula," says M. Huc, "'*Om mani padme houm*,' spread rapidly through all the countries of Thibet and Mongolia. . . . They (the Buddhists of these districts) have written an infinity of voluminous books to explain their famous *mani*. The Lamas say the doctrine contained in these marvellous words is immense, and that the whole life of a man is insufficient to measure its breadth and depth." The Regent of Thibet, however, explained it to M. Huc, who sums up the explanation thus: "The literal meaning of the words is 'O the gem in the Lotus, Amen.' The gem being the emblem of perfection, and the Lotus of Buddha, it may perhaps be considered that the words express the desire to acquire perfection in order to be absorbed in the Universal Soul. So the symbolic formula might be paraphrased thus: 'O may I obtain perfection to be absorbed in Buddha, Amen.'"—Huc's *Travels in Tartary, Thibet, and China*; translated by Hazlitt.

Page 45.—"A clay-clad wingless weak ephemeral," &c.

"Ἄγε δὴ φύσιν ἄνδρες ἀμαυρόβιοι . . .
Ὀλιγοδρανέες, πλάσματα πηλοῦ . . .
Ἀπτῆνες ἐφημέριοι," κ.τ.λ.—*Aristophanes*, Aves, 685.

Page 46.—"Scarab-worship." The beetle (*Scarabeus sacer*, Linn.) was an emblem of the Creative Power, Pthah; also of the Sun, the World, &c. But like other sacred animals, it was worshipped without reference to any type, for reasons difficult or impossible to discover. Wilkinson's *Ancient Egyptians*, vol. v., &c.

Page 48.—"Ding the book," &c. How refreshing the chance to quote a few words that recall the slashing energy and hearty idiomatic downrightness of Milton's wonderful prose! and more refreshing, in these days, when they give us a glimpse of the great free soul of this spurner of every kind of spiritual tyranny: "When every acute reader, upon the first sight of a pedantic licenser, will be ready with these-like words, *to ding the book a coit's distance from him;* 'I hate a pupil-teacher; I endure not an instructor that comes to me under the wardship of an overseeing fist.'"—*Areopagitica.*

Page 50.—"Nature in her insentient Solitude," &c. See Mr. Lewes's admirable *Biographical History of Philosophy.*

Page 53.—"As Dante's heard, &c.:—

"La miserella . . . . . .
Parea dicer . . . . . .
* * * * *
Colui, che mai non vide cosa nuova,
Produsse esto *visibile parlare,*
Novello a noi, perchè qui non si truova."
—*Purgatorio*, Cant. x. 82–96.

Page 67.—"Cold and stony flowers." Described afterwards, Canto xvii. p. 271.

Page 74.—"*Naraka,*" the Hell of the Hindu, as "*Nifl̄heim,*" that of the Scandinavian, mythology.

Page 75.—"Aztec birds." "There was such a multitude of Birds that the Ponds could not hold them, and so extraordinary was their variety for Shape and Feathers that our men were annoyed when they first saw them; . . . Montezuma took such care to have these birds maintained that every sort was supplied with the proper Food they lived upon abroad, &c. Above 300 persons were appointed to attend them; . . . some looked to their Eggs; others did set them when brooding; others cur'd them when sick; others pulled their finest Feathers in hot weather, which was their motive for being at all that Charge and Trouble. They made of them rich Mantles and Carpets, Targets, Plumes, Fans, and several other Things interwoven with Gold and Silver, all of them extraordinary curious and strange Works."—From the description of Montezuma's Palace, Gardens, Aviaries, &c., at Mexico: Herrara's *History of America*, vol. ii.; Stevens's Translation. The finest of these birds were Trogons—the species *Trogon resplendens* and *Trogon Mexicanus*, found only in the gloomy forests of the Southern States of Mexico.

Page 89.—The Maories trace their origin to the occupants of certain canoes, who first came from "Hawaiki," probably "Owhyhee," now spelt "Hawaii."

Page 91.—The reception of missionary teaching attributed to Tangi-moana was that actually given to it by a Maori chieftain. See *Narrative of a Twelve Months' Residence in New Zealand*, by Augustus Erle, Lond. 1832. The remark and gesture relating to divisions of faith were those of Te Hëu-hëu, a famous "heathen" Maori chief. He and a portion of his tribe were stifled in a liquid land-slip as described at p. 97.

Page 102.—Some of these necromantic powers are attributed to a sorcerer in Sir George Grey's *Polynesian Mythology*.

Page 103.—"Central Lake." Lake Taupo, the great lake about the centre of the Northern Island.

Page 122.—"Te Ra, the Sun." A curious coincidence, if nothing more, that the Sun, personified or deified throughout Polynesia under the name "Ra," was worshipped under the same name RA, or Rê, (*The* Sun, *Pi*-Ra, = Phrah, = Pharaoh, the royal title) universally throughout Egypt, and especially at Heliopolis in Lower Egypt, the "On" of the Jewish scriptures. See Wilkinson's *Ancient Egyptians*, vol. iv., p. 287, &c.

Page 135.—For the beginning of motion in the nebulous matter, see *Vestiges of Creation*, &c.

Page 136.—"Himself best proclaims," &c. The following extract will explain this allusion to the doctrine of the "Correlation of Forces:"

"It seems to me," says Mr. Grove, after speaking of magnetism, electricity, light, heat, and chemical affinity, "that it is now proved that all these forces are so invariably connected *inter se*, and with Motion, as to be regarded as modifications of each other, and as resolving themselves objectively into Motion, and subjectively into that something which produces or resists Motion, and which we call Force." Address to the British Association, 1866; *Correlation of Physical Forces, and Address*, &c., by W. R. Grove, President, &c. &c. That *all* the "wisest and best" of our philosophers do not hold the opinion glanced at in the text is shown perhaps from the last paragraph of this philosopher's Address: "In all phenomena, the more closely they are investigated, the more we are convinced that, humanly speaking, neither Matter nor Force can be created or annihilated, and that an essential Cause is unattainable. Causation is the will—Creation the act—of God."—Ibid. For the correlation of sound, see Prof. Tyndall's work on *Sound*, &c.

Page 149.—The desecration of the grave. "To eat in a canoe while passing a spot where the dead had been buried was considered a great impiety; drowning was expected to result."—Polack's *Manners and Customs of the New Zealanders*, Lond. 1840. Spirits of the dead often appeared in the form of birds.

Page 155.—"Fitted up a canoe," &c. A slight undertaking compared to what was actually done by a first-rate settler and pioneer, Mr. Rees, of Otago, who, in the early days of its history, used to navigate and carry provisions up the dangerous Lake Wakatipu (a lake with grand Swiss-like scenery far in the interior of the country) in a boat built by himself of rough frame-work cut in the neighbouring forests, and

"Nailed all over the gaping sides
Within and without, with *red* bull-hides."

Page 165.—The incident of Amohia swimming across the Lake to her lover is taken from the legend of Hinemoa (an ancestress of the Arawa tribe, inhabiting Rotorua), in *Polynesian Mythology*. The shock given to the maiden's feelings which makes her resolve to escape is in the same legend compared to that of an earthquake, and herself at the well to a white crane.

Page 168.—"Dread Spirit," &c. The natives, on coming into a new place, always uttered an incantation to the spirit presiding over the spot, the *genius loci*.

Page 173.—Stumps of trees, remnants of a submerged forest, are found in Lake Rotorua.

Page 182.—"And apprehend," &c. Is it necessary to refer to that profound metaphysical distinction of Hamlet?—"What a piece of work is Man! . . . in *apprehension* how like a God!"—where the word "apprehension" suggests the complement of the thought, "in *comprehension* how like a worm!" as vividly as if it had been expressed—as of course it could not have been *there*. All the distinction between Noumenal and Phenomenal, Ideal and Real, Object and Subject, the Metaphysicians make such a to-do about, rolled up in that little phrase!

Page 213.—"Robe-skirt's splendour":

> "Dark with excessive bright his skirts appear
> Yet dazzle heaven," &c.
>
> —*Paradise Lost.*

Page 221.—"Some earthquake's pant." Such a rupture of a swamp occurred at Wellington after the earthquakes of 1848.

Page 222.—"By all the law the land supplied," &c. "The Maori," says the Rev. Richard Taylor, "seem to differ from almost every known tribe or nation in having no regular marriage ceremony; they had no *karakia* (incantation), or any rite to mark an event which, in nearly every other part of the world is accounted the most joyous in life."—*New Zealand and its Inhabitants*, p. 163.

Page 229.—"The Bounteous Bay." The Bay of Plenty.

Page 236.—"Campaspe."

> "Cupid and my Campaspe played
> At cards for kisses. Cupid paid," &c.
>
> —*Song*, by John Lyly, the Euphuist.

Page 276.—"Savarin." Brillât-Savarin, author of that drily-humorous cookery-book, *La Physiologie du Goût.*

Page 282.—The description of *carriages* in the text was actually given by a Maori, and is recorded in some book of travels, I have forgotten whose.

Page 291.—Origin of Woman. "The first woman was not born, but formed out of the earth by the Arohi-rohi, or quivering heat of the sun, and the echo."—*New Zealand and its Inhabitants*, p. 18.

Page 298.—The Maori to this day have a superstitious dread of ascending the mountain alluded to.

Page 308.—"A cockle-shell." Shells of cockles, whelks, or other marine mollusks, are sometimes found on the banks of rivers or fresh-water lakes in the heart of the country.

Page 315.—"Some hot mead where violets hid," &c. One of the beautiful rural images with which Aristophanes tantalizes the Athenians pent up so many years within their town-walls:

> ἀλλ' ἀναμνησθέντες ὦνδρες
> . . . τῶν τε σύκων, τῶν τε μύρτων,
> τῆς τρυγός τε τῆς γλυκείας,
> τῆς ἰωνίας τε τῆς πρὸς τῷ φρεατί, κ.τ.λ.
> 'Ειρήνη, 565–71.

For the *kind* of well, see Dr. Clarke's *Travels in Greece.*

Page 316.—The readers of good old-fashioned Lempriere will remember the golden grasshoppers the Athenians used to stick in their hair, as emblematical of their nation's origin from the soil, and consequently great antiquity.

Page 319.—"Dynamic energies immense," &c. Referring to our power of converting one mode of force into another, Mr. Grove says, "We may probably be enabled to absorb or store up, as it were, diffused energy. . . . As the sun's force, spent in time long past, is now returned to us from the coal, which was formed by that light and heat, so the sun's rays, which are daily wasted, as far as we are concerned, on the sandy deserts of Africa, may hereafter, by chemical or mechanical means, be made to light and warm the habitations of the denizens of other regions." "Correlation of Forces," &c., quoted above.

"Dynamic energy" is force in motion; when at rest and latent, it becomes "potential energy," with "distance to act in." The law of conservation affirms "the constancy of the *sum* of both." See Professor Tyndall on the "Convertibility of Natural Forces," in "*Heat as a Mode of Motion.*"

Page 323.—"Immeasurable abyss," &c. Let not the English reader think this too high a flight for a Maori girl. It is but a slight amplification of an epithet not uncommonly applied in their songs by a woman to her lover: "*taku torere*—my Abyss!" And a pet phrase of theirs in the like case, given by Mr. Shortland in one of the books above cited, is, "*Taku huia kaimanawa*—my Spirit-devouring Hoopoe!" the hoopoe being, as the Maori describe it, a bird "*nui nui rangatira*—very chieftainlike—very, very much of a gentleman."

Page 326.—"War-chief." Napoleon in Egypt.—*Bourrienne.*

Page 337.—"Diviners bold," &c. As Kepler, in the beginning of the seventeenth century, foretold the existence, between Mars and Jupiter, of the planet required by the laws and analogies he had established; which planet, in its fragmentary condition, was discovered about 200 years later by Baron Zach, Piazzi, D'Olbers, and others, as Ceres, Pallas, &c., and the numerous asteroids in their neighbourhood. Similar instances of the accordance of Nature with the independent deductions of Science will occur to the reader as given in the prediction by Copernicus of the existence in Venus of phases like the Moon's; and in our time, the indication by Leverrier, from intricate and abstruse calculations, to account for the "perturbations of Uranus," of the existence and precise locality of the new planet Neptune, discovered as soon as sought for in the direction pointed out by the prophetical astronomer.

Pages 364 *to* 370.—The reader will, I trust, pardon this digression; written (like the rest of the poem, in New Zealand) at a time when the English Government showed no doubtful symptoms of a desire, or intention, to throw off the Colonies, and so dismember the British Empire.

Page 366.—"Race of War-fleets." Every one knows the object of the French and Spanish fleets was to draw Nelson away from the British seas; but the affair was none the less a flight and a chase, and the grandest in history.

Page 367.—"Bandit in his lair," &c. "There came from the traveller Wolfe, then at Bokhara, a letter saying the General's anger was dreaded there; and at the same time presents and assurances of goodwill arrived from many other quarters, amongst them, from the Affghan Chiefs of Candahar and Herat; and it was at this time the Khan of Khiva, whose dominions border on the Aral and Caspian seas, sent a prince of his family to negotiate an alliance with the victorious General."—Sir W. Napier's *Administration of Scinde by Sir C. J. Napier*, p. 140. Could he but have had 10,000 men and *carte-blanche!*

Page 367.—"Brother of Shay-tan." A name given at first, in their wonderment and terror, by some of the subdued tribes to Sir C. Napier. ——Two or three years of such a man's government would have made the Maories peaceful, industrious, contented, and *loyal.*

Page 369.—Capt. St. George, a young and most promising officer in the Colonial service, was killed while leading the native contingent in a successful attack upon a "pah" or fortified village at Poutou, near Roto-aira, occupied by rebel natives under the religious fanatic, Te Kooti, on the 4th of October, 1869. Being alone ahead of the others, he drew the enemy's fire upon himself as, in the words of an eyewitness and fellow-combatant—Captain Mair, in the same service—he "led his men on in his usual dashing style."

Te Kooti is the principal leader or founder of the "Hau-hau," who attracted his followers with pretensions to revelations from an Angel of the extermination of the whites and their own invulnerability, both of which predictions were speedily falsified.

Page 373.—The author of *Rambles in New Zealand*, 1841, Mr. J. Bidwell, compares the harsh groans of Maories in a war-dance to the sound of a regiment returning ramrods.

Page 385.—"Is this your mutton-fish!" &c. (See note below, "Natural Objects," p. 385.) The proverb is given by Mr. Shortland. The natives make the eyes (or rather the irides of the eyes) of their wooden images, and of spearheads, &c., out of the nacre or mother-of-pearl lining of these shells. Hence possibly, I think, the allusion to this shell-fish with the gesture (attributed to Tangi in the text) may be explained as equivalent to asking, "Is this eye of mine like that of an image? am I a dead or senseless thing like it, you can do what you like with?"

Page 388.—"Tongariro"—a volcano, 6,500 feet high, in the centre of the Northern Island; in active eruption when this was written (May, 1871).

Page 396.—"Mawai, the Gourd," and "Marupo," are real names given for the reasons stated in the text.

Page 398.—"Pry into the wound," &c. "Natives used *kaikatea* and *kaua-kaua* leaves, and other herbs as medicines. . . . Bullet-wounds were well-washed, lead extracted, boiled herbs applied externally."—Polack's *Manners and Customs of the New Zealanders*, vol. ii. p. 99, &c.

Pages 409, 410.—The sounds described here were those which accompanied the approach of spirits in Maori conjurations.

Pages 413 *to* 418.—The deathwound—occupations during his last illness—and the last words attributed to Tangi, were really those of a celebrated Maori warrior, E Hongi, killed in the early part of the century, as narrated in Missionary books. The conduct and exclamations of the Priest are from a description of the death of a Chief in *Old New Zealand*, a very graphic and humorous book by F. E. Maning, Esq., now a Judge of the New Zealand Native Lands Court.

Page 418.—"Made breezes sigh," &c. The "pathetic fallacy," denounced by Mr. Ruskin, is at least undeniably and purely natural, and perhaps universal. Instances of it occur very frequently in Maori songs.

Page 440.—"The gleam iridescent"—called by sailors, a *sun-dog*.

II.—WAIATA, OR NATIVE SONGS.

Page 97.—"Death, degrading," &c. This death-song is an amplification of one given, in his collection of *Poems, Traditions, and Chaunts of the Maories* in the native tongue, by Sir Geo. Grey, late Governor of New Zealand, to whom alone the preservation of what may now be called the "literature" of a savage race, including, besides the above forms of it, their proverbs, &c., is to be attributed.

Page 153.—"Leave me! yes!" &c. A free paraphrase of a song in the same collection.

Page 155.—"Now should he come," &c. No Maori original of this song.

Page 158.—"Tears, tears!" &c. A tolerably close *paraphrase* of a song in Sir G. Grey's collection.

Page 168.—"The freshet is flowing," &c. The idea of the flooded stream and fair wind assisting the maiden's flight while she sits idly twirling the paddle of her canoe, form part of a Maori song in the same collection. Also the appeal to the father at the end.

Page 176.—"As well upbraid," &c. No authority for the song alluded to.

Page 223.—"Praise her—bless her." No Maori original of this song, except that the idea of a girl's decorating herself with flax-work, feathers, and greenstone ornaments, to attract admirers, occurs more than once in the same collection.

Page 245.—"Alas, and well-a-day!" &c. A very free paraphrase of a song in Sir G. Grey's collection. "*Ropa* is a declaration of love by pinching the fingers."—Rev. R. Taylor's *New Zealand and its Inhabitants*, p. 164.

Page 354.—"The clashing of tempests." A free amplification of a song in the same collection.

Page 374.—"How long, how long," &c. A paraphrase of a war-song given in *Traditions and Superstitions of the New Zealanders*, by Ed. Shortland, M.A.

Page 379.—"Hit out, hit out," &c. Paraphrase of a song in Sir G. Grey's collection.

Page 407.—"Be wakeful," &c. Ditto.

Page 412.—"Stars are fleeting." Ditto.

Of the songs above specified, those invented are, it is believed, sufficiently in accordance with the ordinary tone of native feeling and thought; while those paraphrased or amplified will perhaps in their English dress have much the same appearance to an English reader as the originals to a native hearer. In songs or other compositions orally transmitted, it should be remembered that the hearer receives them in most cases from a source which can itself supply the associations, details, or explanations, which so often render paraphrases necessary to make them intelligible to others. The reciter is a *living* book, ready to answer every query, and amplify to any extent desirable; adapt itself, in short, to the greater or less degree of imaginativeness in the hearer. Perhaps this may partly account for the exceeding simplicity and terseness of most early and oral poetry, quite as much as any presumed severity of taste in the composers. Poetry so communicated always had, besides, the expressive looks, tones and gestures of the person communicating it—to facilitate brevity.

III.—LEGENDS.

Pages 116 *to* 120.—The legends alluded to will be found detailed at length in Sir G. Grey's *Polynesian Mythology*. That of Pitaka in the Rev. R. Taylor's *New Zealand and its Inhabitants*.

Page 121.—*Legend of Tawhaki.* Maui and Tawhaki are the two principal hero-gods of the Maori and other Polynesian tribes. The legends relating to Tawhaki are given in full in Sir G. Grey's work just cited; and imperfectly, and with variations, in the Rev. R. Taylor's *New Zealand, &c.*

Page 132.—*The Maori Cosmogony or Theogony* is given in *Polynesian Mythology*, and in one of Mr. Shortland's excellent little works; also in Mr. Taylor's book: in all with variations.

Page 190.—*Legend of Patito.* Mr. John White, in a lecture on Maori customs, printed in the Appendix to Votes and Proceedings of the New Zealand Parliament, 1851, mentions a legend to the effect that a famous Chief, Patito, jealous of his son's warlike fame, came from the Reinga, or abode of departed spirits, to fight him; and the native belief that had the son conquered, Death would have been abolished.

Page 193.—*Maui's Descent to the Reinga.* This is one of the adventures of Maui, narrated in *Polynesian Mythology*, and in Mr. Taylor's book. But the version given by the latter identifies the "Reinga," or kingdom of "Mother Night," in a truly Maori style, with that venerable lady's person.

There is no authority, as far as I am aware, for the description of the *Realm* of Ru. But Ru is really the Earthquake God.

Page 205.—The *Patupaere*, or *Patupaiarehe*, were supernatural beings in some particulars resembling European Fairies, though some were, apparently, Giants. The best account of them is in *Polynesian Mythology*.

Page 303.—*Kidnapping of Hatupatu by the Giantess.* Described before, p. 118.

Page 305.—"The last person who had wings was Te Kahui-rere; he lost them by a woman pressing them down when he was asleep."—Taylor's *New Zealand, &c.*, p. 34.

Page 305.—*Wakatu, the inventor of Kite-flying.* This incident is given in *Polynesian Mythology*, "Adventures of Rata."

IV.—NATURAL OBJECTS.

Though everything introduced into the poem relating to animals and plants is of course from actual observation, I think it as well, in confirmation of my remarks, and as most of the objects themselves must be strange to English readers, to give their scientific names and some brief notices of them, extracted from such books as I could readily come at.

I.—TREES AND SHRUBS.

PAGE.

1. Rata .... *Order*, Myrtaceæ; *Genus*, Metrosideros; *Species*, M. robusta.
A magnificent flowering-tree described afterwards, p. 264.

2. Koromiko .... *O.* Scrophularineæ; *G.* Veronica.
Dr. Hooker describes forty species, and says,—"In New Zealand it forms a more conspicuous feature of the vegetation than in any other country; from the number, beauty, and ubiquity of the species: from so many forming large bushes, and from the remarkable forms the genus presents."

7. Asphodel (*Ti*) ..... *O.* Liliaceæ; *G.* Cordyline; *S.* C. Australis.
"Leaves ensiform, two feet long, one and a half inch broad. Trunk ten to forty feet high. Flowers densely crowded." This genus, with others, forming the family Asphodeleæ, are included by Dr. Hooker in the O. Liliaceæ.

,, Tree-fern .... *O.* Filices; *G.* Cyathæa; *S.* C. dealbata, or Silver-fern, and C. medullaris—two common species.
"Trunk twelve to forty feet high."

11. Flax (*harakeke*, &c.) .... *O.* Liliaceæ; *G.* Phormium; *S.* Ph. tenax.
Profuse in swamps and elsewhere throughout the islands. Used as hemp and flax.

,, Supplejack (*Ka-reao*) .... *O.* Liliaceæ; *G.* Rhipogonum; *S.* R. scandens.

16. Convolvulus .... *O.* Convolvulaceæ; *G.* Convolvulus. Five species—mostly white or rosehued.

,, Clematis.................. (See note to p. 260 below.)

,, Alectryon (*Titoki*) *O.* Sapindaceæ; *G.* Alectryon; *S.* A. excelsum.

103. Tutu or Tupaki.... *O.* Coriariæ; *G.* Coriaria; *S.* C. ruscifolia.
A large bush, with deep green leaves. "The juice of the berries is purple and affords a grateful beverage to the natives." The fruit hangs in thick fringes. The seeds "produce convulsions, delirium, and death."

105. Coffee-bush (Ka-ramu) .... *O.* Rubiaceæ (?) *G.* Coprosma (?) Several species.
Fruit and seeds like small coffee berries, in scarlet colour, arrangement, and taste.

107. Kowhai-flowers.....(See note below, p. 261.)

,, Totára ....*O.* Coniferæ; *G.* Podocarpus; *S.* P. totara.
"The Swamp-totara, P. dacrydioides, grows to 150 feet in height. P. totara, from which canoes are made," to a less height. "Bark used for roofing."

108. Karaka ....*O.* Anacardiaceæ; *G.* Corynocarpus; *S.* C. lævigata.
"Tree, forty feet high; berries, two to three inches long;" orange-coloured, eaten as food.

,, Tawhiri ....*O.* Pittosporeæ; *G.* Pittosporum; *S.* P. cornifolium.
A large shrub; many varieties; leaves of some highly scented.

,, Kiekie (parasite) *O.* Pandaneæ; *G.* Freycinetia; *S.* Freycinetia Banksii.
"A lofty climber; the bracts and young spikes make a very sweet preserve." Grows in forks of trees, &c. Fleshy leaves of flower like soft, bitter-sweet apple.

111. Locust-trees (*Kowhai*).........} (See note to p. 261.)

117. Rimu-tree ....*O.* Coniferæ; *G.* Dracrydium; *S.* D. cupressinum.
"Tree pyramidal, branches weeping, trunk eighty feet high, four to five feet diameter."

123. Fungus-balls..........*O.* Fungi; Sub-order, Gasteromycetes; Tribe, Trichogastres.
"Hymenium or fructifying surface, dries up into a dusty mass of microscopic threads or spores."

131. Fern-root ....*O.* Filices; *G.* Pteris; *S.* Pteris aquilina, of which a variety is Pteris esculenta—edible fern.
"Common in the south temperate zone."

,, Kumara (sweet potato)...............} *O.* Convolvulaceæ; *G.* Ipomœa; *S.* Batatus edulis.

,, Taro ....*O.* Pandaneæ (Aroideæ); *G.* Caladum; *S.* Caladum esculentum.
"A staple article of food in many parts of the Old World." A root something like the kumara—but whiter, firmer, and less sweet.

132. Tupaki or Tutu.....(See above, note to p. 103.)

134. Toë-toë ....(See note to p. 172 below.)
The term "toë!" alluding to the light large flower of this grass is used metaphorically precisely as we use the word "*chaff*."

149. Mánuka ....*O.* Myrtaceæ; *G.* Leptospermum; *S.* L. scoparium, or L. ericoides.
"A large shrub or small tree; leaves used as tea in Tasmania and Australia, where the plant is equally abundant." In the poem it is called indiscriminately manuka, broom, broom-like myrtle, or leptosperm. The settlers often call it 'tea-broom.'

149. Green rushes (*Raupo*) ....} *O.* Typhaceæ; *G.* Typha; *S.* T. angustifolia.
"Extensively used for making walls."

172. Sword-grass (Toë-toë) ..... *O.* Gramineæ; *G.* Arundo; *S.* A. conspicua.
"The largest New Zealand grass; confined to these islands; culms three to eight (ten) feet high; used for thatch and lining houses with reed-work."

213. Ferns ..... Dr. Hooker describes 120 ferns—forty-five species and one genus being peculiar to New Zealand; sixty common to it, Australia, and Tasmania; and nine to it and Great Britain.

221. Azolla-stains ..... *O.* Marsiliaceæ; *G.* Azolla; *S.* A. rubra.
"Plant floating, forming small red patches."

233. Puriri ..... *O.* Verbenaceæ; *G.* Vitex; *S.* V. littoralis.
"A large tree, fifty to one hundred feet high; trunk twenty feet in girth." Common along the northern coasts.

234. Totaras ..... (Note to p. 107.)

236. Laurel-tree (*Tarairi*) ..... *O.* Laurineæ; *G.* Nesodaphne; *S.* N. Tarairi.
"A forest tree sixty to eighty feet high; berry one and a half inches long, purple."

253. Titoki ..... (Note to p. 16.)

254. Savory Palm-tree (*Nikau*) ..... *O.* Palmeæ; *G.* Areca; *S.* A. sapida.

260. Parasite-myrtle (*Rata*) ..... (Note to p. 1.)

,, King-pine (*Kauri*) ..... *O.* Coniferæ; *G.* Dammara; *S.* D. Australis.
"The famous Kauri-pine; some near 200 feet high and forty feet in girth."

,, Fuschia-tree ..... *O.* Onagrariæ; *G.* Fuschia; *S.* F. excorticata.
"Often three feet in diameter. A very large S. American and especially Andean genus of most beautiful plants; found nowhere in the Old World but in New Zealand."

,, Clematis ..... *O.* Ranunculaceæ; *G.* Clematis; *S.* C. indivisa.
"A large, strong, woody climber with trunk often half a foot in diameter. Flowers most abundantly produced; white; sweet-scented; according to Sir J. Banks and Dr. Solander, abundant throughout the islands—festooning the trees." Flowers, seven-petalled stars, three-and-one-eighth inches diameter.

261. Kowhai (yellow or Locust-tree) ..... *O.* Leguminosæ; *G.* Sophora; *S.* S. tetraptera.
An acacia-like tree with abundant yellow pendent flowers.

,, Kowhai (scarlet or Parrot-bill) ..... *O.* Leguminosæ; *G.* Clianthus; *S.* C. puniceus.
"One of the most beautiful plants known." Long fringes of crimson flowers—like lobster claws, or, in the natives' eyes, parrots' bills; so they call it '*ngutu-kaka*' the 'parrot-billed.'

,, Eurybia ..... *O.* Compositæ; *G.* Olearia; Many species.
Broad-leaved shrubs; under-side of leaf furry white.

264. Creeper-fern ..... *O.* Filices; *G.* Polypodium; *S.* P. rupestre (Niphobolus rupestris).

275. Lycopod ....Lycopodium volubile, or L. densum.

289. "Twine of prickles"..... *O.* Rosaceæ; *G.* Rubus; *S.* R. Australis.
"A lofty climber, armed with scattered recurved prickles; branches very slender—pendulous."

302. Amaranthine-green .... All the indigenous trees and shrubs of New Zealand are evergreen except the Fuschia-tree.

311. Downy iron-heart (*Pohutukawa*) .... *O.* Myrtaceæ; *G.* Metrosideros; *S.* M. tomentosa.
This most lovely tree is common about the northern coasts and cliffs of the North Island and the banks of Lake Tarawera.

312. Pepper - spikes (fruit or catkin of the Kawa-kawa) .... *O.* Piperaceæ; *G.* Piper; *S.* P. excelsum.
"Catkins slender, one to four inches long."

,, Poro-poro (potato-apples of) *O.* Solaneæ; *G.* Solanum; *S.* S. aviculare and S. nigrum.
"Berry ovoid, edible, one to one-and-a-half inch long; three-quarters inch thick." Sweet and rather richly flavoured when quite ripe.

360. Hinau-berries .....*O.* Tiliaceæ; *G.* Elæocarpus; *S.* E. dentatus and E. Hookerianus.
"A small tree with brown bark which yields a permanent dye. Drupe one-third to one-half inch long; pulp edible."

All the above names (with the exception of that in the first note to p. 105), and all the remarks included in inverted commas, are from *The Handbook to the Flora of New Zealand*, by Dr. J. D. Hooker, whose very valuable services in connection with the botany of that country are highly appreciated by the Colonial Government and Parliament; as well as by the numerous colonists interested in the subject.

2.—BIRDS AND INSECTS.

94. Hoopoë-feathers *Fam.* Upupidæ; Heteralocha Acutirostris.
A beautiful bird; black shining plumage; tips of tail feathers white; bright orange wattles. "That it possesses strong affinities to the Hoopoes is certain."—DR. BULLER (*History of New Zealand Birds*, now publishing.)

103. Wingless locust.....Deinacrida heteracantha.
From some rough notes on this (not attractive) insect I made years ago I extract the following:—"This curious locust is found in soft decaying trees; its body and hind legs are in shape like a grasshopper's; its colour is pale reddish or

yellowish white beneath, and, up the edges of the abdominal rings, head, and back, deep brown. The head of the male is set on perpendicularly, with a hard round forehead, like an elephant's, the head being with the jaws two-thirds as long as the rest of the body. Eyes staring and prominent, two very long antennæ" (sometimes, says Dieffenbach, with the body reaching to fourteen inches) "between them; the labrum long and large; from beneath it falls a fleshy kind of curtain, triangular, on a broad neck, which it raises and lets fall like a portcullis, over the two enormous toothed mandibles hanging on each side curving towards each other at their ends; black and an eighth of an inch in breadth and thickness each, which increase the resemblance to the elephant's head, &c. . . . . (Much more about 'geniculated palpi,' 'fleshy tongue,' &c.) Tibiæ of hind legs have a row of strong spines at the back, on each side, projecting outwards. . . . . It has a large stomach opening into a gizzard, which is of really beautiful structure; more than one-eighth of an inch in diameter, bluish-white in colour, oval-shaped, hard; cut open, shews interior surface fluted with a number of toothed or serrated ridges meeting at the ends like lines on a currant or meridian lines on a globe; the green vegetable-looking wet ground contents of stomach evidently passed through it. . . . . These creatures hop feebly, and being teased, run towards the teasing object as if butting with the head. They smell like shrimps or shell-fish."

105. Green parrakeet.....Psittacidæ; Two species, Platycercus Auriceps and P. Novæ Zealandiæ.

First has a yellow, second a crimson crest. "General plumage bright grass green."—BULLER.

,, Kingfisher ....Alcedinidæ; Halcyon vagans.

,, Ichneumon fly .....Ichneumonidæ.

The species alluded to is about the size and shape of a wasp; thorax pure golden; abdomen bright ruddy brown; both very hard.

119. Cuttlefish ....Cephalopods are common about the coasts of New Zealand.

131. Crayfish.....................three or four inches long are caught in abundance in the central lakes in manner described.

138. 'Tui,' the Parson-bird or Poe-bird of Capt. Cook.....Melliphagidæ; Prosthemadera Novæ Zealandiæ.

"Splendid bird — woods resound with its tuneful notes."—KNIGHT'S *Museum of Animated Nature.*

140. Hawk.........................Falconidæ.

The most common species appears to be the Cercus Gouldi: or New Zealand Harrier.—BULLER.

159. Cicada ....Cicadidæ; Cicada cingulata or Cruentata (?)

These beautiful insects abound in the islands—biggest one and half inches long, near half inch broad at the head.

168. Night-hawk or New Zealand Owl ....Strigidæ; Spiloglaux Novæ Zealandiæ: (Buller).

The "morepork" of the colonists.

173. Wild-pigeon ....(See note to p. 223.)

194. Jelly-fish......................*C.* Acalephæ; *O.* Pulmonigrada; *G.* Medusæ.
Size of a dinner-plate and smaller; abound in the bays and harbours; some beautifully marked on the upper surface of disc with radiating scarlet lines.

202. Korimako ....Melliphagidæ; Anthornis melanura.

208. Lizard..........................Scincidæ; Hinulia N. Zealandica (Gray).

209. Phasmid. The "Walking Stick" ....*O.* Orthoptera; *G.* Phasmidæ.
Several species in New Zealand: mostly admirable imitations of withered twigs or sticks; one with wings like delicate leaves. Some are brilliant green, covered with thorns—like new shoots of some plants. In my rough notes, alluded to above, I find the following description of some of these very interesting insects I kept under a tumbler:—"These creatures are slow in their movements; leave any limb in the position you place it in; legs sticking up in the air like sprays of branches. The forelegs are joined to the body by a sort of foot-stalk thinner and tinged with red exactly like the petioles or leaf-stalks of some plants; curious, as these legs can most conveniently be kept up in the air. Bodies and limbs long and slender; three to six or seven inches in length—from an eighth to a quarter of an inch in thickness; colour, pale brown inclined to grey, like dry sticks. Along their backs are rows of protuberances like incipient thorns. The female laid several eggs, eighth of an inch in length, oblong, grey, or French white in colour, dry and looking exceedingly like seeds of plants; but crack in breaking and are full of a yellow liquid like yolks of bird's eggs. If the outer skin of the egg dried and broke off on being touched—the yolk had hardened into a gold-coloured grain. . . . . They thrust out their forelegs like antennæ, though they have two of these latter. As they walk they frequently stop and sway their stick-like bodies, on their legs as if on springs, from side to side, with a slow regular motion, ceasing gradually, as if shaken by a light wind. Stride along pretty quickly if much handled or alarmed. But they will remain a considerable time in any attitudes they may be thrown into, upon their own or each others' backs, perfectly motionless; with their long slender legs up in the air: mimics to the last. They have nine abdominal rings, not very strongly marked, but like small bamboo. Eyes of the colour of their bodies; feet hooked. They will stand upright on two hind legs and tail if so placed, their arms (as you are tempted to call them) or rather their middle pair of legs stretched out and upwards, motionless; their forelegs and antennæ held perpendicular and close-joined as if a continuation of their body, which is no thicker. . . . . As they walk they lift their legs high off the ground as if on stilts. . . . . These Phasmids lived a fortnight or more among manuka-sprigs as lively to all appearance as ever. Then the smallest was found dead; limp and as if sucked dry—part of its neck eaten away by its companions. So the rest were killed with spirits of wine. Though looking so dry externally they seem full of a thin watery sap-like fluid."

213. Porphyrio ....(See note to p. 223.)

218. White Crane (*Kotuku*)..........Ardeidæ; Herodias flavirostris (?)
The Rev. R. Taylor mentions a native proverb that "A man only sees it once in a life-time;" but it is much less uncommon in the Middle Island.

223. Stock-doves ....Columbidæ; Columba spadicea, Chestnut-shouldered pigeon.

"All the upper part and throat of this beautiful bird are of a changeable hue, with rosy-copper reflections running into brilliant iridescent tints."—KNIGHT's *Museum of Animated Nature.*

,, Sultana-birds (*Pukeko*) .... *F.* Rallidæ; *G.* Porphyrio (the 'Poule Sultane' of the French—Pollo Sultano, Ital.), Porphyrio Melanotus, *ib.*

The New Zealand species has crimson bill; red legs; rich deep-blue breast, rest of plumage velvet-black.

,, Cuckoo ....*F.* Cuculidæ; Chrysococcyx lucidus (Gray), Cuculus Nitens (Forster).

,, Parrots ....Trichoglossidæ; *G.* Nestor.

Dr. Buller gives nine varieties, some splendidly coloured. They are "true flower-suckers."

224. Albatross ....Procellaridæ; Diomedea exulans.

232. Kiwi, the Apteryx .... Struthionidæ; Three species. 1. Apt. Australis, 2. A. Mantelli, 3. A. Owenii.

"So extraordinary a bird that the existence of a species possessing such a combination of anomalous characters was long denied. Wings, trifling rudiments buried beneath general plumage, discovered with difficulty; nostrils at *tip* of long beak; no vestige of a tail; feathers long, lanceolate, only a single plume from each quill."—KNIGHT's *Museum*, &c., from descriptions in *Transactions of the Zoological Society*, by PROFESSOR OWEN and others.

239. Whitebait ....Eleotris basalis.

Abundant.

265. Cormorant........ Pelicanidæ; Graucelus punctatus, &c.

"Social birds, and build their nests many together on high trees overhanging rivers and coasts."—GRAY.

274. Oyster-catcher . *G.* Hæmatopus.

,, Avocet .... *G.* Recurvirostra.

282. Moa .... Struthionidæ; *G.* 1. Dinornis, 3-toed; 2. Palapteryx, 4-toed; *S.* 13 or 14 described by Prof. Owen.

Gigantic wingless birds, the massive bones of which are dug up in many parts of the country: nine to ten feet six inches high according to Owen—thirteen or fourteen feet according to others—Kiwi (note to p. 232), apparently the only living representative of the family.

289. Bittern ....Ardeidæ; Botaurus Melanotus (Gray), Ardea [B.], Australis (Cuvier).

"Total length two feet two inches."

301. Honey-bird ....Several species of Melliphagidæ common: including the—

,, Mocking-bird or "Tui" .... (Note to p. 138).

So called by Captain Cook: and the—

301. Bell-bird or Korimako.............. (Note to p. 202.)

308. Grebe........................Colymbidæ ; *G.* Podiceps ; *S.* P. cristatus (?)
A beautiful crested grebe is found about the lakes in the Middle Island.

314. Dragon-flies ....Libellulidæ ; Petalura Carovei.
Total length four inches five lines to four inches eight lines.—Gray. This species barred black and white. Other commonest species or varieties are about two inches long—bright scarlet or bright blue.

347. Blue crane............Ardeidæ ; Herodias Matuku ?

385. Mutton-fish ....Haliotis Iris.
"These are found in colossal specimens."—Hochstetter.

474. Sea-windflower.....Sea-anemones ; Actiniæ.
Common on some of the rocky coasts.

481. 'A slender beetle' *O.* Coleoptera ; *F.* Longicornes ; Callichroma (Calliprason) Sinclairi.
Gray—who calls it, "This delicately-pretty little longicorn beetle."

487. Animalcule ....Allusion to one of the Diatomaceæ (vegetable or animal?) placed under a microscope.

The above chiefly taken from the list of the Fauna of New Zealand, by Dr. Gray of the British Museum, appended to Dieffenbach's *New Zealand*, vol. ii.

THE END.

London: Printed by Smith, Elder & Co., Old Bailey, E.C.

ERRATA.

Page 46, line 2, *for* "mere Scarabeus-worship" *read* "unsymbolled Scarab-worship."
,, 53, ,, 16, *after* "rest" *insert* semicolon.
,, 69, ,, 5, *for* "Sailor life" *read* "Sailor-life."
,, 125, ,, 24, *for* "wild wood" *read* "wildwood."
,, 185, ,, 15, *for* "nigh" *read* "near."
,, 188, ,, 24, *for* "tipped" *read* "lipped."
,, 213, ,, 12, *after* "below" *for* full stop *insert* comma.
,, 221, ,, 22, *after* "ruddiest hue" *omit* full stop.
,, 256, ,, 15, *for* "abandoment" *read* "abandonment."
,, 259, ,, 28, *after* "*knowing*" *for* full stop *insert* comma.
,, 261, ,, 31, *after* "nature" *omit* full stop.
,, 301, ,, 15, *for* "wild ducks'" *read* "wild duck's."
,, 302, ,, 13, *for* "guest" *read* "quest."
,, 343, ,, 8, *for* "life blood" *read* "life-blood."

CPSIA information can be obtained
at www.ICGtesting.com
Printed in the USA
LVHW112010030423
743357LV00006B/450

9 783382 133368